REDEMPTION

Sarah Fisher

Book Three in the Dragonscale series

First published in Australia in 2018 by Sarah Fisher

Copyright © Sarah Fisher 2018

Website: www.sarahfisherauthor.com
Email: sarah@sarahfisherauthor.com

The moral right of the author has been asserted.

ISBN: 9780648182429 (paperback)

A catalogue record for this book is available from the National Library of Australia

Disclaimer

This is a work of fiction. Names, characters, places, incidents and events, other than those clearly in the public domain, are fictitious and any resemblance to actual persons, living or dead, is entirely coincidental.

To Angus, for walking beside me

Acknowledgements

This book would not have made it into the world without the support and encouragement of my wonderful family. And I don't just mean those I am related to. You know who you are.

Thank you, Lucy for bringing my vision for this cover to life.

My gratitude also goes to Patrice and Kirsty, whose technical skills in editing and design have been indispensable.

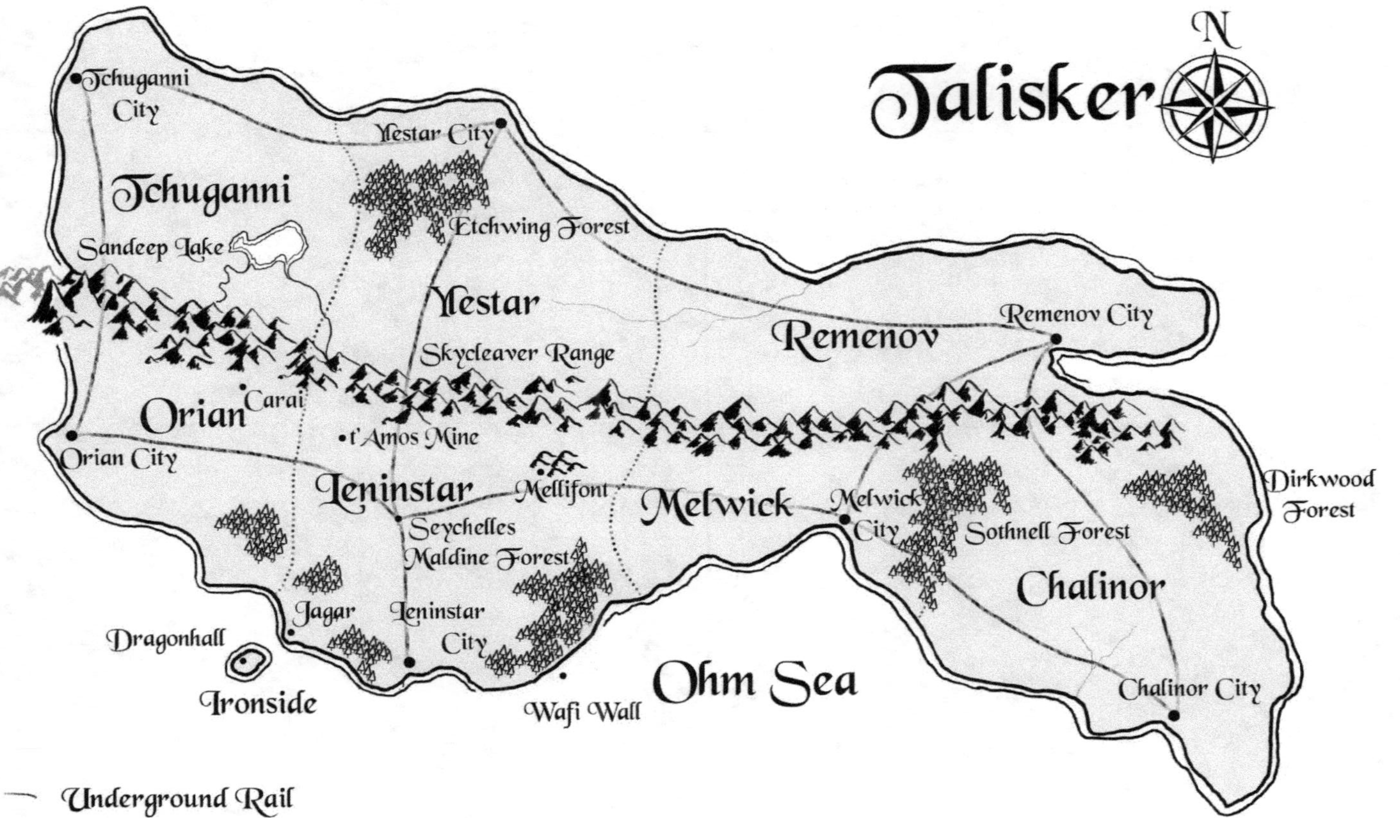

Talisker
N
Tchuganni City
Tchuganni
Sandeep Lake
Yestar City
Etchwing Forest
Yestar
Skycleaver Range
Remenov
Remenov City
Orian
Orian City
Carai
t'Amos Mine
Leninstar
Mellifont
Melwick
Melwick City
Sothnell Forest
Dirkwood Forest
Chalinor
Chalinor City
Seychelles
Maldine Forest
Jagar
Leninstar City
Dragonhall
Ironside
Waft Wall
Ohm Sea
Underground Rail

Characters

<table>
<tr><td>

Academy adepts
Major Noah Chord, viola
Chief Examiner Sachin, flute
Major Jacin, flute
Major Alan, recorder
Major Anok, lyre

</td><td>

Royals
King Catriona, Leninstar
King Henrik, Orian
King Mallory, Melwick
King Tara, Chalinor
King Severine, Carai

</td></tr>
<tr><td>

Noah's crew
Raven Chord, Leninstar's Army
Commander
Emir Delorian, Noah's adviser
Jemima Chase, Noah's best friend
Jaxon, Emir's brother
Gillette, Emir's nephew
Montana, High Priestess of Talisker
Ardis, Elani warrior
Dr Grainger, Dragonsbane
Brinn, cat
Xan, ancient dragon

</td><td>

Dragons
Horatio, dragon elder
Fontina, dragon elder
Piper, Noah's dragon
Chain, Emir's dragon
Vespa, Raven's dragon

Gods
Elani, creator
Jong, destructor
Temperance, mediator

</td></tr>
<tr><td>

Elves
Councillor Talyn, sein-Jong
Theo, woodland elder
Seamus, Theo's grandson

</td><td>

Other
Avril Jane, historian
Sorcerer-master Percival, Somyni's
ruler
Sorcerer Sagan, Percival's acolyte

</td></tr>
</table>

Prologue

Temperance sipped her tea while Elani massaged his temples. She hadn't seen him troubled like this in aeons.

'What troubles you, Brother dear?' Temperance asked.

Elani sighed. 'The vortex is growing much faster than I'd anticipated.'

'Yes,' Temperance said. 'Comets and asteroids won't appease it for much longer. It's going to have an appetite for bigger things.'

'Talisker,' Elani said. 'It's going to swallow Talisker.'

Temperance placed her teacup on the saucer. 'Yes.'

'I don't want to sacrifice Talisker, Temp,' Elani said, 'but it's the only way.'

Temperance shook her head, setting her brown ringlets jiggling. 'No it isn't.'

Elani drummed his fingers on the table but said nothing.

'The Pyranhi foresaw this,' Temperance said. *'The thirteenth key the world shall need, for evil to be brought to heel – One of two, the Dragon's bane must rise; and the music wield.* The 13th key has been made.'

'The human?'

'Her name is Noah.'

'She's not ready.'

Temperance sniffed. 'Of course she's not … but she will be.'

'Temp, you can't help her. *We* can't intervene.'

Eyes smouldering with ageless wisdom, Temperance smiled. 'Not *directly*.'

Elani stood up and strode to the archway. Temperance took a deep breath before joining him. Beyond their celestial palace, the galaxies sprawled gloriously across the universe. All Elani's wonderful creations. But the shimmering tapestry of star-studded gas clouds and swirling planetary clusters brought Temperance no joy today. In a distant galaxy, Talisker – her favourite of all Elani's worlds – sailed through the heavens on a collision course with a rapidly expanding vortex.

Talisker was a paradox. Both a shrine and a prison. The mighty dragon, Xan had been mortally wounded when she'd battled the destructive god, Jong – and then devoured him – to end his campaign to destroy all Elani's creations. Elani had built a world around her, a protective cocoon in which the injured dragon could continue to contain the vanquished god. It was a precarious situation though. Jong still lived, waiting for his chance to break free.

Talisker must be saved, Temperance thought, *and we're desperately short of time.*

'What if Noah were to find the illestial?' she said.

Elani spun round. 'No! That'd be playing into Jong's hands. That's exactly what our brother wants.'

'But with the illestial, Noah could extract Jong from Talisker and re-home him in the vortex. That's what we need, isn't it? We've got a voracious vortex and a delinquent god – a perfect match.'

Elani frowned. 'I agree it's a perfect match, Temp. Xan cannot contain Jong much longer. The vortex is definitely the solution. Jong wouldn't be strong enough to break free of the vortex, but he'd suck enough energy from it to stop it growing.' He sighed. 'It weighs heavily on me that the vortex will consume Talisker, but it's the safest way to get Jong in there.'

Temperance glared at her brother. 'How can you talk like that? Noah could do this. Talisker could be saved.'

'The human is brave and well-meaning,' Elani said, 'but no match for Jong.'

'Noah is part dragon. Xan's power is in her veins.'

'She is mortal.'

'So because her life – *human* life – is fleeting, it is meaningless?' Temperance said. 'We should just let them all die?'

Elani faced her. 'Don't do that.' He put his hands on her shoulders. 'You know that's not what I meant.'

Temperance waited.

'Temp, Xan was a mighty dragon,' Elani said. 'The mightiest. She fought Jong and …'

'Contained him,' Temperance said. 'With the illestial, Noah could do the same. She wouldn't have to do it for long – just long enough to get Jong into the vortex.'

Elani returned his gaze to the cosmic landscape. 'The illestial was designed to *free* Jong. We can't risk that. If Jong is free – he will destroy everything. Not just Talisker … *everything.*'

Chapter 1

Noah glanced at her watch as she and her companions strode along the footpath.

'How late are we?' Chase asked.

'Half an hour,' Noah said.

Chase shook her head. 'I can't believe there was so much traffic.'

Raven adjusted his cap as they approached the museum forecourt. 'Is it even possible for VIPs to be late?' he said. 'I thought they could arrive whenever they liked.'

'I told Avril we'd be here at opening time,' Chase said, fanning herself with a vintage lace fan. 'I don't like being late.'

Sayle Museum loomed over them; its sandstone façade taking the brunt of the morning sun's baking heat. The four long queues snaking out from the main archways wrapped and curled through a maze of temporary rope barriers. Progress was slow. Though the massive shade sails over the forecourt protected the waiting visitors from direct sunlight, it was still oppressively hot in the marshalling area.

'I'm so glad we don't have to queue,' Noah said as they bypassed the shuffling horde on their way to the museum's rear entrance.

'Agreed,' Raven said. 'Bring on the air-con.'

Chase huffed. 'You think you're hot? Try being five months pregnant.'

'No chance,' Noah said.

Raven shrugged. 'Yeah, think I'll pass on that too.'

Chase sighed. 'I should've known better than to expect any sympathy from you two.'

The lone guard in the security booth was dozing in her chair when they reached the window. *She looks old enough to be one of the exhibits,* Noah thought. It appeared that someone had papier-mâchéd over a skeleton then topped it with a dusty old brown wig from the props box. The guard's faded uniform was crumpled and bore several coffee stains.

'Do you think she's alive?' Chase whispered.

Raven raised his fist. 'Let's see.'

He knocked on the window. The guard jerked in her seat but was slow to look up. When she did, she stared at them with eyes so devoid of expression they might have been made of glass.

'Help you?' she drawled.

'I'm Jemima Chase,' Chase said. 'Avril Jane is expecting me and my two guests.'

The guard turned her attention to the monitor on the desk. 'Yes,' she said. 'You're on the list. I'll page her … once you sign for your passes.'

While Chase attended to the paperwork, Raven sidled closer to Noah. 'So, Sis, what are you going to do if you happen to run into one of your old school friends today?'

'I'll hide behind one of the exhibits,' Noah said.

'Seriously?'

'Seriously.'

'You wouldn't want to talk to them? Find out what they've been doing?'

Noah considered it for a moment. 'I'd be interested to find out what they've been doing, but the conversation might get a bit awkward if they ask me what I've been up to.'

Raven grinned. 'Really?'

'Don't be a jerk,' she said.

'I'd love to hear *that* conversation,' he said. Doing his worst to imitate his sister's voice, Raven continued, 'Well, I've travelled to another world where I had my hearing restored and I learned to speak. To repay the favour, I saved the world from destruction by becoming a living weapon. I attained the position of King's Tailor and from there I went on to be a king myself – King of the Goblins actually. I have also achieved the highest raiki honour in the land – that of Major – by curing the effects of a toxic parasitic worm. I am dating the king's adviser, my brother is the king's army commander, and I am about to be godmother to the child of one of Earth's most successful authors.'

Noah stomped on his foot. 'Knock it off, Commander,' she said. 'Geez, I'm glad you're my brother and not my biographer. That was worse than awful.'

'But all true.'

'And what about you?' Noah said. 'Though born human, I was secretly turned into a dog when I was a baby by a seer on another planet. I lived on Earth for sixteen years as an Alsatian before returning to my homeland to have my true form reinstated. I helped my sister become the 13th key. I am the army's chief commander and the king's consort. I—'

'Okay, okay,' Raven interrupted, raising his hands in surrender. 'I get it. Maybe we should leave the biographical details to Chase.'

'Forget it,' Chase said, handing each of them a VIP pass. 'I'm a fictioneer, not a journalist.'

The steel door behind them squeaked open.

'Jemima!' a smartly-dressed young woman said. 'I'm so pleased you could come.'

'Pleased to be here,' Chase said, shaking the hand that was offered to her. 'Avril, this is my dearest friend, Noah Chord and her brother, Raven.'

'Avril Jane,' the woman said, extending her hand to Raven. 'Archaeologist, historian and curator of my grandfather's collection which is currently on display here at the museum … *and* I'm Jemima's biggest fan!'

'Nice to meet you,' Raven said. 'So, you've read all her books?'

'Read them and brought them in today for Jemima to sign.' Avril turned to Noah. 'Noah? That's an unusual name for a girl.'

With a practised smile, Noah said, 'So I'm told.'

Noah guessed Avril was in her early twenties. Subtle makeup accentuated her doll-like features while loose blonde curls cascaded from a high pony tail. But what impressed Noah most was her outfit. Her halter-neck chiffon swing top was emblazoned with an elaborately sequinned and beaded daffodil – the bright flower radiating a dazzling blend of colour and energy. She'd teamed her top with faded designer jeans and yellow stilettos, giving the ensemble a casual sophistication.

Noah's designer's instincts took over. 'Where did you get your top?'

The young woman beamed. 'Elzaba. You like it?'

'Yes,' Noah said. 'I do like it.'

'Well, come in, come in,' Avril said, ushering them towards the door. 'It's lovely and cool inside and there is much to see.'

Inside, a floor-to-ceiling poster advertising the current exhibition dominated the small foyer.

'Wow!' Raven said. 'If that's the poster you've got at the back door, I'd like to see the one at the front.'

'There are actually four designs,' Avril said. 'You'll see a full set in the main foyer.'

'Impressive,' Chase said.

'Thanks,' Avril said. She pointed to the dates on the poster. 'As you can see, the exhibition has only a week left to run. I'm so glad you're in town to see it. Your VIP passes are valid for the rest of the week. Feel free to come as often as you like.'

'Thank you,' Chase said, looping her lanyard over her head. 'That's very kind of you.'

'Absolutely my pleasure,' Avril said. 'Shall we get started?'

'Yes indeed,' Chase replied.

Avril smiled. 'Excellent, follow me.'

Noah walked beside Chase as they followed their guide through corridors that were strictly off-limits to *un*official museum patrons. When they reached the main hall, Noah shook her head in wonder. Though she'd visited the museum several times as a youngster, the intricately carved sandstone columns supporting the vaulted ceiling enchanted her all over again.

As they crossed the geometric mosaics on the tiled floor, Noah wondered how long the magnificent old building would survive in the face of Sayle's unrelenting scramble for modernity. Noah enjoyed Earth's state-of-the-art technology but preferred the simple life on Talisker. Electricity was still in its infancy there and she hoped it would take a long time for them to catch up.

'This is the *Warriors of the World* exhibit,' Avril said as they entered the first auditorium. 'A good portion of what's on display throughout the museum is from my grandfather's private collection and since I've helped him collect some of the pieces, I can give you extra information that you won't get from the other guides.'

When she winked at them, Noah cringed.

'I hope you'll find this interesting, Jemima,' Avril said. 'I know you do lots of research for your books and I thought all this history and these relics might inspire you.'

'That's very thoughtful,' Chase said. 'I'm sure it will be wonderful.'

'Please,' the young historian said, taking Chase's elbow, 'this way.'

A few steps behind Chase and Avril, Raven walked with Noah. 'And it certainly doesn't hurt to have a famous author at your exhibition,' he said so only his sister could hear. 'A great way to drum up business for the last week of the show.'

'So cynical, Brother,' Noah said.

'You disagree?'

'No.'

Raven grimaced. 'Maybe Avril wants to be a character in Chase's next book?'

'She seems to be sucking up for something,' Noah said, 'and maybe something more than just getting her book collection signed.'

'There are two more displays after *Warriors of the World*,' Avril said. 'In the next hall, you'll find ancient burial practices of different societies and then, after that, there are rare and intriguing relics from around the globe.'

Raven clapped his hand on Noah's shoulder. 'I think I can pretty much keep myself entertained in this hall right here.'

'I'm sure you can, Army Commander,' Noah said. 'Hoping for some tips from these ancient warriors, are you?'

'Very funny,' Raven said. 'Just pick me up from here when you're done,' he added, before wandering off to look at a life-size wax model of a Viking warrior.

Noah tagged along with Chase and Avril, doing her best to ignore the conversation. Chase didn't need any help dealing with crazy fans. She'd had lots of practice.

Though military history wasn't of interest to Noah, she examined all the weaponry and read the plaques. At least the models of the different fighters and soldiers gave her the chance to indulge in a critique of their uniforms.

When they entered the *Death and Beyond* exhibit, a feeling of foreboding crept over Noah. Instantly wary, she scanned the hall but saw nothing to explain her apprehension. She thought about getting Raven but dismissed the idea. He'd only give her a hard time about being scared of mummies and dead bodies. *Don't be silly,* she thought. *It's only the living that are dangerous.*

'Avril, where are the toilets?' Noah asked.

Avril smiled. 'The toilets are in the next hall, Noah,' she said. 'Are you maybe trying to sneak ahead to see the rare artefacts?'

'You got me,' Noah said.

Chase patted Noah's shoulder. 'It's okay. We'll catch up with you next door.'

Noah threaded her way through the crowd towards the next hall, scrutinising the exhibits she passed for anything unusual. She paused at a scale model of a cliff-face, joining a tour group and standing beside an elderly lady with a young boy in tow.

'The great mystery of this ancient culture is how they got their dead into the niches,' the young female guide said. 'The niches are high in the cliffs. They certainly couldn't have climbed up from the bottom and it is difficult to imagine how they might have scaled down from the top – especially with a mummified body to carry.

'As you can see' – she pointed to one of the mummified bundles – 'the corpses were not laid out flat. They were arranged in the foetal position before binding. These people believed that since they were curled up this way in their mother's womb before being born into this world, they should take the same position before being born into the next world.'

'Neat,' the young boy said, clapping his hands enthusiastically.

Noah smiled as the elderly woman accompanying him flinched.

'Toby, remember what we talked about?' the old lady said. 'You can be interested without being creepy.'

Creepy, Noah thought, rubbing her hand absently over the goose-bumps on her arm. *There is* definitely *something creepy here.*

'Noah.'

At the sound of Raven's voice, Noah turned. 'Bored with the warriors already?' she said.

He didn't answer her question but looked her up and down. 'Are you alright?'

Her unease rising as he studied her, she said, 'I think so. Why?'

Raven frowned. 'I dunno. I just had a feeling …'

'Yeah, I know what you mean,' Noah said. 'There's something not quite right here but I can't put my finger on it. Come next door with me.'

'Yep.'

Raven strode towards the final exhibition hall, leaving Noah scrambling to catch up. They walked through the short tunnel side by side, but Noah stopped as soon as she set foot inside the next hall. Raven pulled her out of the entranceway.

'You want to get trampled?' he said.

Noah put her right hand over her chest and pinched her locket between her fingers. 'My slider,' she said. 'It's warm.'

'That sounds bad.'

Noah nodded. 'It is. Firestone is attuned to Talisker, not to here.'

'But something is setting it off?'

'Yes.'

Raven looked over his shoulder towards the entranceway. 'Where should I be?' he asked. 'Should I check on Chase or am I more useful here?'

'Stay with me,' Noah said.

Raven folded his arms across his chest. 'Then there's something in here – a relic – from Talisker?'

'That's what I'm thinking,' Noah said.

'Then we need to find it.'

'You got that right.'

They jostled their way through the sea of people and at the far end of the hall, Noah stopped in front of a glass case. 'This is it.'

A solid metal triangle about the size of Noah's open hand lay on a black velvet cushion. Its centre had been drilled out to the size of a half-dollar coin, and then filled with a piece of firestone. The shiny metal around the multicoloured gem was smooth but for three identical carvings. Running parallel with the triangle's edges, three straight lines had been etched in black into the metal. *Almost a triangle within the triangle,* Noah thought, *but the lines don't quite join up.* On the ends of each line was a circle – an unfilled circle at one end and a black circle at the other. Noah read the plaque on the case.

Iron and copper triangle with opal inset – origin unknown.

'Not a very helpful description, is it,' Raven said.

Noah gaped at the artefact, his words barely registering with her.

'It can't be,' she whispered.

Noah's heart beat painfully in her chest as an image of Gillette flashed in her mind. She had saved Emir's nephew from King Franco but she'd had no chance against Jong. The God of Destruction had abducted ten-year-old Gillette and given Noah a mission. In exchange for Gillette, she was to free Jong. Set him loose in the universe. And with the relic before her, she could do it!

Raven nudged her with his elbow. 'Noah?'

'It can't be,' she said again.

'It can't be what?'

Noah decided against mentioning Jong in a public place. Instead, she reread the inscription.

Iron and copper triangle with opal inset – origin unknown.

'Origin unknown, my arse,' she muttered under her breath.

'Beg your pardon?' Raven said.

Noah turned to him. 'Where's Avril? I need to know who donated this piece.'

A voice behind her interrupted whatever response Raven might have made. 'Excuse me, Miss?'

Noah spun round. A freckle-faced young man in a museum uniform waved a booklet. 'Would you like a program?' he asked. 'It's full of information on all the exhibits, including the contributors.'

'How much?' Noah asked.

'For you, Miss, a tenner,' he said, smiling.

Noah fished her wallet out of her handbag and found a ten-dollar note. 'Here you go,' she said, 'a crisp, new tenner.'

He took the note and slipped it in the money pouch around his waist. 'Pleasure, Miss,' he said, handing her a program. 'Enjoy the rest of your visit today.'

'Thanks,' Noah said, opening the glossy booklet. 'Let's see who owns …'

She stared at the inside cover for several moments.

'Noah?' Raven said. 'What is it?'

'Guess whose exhibition this is,' Noah said as she leafed through the program in search of information about the artefact.

'Whose?' Raven said.

'Bernard Kurz.'

Raven's eyes widened. '*Kurz?* Really?'

'Really.'

'Do you think he's related to … you-know-who?'

'Yep,' Noah said. 'I'm pretty sure "Bernard" was Orville's grandfather's name.'

'Crap!'

'And, according to the program,' Noah said, glancing at the photo of the iron triangle, 'that artefact belongs to him.'

Raven frowned. 'Avril Jane said that she had curated this exhibition of her grandfather's work, didn't she?'

'Yep.'

'So Avril is Bernard Kurz's granddaughter?'

'It looks that way.'

Raven exhaled slowly. 'So what do we do now?'

The question hung in the air for long moments while Noah marshalled her thoughts.

'We tread very carefully,' she said at last.

'A trap?'

Noah nodded as she clutched her locket. 'It's gotta be.'

'Do you think Chase is in danger?' he asked.

'Not at the moment,' Noah said, 'but I'll go and hurry her along. You wait here.'

'Yep.'

Noah's stomach churned as she retraced her steps across the hall. As if dealing with Jong wasn't bad enough, Bernard Kurz promised to further complicate things. His grandson, Orville Kurz had almost obliterated Talisker three years ago and his face still lurked in Noah's nightmares. And Orville hadn't had the artefact that Bernard possessed.

When Noah found Chase, her friend was so engrossed in the mummified cat display that she didn't notice Noah's arrival. Not wanting to startle her, Noah hung behind her.

'Ah, Noah,' Avril said, 'back already?'

'Checking on progress,' Noah said. 'There are certain places writers should not be left unchecked. Museums, libraries and second-hand shops top the list.'

Far from being offended, Chase smiled.

'I see you got yourself a program,' Avril said.

'Yes,' Noah said. 'It's for Chase actually. She likes to collect this kind of stuff.'

'She can have as many copies as she likes – on the house,' Avril said magnanimously.

'A couple of copies would be great,' Chase said. 'I like to cut out the pictures.'

'You keep your copy as a souvenir, Noah,' Avril said. 'It actually makes for very interesting reading.'

'I'm sure it does,' Noah said, 'but, unless there's *fashion* in there, I'm unlikely to get to it anytime soon.'

Avril tilted her head to one side. 'So you haven't had a little peek inside?'

A tingle trickled down Noah's spine as she studied the young woman. If Avril was Bernard Kurz's granddaughter then Avril and

Orville were related. *Siblings or cousins?* Noah wondered. Right now, that didn't matter she decided.

'I've been too engrossed in the exhibits to read the program,' Noah said. 'It's an excellent display.'

'Well thank you, Noah. I'll take that as a compliment.'

Noah nodded but said nothing more. She checked her watch. They'd been at the museum for less than an hour.

The tour ground on, Chase taking photos of almost everything. By the time they reached the firestone relic in the last hall, Noah was desperate to leave.

'This display here,' Avril said, 'contains items of unknown origin. My grandfather has acquired these from collectors over the years but, despite extensive investigation, has found little information on them. As you can probably appreciate, artefacts are much easier to analyse in context when you're on a dig – but when you purchase them from dealers it's much more difficult.'

'I can imagine,' Noah said.

Chase stared at the firestone relic for a long moment before looking at Noah. Noah tapped her watch.

Chase took the hint. 'Well, it's been a wonderful tour, Avril,' she said, 'but I'm afraid we have to run. We have a lunch engagement to attend.'

'I completely understand,' Avril said. 'Being a famous author, I'm sure your diary is always full.'

'It is tricky to juggle all my commitments,' Chase admitted.

Avril clasped her hands over her heart. 'Would you have time to sign my books before you go?'

Chase smiled. 'Of course. It's the least I can do to thank you for your generosity. The passes' – she waved the VIP tag on her lanyard – 'and the guided tour are much appreciated.'

Avril blushed. 'Do you think you might use the passes again?'

'I have a few appointments this week, but I'll see what I can arrange,' Chase said.

Oh, we'll be back, Noah thought. *We'll* definitely *be back.*

Chapter 2

'You're sure it's firestone?' Chase said as she and Noah waited outside the museum for Raven to bring the car around.

'Totally sure,' Noah replied.

'And it definitely belongs to Bernard Kurz?'

'That's what it says in the program.'

Chase rubbed her hand over her swollen belly. 'That can't be good.'

'Agreed,' Noah said. 'It's part of the illestial.'

'The what?'

'The illestial,' Noah said again. 'I read about it in the archives in Carai. It's part of Pyranhi folklore.'

Chase's eyes narrowed. 'And what does it do?'

'Hold that thought,' Noah said as the car pulled up in front of them. 'Raven needs to hear this too.'

Chase took the front seat while Noah climbed in behind Raven.

'All set?' Raven said, watching Noah in the rear-vision mirror.

Noah nodded. 'Yep. Let's go. If we're late for Aunt Polly's birthday lunch, she'll never let us forget it.'

Though Noah's relationship with her guardian had improved over the last few years, she wasn't prepared to do anything that might jeopardise the fragile bond.

Raven saluted before pulling out from the curb.

'So Noah,' Chase said. 'The illestial?'

'The illestial was made by a faction of the Pyranhi called the Jongu,' Noah said.

'Hang on,' Raven said, changing lanes to merge onto the freeway, 'remind me – who were the Pyranhi?'

'I know this!' Chase said. 'The Pyranhi were an ancient race of Taliskeran beings, predating the Descera. They were small creatures, powerful in magic, who built magnificent cities deep underground. For millennia upon millennia they celebrated subterranean life in art and architecture. Ultimately though, as they drained the world's dragonsong and their race declined, they split into two main groups. One group – the Elanu – supported the ideals of the god, Elani. The Jongu, on the other hand, followed Jong. Each group thought that their way was the way to save their civilisation, but the war that resulted from the conflict of ideas ended their race.'

'You sound like a journalist, Chase,' Noah said.

Chase turned in her seat and poked out her tongue.

Noah took up the narrative. 'The Jongu, who wanted to leave what they saw as a doomed world, were thought to have created the illestial. It's a four-sided pyramid – designed to break Jong free of Talisker. There are three plain metal triangles plus the piece we saw – the pyrohm – that activates the device.'

'But releasing Jong – that would destroy Talisker,' Raven said. 'How did the Jongu think that would save them?'

'The Jongu thought that their revered god would be so grateful for his freedom that he would give them sanctuary on another world.'

'Risky play.'

Noah nodded. 'But there was a third, lesser known sect of the Pyranhi in the game too. One that followed the goddess, Temperance – Elani's and Jong's sister. She doesn't get a lot of press. I hadn't even heard of her until I started trawling through Carai's archives. There are very few references to her, but they indicate that she was a kind of mediator. She settled disputes between her brothers. So following Temperance's example, her disciples tried to keep the peace between the Elanu and the Jongu. One account I read suggested that although they failed to unite the Elanu and Jongu to save the Pyranhi race, Temperance's followers saved the planet by stopping the Jongu from using the illestial – by stealing the pyrohm and hiding it.'

Chase swivelled around to look at Noah. 'So if it was hidden by Temperance's disciples, how did Bernard Kurz get hold of it?'

Noah frowned. 'I don't think *how* he got it is as big a problem as what he intends to do with it.'

'He wanted us to see it,' Raven said. 'He had Avril lure us to the museum so we would.'

For a few moments, the only sound in the car was the clicking of the indicator as Raven changed lanes.

'I can't believe I fell for that ruse,' Chase said.

'I'm sure Avril really is a fan of yours, Chase,' Raven said. 'She did have *all* your books and they were hardly in top condition. Someone had read them.'

'Maybe,' Chase mumbled.

'Well, if she's not a true fan, then that's her loss, Chase,' Noah said. 'You're the best.'

Chase sighed. 'Thanks, Noah.' Straightening in her seat, she added, 'Do you think old Bernard wants revenge for Orville's death?'

Noah shuddered. Orville Kurz had planned his assault on Talisker meticulously – detailing it in a novel dedicated to his grandfather. *Taliskeran Terror* was Orville's idea of life imitating art. He was the protagonist – the embodiment of the evil foretold in the prophecy of the 13th key, who planned to compromise Talisker's dragonsong and unleash Armageddon. When Noah had used firestone to blast the portal to Earth to prevent his escape, Orville was incinerated in the explosion.

Noah winced at the memory. She hadn't meant to kill him.

'Yes,' Noah said. 'I think Bernard wants to succeed where Orville failed. He wants to destroy Talisker.'

'We need to steal the illestial then,' Raven said.

'The pyrohm,' Noah said. 'We need to steal the pyrohm. As far as I know, no one knows where the other three pieces of the illestial are – and let's hope it stays that way.'

'Let's hope Bernard doesn't have them,' Raven said.

'If he does,' Noah said, 'then it's even more important we get the pyrohm from him.'

Raven veered off the freeway and, as he slowed the car, Noah caught him watching her in the rear-vision mirror. She avoided his gaze, leafing through the program from the exhibition until she found the photo of the pyrohm. Goosebumps broke out on her arms again as she studied the Pyranhi relic. She recalled what Jong had said about Gillette.

I will not harm him. When you return to free me, he will be hale. I promise you this – as proof to you that I am not evil.

'Noah?' Raven said.

She kept her eyes on the photo. 'Yes?'

'What else?'

Noah sighed. There was no point trying to deflect him. Raven was her twin. If she lied to him, he'd know. She gave him only one word.

'Gillette.'

Chase's head snapped round. She stared at Noah. 'This is what Jong wants from you – in exchange for Gillette?'

'Pretty sure,' Noah said.

'Pretty sure?' Chase echoed, the colour fading from her face.

'All the research I did in Carai points to the Jongu city of Somyni … and this' – Noah stabbed her finger at the picture of the pyrohm – 'being what Jong needs to break free of Talisker.'

'Then not only do we need to steal it,' Chase said, 'we need to destroy it.'

'Eventually it needs to be destroyed,' Noah agreed, 'but in the meantime …'

'It *must* be destroyed,' Chase insisted, resting one hand on her belly. 'I know it's selfish, but now that I'm about to be a mother … if we take it back and Jong succeeds … my baby …'

'I won't let that happen,' Noah said.

'You know I think you're awesome, Noah,' Chase said, 'but you can't control everything. I know you want to rescue Gillette – we all want that. But Jong is a god! What if something goes wrong? You've been really lucky so far, but what if your luck runs out?'

'You think Noah's success has all been luck?' Raven said.

'*Luck* isn't the word I would've used,' Noah muttered.

'Not all luck, Raven,' Chase said defensively, 'but even *you* have to admit that she *has* been lucky. Who else could possibly have survived everything she has?'

'Exactly,' Raven said. 'No one else *could* have. Think about everything she's done. Do you really think she can't do this?'

Chase frowned. 'Don't do that,' she said. Fixing her gaze on Noah, she added, 'You know I have absolute faith in you, but this device sounds really dangerous. It's *designed* to release Jong. If even the smallest thing were to go wrong – Talisker is no more.'

'I know,' Noah said, 'but think of it this way, Chase. We only have one piece of the illestial …'

'And if Jong's been planning this, he's probably got the other three!' Chase said.

You have a higher purpose, Noah, Jong had said, *and you will fulfil it. Releasing me will make the universe a greater place and you will make sure it happens.* Jong was relying on her to set him free. No one else. Noah knew better than to share that with Chase though.

'Jong couldn't have them,' Noah said, shaking her head. 'The Jongu made the illestial long after his incarceration. There is no way he could have got his hands on them.'

Raven parked the car and switched off the engine. No one made any move to get out.

'So how does old Bernard fit into all this?' Raven said. 'Is he working for Jong?'

Again, Noah refrained from sharing her suspicion that she was Jong's sole operative. 'I don't think Bernard is on Jong's radar,' she said at last. 'Maybe it's just a fluke that he's got the pyrohm.'

Raven scoffed. 'And the fact that his grandson tried to destroy Talisker? That's a fluke too? I don't believe that, Sis – and I don't think you do either.'

A rapping noise on the window beside Noah made her jump. Aunt Polly stared in through the glass, frowning.

'Are you coming out?' Polly said, her voice muffled by the glass. 'Or do you want me have lunch delivered to the car?'

'Coming,' Noah said as she reached for the door handle.

Once out of the car, Noah hugged her aunt. 'Happy birthday, Aunt Polly.'

'Thank you, Noah,' Polly said.

Raven and Chase each took their turn hugging Polly before they moved inside the restaurant. Noah marvelled at the antics in the open kitchen as she passed. It was a frenzy of activity. From within a pall of steam, chefs barked orders and junior cooks scrambled to follow them. Bursts of flame erupted from different sections of the kitchen in an hypnotic pyrotechnics display. And Noah was sure that even when the restaurant was closed, the pungent aroma of exotic spices and coriander would be ever-present – the walls and furnishings had had four decades to absorb the smell of the traditional Thai cuisine.

'I love this place,' Polly said as Raven pulled out her chair for her.

Noah smiled. 'Food's always good here.'

'I first came here for my thirtieth birthday,' Polly said, 'and I've come every birthday since.'

'And no doubt – since it's a *special* birthday today – they'll fuss over you even more than usual,' Raven said.

'Choose your next words very carefully, Raven,' Polly said. 'Remember, it's bad manners to mention a lady's age.'

'I wouldn't dream of it, Aunt Polly,' he said.

'Do we get menus?' Chase asked.

'Hungry *again*, Chase?' Raven said. 'Are you sure you're only eating for two?'

Chase shot him a withering look. 'Very sure,' she said.

Polly waved her hand. 'No menus today, Jemima. The head chef has planned a special banquet for us.'

Chase's eyes widened. 'Sounds exciting.'

'It will be fabulous,' Polly assured her, 'and no one will go hungry.'

As pitchers of drinks arrived, Noah thought of her parents. She had only vague memories of Polly's birthdays here with them. *I was five years old the last time we were all here together,* she thought. A car accident had claimed her parents only a few months later.

Raven leaned over and put his arm around Noah's shoulder. 'You okay?'

'Yeah,' she said. 'I'm good.'

'You?'

'Fine.'

Though losing her parents had devastated Noah, she felt worse for Raven. The only time he'd spent with their parents was as an Alsatian.

Polly raised her glass, interrupting Noah's reverie. 'To my late brother, Striker and his lovely wife, Isla,' she said. 'They should be here with us.'

'To Mum and Dad,' Noah said as Raven and Chase echoed the toast.

Everyone sipped their fruity drinks.

'So how was the museum?' Polly asked.

'Pretty good,' Noah said.

Raven nodded. 'The Warrior section was good.'

'It was well laid out,' Chase added.

Polly studied each of her guests in turn. 'Noah,' she said, 'spill.'

Noah took a deep breath. She'd withheld a significant amount of information from Aunt Polly about her exploits on Talisker. On her infrequent visits to Earth over the past three years, Noah had talked up her role as King's Tailor but had given away little else. *She deserves to know more,* Noah thought.

'Chase,' Noah said, 'do you have a copy of the program from the museum? I left mine in the car.'

Chase reached into her bag and retrieved one of her programs. 'Here,' she said, handing it across the table to Noah.

Noah flicked through the glossy brochure until she found the picture of the pyrohm. 'This artefact,' she said, 'is from Talisker.'

'It's a lovely piece,' Polly said. 'That opal is magnificent.'

Noah shook her head. 'It's not an opal. It's firestone.'

Polly studied the photo. 'A rose by any other name is still a rose.'

'That's true for roses,' Chase said, 'but that isn't a rose.'

'Well, obviously …' Polly said, frowning.

'It's firestone,' Noah said. 'Firestone is a source of great power on Talisker. *Very* great power. Opals are gems, made of minerals. Firestone is … fragments of dragonscale.'

'Dragonscale?' Polly said. 'As in the scales of a dragon?'

'Yes. In Talisker's case, firestone comes from the scales of one particular dragon,' Noah said. 'The story goes like this … Millions of years ago, the great god, Elani was busy creating beautiful worlds across the galaxies. His brother, Jong, who was equally powerful but destructive, rode through the galaxy on his trusty dragon, Xan, destroying Elani's worlds as he came across them.

'One time, Elani came across Xan while she was sleeping. As Jong was nowhere in sight, Elani disguised himself as his brother and tricked Xan into riding with him. He created a world for her that was the most beautiful he'd ever made. For the first time, Xan saw the beauty of creation and was instantly sorry for the destruction she'd been party to. She was angry and decided to eat her evil lord, but Elani threw off his disguise just in time to save his life.

'Xan vowed to find Jong and kill him and when she found him there was a great battle. They fought for an age. Xan did finally consume Jong but he didn't die. She was mortally wounded and begged Elani for help to contain Jong. To honour Xan's sacrifice and to contain his wicked brother, Elani made a world around them. Talisker. The dragon Xan didn't die though – she is sleeping. Her blood still flows as lava through the earth and pieces of her scales are scattered throughout the underground.'

'That's an … interesting story,' Polly said.

Noah was about to continue when two waiters arrived bearing tasty entrees. She surveyed the plates and selected a few of her favourites. The coconut prawns made her mouth water.

'Looks delicious,' Raven said.

'Is delicious,' Noah said through a mouthful of prawn.

Polly grimaced. 'Noah,' she said, 'for someone who lives and works in a palace, your manners are deplorable.'

Noah swallowed. 'Sorry, Aunt Polly.'

'I should say so,' Polly said. 'Now what were you saying about firestone?'

'When I arrived on Talisker,' Noah said, 'there were twelve small pieces of firestone embedded in musical instruments. The Taliskerans called them keys and skilled musicians used the keys to maintain the natural order of the world.'

Polly frowned.

'We'd call it magic here,' Noah clarified. 'Anyway, there was a prophecy that a great evil would destroy the world unless the 13th key was found. As it turned out, the 13th key didn't need to be found – it needed to be made. I had the thirteenth piece of firestone to make it with.'

Polly cocked her head. '*You* had it? How's that?'

Noah pointed to her ring. 'Mum's ring. It wasn't a sapphire. It was a piece of firestone.'

Polly looked at Noah's ring and then at the photo in the program. 'I don't remember it ever looking like that.'

Noah stared at her ring. 'There was a charm – a spell – on it so no one would know what it really was. This isn't firestone though. My firestone's inside my locket now.' She unclasped the chain around her neck and placed the necklace on the table in front of Polly. 'Open it.'

Polly flicked the catch on the locket and a glittering piece of firestone slid out onto the table. Inside its silver frame the dragonscale glinted and sparkled.

Polly gasped.

'It's called a slider,' Noah said. 'I can insert it into the bridge of Mum's viola and the instrument becomes a key.'

Polly stared at her. 'And what do you do with it? Magic?'

'Sort of,' Noah said. 'We call it raiki, and I've been learning how to use raiki to heal people. I'm actually moving away from fashion to be a doctor.'

'You play music to heal people?'

'Yes.'

'I'd like to see that sometime,' Polly said.

'Well, you'll have to come to Talisker,' Noah said. 'It doesn't work here.'

'Maybe I will.' Polly pointed to the slider. 'May I pick it up?'

'Sure. It won't hurt you.'

Polly picked up the slider and cradled it in her hand. Without taking her eyes from the stone, she said, 'You said you had this piece to make the 13th key because the world was under threat from a "great evil". What happened?'

Noah wasn't ready to admit to her aunt that she was the 13th key, but she wouldn't lie. 'With help, Raven and I made the 13th key to defeat the "great evil" that threatened Talisker. The "great evil's" name was Orville Kurz – the grandson of Bernard Kurz.'

Polly shook her head. 'I don't recognise the name.'

Noah pointed to the photo of the artefact. 'Bernard Kurz owns that artefact. And it was his granddaughter, the curator of the exhibition, who lured us to the museum by giving Chase VIP tickets.'

Polly's eyes widened. 'Well, well, well,' she said. 'That *is* interesting.'

'And not a coincidence.'

'No,' Polly said slowly. 'I don't suppose it is. You said you defeated Orville. Do you know where he is now?'

'Dead.'

'Dead … how?' Polly said, handing the firestone slider back to Noah.

'He died when we tried to stop him destroying Talisker.'

'Oh.'

Polly's brow furrowed and the corners of her mouth twitched as she digested what Noah had told her. Raven loaded their aunt's plate with curry puffs, but she seemed not to notice. Noah exhaled slowly as she waited for her aunt's reaction.

At length, Polly said, 'Do you know anything about this … Bernard Kurz?'

'Not really, only what Orville told me.'

'You talked to Orville?'

Noah nodded and told her aunt of the book Orville had read – his inspiration for trying to destroy Talisker.

Polly's brow furrowed. 'Let me get this straight … Orville read about the prophecy of the 13th key in a book and decided that he wanted to be the evil that ended the world?'

'Yes.'

Polly tapped her fingers on the table. 'How was he planning to do it?'

'Using a combination of blood magic and the 13th key.'

'But he didn't have the 13th key.'

'No, he planned to find it though.'

'That doesn't make sense,' Polly said. 'Why look for the 13th key when your grandfather has a piece of firestone lying around? If dragon-scale is as powerful as you say, surely that' – she pointed to the photo – 'would be powerful enough to do the job.'

'Orville might not have known about it,' Noah said. 'Maybe Bernard didn't share everything with his grandson.'

Polly nibbled a fishcake. 'What are you going to do now?'

Noah's gaze flicked from Raven to Chase and then back to her aunt. 'We're going to steal it.'

Polly's eyes bulged. 'Seriously?' she said. 'How about you go and talk to Bernard first?'

'*What!*' Noah, Raven and Chase chorused.

'Go and talk to him,' Polly said.

Noah leaned forward and kept her voice low. 'Did you not hear the part about how I killed his grandson?'

'And the part about him luring us to the museum?' Raven added.

'I heard,' Polly said. 'But before you resort to a life of crime, get on the front foot and go and talk to him.'

'Do you really think he'll tell us what he's up to?' Noah said.

'Probably not, but don't let him push you around,' Polly said. 'Don't let him have it all his own way.'

Chapter 3

Noah stared through the windshield of Aunt Polly's mini as she approached the main building on the Kurz estate. The medieval garrison presided over the hilltop with an ominous air. As the tyres crunched the gravel on the circular drive, Noah thought she saw movement in one of the many windows. Was Bernard watching? It could have been anyone, she told herself. There was bound to be an enormous staff.

Dozens of cars filled the carports adjacent to the building so Noah pulled up in front of the main door. *Might as well be really bold,* she thought.

She turned the key and the engine rattled to a stop.

'Rest up, old girl,' Noah said. 'It's all downhill on the way home.'

She stepped out of the car, strode to the front door and lifted the ornate iron knocker. Noah announced her arrival with three loud strikes. Within seconds the door opened soundlessly.

An old man in a maroon velvet suit stood in the doorway. Though his body was frail and his shoulders stooped, the blue eyes straddling his bulbous nose twinkled with mischief.

'Good morning, Miss Chord. I'm Bernard Kurz,' the man said. 'I must say that I'm surprised to see you here.'

'Really?' Noah said, pulling the exhibition brochure from her satchel. She held up the picture of the pyrohm. 'I thought this was an invitation.'

Bernard smiled. 'I wasn't sure that you'd recognise it.'

'Then you underestimated me,' Noah said.

'We'll see,' Bernard said, making a sweeping gesture with his arm. 'Won't you come in?'

Noah stepped inside and surveyed the entrance hall as Bernard secured the door. Life-size paintings of aristocratic folk adorned the walls. *The Kurz family tree,* she thought. *Arrogant lot, by the look of them.* Ignoring the disdain on their faces, Noah catalogued the changes in fashion that marked the different generations. She'd like to have spent more time studying the haute couture, but Bernard beckoned to her.

'This way,' he said.

Noah fell in step with him. 'There are a lot of cars out front,' she said. 'Big staff here?'

'Yes. It takes many hands to maintain a place like this,' he said. 'Would you like a tour?'

Noah knew it would be polite to say yes, but that would jeopardise Raven's mission. She wasn't here just for information. She was a diversion. Someone to keep Bernard and his staff distracted while Raven completed his reconnaissance. Noah checked her watch. Raven would be on the estate grounds now and Chase would soon be at the museum, scoping the security measures there. Noah had taken Aunt Polly's advice about confronting Bernard but stealing the pyrohm was still the priority.

'I don't want to impose,' Noah said. 'I'm sure you're very busy.'

'It's no trouble,' Bernard said, 'but let's have tea first.'

Noah smiled. 'Sounds lovely.'

I survived a year and a half in a goblin city, Noah thought. *I can do this.*

Bernard led her down the hall to glass doors at the rear of the building. Beyond the doors Noah spied a swimming pool – or a small lake – shimmering under a bank of hedges that skirted the perimeter of the courtyard. As she stepped outside, she saw two waiters standing by the deck chairs under the shade sails.

'Please,' Bernard gestured. 'Take a seat.'

When Noah had made herself comfortable on her chair, the waiter nearest her handed her a brochure.

'Today's menu, Ma'am,' he said. 'Just let me know when you're ready to order.'

Noah waved the menu away. 'Just a jasmine iced tea will be fine, thank you,' she said.

The waiter bowed then left, leaving Noah hoping she'd chosen a non-poisonous option.

'So Mr Kurz, how long's this estate been in your family?'

'Three hundred and sixty-four years,' Bernard replied. 'Fourteen generations of my family have graced these halls. Do you like the place?'

'I'd like to reserve judgement until I've seen more of it,' Noah said.

Bernard nodded. 'Very sensible.' He studied her. 'You're a sensible girl, are you, Noah? Perhaps that's the reason you're alive and my grandson isn't?'

Noah looked at him, remembering her aunt's advice. *Get on the front foot*, Polly had said. *Don't let him push you around.* With an opening like that, it was difficult to imagine how she'd get ahead of him.

'Possibly,' Noah said. 'I certainly wouldn't run *into* an inferno.'

'Is that what happened?' Bernard said.

'Yes.'

'Ah, my Orville,' Bernard said. 'He was impetuous, I'll grant you that.'

'You were close?'

'No,' Bernard said. 'He was a strange child. I tried to set him straight but he was just … odd.'

'What about his siblings?' Noah asked.

'Siblings?'

'I heard he was one of thirteen children.'

Bernard laughed. 'You talked to his biographer?'

'Indirectly.'

'Hmm. Load of rot that. He was an only child. His biography was a greater work of fiction than his novel.'

'And better written, I'll bet,' Noah said.

Bernard nodded. 'Yes, though that wouldn't have been difficult.'

'You read his novel?' Noah asked.

'Yes,' Bernard said. 'Utterly terrible.'

When the waiter delivered her drink, Noah was thankful for the distraction. She sipped her tea and gazed at the pool. This wasn't going at all as she'd thought it would. Bernard Kurz was not what she'd expected.

'So this isn't about revenge then?' Noah said, placing her drink on the table beside her.

Bernard recoiled. 'Of course not, Noah. I should probably be thanking you. Orville was a frightful twerp. He broke his mother's heart – and her mind. Poor Lillian. The world … the world*s* … are better off without him.'

'Worlds?' Noah said. 'You mean Earth and Talisker?'

'Yes.'

'And what about Avril?' Noah said. 'Does she meet with your approval?'

Bernard smiled. 'My dear Avril. Yes. She meets with my approval.'

'Because she does your bidding? Like luring authors and their friends to museum exhibitions?'

Bernard cocked his head. 'Only one author.'

'How much have you told her?' Noah asked. 'Does Avril know where the artefact is really from?'

'She knows about the *artefact*,' Bernard said. 'She doesn't know about *you* though.'

Noah held his gaze. What did *he* know about her? If he'd read Orville's book, he'd know lots. Orville had known things. He'd known her mother was from Talisker. He'd known about her Academy ring. But did Bernard know more than Orville? Orville hadn't known she was the 13th key and she prayed that Bernard didn't either. Hopefully he hadn't found out she was Dragonsbane or had been King of Carai.

'Can you trust her?' Noah said.

'Yes.'

'Why? What makes her different from Orville?'

'You've met them both,' Bernard said. 'You tell me.'

'She's a better actress,' Noah said. 'Orville could never have pretended to be a fan of Chase's books.'

'She wasn't pretending,' Bernard said. 'I'd wager that Avril *is* Ms Chase's biggest fan.'

'Her taste in literature, if nothing else, weighs in her favour then, I guess,' Noah said.

'She's a good girl,' Bernard said, as Noah drained her glass. 'Did you enjoy your tea?'

'Very refreshing.'

'Perhaps we could start our tour of the estate now?'

'Sure,' Noah said, placing her glass on the waiter's tray.

She walked alongside Bernard across the spongy lawn. He was surprisingly spritely for an old man. They approached the hedge and then walked through an archway cut into the luxuriant green barricade. Where the ground sloped away she saw a stand of old gravestones by a gargantuan oak. At least there didn't appear to be any open graves.

Other people might be dying to come here, Noah thought, *but I'm not.*

'This might seem like an odd place to start,' Bernard said, 'but there's a reason I brought you here.'

Noah studied him. 'Which is?'

'I wanted to show you my wife's grave,' Bernard said, resting his hand on a carved marble obelisk. 'My late wife – Alina – was Taliskeran.'

Noah studied the headstone.

> *Alina Kurz (nee Jane)*
> *02.03.1945 – 20.08.2019*
> *Beloved wife of Bernard Kurz*
> *Mother of Lillian and Gillon*
> *Grandmother of Orville and Avril*
> *Our eternal light*

'She visited you and your mother once,' Bernard said.

'I don't remember that.'

'No, I don't suppose you do. You were only a baby at the time.'

Orville had told Noah that he'd accompanied his grandmother on the visit.

Bernard sighed. 'My wife is here because of Orville. He broke *her* heart too.'

Noah said nothing, waiting for the old man's explanation. But as she stood under the exotic oak that shaded the gravestones, a cool breeze snaked around her ankles and wound its way up her legs. It took hold of her fingers and then her arms. When the chill seized her chest, Noah struggled to breathe. She shivered and inhaled deeply, forcing air into her lungs. Bernard, staring at Alina's headstone, appeared not to notice her discomfort.

Thankful for a short reprieve from Bernard's scrutiny, Noah scanned the small burial ground. Dozens of headstones poked up amongst the shrubs and flowers in the dappled shade. It looked peaceful – almost cheery – but Noah sensed something stirring.

'I met Alina at university,' Bernard said. 'We were both studying history. Of course, I had no idea initially that she was from another world. That came later. I just saw a beautiful, passionate, driven historian.'

The cold that gripped Noah started to dissipate and the pressure on her lungs eased.

'Why was she here?' Noah said. 'Why was she so interested in Earth's history?'

'Alina was convinced that many ancient Taliskeran relics were hidden here and she wanted to find them.'

'And return them?'

Bernard nodded.

'But you didn't want to?' Noah guessed.

'We returned many relics, I'll have you know,' he said. 'The one *you* saw was one of only a few that remain here.'

In place of the cold, there was warmth now. It started in her chest, tentacles of heat reaching through her body like an octopus stretching after a long sleep. Strange visions cascaded through Noah's mind, of foreign landscapes and exotic treasures. Armed with miniature tools and brushes, small armies of archaeologists combed deserted cities forgotten by time. In forests, deserts, mountains and caves, people sifted through layers of earth for clues about civilisations long gone. The pictures kept coming, so fast that Noah could barely distinguish them. *They're memories,* she thought, *but they're not mine.*

The heat continued building inside her, and Noah glanced at Alina's headstone as she fought to find her own thoughts amongst the chaos.

'You went to a lot of trouble to make sure I saw the firestone relic in the museum,' Noah said. 'Why?'

'I'm not going to live forever, Noah and it's important that my knowledge is preserved. You need to understand why it's here and why it must stay here.'

'Why do *I* need to know? Couldn't you have just told Avril? You said you trusted her.'

'I do trust her,' Bernard said, trailing his fingertips over Alina's headstone. 'But I'm worried that she's not as … persuasive as I am. I can foresee a time, after I'm gone, that you come across this relic here. You'll want to return it but you need to understand why that can't happen.'

Noah stared at the headstone, which appeared to be shimmering now. 'So why all the theatre? There were simpler ways to tell me.'

'Simpler, yes. But I do like a bit of drama,' Bernard said.

When he smiled, the pictures clattering through Noah's mind finally stopped. She shook her head in surprise.

'Are you okay?' Bernard asked.

'Yes,' Noah lied.

Though the heat had vanished along with the foreign memories, Noah's heart still raced. Something was stirring in the graveyard. *Is that you, Alina?* Noah thought.

Creak. Creeeeaaaak.

'Look out!' Noah cried, as her eyes flicked to the oak tree.

Crack!

Noah launched herself at the old man, skittling him out of the way of the falling branch. Almost.

'*Ouch!*' Bernard cried. 'My foot! My foot! *Ooooouch!* My foot is caught!'

Noah jumped to her feet. 'I'll lift the branch, you pull your foot out.'

Bernard nodded, panting. Noah heaved on the fallen bough and he yanked his foot clear.

'Take a deep breath. Take a couple,' she advised as she knelt next to him. 'How bad is it?'

'I don't think I'll be able to walk on it. Run up to the house would you, and get some help?'

'Okay.'

Noah glanced up at the oak. Where the branch had been attached to the tree, it was … smouldering. She frowned as she watched tendrils of smoke curling away towards the sky. Keen to be away from the graveyard, Noah pushed to her feet and jogged back towards the main building on the estate. *It's not only the living I have to watch here,* she thought. *It seems the dead could be just as big a problem.*

♪♫

Noah watched the nurses as they adjusted the pillows under Bernard's bandaged foot. It was far from riveting viewing but she kept her attention there. Any distraction from the book that had just been delivered by Bernard's butler was a good thing. The leather cover of the ancient text was scuffed and bore a dark stain that Noah suspected was blood. She'd seen similar books – minus the blood splatter – in the restricted sections of two of Talisker's royal libraries.

'I'm fine,' Bernard said with a wave. 'Leave us.'

The male nurse nodded. 'Yes, sir. Just buzz if you need anything.'

'Yes, yes.' When the nurses were gone, he said, 'Well, Noah, this isn't how I'd imagined this day going.'

'At least it's only your foot that's injured,' Noah said. 'You can still tell me about the pyrohm.'

'So you *do* know what it is?'

Noah nodded.

'Good.' He reached for the book on the sideboard. 'Alina had several books that she brought from Talisker. She came from a long line of librarians.'

Noah's grip on the arm of her chair tightened. 'Is this the one that inspired Orville to write his novel?'

'No,' Bernard said. 'He took that one. I don't know what became of it. *This* one,' he continued, 'was one of Alina's most treasured possessions. It's a goblin text actually. I guess you'd have seen lots of those during your time in Carai?'

He studied her, awaiting her reaction.

Keen to disappoint him, Noah kept her expression neutral. 'Yes,' she said. 'I did.'

'This book details the fall of the Pyranhi culture. Did you know there was only one war in the history of the Pyranhi?'

Noah nodded. 'Yes. It was the one that ended them.'

'And you know that the war was over the illestial?'

'I know the war resulted from their different ideas – between the Elanu and Jongu – on how to save the Pyranhi race.'

'The illestial,' Bernard said, 'was the biggest problem. That was the cause of the war. Do you know how the piece – the pyrohm – that you saw in the museum, came to be here?'

'You stole it?' Noah guessed.

Bernard frowned, his wiry eyebrows bristling dangerously. 'I found it on a dig.'

'When?'

'Last year.'

'Where?'

He smiled. 'An island in the Pacific is all I'm willing to tell you, Noah. Its exact location will go to the grave with me.'

'You found it on Earth?' Noah said.

'I did.'

'*You* did? Personally?'

'I'm quite active and mobile,' Bernard said, 'when I'm not being viciously attacked by murderous tree branches.'

His tone did little to cloak his accusation.

Where does he get off? Noah thought. *His dead wife just tried to kill me* and *he's making out that I attacked him!*

'Right,' she said at last.

'So anyway,' Bernard said, patting the cover of the book, 'in here is the legend of how the pyrohm was stolen by one of Temperance's followers. Until I found it though, no one knew where it had gone.'

'So, you've re-written the ending then?' Noah said. 'Orville must have got his writing "talent" from you?'

Bernard held her gaze for several long moments before handing the book to Noah.

'See for yourself,' he said.

Noah took the book – fingers tingling – and opened the cover. The parchment inside was brittle and discoloured, the script small and spidery. The style was consistent with other goblin texts she'd seen.

'Take it,' Bernard said. 'Read it at your leisure.'

'Really? You'd let me take this?'

'It's important you understand the gravity of this situation, Noah. I do want the book back though – after you've read it.'

Get on the front foot. Polly's words echoed in Noah's mind. *Find out what he's up to.*

'Well, if the illestial is so dangerous,' Noah said, 'how about we destroy it?'

'An elegant solution, but fraught with danger.'

'Because?'

'The illestial can only be destroyed on Talisker, and only with all the pieces together.'

'Convenient,' Noah said.

'Hardly,' Bernard retorted. 'I can see you don't believe me. Take the book, read it. You don't have to take my word for it.'

Noah closed the book. 'I will read it … but what's *your* plan for the pyrohm now? If what you say is true, and the Pyranhi hid it here, then the secret's out – since you've displayed it at the museum. It clearly can't stay here.'

'I displayed it, yes,' Bernard said, 'but you're the only one who'd recognise it, Noah. Its secret is still safe. When I'm gone, Avril will be its protector. This relic must stay here. While it's here, Talisker is safe. If it returns – well you know what could happen …'

'I'll do whatever I think is in Talisker's best interest.'

'I really hope you do, Noah,' he said, 'because if you try to steal the pyrohm, I will not hesitate to neutralise the threat that you pose to Talisker.'

A knock at the bedroom door saved Noah the trouble of a reply. The male nurse stuck his head around the door. 'Phone call for you, sir. Mrs Potter,' he said. 'Would you like to take it?'

'Yes, I'd better speak to Mrs Potter.'

Noah stood up. 'I'll leave you to it,' she said. 'Thank you for your time. It's been a very interesting morning. I'll show myself out.'

Chapter 4

Noah walked along the polished marble floor on the third storey of Bernard Kurz's palatial home with Alina's book under her arm. The glass panels along the eastern wall of the garrison allowed a spectacular view of the estate's sprawling gardens. On the opposite wall, ornate doors silently guarded the rooms behind them. Noah wondered where Raven was. Was he in any of the rooms she'd walked past? He had a lot of ground to cover to document the security arrangements, as well as looking for any files Bernard had on the illestial. Noah hoped she'd bought him enough time to do his job.

Click.

Noah stopped. She scanned the corridor and saw a flicker of light ahead. One door was ajar.

Raven? It wasn't like her brother to be careless.

Noah tiptoed to the door and listened. Nothing. She peered through the small gap and spied a dressing table. Below a large scalloped mirror, the wooden dresser was under siege from an army of crystal and porcelain figurines. Dustables, Aunt Polly would call them. On the raised section on the far side, an ornate pewter hairbrush rested on a crystal platter, wisps of white hair tangled through the bristles.

Noah pushed the door open a little further. Dark blue curtains fluttered in the breeze. Apart from the curtains though, nothing moved.

'Raven?' Noah whispered.

A woman's voice answered. 'Who's there?'

Noah's eyes flicked to the four-poster bed that dominated the bedroom. Behind the delicate mosquito netting, lay a middle-aged woman. She wore a white gown and amongst the white sheets and pillows, Noah hadn't noticed her. Orville's mother? Bernard had said that Orville had broken his mother's heart and mind. *This must be her*, Noah thought, wondering if the woman's presence here was Bernard's way of caring for his daughter or saving himself the embarrassment of having her in a public facility.

'Who are you?' the woman said.

Noah briefly considered lying. If the lady recognised Noah's name, there was no telling how she might react, but Aunt Polly always said that honesty was the best policy.

'I'm Noah Chord, Ma'am,' she said. 'I've been visiting with Mr Kurz today.'

The lady sat up. Long snowy hair cloaked her shoulders and framed her gaunt face. Her skin was pale, almost translucent, no longer able to conceal the blue veins beneath. Eyes as cold as flint considered Noah.

'And what do you want with me?' she said.

'I was on my way out when I saw your door was ajar. I thought to close it but I was intrigued by your dresser, and I just …'

'Thought you'd nosy around,' the lady finished, turning her attention to the dressing table. After scanning the dresser, she added, 'At least you haven't stolen anything' – her eyes then went to the book Noah carried – 'of mine anyway. What have you got there?'

Noah presented the book for inspection, thankful that the lady hadn't recognised her name. 'Mr Kurz loaned it to me, Ms …?'

'Kurz. Lillian Kurz,' she said, still eyeing the book. 'That is one of my late mother's books. What is your interest in Talisker, Noah?'

'I'm from Talisker, Ms Kurz.'

Lillian gasped, then leant over and parted the gauze curtain. 'Sit.'

Noah did as she was told, perching lightly on the edge of the bed.

'You wear an Academy ring,' Lillian said. 'What rank are you?'

Noah flinched. 'I'm a Major, Ma'am.'

The corners of Lillian's mouth curled into a smile. 'You're surprised I would ask such a question?'

'A little.'

'My father told you I was crazy, didn't he.'

'He said you'd struggled with … your son's disappearance,' Noah said, glancing at the pill bottles on the bedside table.

Lillian's smile faded. 'And did he tell you that he's the one responsible for Orville's situation?'

'Ah, no,' Noah said slowly, her stomach knotting painfully.

'Orville read one of my mother's books,' Lillian said, 'one that contained the prophecy of the 13th key. I assume you've heard of it?'

Noah nodded.

'Orville was just a boy and he was captivated by the idea of finding the 13th key. It was like a treasure hunt for him and my father kept encouraging him. I could see Orville was obsessed but my father … he wouldn't stop. My mother was worried too but neither of us could make them see reason. Orville never let go of the idea. He left here five years ago. I don't suppose you know if he found it?'

'The 13th key was found and subsequently destroyed,' Noah said, giving Lillian the official version of what had transpired the night she'd confronted Orville with a decoy key.

'When?'

'Nearly three years ago.'

'Orville?'

She doesn't know? Noah thought. *Why hasn't Bernard told her?*

Noah cursed herself for entering Lillian's room, and she saved a curse for Bernard too. He knew Orville's fate and hadn't told Lillian. Despite her delicate mental state, surely it was better that she knew her son was dead, rather than waiting and wondering if he'd return.

'There was a great explosion when the 13th key was destroyed,' Noah said. 'The king's adviser was listed as one of the victims.'

'King's adviser?' Lillian whispered. 'Orville was the king's adviser?'

Noah nodded. 'He was adviser to King Tambian – Leninstar's king.'

A tear slid down Lillian's cheek. 'My Orville,' she said. 'He was such a clever boy.' As she stared at Noah, her gaze sharpened. 'Did my father know this?'

Noah took a breath. 'Yes.'

Lillian frowned. 'Why did you come here, Noah?'

'I saw the firestone artefact in the museum,' Noah said. 'I wanted to know more about it.'

The woman's eyes widened. 'The pyrohm,' she murmured.

Noah nodded.

'I think it needs to go back to Talisker,' Lillian said.

Surprised, Noah said, 'Because?'

'It needs to be unmade and that can only be done on Talisker.'

'It is risky to take it back there, though.'

'Agreed,' Lillian said, 'but it's going to get there one day – mark my words. Whether it's now, or in a hundred years, or in a thousand years … it'll get back there. These things have a way of finding their way home.' She sighed. 'I worry that it'll be taken back by someone well-intentioned but with no idea of the danger. It needs to go back with someone who understands what's at stake and can destroy it once and for all.'

As Noah listened, she wondered why, if Lillian believed the relic should go back, she hadn't taken it herself. Her mother had been Taliskeran. Had Lillian ever visited Alina's home world? Aside from that, it would have been the perfect opportunity to search for Orville.

Unable to find a tactful way of asking, Noah said, 'Why haven't you taken it back?'

'I find it difficult to get around these days,' Lillian said, pulling down the bedcover and hitching up her nightdress. Short stumps were all that remained of her legs. 'Blood poisoning.'

'Oh,' Noah said.

'I think you're the person to do this, Noah.'

'You only just met me,' Noah said, 'and only because I'm a stickybeak.'

'You're from Talisker and you're a Major – I can't see anyone more qualified coming by anytime soon.'

'Maybe give it a hundred years …'

'Noah,' Lillian said, 'you simply must do this.'

Before Noah could respond, a nurse entered the bedroom. 'Oh, Miss Chord,' she said, 'I didn't realise you were still here.'

Noah stood up. 'I was just on my way out actually.'

'Very good,' the nurse replied. 'It's time for Ms Kurz's medication.'

Noah looked at Lillian. 'It was nice to meet you, Ms Kurz.'

'Nice to meet you too, Noah,' she said. Lillian cocked her head to one side and pointed to her dresser. 'So you'll let me know when those figurines I want come in?'

Noah glanced at the nurse who shrugged apologetically.

'She's not all there,' the nurse whispered behind her hand. 'Just humour her.'

Noah nodded and picked up Alina's journal. 'I'll be sure to let you know the moment they arrive, Ms Kurz.'

Noah turned, leaving the nurse to her patient. As she walked back to her car, Noah tried to untangle the day's events in her mind. If Jong were to get hold of the pyrohm, Talisker was doomed, but could a Kurz be trusted to protect it? She'd thought dealing with Orville had been difficult, but at least he'd been only one person. From what she'd seen today, dealing with his grandfather, mother and cousin promised to be a good deal more challenging.

♪♫

Noah checked her watch. 'Raven really should be back by now.'

Chase fidgeted with the replica artefacts on the kitchen table while Polly kneaded her pizza dough.

'Should we call the police?' Chase said.

Polly scowled as she slammed the dough onto the floured benchtop, sending a puff of white dust into the air. 'The police?' she said. 'If I had to bet, I'd say *they're* the reason he's not back yet. No doubt they're inter-rogating him as we speak.'

Noah and Chase glanced at each other. When Polly had found out about Raven's mission to scope Bernard Kurz's estate and look for secret files, she'd been furious. Noah thought her aunt was secretly worried about Raven but there was no way she'd admit it.

The door chime sounded. Noah froze and Chase fumbled the replica firestone artefact. Aunt Polly wiped her hands on her floral apron.

'I'll get that, shall I?' she said. 'It's probably the police – returning your lost property.'

When Polly cleared the doorway, Chase said, 'I don't suppose she's talking about the pyrohm, is she?'

Noah shook her head. 'No. She's talking about Raven.'

'I hope he managed to get hold of some more information. I know Bernard gave you that book, but we need to know everything we can about this thing.'

'I guess we're about to find out,' Noah said when she heard her brother's voice.

Raven entered the kitchen with Polly as his sole escort.

'Any luck?' Noah asked.

Her brother shook his head as he took a seat at the table. 'Couldn't find any files on the illestial.'

Polly whacked him on the back of the head on her way to the fridge.

'What was *that* for?' Raven said.

'*That*,' Polly said, 'was for making Noah and Chase worry about you. I can't believe you've been sneaking around Bernard Kurz's house all this time looking for files. What would've happened if you'd been caught?'

Raven smiled. 'I'd have escaped.'

Polly put her hands on her hips. 'You'd have escaped?'

'I'd have escaped,' he said. 'I've been in some pretty hairy situations before, Polly. I'm Army Commander, you know.'

'Yes, I'm aware of that, *Army Commander*, but I don't see your army anywhere.'

'No, well, luckily I didn't need it. But unfortunately, no files on the illestial either. They must be locked away—'

'Maybe they're on Bernard's bedside table?' Chase suggested.

'Definitely not there,' Raven said. With a sideways glance at Polly, he added, 'I checked.'

Polly shook her head and sat down beside Noah.

'There is a secured wing on the ground floor,' Raven said. 'I found the entrance but it needs an access code, so I couldn't get in to investigate. Any files old Bernard has are probably in there.'

He probably has some other Taliskeran artefacts in there too, Noah thought.

Raven pointed to the assortment of artefacts on the table. 'Chase, did you decide to steal a variety of artefacts to hide the one we're really after?'

'They're souvenirs,' Chase said, tossing a replica pyrohm to him. 'You weren't the only one with a mission today, Army Commander.'

Raven caught the souvenir. He turned it over in his hands, inspecting the markings. 'I don't think stealing souvenirs is a good idea,' he said, holding it up to the light to examine the fake firestone core.

'I didn't steal them,' Chase said, shaking her head. 'Avril offered them to me. She said I could take as many as I liked.'

'Yes,' Raven said slowly, 'when people say that though, there's usually an expectation that one might make a *selection* from what is on offer, and perhaps just take one of each. I'm surprised you could get so many in your bag. It looks like you took half a dozen of everything. Have you no manners?'

Noah's eyebrows arched. 'You've spent your day breaking and entering and snooping through someone's house. Who are you to be lecturing Chase on manners?'

Raven raised his hands in surrender. 'Fair enough. So what's the plan now? You're going to give these away as presents?' he asked. 'Can I choose mine now?'

'No,' Chase said. 'You can wait for your birthday like everyone else.'

Polly threw her arms up. 'Can you people be serious? This is no laughing matter.'

'Quite right,' Raven said. 'Chase, what did you find out at the museum today?'

'Security is tight,' Chase said. 'Obviously all the exhibits are monitored by CCTV, but many have weight sensors too.'

Raven nodded. 'And the pyrohm?'

'Still there,' Chase confirmed, 'and the cabinet it's in is different to the others. It has more buttons on it.'

'Buttons?' Raven said. 'Sensors maybe? Monitors?'

Chase sniffed. 'Could have been,' she said. 'I'm not a security tech expert. But I will say that I think the extra security on that cabinet means that Bernard anticipates that we might try to steal it.'

Polly groaned. 'Noah, tell your brother what Bernard said would happen if you tried to steal it.'

'He said he would "neutralise the threat I pose to Talisker",' Noah said.

'Meaning he'll neutralise *you*?' Raven said, rubbing his chin.

'Yep.'

Raven turned to Chase. 'And what about Avril?'

'Avril spends most of her time on research and maintaining her grandfather's collection,' Chase said, 'but has plans to branch out and make a documentary on the history of mathematics in pre-Columbian societies.'

'Sounds riveting,' Raven said.

Chase grimaced. 'I know.'

'So is Avril Bernard's patsy or is she in league with him?' Raven asked.

'Difficult to say,' Chase said. 'Avril is loyal to him, but it's hard to figure out if her devotion is from the heart or if she's protecting her inheritance. She's certainly pleased that Orville's out of the picture. She had nothing good to say about him.'

Noah nodded. 'That's not surprising,' she said. 'I don't know that I could find much good to say about Orville either.'

'Avril has taken her grandmother's maiden name – Jane,' Chase continued, 'apparently because she wants to be an historian in her own right. She's not content to trade off the Kurz name.'

'There's an older woman at the estate,' Raven said, 'heavily sedated if the pill bottles on her bedside table are anything to go by. Avril's mother?'

'*Orville's* mother,' Noah said. 'Lillian Kurz.'

Raven's eyes widened. 'How do you know that?'

'I talked to her,' Noah said.

Raven whistled. 'That must have been awkward.'

'It was a little,' Noah said. 'Anyway, Lillian thinks the pyrohm should go back to Talisker so it can be destroyed.'

'Really?'

Noah shrugged. 'That's what she said.'

'I wonder then,' Raven said, studying his sister, 'if we could count on her to help us to … return it to Talisker?'

'You mean *steal it*,' Polly said.

Without taking his eyes from Noah, Raven said, 'Yes. I mean steal it.'

'She's a Kurz,' Chase said. 'Maybe she's setting us up. It could be a trap.'

'Possibly,' Noah said, 'and I'll tell you something – I'm not keen to go back to find out.'

Chapter 5

Aunt Polly's car shuddered to an asthmatic stop and Chase swivelled in the driver's seat. Noah looked up from the letter in her lap and exhaled slowly.

'Okay you two,' Chase said, glancing at each of her passengers, 'this is your stop.'

'Yes, Ma'am,' Raven said. 'Noah?'

It could be a trap. The words swam around inside Noah's head as she returned her attention to Lillian's letter and reread it for the hundredth time.

Dear Noah,

You MUST take the pyrohm back to Talisker and destroy it. I have given this much thought since your visit the other day, and I want to help.

My father will be at a function at the museum on Sunday night to mark the close of the exhibition. I anticipate he will be away from the estate from about four in the afternoon until at least ten o'clock that night. This will be your best opportunity to acquire the pyrohm, which is now back at the estate. My father suspects you might try to steal it from the museum so he brought it back today, leaving a replica in its place at the museum.

The code for the security gate is Z78VR91. Once you're on the grounds, come to my bedroom window. Scaling the wall and climbing in through the window will be the best way to avoid the security guards in the house. I will be waiting for you and will give you directions and codes for the vault.

Please do this, Noah. If my mother were alive, she'd say the same thing. She and my father searched for the pyrohm for many years, but she died before it was found. It was always her intention to destroy it.

I hope to see you Sunday,

Lillian

Raven waved his hand in front of his sister's face. 'Noah?'

Noah folded the paper and tucked it into her pocket. 'I really hope we can trust her.'

'Either way, we'll get the pyrohm,' Raven said.

The letter's arrival at Aunt Polly's house had surprised them all. A young woman claiming to be Lillian's nurse and confidante had hand-delivered it. She'd said that Bernard Kurz had appointed her to keep his daughter "comfortable", which meant sedated. But the nurse had apparently taken pity on Lillian, secretly weaning her off her medication over several months. As Lillian's wits had returned, she'd set her sights on travelling to Talisker in search of Orville. Now that she'd learned of her son's fate though, she had new goal – destroying the illestial. It was a plausible story. Noah hoped it was true.

'Well, get on with it,' Chase said. 'The sooner you're back, the better I'll like it.'

Raven opened his door. 'Remember, Chase,' he said, 'if anyone else shows up, you leave – pronto!'

Chase frowned. 'Thanks for the advice, Army Commander, but I can take care of myself.'

Noah climbed out of the car and closed the door as quietly as she could. She poked her head through the open window on the front passenger side.

'Be safe,' Noah said. 'I don't want to have to explain any … incidents to Ardis.'

Chase waved her away. 'My husband need never know what we're up to.'

'Let's hope,' Noah murmured.

Ardis had been keen to accompany Chase to celebrate Aunt Polly's birthday, but the facial tattoos that marked him as an Elani warrior would have been too conspicuous on Earth, so he'd stayed on Talisker to help Emir manage the farm.

'You be careful too, Noah,' Chase called. 'I don't want to have to explain any *incidents* to Emir either.'

Raven snorted. 'She *was* King of the Goblins,' he said. 'I doubt this would surprise him.'

It wouldn't surprise him, Noah thought, *but he definitely wouldn't be happy about it.*

She inhaled deeply, the cool night air making her nostrils tingle, and followed Raven as he trekked along the roadside towards the estate's main gate. In contrast to her previous visit to the estate, tonight the gate was shut. The smooth, five-metre high, solid metal wall across the roadway gleamed in the moonlight. Too slippery to climb and too thick to ram with anything other than a military tank, it was an effective deterrent. Unless one had the security code.

Noah pulled Lillian's letter from her pocket as she approached the pin-pad. Before she entered the code, she glanced at Raven who stood by the gate. He nodded. Noah held her breath as she typed the alphanumeric sequence, hoping the code wasn't designed to alert security to their arrival.

The gate rolled aside silently. *Obviously well-maintained,* Noah thought as she slipped inside the grounds behind Raven.

'Freeze!' a voice said. 'Turn around! Hands in the air!'

Noah and Raven spun round. A lone security guard pointed his pistol at Raven.

'That doesn't make sense,' Raven said.

The guard frowned. 'What doesn't make sense?'

'You said "freeze" and then "turn around" and "hands in the air",' Raven said. 'If you tell someone to freeze you can't really expect them to follow the next instructions.'

'And yet you seemed to manage okay,' the guard said, stepping towards Noah. 'What's your business here tonight?'

'We're here to collect the pyrohm,' Noah said.

'Ah,' the guard said. 'Mr Kurz thought you might drop in. And he said if you did, we were to detain you until he could speak to you.'

'Who's we?' Noah said.

'What?'

'Who's we?' Noah said again. 'You seem to be the only guard here.'

The guard waved his weapon. '*We* is me and my gun.'

Raven launched himself at the guard and tackled him to the ground. He snatched the gun from the man's grasp before jamming it against his forehead.

The man glared at Raven. 'You gonna kill me?'

Raven shook his head as he reached for the guard's handcuffs. 'Not worth it.'

'I'll find a gag,' Noah said as she slipped into the booth beside the gate.

She rummaged through the drawers under the desk until she found a dusting cloth. *That'll do,* Noah thought, whipping the cloth from the drawer.

'I can take care of …' Noah said, nodding towards the now unconscious guard. 'What happened to him?'

Raven secured a second set of cuffs around the guard's ankles. 'He was going to yell for help. He'll sleep for a while, but he'll be fine.'

'Okay,' Noah said. 'I'll still gag him. You go on ahead.'

Raven saluted. 'Six minutes.'

Noah checked her watch. 'Six minutes.'

Search lights swept back and forth across the grounds behind Noah as she wrestled the gag into place. When she'd secured it, she dragged the guard into the booth.

Noah's stomach churned as she moved to her next position. Crouching beside a shrub, she studied the search lights while she waited. Five beams crisscrossed the grounds. She'd need to time her run precisely. Six minutes didn't sound like long but it felt like an eternity behind enemy lines. Once Raven had neutralised the guards outside, they'd meet under Lillian's window.

Noah glanced at her watch. Two minutes. She scanned the windows on the third floor. Lillian's, like all the others, were closed but through parted curtains Noah saw a light on inside. Maybe Lillian *was* waiting for them. Noah still harboured doubts about the letter. Bernard could have written it to lure her to the grounds. But the bedroom light gave her hope that the letter might be authentic.

She checked her watch again. *Time to go,* she thought.

Noah tracked the lights as she dashed from her spot. It wasn't a direct route to the rendezvous point. She had to dodge the crisscrossing beams. Arms pumping, Noah raced across the manicured lawn. As she approached the hedgerow under Lillian's window, Raven waved to her from his hiding place behind the hedge. She battled her way through the shrubbery to join him.

'Glad you could make it,' he said, uncurling his fingers to reveal a selection of pebbles in his palm.

'Thanks,' she said as she took the small stones from him.

Noah pushed back through the hedge and took three steps out onto the lawn. She stopped and turned to face the building. Heart racing, she took aim at Lillian's window and pitched a pebble towards it. *Plink.* She waited a few seconds before launching her second one. *Plink.* Noah ducked back through the foliage, craning her neck so she could watch the window. The casement window creaked as it opened and Noah held her breath. Lillian's head appeared, her white hair catching the moonlight and shining like a halo. The woman peered down.

'Noah?' she said. 'Is that you?'

'Yes, Ma'am. I'm here with my brother.'

Lillian nodded curtly. 'Come on up.'

Raven unslung the coiled rope from his shoulder as he cleared the hedge. Noah, peering through the shrubs, watched the grappling hook arc in graceful circles as her brother lined up his shot, letting out a little more rope with each cycle.

'Lillian, move back,' Noah said, gesturing for her to stand clear of the window.

'Settle down,' Raven said. 'I'm not going to hit her.'

'Not everything's about you,' Noah whispered as she struggled into her harness in the narrow space behind the hedge. 'I'm worried she might try to catch it.'

When Raven was satisfied with the rope length and momentum he released the rope. The hook sailed upwards. *Thud.* As Noah had expected, the hook caught the window sill.

Noah motioned to Lillian. 'Pass the rope around the window frame,' she said, 'and drop the hook back down to me.'

Noah knotted a loop into the rope while Raven crept back through the hedge.

'Ladies first,' he said, clutching the slack end of rope.

'You're too kind,' Noah said as she attached the carabiner on her harness to the loop she'd made. 'Don't let me fall.'

Raven tugged the rope. 'I've got you.'

Noah scaled the ivy-clad wall carefully. When she reached Lillian's window, the woman put her hand out to help.

'It's okay,' Noah said. 'I can manage.'

Noah dragged herself over the sill before unhooking herself from the rope.

'Is your brother coming?' Lillian asked as Noah climbed out of her harness.

'Yes,' Noah said. 'He'll be fine. He doesn't need the rope.' She looked at Lillian. 'It's good to see you out of bed.'

Lillian untied and then discarded her robe. Dressed in trousers and a skivvy, Lillian smiled at Noah. 'State-of-the-art prosthetics,' she said. 'There are some advantages to being a poor little rich girl. With these, I'm a few centimetres taller than I used to be.'

Not sure what to say, Noah smiled weakly.

Lillian drew a slip of paper from the back pocket of her trousers and handed it to Noah. 'Codes to get us to the vault.'

'Us?' Noah said.

Lillian nodded. 'I'm coming with you.' Noah stared. 'Are you sure you're—'

'Capable?' Lillian finished.

Noah shrugged apologetically as Raven's head appeared over the window sill.

'I'm not crazy,' Lillian said. With a glance at the pill bottles on her bedside table she added, 'As my nurse told you when she delivered my letter, I haven't taken any of those for months. I've been *acting* like I'm crazy – that's what they expect. I was planning to go to Talisker to look for my son.' She sighed. 'But now I know he's gone, returning the pyrohm so it can be destroyed is the next best thing I can do.'

Raven stood beside Noah and extended his hand to Lillian. 'Raven Chord,' he said.

'Lillian Kurz,' she said, shaking his hand. 'Nice to meet you.'

'So you want out of here?' Raven said. Lillian nodded. 'Yes.'

'Noah will get the pyrohm,' he said. 'You come with me.'

'I should go with Noah,' Lillian argued. 'I know where the vault is.'

'We've studied the blueprints. Noah knows where the vault is,' Raven said. 'You're coming with me.' He turned to Noah. 'You've got your explosives?'

Noah nodded. 'Yep.'

'Good.'

Raven strode to the window and straddled the ledge. He reached his hand towards Lillian. 'Ready?'

'We're going out *that* way?' Lillian said, wide-eyed.

Raven smiled. '*We* need to be outside. This is the quickest way. Noah, give her your harness.'

Noah helped Lillian into the climbing gear and then with a grace Noah thought would have been impossible on prosthetic legs, Lillian strode to her dressing table. She snatched up two small figurines and slid them into her pockets. 'Ready.'

Raven winked at Noah. 'Get going. See you soon.'

Noah nodded and padded towards the bedroom door, alarm codes and explosives in hand. She pushed on the handle and cracked open the door to listen. The hall was quiet. She pulled the door back far enough to poke her head out. A glance up and down the hallway revealed no movement. *Well*, she thought, *here goes.*

Noah scooted westward along the third-floor corridor and tossed two explosives over the balcony.

Boom!

The walkway trembled as Noah raced to the staircase at the end of the corridor. She bounded down two steps at a time. An alarm wound up to an eardrum-piercing whine, drowning out the shouts and screams of panicked staff. Noah hurdled the railing and bolted for the door to the west wing, eying the devastation the blast had caused as she ran.

Another explosion sounded, this one outside. *Good job, Raven,* Noah thought as she reached the door. She unfolded Lillian's piece of paper. Four codes were scrawled on it. Noah keyed in the first one and when the latch clicked, she shoved the door with her shoulder.

One of Bernard's minions sprinted down the hall towards her, gun drawn.

'Stop!' the man yelled.

Noah hesitated. *Guns,* she thought. *I hate guns.*

The man took aim and Noah dropped to the floor.

Bang!

Noah rolled to her left, sprang to her feet and launched herself forward. Adrenaline surging through her, she zigzagged down the corridor as the guard fired another shot.

The man snarled. 'Stop!'

Noah lunged and rolled, narrowly avoiding his next shot. She gained her feet and ran at him again. When the man was within range, she dived at his ankles, sending him sprawling on the floor. Though he recovered his feet quickly, Noah was faster. She spun round and punched him in the throat with her left hand, then in the temple with her right. He crumpled to the floor without a sound. Noah winced and shook her right hand. It was an effective strategy but it hurt.

Whipping two zip-ties from the man's utility belt, she secured his wrists and ankles. Noah snatched the man's gun from the floor and tucked it into the back of her trousers. She didn't like guns but she was thankful now that Raven had taught her how to use one.

Noah stole along the corridor. When she reached Bernard's study, she keyed in the second code on Lillian's list and the door opened. Two guards stood waiting, guns drawn.

'Mr Kurz knew you'd come,' one said.

'And despite your little show, you're not going to get what you came for,' the other added.

Noah scanned the room and dived behind the chaise lounge to her right. Three gunshots rang out. She didn't hesitate. Drawing her stolen weapon, she fired at the men's ankles. They screamed as they sank to the floor. Now they were grounded they'd get a better shot at her if she didn't move quickly. Noah thrust her hand into her pocket and pulled out a smoke bomb. She threw it in the guards' direction and sprang from her spot. More shots sounded but Noah ran for the door behind the ornate wooden desk. She steadied her hand and punched in the third code.

The door opened – not to a room, but to an elevator.

Breathing hard, Noah strode in. With her back against the side wall, she jabbed the button for the vault and keyed in the next code. More shots rang out and five bullets lodged in the elevator's back wall. Noah pressed the "Close" button repeatedly. The lift lurched into action as she tucked the gun back into her waistband. As the lift descended, Noah raised a hand to her locket. Her slider was warm again. Relief washed through her. The pyrohm was close.

The elevator slowed and then stopped. The doors slid open silently.

Noah peered into the gloom. The vault was narrow but long. Shelves affixed to the walls ran the length of the underground storeroom and were crowded with artefacts. Between the walls was a series of shelves on tracks so the units could be rolled side to side for easy access.

Noah stepped out of the lift and had taken only three steps when something slammed against her head. Staggering sideways, she reached for the gun.

Bang!

A bullet whizzed close to Noah's ear.

'Don't,' a voice warned.

Noah shook her head, trying to focus.

'Put your hands in the air,' the man said. 'I won't miss next time.'

Noah raised her hands as she studied the young man. Despite his tailored black suit, he looked like a prison escapee. His neck and bald head were heavily tattooed, his face puckered with acne scars. He held a pistol in his right hand, but it was the artefact in his other hand that captured Noah's attention. The firestone glimmered in the soft light of the vault.

'Looking for this?' he asked.

'Yes,' Noah said. 'Thank you for getting it for me.'

The man sneered. 'It's not *for* you. I'm here to make sure you don't get it. Mr Kurz said you'd come.'

'Well, here I am. When's he going to be here?'

'Soon,' the man promised. 'Very soon.'

'Good,' Noah said. 'Then I can get this mess sorted out and be on my way.'

The man laughed, but without humour. 'Think again,' he said. 'Since you seem to like it here so much, Mr Kurz has organised that you'll stay here *permanently*. I've spent the afternoon overseeing a new plot in the graveyard.' He looked her up and down. 'I think it'll fit you perfectly.'

'Unfortunately, I have other plans.'

'You think your brother will save you? Think again. My men have already picked him up.' He tapped his earpiece. 'In fact, I'll take you to him now.'

His gun still pointed at her, the man stepped forward then back-handed her hard across the face. Pain exploded in her head and she staggered backwards, barely managing to stay upright. The man grabbed her arm, spun her round and then kicked her in the back. She landed face down on the slate floor. She spat. Blood and saliva sprayed across the tiles.

Noah put her hands under her shoulders to lever herself up but the man caught her wrists in a vice-like grip, wrenched her arms behind her and tied them.

Noah winced. 'Do you have to make it so tight?' she said. 'You'll cut my hands off at this rate.'

'Stop your whinging,' he said. 'You won't have long to worry about it anyway.'

The man hooked his hand under her armpit and hauled Noah to her feet.

She glared at him. 'You won't get away with this.'

'I *will* get away with this,' he said with a reptilian smile. 'Now move.'

♪♫

'This looks cosy,' Noah said as her captor slid a key into the circular metal door set into the hillside. The trek across the hilly terrain had taken over half an hour, and Noah wondered if the estate's dungeon saw many visitors these days. Though the Kurz family had resided on the hilltop estate for three hundred years, the garrison itself was over a thousand years old. Noah shuddered at the thought she might find human remains.

The man turned the key and pushed the door. 'In.'

Though she had to duck her head to get through the doorway, Noah could walk upright once inside the passageway.

'Is Bernard really going to come out here to visit?' she asked. 'It's not going to be an easy trek for someone with a twisted ankle.'

'Mr Kurz is a tough customer,' the man said. 'That's your problem, Noah – you underestimated him. Badly. He'll get himself down here and he'll deal with you and your brother and then life will go on for him.'

'We'll see,' Noah said.

He pushed her in the back. 'Move. Let's see how cocky you are once you're locked in a cell.'

They'd walked only a few metres before the passageway veered right. Noah shuffled a dozen paces until she reached the first of the cells. The two on her left were occupied, Lillian in one and Raven in the one adjacent. They both stood with their hands gripping the bars, watching Noah as she approached.

'First on your right,' the man said. 'Door's open.'

'Can you cut these ties now?' Noah asked.

The man drew a blade from his belt and flicked it open. He cut the ties and shoved her into the cell almost in one motion. The door slammed shut before she could turn around.

'Now you all enjoy your stay,' he said, chuckling to himself as he retreated down the corridor.

No one spoke until they heard the outer door close.

'So what do we do now?' Lillian asked.

'We wait for your father,' Noah said.

Lillian nodded and took the figurines from her trouser pockets.

'Tell me what happened to my father,' she said, as she nursed the porcelain wrens.

'I'm sorry?' Noah said.

'How did he get injured the day you were here? He said a tree branch fell on him.'

Noah nodded. 'Yes, a tree branch did fall on him.'

'At the graveyard?'

Again, Noah nodded.

'There's more,' Lillian said, staring at her. 'Tell me.'

Noah trawled through her memories of the day. 'It was really strange actually. The branch cracked and fell, but where it splintered – both the tree and the branch were charred black. Like they'd been burned.'

Lillian pressed her face between the bars. 'What else?'

'Before the branch fell, I had strange visions inside my head – like someone's memories. They were of archaeological digs in all kinds of places. Random people, random places, random objects. And I felt really hot, like I was going to burst into flame, and my vision was blurry.' Noah paused. 'And then, all of a sudden, the heat vanished and the visions stopped … and the tree branch fell.'

'My mother,' Lillian said softly. 'She wants revenge against Father too.'

Noah frowned. 'Against your father? I thought she was after me.'

'What could she have against you?' Lillian said.

Lillian didn't know about Noah's role in Orville's demise and now wasn't the time to share that.

'Noah thinks everything's about her,' Raven said.

Noah glared at him.

'Mother never forgave my father for what happened to Orville,' Lillian said. 'I think she was drawn to your Academy ring, Noah. I think she acted *through* you to get to Father.'

Lillian cradled the two porcelain figures. 'These were my mother's. I've always loved them. Right from when I was a little girl. They remind me of her in the old days – beautiful, energetic, adventurous and free. After Orville read that book, everything changed. She died of a broken heart.'

Noah watched her.

'Noah,' Lillian said, 'the illestial must be destroyed. My mother will rest easy if we do that.'

'We have to get hold of the pyrohm first,' Noah replied.

'We will,' Lillian said. 'Promise that you'll destroy it?'

Noah's stomach knotted. She wanted to say something to ease Lillian's pain, but she was wary of making false promises.

'I will do everything in my power to destroy the illestial,' Noah said at last.

'Good,' Lillian said.

Raven spoke up. 'So what now?'

Lillian sighed. 'Like Noah said – we wait for my father.'

Chapter 6

The hinges on the exterior metal door groaned. Noah stood up and padded to the front of her cell, curling her hands around the bars. She glanced across at Raven who'd done the same. Only Lillian remained sitting on the floor.

'Here we go,' Raven said.

Noah nodded.

Two guards appeared around the corner followed by Bernard who limped, cane in hand. His face was flushed. Noah felt a sense of satisfaction that the old man had had to traverse the hilly terrain to visit them.

'So Noah,' he said. 'We meet again. This is getting quite tedious.'

'You don't say,' Noah replied.

'You could just give us the pyrohm and we'll be on our way,' Raven suggested.

'Hardly,' Bernard said, turning to look at Lillian. 'And now you've dragged my daughter into this too?'

Lillian pushed to her feet slowly. 'They didn't drag me into this. I *chose* this. Noah can destroy it.'

'Well, she *is* good at destroying things,' Bernard said, pulling the triangular artefact from his shoulder bag, 'but I don't think she can be trusted to do this.'

The dragonscale in the artefact splashed the walls with its vibrant colours as Bernard held it up to the light. Noah felt a small patch of warmth on her chest where her locket rested against her skin.

'I trust her,' Lillian said. 'At least she was honest enough to tell me that Orville was dead. *You* should have told me.'

'I *could* have told you, if I'd wanted to see you suffer the same fate as your mother,' Bernard said. 'But I didn't want that for you, Lillian.'

'I deserved the truth.'

'I don't think you'd still be here if I'd told you the truth,' Bernard said.

'Maybe not,' Lillian said, 'but that wasn't your decision to make.'

Bernard looked at his feet. 'I couldn't bear to lose you too.'

'You selfish bastard!' Lillian yelled. 'It's always about you, isn't it! *You* didn't want to lose me? Did you care about me? What I wanted? No, of course you didn't.'

'Lillian, I—'

'No!' Lillian said. 'I don't want to hear it. This ends now. The pyrohm goes back to Talisker.'

She reached into her trouser pocket and withdrew not a porcelain wren, but a metal marble. Lillian cradled the device in her palm as she glared at her father.

'Give the pyrohm to Noah,' she said.

Bernard glared at the guard closest to him whose face paled a few shades. 'She *was* searched,' the guard said.

'I was patted down,' Lillian said, 'and when they felt lumps in my pockets, I showed them my porcelain figurines, which they generously allowed me to keep. I *may* have forgotten to show them this.'

'Where did you get it?' Bernard asked.

Lillian smiled. 'From Raven.'

Bernard extended his hand. 'How about you give that to me, Lillian. We can discuss this calmly.'

'We're past that. Give the pyrohm to Noah or I'll drop this.'

Movement in Raven's cell caught Noah's attention. Raven held up his hands and started signing to her.

'If she drops it,' he signed, 'shelter behind the wooden bench to protect yourself from the flames.'

She nodded in acknowledgment. Being deaf for the first sixteen years of her life had been a real pain, but Noah had lost count of the number of times knowing sign language had come to her rescue. She scanned her cell. A bench seat was the only furnishing.

Bernard spoke again, but this time it wasn't to Lillian. 'Take my daughter back to the house,' he said to the guard.

'Yes, sir,' the man replied.

'I won't go!' Lillian yelled at the guard as he unhooked the keyring from his belt. 'Noah! Do as you promised. Take the pyrohm back to Talisker and destroy the illestial!'

Noah nodded.

Lillian thrust her hand out between the bars. 'Go now!'

As Lillian turned her hand over, Noah spun and grabbed the wooden bench. She wrenched it around, kicked it on its side and jammed it against the bars – then wedged herself behind it.

Whoomp!

Flames exploded through the underground prison. Noah huddled behind her barricade as fire scorched her shirt sleeve. A tortured scream reverberated off the stone walls. Noah counted to five before chancing a look over the bench. Bernard was pinned under the unconscious form of one of his bodyguards and he strained to push the burly man's body off him. The other guard screamed as he rolled on the floor, trying to extinguish the flames that consumed him.

Lillian was dead, her charred remains smouldering on the dirt floor of her cell. Anger burned inside Noah. She watched tendrils of smoke curl into the air, as if carrying away Lillian's last hopes of appeasing her mother's restless soul.

Keys jangled. Noah looked towards Raven. He'd retrieved the guard's keys and opened the door to his own cell.

'Raven, hurry,' Noah urged.

'Yep,' he said, nimbly sidestepping the thrashing guard on his way to her.

He glanced in Lillian's cell and his lips disappeared in a thin line. Without words, he set the key in the lock of Noah's cell as she kicked the smoking wooden bench out of the way. The latch clicked.

'Be careful,' he warned. 'The bars are hot.'

Noah used her boot to open the cell door before stepping into the passageway. The metal triangle lay at her feet. She bent down and picked it up. It was warm but not too hot to handle. The firestone twinkled at her as she turned it over in her hands. Noah shivered. *This is going to be a whole new world of trouble,* she thought.

Bernard groaned. 'Help me.'

'Someone will come looking for you, I'm sure,' Noah said. 'Until then, think on your sins.'

Bernard glared at her. 'I will if you will.'

♪♫

Noah cringed as Chase pulled into Aunt Polly's driveway. The car engine rumbled, blissfully unaware of the late hour. Unlike the other houses in the street, the lights in Polly's house burned brightly.

Raven looked sideways at Noah. 'Are you ready for Aunt Polly?'

Noah tugged on the door handle and swung her legs out. 'I'm ready to go home,' she said.

'If we're to be gone before the cops get here,' Chase said, 'then we need to move fast.'

The trio climbed the front stairs to find Polly waiting for them.

'Did you get it?' Polly said.

Noah nodded. 'Yes, so we need to get going.'

Polly nodded as she stepped aside. 'Quick, all of you inside.'

Noah headed for the lounge room with Raven at her heels.

'Jemima, put the kettle on,' Polly said.

'There's no time for tea,' Noah said as she surveyed the luggage in the lounge.

'Noah! Kitchen, now!' Polly said. 'You too, Raven.'

Noah stormed into the kitchen.

Polly thrust a plastic container into her hands. 'Jam drops,' she said. 'We'll need to keep our strength up.'

'We?' Noah said.

Polly rounded on Chase. 'Get that kettle on, girl!'

'Yes, Ma'am,' Chase said, swiping the kettle off the bench.

'We?' Noah said again. 'What do you mean, we?'

'I'm coming with you,' Polly said.

Noah stared at her aunt.

Polly said, 'I've decided I need to see this Talisker place for myself. I'm seventy years old and, let's face it Noah, your visits are … infrequent. If I don't take my chance now, I'll never get to see it.'

Noah peered at Chase.

'Don't look at me,' Chase said. 'It wasn't my idea.'

'Look, we don't have time to argue about this—' Noah began.

'Exactly right,' Polly said. 'So you'll just have to agree. Once the kettle's boiled, we can be on our way. You might have noticed my bags in the lounge.'

Noah had noticed there were more bags than they'd arrived with, but she'd assumed the extras were stuffed with the fruits of Chase's shopping adventures. For a few moments, the only sound in the kitchen was the kettle's gurgling. Noah's eyes flicked to the counter where two insulated flasks sat open. Her aunt was prepared to risk police capture just so she could have tea for the road. Noah took a deep breath. She wasn't willing to wait.

'I think it would be best if *we* left now,' Noah said, gesturing towards Raven and Chase. 'We could come back for you.'

'What? And leave me to deal with the cops?' Polly said with a sniff. 'I don't think so.'

'She could dob us in,' Chase said.

'She won't,' Noah said.

'Damn right I won't,' Polly said. 'Who'd believe my story?'

'I would,' Chase said.

'Yes, but you're *special*, Jemima,' Polly said. 'What *police detective* would believe me?'

Chase thought about it for a moment and said, 'A police detective who is a fan of my stories?'

'You're impossible,' Polly declared, turning back to face Noah. 'Look, we don't have time to argue. Time is of the essence.'

'If time is of the essence,' Noah said, 'why are you making tea?'

Polly threw her hands in the air. 'Have I taught you nothing?'

The kettle clicked off, and the distant wail of a siren intruded. Noah flinched. 'Time to go.'

'Jemima, fill the flasks,' Polly said. 'We'll get your bags.'

♪♫

'Does this bring back memories, Noah?' Raven said as he dragged his and Polly's luggage through the eucalypt forest behind their aunt's house.

'Yeah,' Noah murmured. 'It's so weird.'

'It's definitely weird,' Raven agreed. 'The first time I came through here, I was a dog.'

'And I was deaf,' Noah said.

Raven gave her a sidelong glance. 'And how we all miss *those* days.'

'This might surprise you, Brother,' Noah said, 'but there are days when I wish you were still a dog. You were cuter then.'

'And more obedient?'

'No. You were never obedient.'

Without warning Noah stopped.

'Noah?' Polly said. 'Is something wrong?'

'No,' she said. 'It's just … this is where I first met Emir.'

'How romantical,' Chase said.

Noah grimaced. 'It was hardly *romantic*,' she said, refusing to repeat one of Chase's favourite made-up words. 'I thought he was a bit stuffy and his cat was positively revolting.'

'Brinn?' Raven said. 'Surely you're not saying Brinn was revolting.'

Noah rolled her eyes. 'Brinn was—'

'—brilliant,' Raven finished.

'You know, I never got that,' Chase said, shaking her head. 'You always hated cats but Brinn – you followed her everywhere, you let her ride on your back, you even brought her presents. Why?'

Raven adjusted his rucksack. 'I dunno,' he said. 'She *looked* like a cat, she *acted* like a cat but … there was something else about her that wasn't like a cat. I can't explain it.'

'No,' Noah said. 'You really can't.' She turned to her pregnant friend. 'Are you okay? Do you need a rest?'

'No, I'm fine,' Chase said, puffing slightly. 'It's not much further is it?'

'About another twenty minutes,' Noah said.

'I'll make it.'

'So Noah,' Polly said, cradling her two tea flasks protectively, 'explain this to me. You go for a walk in the forest one afternoon and meet a stuffy stranger with a surly cat. How is it that you ended up romantically involved with this man?'

'I had several reasons to give him a chance,' Noah said. She counted them off on her fingers as she went. 'He wore a very nice suit; he promised me that if I came to Talisker, I'd be able to hear; and he gave me a lovely scarf.'

'In that case, I'm surprised you didn't fall for him straight away. What was the problem?'

Chase said, 'If I may just jump in here—'

'No, you may not,' Noah said.

'Let her speak, Noah,' Polly said.

Noah groaned. 'Here we go.'

'For the record,' Chase said, 'it took an impending apocalypse and some rather direct intervention from Raven and myself to make them realise – eventually – that they liked each other.'

Noah raised her hand in protest. 'That's not exactly how it happened.'

Chase raised one eyebrow. 'You're right,' she said, 'I forgot to mention the part where we saved your life when Emir threatened to slit your throat.'

Polly's jaw dropped.

Noah patted her aunt's shoulder. 'It's not what it sounds like.'

'Show her your arm, Noah,' Chase said.

'Look, it's—'

'Show her the scar, Noah.'

Noah pulled up her sleeve to expose her inner left forearm, hoping that the moon wouldn't provide enough light for Polly to see the scar that ran from her wrist to her bicep. Luck wasn't with her. The white line was clearly visible.

'Emir did that with a sword,' Chase said.

Polly gazed at Noah, eyes wide.

Heat flushed Noah's cheeks as she endured her aunt's scrutiny. 'Well, show and tell is done,' she said, yanking her sleeve back in place. 'Perhaps we can now focus on getting out of here. In case you'd all forgotten, the cops are after us.'

Chase frowned. 'What's wrong, Noah? You usually enjoy that story.'

Noah fought for calm. True, she'd often joked about her and Emir's unconventional courtship, but only with people who'd been there and witnessed it unfolding. People who knew them both. Polly, though family, was an outsider to the story and the horror in her eyes at what Emir had done ignited Noah's indignation. Polly hadn't met Emir yet, and now her opinion of him would be tainted by what she'd just heard. He didn't deserve that.

'There's more to the story,' Noah said to her aunt, 'which I'll tell you another time. Just promise me you won't mention it to Emir.'

'Okay,' Polly said. 'Not a word.'

Noah tightened her grip on her duffel bag and quickened her pace. The sooner they reached the portal, the better.

'Noah, I'm sorry,' Chase said, when she caught up. 'I didn't think. You know I'd never do anything to upset you – or Emir.'

Noah sighed. 'I know. I'm sorry too. I didn't mean to be snippy.'

'Let me make it up to you,' Chase said. 'Let me tell Polly the whole story. You know I'm good at stories. What do you say?'

Noah felt it was her responsibility to tell her aunt about her exploits on Talisker, but she knew Chase would do a better job.

'Okay, that'd be great,' Noah said. 'Thanks, Chase.'

'Great,' Chase said, smiling. 'You find the portal, I'll deal with the narrative.'

Raven arrived at Noah's side, as Chase dropped back to walk with Polly.

'Are you ready to give up one of those bags?' Noah said. 'I have a free hand.'

'Nope,' he said. 'I've got this.'

Noah shrugged. If he insisted on carrying Polly's two bags as well as his own, she wasn't going to argue with him.

'It's not far now anyway,' Raven added.

The twins walked the rest of the way in silence, alert for any sounds of pursuit. Though the moonlight would help those tracking them, they'd still be at a disadvantage. They wouldn't know the forest as well as Noah and Raven did.

'Where is it?' Polly said when Noah and Raven stopped. 'I don't see anything.'

Noah pointed to a slender tree that appeared to have been mercilessly savaged by woodpeckers. 'That is a branch of an olluka tree,' Noah said. 'Olluka trees serve as pathways between here and Talisker.'

'It doesn't look like a pathway,' Polly said.

Noah nodded. 'That's the idea.'

Chapter 7

The lush, undulating pastures of her farm on the outskirts of Seychelles always brought Noah a sense of peace. Of her prized herd of shaggy cows, some grazed sedately in the last of the day's light while others had already retired for the evening, reclining contentedly in small groups. Until they bellowed or shook their heads, the resting bovine looked like lumps of caramel-coloured sandstone scattered across the meadow. Noah gripped the reins a little tighter as the horse-drawn coach rounded the last bend.

Raven turned in his seat beside Noah in the driver's box and rapped on the top of the coach.

'We're almost home ladies!' he called.

Polly stuck her head out the window. 'Excellent,' she said. 'I need tea.'

Chase's head appeared out the adjacent window. 'And I'm starving.'

Raven saluted them.

'Situation normal,' he said, turning back to Noah. 'Polly wants tea and Chase is hungry … again.'

'Yes,' Noah said. 'I heard. I'm sitting right next to you, you know.'

He grinned. 'Oh yeah.'

When Noah pulled up outside her beloved double barn, Raven jumped down to help Polly and Chase out of the cabin.

'Wow!' Polly said. 'What a lovely home! Very nice indeed.'

'We like it,' Noah said, jumping down from her seat. 'Raven, Emir and I share the barn on the left. Chase and Ardis have the one on the right.'

Woof. Woof.

Kane appeared from around the side of the house and bolted towards Noah, tail wagging furiously.

'Oh!' Polly said.

'It's okay,' Noah said as she knelt down to hug her Alsatian. 'He won't hurt you.'

Polly pointed to the elevated walkway that linked the upper storeys of the two timber barns. 'How much traffic does that walkway see from you two girls?' she asked.

'We're quite restrained … now,' Noah said.

Polly nodded. 'I can just imagine what it would have been like at the start.' She took a few steps towards the houses. 'So this is where my brother settled down.'

'My mother's grandfather built this farm,' Noah said.

'Are those olive trees?'

'Yes,' Noah said. 'Mum planted those. Shall we go inside?'

'Absolutely,' Polly said.

'I'll unload the bags,' Raven said, as he clambered up onto the coach again.

The front door of one barn opened.

'Emir!' Noah said, jogging to meet him.

'Welcome home,' Emir said, wrapping his arms around her and kissing her forehead.

Emir's cotton shirt smelled of sweat and freshly cut hay. Noah smiled. *It's good to be home,* she thought.

'Is that your aunt?' he whispered in her ear.

Noah released her hold on him. 'Yes. Come, I'll introduce you.'

She took his hand and led him to where Polly was fussing over her bag.

'Aunt Polly,' Noah said, 'this is Emir.'

Polly turned and extended her hand. 'Nice to meet you at last, Emir,' she said, smiling.

'It's nice to meet you too, Ma'am,' Emir said, wiping his hand on his shirt before shaking Polly's hand.

'Call me Polly.'

Emir bowed his head. 'Welcome to our home, Polly.'

'Chase, put down that bag!'

Everyone turned towards the olive grove.

'Ardis!' Chase cried, dropping her bag.

When the Elani warrior reached his wife, he wrapped his arms around her and hugged her tightly. 'I'm so glad you're home,' Ardis said. 'I missed you.'

Chase kissed his tattooed cheeks. 'I missed you too.'

'You shouldn't be carrying those bags though,' he said. 'You should be taking it easy.'

Chase wrinkled up her nose. 'I'm pregnant, dearest – I'm not an invalid.'

'We made her ride inside the coach,' Raven said.

Ardis gave him two thumbs up.

Chase hooked her arm around Ardis's elbow and steered him in Polly's direction. 'Aunt Polly, this is my husband, Ardis.'

Ardis bowed his head. 'Nice to meet you,' he said. 'Welcome to Talisker.'

Polly reached out tentatively and shook Ardis's hand. Noah suppressed a smile. Ardis's overalls and boots bore the stains of a hard day's work on the land, but there was no mistaking him for a mere farmhand. Aside from his facial tattoos and brooding dark eyes, there was something in his bearing that put people on edge. Noah had seen seasoned soldiers cower before him.

'Right,' Emir said, 'everyone inside and get cleaned up. Ardis and I will get the bags.'

As Chase walked towards her house, she said, 'I'll be over in a while. I need a nice, long bath.'

'Don't be too long,' Noah said, 'or I'll start the show without you.'

Chase stopped. 'You *wouldn't!*'

'Don't tempt me,' Noah said. Turning to Polly, she said, 'You can use the guest room at Chase's place. You're welcome to bathe at my place though, since you could be waiting awhile next door apparently.'

'But tea first?' Polly said.

Noah smiled. 'Absolutely.'

♪♫

By the time everyone was gathered around the dinner table, the sun had long gone for the day. Fresh bread, cold beef and baked pumpkin with relish filled the platters along the table.

'Simple dinner tonight,' Emir said, 'but there should be enough to fill empty stomachs.'

'Yes,' Aunt Polly said. 'Is Raven's army coming to help us with this?'

Chase said, 'We won't need them. You'd be surprised how much these boys can put away.'

Noah shook her head but decided against ribbing her friend again about her appetite.

'So, Noah,' Ardis said, 'when are you going to tell us your little secret?'

'How do you know I have a secret?' she asked.

'Noah,' Emir said, 'we're not going to beg. Just tell us.'

'After dinner,' Noah replied. 'There is something we need to *show* you. Once we've eaten and the dinner table is clear, I will get it and we will tell you the whole story.'

'Good. Let's eat then,' Ardis said.

The group chatted about the farm as they enjoyed their dinner. Several of the cows had given birth in the previous few days, keeping Emir and Ardis very busy. At Polly's request, Ardis gave her a rundown on the process for harvesting and preparing olives. Noah watched him as he elucidated every step. Clearly passionate about his subject, his recital was almost mesmerising. Polly hung on every word.

Noah refilled her aunt's wine glass as everyone tidied up their plates. 'What do you think of our wine?' she asked.

'It's wonderful, but quite hard to describe,' Polly said. 'It's sweet and very smooth but hearty and robust at the same time.'

As Raven collected the last of the plates from the table, Emir said, 'Right, Noah. Go and get whatever it is. We're ready.'

Noah winked. 'Prepare to be amazed.'

'I don't really want to be amazed, Noah,' Emir said. 'With you, *amazing* usually means *trouble*.'

'Don't be like that,' she said as she headed for the bedroom to retrieve the pyrohm.

Noah returned to the kitchen with her hands behind her back to find Chase positioned at the head of the table.

'*Please* may I tell the story?' Chase asked.

'You're not a journalist though …' Raven said.

Chase snorted. 'I'm telling it anyway. I was just trying to be polite by asking.'

'Fair enough,' Noah said as she lay the metal triangle on the table.

'Is that firestone?' Emir asked.

'Yes,' Noah said.

'And what does it do?' Ardis said.

'Allegedly,' Noah replied, 'it was made by the Pyranhi to break Jong free of his prison.'

Emir looked at Chase. 'I think you'd better tell us the story now.'

'Right,' Chase said. 'So I was invited to an exhibition at the Sayle Museum by a young lady named Avril Jane … who happens to be the granddaughter of Bernard Kurz.'

Noah watched the colour drain from Emir's face. He looked at Ardis and mouthed one word … *trouble*.

Ardis nodded.

Unperturbed, Chase continued. 'Avril Jane is an archaeologist and historian whose main focus for the past few months has been her grandfather's exhibition. Bernard Kurz owns a mighty collection of historical artefacts which has been on loan to the museum.'

'And you found this artefact amongst his collection?' Ardis said.

'Correct,' Chase said.

Emir looked at Noah. 'And you recognised the firestone and thought it must have come from Talisker?'

Noah nodded.

'And when you told Avril Jane this, she gave the artefact to you?' Emir said.

Noah looked at Chase, who shrugged. 'Two out of three ain't bad.'

Emir held up his hand. 'I don't want to hear how you got it—'

'But it's really brilliant,' Chase said. 'You have to hear it.'

'Jemima,' Emir said, 'I really *don't* have to hear it. And I don't *want* to hear it. All I want to hear is … the plan from here. Now that we *have* it, what do we *do* with it?'

'Right,' Chase said. 'Noah … all yours.'

Noah had her spiel prepared, but as she began to speak, the firestone started to glow.

'That's new,' she said.

Emir showed no surprise. 'And let the trouble begin.'

As if on Emir's command, a beam of light burst from the dragon-scale, illuminating a small spot on the ceiling. After a few seconds, the beam widened until light drenched the room. But it wasn't the daz-zling light that drew everyone's attention. Hovering just above the table, colours whirled and then coalesced into a face.

The spectre grew until Jong's head dominated the table, floating above it like a gigantic helium-filled balloon. A scarlet ribbon contained his mane of dark hair at the nape of his neck, while piercing green eyes punctuated his pale complexion.

'Hello, Noah,' Jong said.

'Hello, Jong,' Noah said. 'Where's Gillette?'

Jong's thin lips stretched into a smile. 'He's still here. As I promised, he is whole and hale and awaits your return – as I do. Now that you have found my little trinket, when might we expect you?'

Noah's heart hammered in her chest. 'That's not up to me. I'm handing it over to the Firestone Alliance. They will decide its fate.'

Jong sighed. 'Tut-tut, Noah. You're just wasting time doing that. You know you're going to have to bring it to me sometime … why wait? Gillette will be most upset at the delay.'

'We'll get Gillette,' Noah said.

Jong's ghostly head tilted to one side, eyes twinkling with ancient malice. 'You need to take the pyrohm to Somyni – the other three pieces of the illestial are there.'

Noah drummed her fingers on the table. 'Good to know. I believe we need *all* the pieces if we're going to destroy it.'

Jong laughed. 'You can't destroy it, Noah.'

'It can be destroyed if—'

'I didn't say it couldn't be destroyed, Noah,' Jong said. 'I said that *you* can't destroy it.' Jong's head swivelled, eyeing each person at the table in turn. 'None of you can destroy it. *Theoretically* it can be destroyed … but even the Pyranhi couldn't do it. Why do you think the pyrohm was stolen and hidden?'

Noah knew why. She'd read the book Bernard had loaned her. The Pyranhi who'd tried to destroy it had perished.

As she considered her response, Jong's image dissolved and a new one took its place.

Noah gasped. 'Gillette!'

'Noah!' the boy cried.

Noah glanced at Emir. His face, usually a mask of calm, had contorted into something she rarely saw on him. Shock.

'Gillette,' Noah whispered again.

Gillette's head turned. 'Uncle Emir! Commander Raven! Wow! I can't believe you're all here. It's so good to see you.' He scanned the group again. 'My Dad? Is he …'

'You dad is fine now, Gillette,' Noah said. 'His body is strong and his mind is clear. He spends every day planning to rescue you.'

Alarm flashed across the boy's face. 'Dad mustn't come,' he said. 'And you mustn't come either, Noah. No one can come. That's what Jong wants! He plans to escape and destroy everything. *Everything!*'

'Anyway,' Jong said, reappearing in Gillette's place, 'you need to take the pyrohm to Somyni, Noah. I look forward to seeing you there soon.'

With that, the light went out.

To Noah's surprise, it was Polly who spoke. Clearly shaken, she whispered, 'Gillette is your nephew, Emir?'

Emir nodded.

'So how did he …'

'My fault,' Noah said.

Raven frowned. 'Noah—'

Noah picked at her fingernails. 'It *is* my fault.' She fixed her gaze on her aunt. 'Gillette and I were abducted by King Franco a year and half ago. Franco, along with two other kings, had stolen a large piece of firestone from the Alliance. In trying to … reclaim it, Gillette and I ran into Jong.'

Polly frowned. 'I thought you said Jong was a god – defeated by a dragon and contained. How did you run into him?'

Noah explained how the firestone had given them physical access to Xan's consciousness and how Jong had found them there.

'And you escaped but Gillette didn't?' Polly said.

Noah nodded. 'Jong sent me back but kept Gillette so one day I would return for him.'

'Jong always intended for you to release him?'

Again, Noah nodded.

'I can't believe you would risk bringing it here then,' Polly said.

'I think it's a bigger risk to leave it with Bernard Kurz,' Noah said.

'We need counsel,' Ardis said.

'Agreed,' Noah said, scooping up the pyrohm from the table. 'I'm going to take it to Mellifont and they can convene a meeting of the Firestone Alliance.'

'You're not tempted to try to rescue Gillette first?' Ardis said.

Noah sighed. 'Of course I am, but this is … seriously dangerous. This isn't something I can make a decision about. Dark forces are at work.'

'Are you talking about Jong or Bernard?' Raven said.

'I don't know who I think is worse,' Noah said with a shrug.

'It's possible Bernard really did want to protect it,' Chase said.

'It is possible,' Noah conceded, 'but even if that's true – he's not going to be around for much longer. Who knows what might happen after he's gone?'

'And if his plan was for you to bring it here?' Emir said.

'Then between us and the Alliance, we'll outsmart him. He can't be smarter than all of us together.'

Emir rubbed his chin as he studied Noah. 'In the morning, you and I will take that to Mellifont.'

'I'll return to Leninstar City and brief Catriona,' Raven said.

'I will come with you,' Ardis said. 'Chase and Polly can stay here at the farm.'

Emir looked at Polly. Without a trace of humour, he said, 'I hope you're good with cows.'

Chapter 8

Mellifont's magnificent stone domes towered over Noah as she and Emir wound their way through one of the city's many canyons. The beehive-like structures that sprouted from the ground for miles around had formed by natural geological processes, but the city within and under the rock had been fashioned by the magic of the Descera. Though none of the ancient race remained, their magic endured in the hands of Academy adepts who'd inhabited the city for millennia. Noah hoped that once they were inside she would find the peace, calm and counsel she needed, but she wasn't optimistic.

Where the gorge ended, Noah reined in her horse and admired the view. 'It's amazing, isn't it?'

'Yes, it is,' Emir agreed, 'but let's get inside.'

Noah sighed. 'Yep,' she said, nudging her horse into motion again.

She led the way towards Elani's Chamber. The great hall was the hub of all that happened in the city and Chief Examiner Sachin's quarters were right next door. If anyone had any ideas on what to do with the pyrohm, it would be Sachin. He was only fourteen years old but his prodigious musical talent had seen him achieve the rank of Major when he was just eight. Without him, creating the miraculous tonic to reverse the effects of the toxic ilanxis worm that had afflicted Emir's brother would have been impossible.

After they had tied up their horses, Noah extracted her slider from her locket and pressed it onto the latch plate. The door slid aside without a sound. They navigated the corridors without encountering anyone who wanted to engage them in prolonged conversation, and Noah was relieved to find that Sachin's assistant was absent from his post. She walked straight into Sachin's office with Emir at her side.

From behind his cluttered desk, Sachin looked up. 'Ah, there you are, Noah,' he said. 'Nice to see you too, Emir.'

Noah frowned. 'You're not surprised to see us?'

'No,' Sachin said. 'I had word you were coming.'

'From whom?' Emir asked.

'From me,' a voice said.

Noah pointed at Sachin. 'How did you say that without moving your lips?'

Sachin rolled his eyes. 'I didn't say anything.'

'I did,' said the voice.

Noah looked down at the desk and saw something stirring among the paperwork. Something stripy. Something furry.

'Brinn?' Noah said. 'Is that you?'

'Is that a rhetorical question or a stupid question?' the miniature tiger said as she put her front paws on top of a mound of papers and stretched extravagantly. 'I always get those confused.'

Noah stared at the feline. 'Sachin, you might want to clean up your desk. You never know what else might be lurking under all those papers.'

'Never mind about that,' Brinn said as she picked her way across the table to perch on a stack of books so she could study Noah at eye level. 'There couldn't be anything on this desk that is anywhere close to being as dangerous as what you've brought with you.'

Noah caught herself before she asked the cat how she knew about the pyrohm. This was no ordinary cat. This cat talked, appeared and disappeared at will, counted the high priestess of Talisker as her friend and had Raven wrapped around her silky paw. She defied all rules, even rules of nature.

Noah reached into the pocket of her Academy-issue trousers and extracted the triangular relic. She placed it gently on the stack of papers next to where Brinn sat. Sachin leaned forward for a closer look.

'Sachin, do you know what that is?' Brinn asked.

Sachin shook his head. 'The firestone I recognise, but the triangle and the etchings don't mean anything to me. The fact that you're here' – he looked directly at the cat – 'tells me that it's a serious problem though.'

'You got that right,' Brinn said, licking her paw. 'Tell him, Noah.'

Noah glared at the cat for a moment. Brinn had given her an order and Noah felt like she'd been hauled into the principal's office and, regardless of her response, was going to get a serious telling-off. Reluctantly, Noah related how she'd obtained the relic and about her conversation with Jong and Gillette, and then braced herself for Brinn's reaction.

'I can't believe you brought it here,' Brinn muttered when Noah had finished her story. 'Sometimes I wonder how you got an opposing thumb, Noah. You don't deserve it.'

Noah's cheeks burned but Emir spoke in her defence. 'Noah is turning it over to the Alliance,' he said. 'I happen to agree that that is a *very* good idea. Brinn, perhaps you could tell us what you know. If we're going to put this right, we need information rather than insults.'

'Noah, come here,' Brinn said.

Instantly wary, Noah took a tentative step towards the desk.

'Closer,' the cat said.

Noah took another step, stopping only when her hip touched the desk. 'That's as close as I can get.'

To Noah's surprise, Brinn rubbed her head against her arm. 'You know I don't mean to be offensive when I insult you, don't you?'

Shocked but unwilling to risk saying anything that might draw another insult from the feisty feline, Noah looked at Emir.

'You do know that's the point of an insult, don't you?' Emir said. 'It is to be offensive.'

'Not when *I* do it,' Brinn said. 'I'm simply trying to inspire Noah to be the best she can be.'

Sachin laughed. 'You're such a cat.'

'I'm going to assume that's a compliment,' Brinn said.

'Assume whatever you like,' Sachin said.

'Watch yourself, Chief Examiner,' Brinn warned. 'You might be the most talented Major on Talisker but if I think you need a little … inspiration, I'm happy to insult you too. Now stop distracting me. We have a job to do.'

'We?' Noah said. 'You're going to help us?'

'Of course I'm going to help you,' Brinn said. 'Have I ever *not* helped when Armageddon is nigh?' Without waiting for an answer, she continued. 'The illestial was made around a million years ago by a sect of the Pyranhi called the Jongu – Jong worshippers. Their goal – as you can probably guess – was to set Jong free. It did take them a few hundred years but eventually they created the illestial. The illestial is a four-sided pyramid. This piece' – she indicated the relic on the desk with her paw – 'is the pyrohm – the piece that activates the illestial. The other three sides have no firestone inset. They are solid metal, though each has the alume symbol etched into it.'

'Alume?' Noah said. 'What's that?'

'The alume is the symbol of the trinity,' Brinn said.

'Elani, Jong and Xan?' Sachin ventured.

'Close,' Brinn replied. 'Elani, Jong and Temperance.'

'Who's Temperance?' Sachin asked.

'Temperance is the sister of Elani and Jong,' Noah said.

Sachin leaned back in his chair. 'Since when? I've never heard anything about a sister.'

'So, Sachin, it seems you don't know everything,' Brinn said.

'And you do?' Sachin said.

'I am a cat,' Brinn said, as if that was explanation enough.

Sachin looked at Noah. 'How did you know about Temperance?'

'I am allowed to know things that you don't,' Noah said.

Sachin's eyes narrowed.

'Okay, okay,' Noah said. 'I found out while I was trawling through Carai's library.'

'While you were researching Jong to find a way to rescue Gillette?'

Noah nodded as she picked up the pyrohm to study the alume symbol more closely. 'What do the circles mean?'

'The alume is the generic sign for a god,' Brinn explained. 'At one end there is an unshaded circle – representing emptiness or nothing, at the other end there is a filled circle which symbolises all or everything. The line that connects them shows that gods are the link between noth-ingness and everythingness.'

'Everythingness?' Emir said.

'Everythingness,' Brinn confirmed. 'This triangle shows a family of three gods. The dragonscale – the quintessential symbol of Talisker – harnesses the energy of Xan. The pyrohm connects the siblings, allowing the illestial to draw on their power.'

'You said the alume was a generic symbol for a god,' Noah said, 'so does that mean Jong could connect to any god, rather than just his siblings?'

'That is a logical deduction,' Brinn said, 'but it doesn't work that way. The connection works by virtue of the *relationship* between the gods rather than through the symbol.'

'Fascinating,' Sachin said.

'Indeed it is,' Emir agreed, 'but what do we do with it now?'

Brinn stood up and jumped down from Sachin's desk. 'We're going to take the pyrohm to Somyni.'

'We have to see what the Alliance decides,' Noah said.

'Somyni is where it was made,' Brinn said, 'Somyni is the only place it can be *un*made. Noah, you need to convince the Alliance to let us take it there.'

'Why do I have to convince them?' Noah said. 'You know more about it than I do so how about you do it?'

'Speak in front of the Alliance?' Brinn's ear twitched. 'I'm not really a people person.'

Noah rolled her eyes. 'At least we agree on something,' she muttered.

'We're going to need more than that,' Emir said. 'If we're to con-vince the Alliance of anything, *we* need to be convinced.'

Noah reached into another pocket on her trousers and extracted the book that Bernard Kurz had loaned her.

'According to this,' Noah said, opening the journal, 'Temperance's followers stole the pyrohm and tried to destroy it. They failed – died trying. If the Pyranhi couldn't do it, what makes you think we can?'

'We have the 13th key,' Brinn said.

Noah sighed. 'That's wearing a bit thin now.'

'Maybe for you,' Brinn said, 'but you're Talisker's protector and it's your job.'

Noah clenched her fists in frustration. 'I would do it … if I knew how. The Pyranhi were skilled and powerful sorcerers and I'm not. How am *I* supposed to do something they couldn't do?'

'None of them was part dragon,' Brinn said. '*You* are.'

'Part dragon?' Sachin said.

'One smart comment,' Noah said, stabbing her index finger in his direction, 'and I'll—'

'Firestone flows in her veins,' Brinn said. 'Xan recognises Noah as her child.'

Emir ran his hands through his hair. 'Of the Alliance members, only King Catriona knows that Noah is the 13th key,' Emir said.

'Well, keep your secret if you can, Noah,' Brinn said, 'but you might need to give it up to get their support.'

'Right. Even if they *do* believe me,' Noah said, 'I still don't know how to do it. They'll want details.'

Brinn eyed her like prey.

This cat's going to be the death of me, Noah thought.

'The four triangles that form the pyramid – the illestial – sit atop a tripod,' Brinn said, 'which straddles a larger piece of firestone set into the floor in one of Somyni's temples. The piece of firestone in the pyrohm acts as a magnifier, to channel and concentrate the energy of the large piece of dragonscale. The flow of energy from the large piece through the magnifier draws Jong from his dragon prison and catapults him to freedom.'

'Drawn like pus from a wound …' Sachin said.

Brinn screwed up her nose. 'Accurate, though revolting.'

'And we destroy it how?' Emir said.

'Destroying one piece doesn't work,' Brinn said. 'That's because when the Jongu made the device, they interconnected all the components with powerful magic. If one piece is attacked, the others react to protect it.'

'And that's what killed the Pyranhi who tried to destroy the stolen piece?' Noah said.

Brinn nodded.

'How many died?' Sachin said.

Brinn's eyes flashed. 'Twenty-six.'

For a few moments no one spoke. Noah looked at Emir, who rubbed his chin and she wondered if he was thinking the same thing she was. Had Brinn been there when the Pyranhi tried to destroy the pyrohm?

'Stripping the binding magic away is the key,' Brinn said. 'And all the components need to be together – including the piece of firestone in Somyni – for that to happen. Once the spell is neutralised, the magnifier can be removed and the metal pieces can be melted down in a lava pit.'

'And what about the magnifier?' Noah said, squinting at the firestone. 'What do we do with it after it's removed?'

'Whatever you wish,' Brinn said. 'Once the spell is broken, it's safe.'

'It sounds straightforward in theory,' Emir said, 'but I'm not sure the Alliance will have much faith in our ability to unravel the ancient Pyranhi magic that protects this device.'

'Sachin'll do it,' Noah said. 'There's nothing he can't do. Isn't that right, Sachin?'

Sachin drummed his fingers on the desk. 'If we talked to Dragonsbane Grainger, I reckon we—'

'Not seriously!' Noah cried. 'Sachin, I was joking. This can't be done. This isn't raiki – this is ancient Pyranhi magic we're talking about. You can't mess with this stuff.'

'Noah, you're the 13th key …'

'Yes – and if it was just firestone, I'd deal with it. But it's not. If you'd seen what I saw in Tisaan, you wouldn't even be thinking about it.'

She shuddered. When she'd retrieved thirteen pieces of firestone from the Elanu city of Tisaan, she'd barely escaped the Pyranhi magic there. She had no wish to risk it again.

'Yes, make sure Grainger addresses the meeting,' Brinn said. 'The research he's done since your little adventure in Tisaan will be very helpful.'

'It'll take a week to convene an extraordinary meeting of the Alliance,' Sachin said, 'so we've got some time to get our ideas in order.'

Noah massaged her temples with her fingertips. *Our ideas?* Brinn's *ideas more like it.*

She sighed. As tantalising as the idea was that she might have been able to use the illestial to save Gillette, she'd been wholly prepared to entrust the pyrohm to the Firestone Alliance and let them determine its fate. In fact, it had been something of a relief to abandon responsibility for such a crucial decision. Now though, Brinn expected her to bully the Alliance into letting her take it to Somyni to attempt the impossible.

'No expedition has returned from Somyni in over three thousand years,' Noah said.

'I didn't say it would be easy,' Brinn said. 'It just needs to be done.'

Chapter 9

Raven clicked his fingers. 'That's it!'

'What's it?' Noah asked.

'I've just had a brilliant idea,' he said. 'I think it must be being back in Mellifont, surrounded by all you Academy types—'

'Adepts,' Sachin said. 'We're adepts – not "Academy types".'

'Right … adepts,' Raven said. 'Anyway, I've just had a brilliant idea about how you can get the Alliance to agree to your crazy plan, Noah.'

Emir rubbed his chin. 'It's Brinn's crazy plan, actually.'

'Fine. Brinn's crazy plan,' Raven said, pacing back and forth across Noah's rehearsal studio. 'So now that the kings are all here in Mellifont, you have to convince them to approve a mission to Somyni to destroy the illestial, right?'

'Yes,' Noah said.

Raven rubbed his hands together. 'Is it possible to put a firestone slider in a dog whistle?'

Noah, Emir and Sachin frowned at him.

Raven folded his arms across his chest and frowned back. 'What?'

Sachin snorted. 'Part of me is curious about why you would want to do that,' he said, 'but another part of me is afraid my IQ will drop twenty points if I listen to your answer.'

'No, hear me out,' Raven said. 'I was thinking you could use raiki to "convince" the Alliance that destroying the illestial is the only option.

But there's a problem – as soon as you start playing a tonic, they'll hear the music and know you're up to something.'

Sachin clapped his hands over his ears. 'My IQ is dropping … I can feel it.'

Raven ignored him. 'But humans can't hear dog whistles,' he said. 'If you could write a tonic for a dog whistle, that just might work.'

Emir's brow furrowed. 'Raven, your girlfriend is one of those kings. Do you really want Noah using a dog whistle on Catriona?'

Raven grimaced. 'Ah … no. That idea probably needed a bit more thought, huh?'

Noah shook her head. 'Let's pretend that conversation never—'

The doors to Noah's suite swung open and Sabre, King Catriona's adviser, swept into the room with her usual energy.

'No, don't get up,' she said with measured sarcasm.

Raven's eyebrows betrayed his surprise. 'Since when do we have to stand for the king's adviser? I must have missed that memo.'

'Yes, yes,' Sabre said. 'It's only me *now*, but the king won't be long. You might want to limber up.'

'Limber up?' Sachin said. 'Gee, I reckon I could risk standing without a warm up.'

For Noah's part, she had no intention of standing up when King Catriona arrived but she didn't say so. She liked Sabre. The middle-aged widow who'd taken the adviser's post vacated by Emir was cool, clever and compassionate and had an unquenchable enthusiasm for her job.

'Sachin, is there some pressing Academy business you could be attending to?' Emir asked.

The young Major shook his head. 'I cleared my schedule and if anything crops up, Alan will deal with it. You're not trying to get rid of me, are you?'

Before Emir could respond, King Catriona burst through the doorway.

'All rise,' Sabre intoned.

'Stop that, Sabre,' Catriona said. 'We've talked about this. We don't need to stand on ceremony with these people.'

'Because we're family?' Noah said.

Catriona glared at her. 'No … because whenever you're around there's usually trouble and we don't have time to waste.'

Noah held the king's gaze. Catriona was two months older than her and had taken Leninstar's throne after her father's murder eighteen months ago. In the time Noah had worked in Leninstar's palace as King Tambian's tailor, the then-Princess Catriona had been less than cordial to her. But after the collapse of the Sovereign States Alliance, she and Catriona, as Talisker's newest and youngest female kings, had had to collaborate to engineer a new Alliance. The resulting Firestone Alliance, incorporating the four southern states and the goblin city of Carai, was a fabulous achievement but the negotiations had been harrowing. Catriona was a formidable force.

'That's a bit harsh,' Noah said. 'In my defence, the trouble isn't usually of my making.'

'But it *is* this time from what I've heard. Raven's told me his version of the story – now let's hear yours.'

Noah related the story of how they'd discovered the pyrohm and subsequently purloined it. She then gave a detailed account of her communication with Jong and his desire for her to take it to Somyni.

Catriona studied Noah. 'And let me guess, you want to take it there because that's the only place it can be destroyed?'

'I actually *don't* want to take it there,' Noah said, 'but your guess that Somyni is the only place it can be destroyed is correct.'

'In fact, that wasn't a guess,' Catriona said. 'I've been talking to a friend of yours, Noah. I know a great deal about the illestial.'

Noah glanced at her brother, who was taking an uncharacteristic interest in his fingernails.

'Not Raven,' Catriona said. 'Though he has told me much. I have another source of information on the pyrohm and illestial.'

'Brinn?' Noah guessed.

Catriona frowned. 'No. Who's Brinn?'

'Brinn is a cat,' Emir said.

'A cat?' Catriona frowned. 'I know you don't have many friends, Noah, but a cat? Really? And anyway, how would I talk to a cat?'

'Brinn can talk,' Sachin said. 'She's superior, bossy, opinionated and loves to flout rules—'

'Aside from the talking part,' Catriona said, 'she pretty much sounds like any other cat. That's why I don't like cats.'

Sachin smiled. 'I've met people with those attributes.'

'I don't like *people* like that either,' Catriona said.

Noah looked around the room. Only Emir maintained a neutral expression. Even Raven, Catriona's consort, raised an eyebrow.

'So,' Catriona continued, 'need I point out that anyone who mentions a talking cat at the Alliance meeting will find themselves in a world of unimaginable pain?'

Noah, Emir, Sachin and Raven all shook their heads while Sabre jotted a note on a piece of parchment.

Catriona tapped her fingers on the table. 'As I was saying, I spoke to a friend of yours, Noah. Her name is Avril Jane.'

'We're not friends,' Noah said. 'I barely know her.'

'Well, she was so keen to see you again that she followed you here. I'm currently holding her on a charge of possessing outlawed technology. You should check your luggage, Noah. There's a tracking device in there somewhere.'

'I'll be sure to do that later,' Noah said.

'Good. Now, when Avril addresses the Alliance, she will no doubt say that—'

'I'm sorry,' Noah interrupted, 'did you say that Avril is going to address the Alliance?'

Catriona nodded. 'Of course,' she said. 'The Alliance needs all the information it can get to make a decision on what to do with this pyrohm. Actually … may I see it, please?'

As Sachin unbuttoned one of the pockets on his trousers, Noah said, 'You do know Avril is Orville Kurz's cousin?'

'I am aware of that, yes.'

Sachin unwrapped the velvet cloth and handed the artefact to Catriona. The king's brow furrowed as she accepted it.

'Avril will contend that it should return to Earth to protect Talisker from destruction,' Catriona said as she studied the firestone relic.

'Avril will no doubt say that it should return to Earth,' Noah said, 'but not to protect us. She wants it to remain in her grandfather's collection, because when he dies it will become part of *her* collection.'

'And there's a book that you "borrowed"?' Catriona said.

'Bernard loaned it to me,' Noah replied. 'He insisted that I read up on the illestial.'

'Then I'll take that now too.'

Noah took the book from her pocket and dropped it on the table.

Catriona glanced at the journal and then returned her attention to Noah. 'And what will *you* say to the Alliance, Noah?'

'It needs to be destroyed,' Noah said.

Catriona looked at Emir who nodded his agreement. She leaned back in her chair, interlacing her fingers over her abdomen. 'And do you know how to do that?' she asked.

'Brinn told us—' Sachin began.

Catriona held up one hand. 'Consider your next words very carefully, Chief Examiner.' The king turned to her adviser. 'Sabre, put your pen away.'

Noah braced herself. Sachin had already considered his next words carefully and he'd say them regardless of Catriona's warning.

'Brinn, though not great company,' Sachin said, 'has proven herself a protector of Talisker. She was invaluable in thwarting Orville Kurz's plan to destroy us three years ago, and she knows how to destroy the illestial.'

With her eyes on Noah, Catriona said, 'And you think the Alliance will back you on this?'

'Will you?' Noah said.

Catriona got to her feet. 'I haven't decided yet.'

♪♫

Noah settled herself in her seat. Elani's Chamber was Mellifont's largest auditorium. It could seat twenty thousand people, but today fewer than twenty would be in attendance.

'Showtime,' Sachin said as the chamber doors opened.

Noah shook her head but thought better of telling him to behave. Let Talisker's kings deal with him. They were more than capable.

King Tara of Chalinor escorted Carai's new young goblin king to her seat. Though ten-year-old Severine had been happy to accept her crown from Noah, Noah still had reservations about the appointment. Goblin politics was brutal, but at least her human counterparts on the Firestone Alliance would do their best to guide her.

King Catriona placed the pyrohm and Alina Kurz's book on the table before taking her seat between King Mallory and King Henrik.

'I welcome you all to this meeting,' King Tara said. 'I suggest we get down to business … I think we're in for a long day.'

'Major Alan,' King Henrik said, 'I charge you with recording attendance and keeping minutes of the testimonies and conversations we hear today.'

'Yes, Your Highness,' Alan said. 'Absolutely. You can count on me.'

'And Major Alan,' Tara said, 'I charge you with *not* speaking today … unless you are asked to do so.'

Noah smiled. Alan discharged his duties as Mellifont's chief auditor and Sachin's personal assistant with supreme efficiency, but also relentless enthusiasm.

Alan raised a pudgy hand in salute. 'Yes, Your Highness.'

'Major Alan,' Henrik said, 'please confirm the attendance list so we can proceed.'

Alan bowed his head and read from his parchment. 'Present today are King Henrik of Orian, King Catriona of Leninstar, King Mallory of Melwick, King Tara of Chalinor and King Severine of Carai. Also present are Majors Sachin, Noah and Anok of Mellifont. We welcome too, High Priestess Montana and her warrior, Ardis, as well as former adviser Emir Delorian.'

'So, Noah,' Tara said, 'I believe you have brought us a little gift. Perhaps you could share what you know first.'

'Certainly, Your Highness,' Noah said.

Everyone at the table listened as Noah detailed their meeting with Avril Jane, their visit to the museum and the acquisition of the firestone artefact. She related her interactions with Bernard Kurz and his daughter

Lillian, and how Alina's journal had come to be in her possession. After she'd recounted her conversation with Jong and Gillette, she paused.

'So,' King Mallory said, 'our choices are return it, hide it or destroy it. Have I missed anything?'

'I think that about covers it,' Henrik said. 'Destroying it seems preferable, but I don't suppose that's a straightforward exercise, is it?'

'No,' Noah said. 'According to what I read in the journal, the Pyranhi who stole that piece were unable to destroy it. The current theory is that all the pieces are bound by magic. Trying to destroy one piece causes the other pieces to react to protect it.'

'Could you deal with this? Could you destroy it?' Henrik asked.

'*I* couldn't,' Noah said, 'but that's not to say it can't be done.'

'Dragonsbane Grainger?'

'He'd be the one to talk to.'

Henrik turned in his seat. 'Dr Grainger, please,' he said to the door guard.

The herald opened the door and called for Grainger.

When Dr Grainger appeared in the doorway, Alan said, 'The attendance log now reflects the arrival of Dr Grainger Brimblecombe, Dragonsbane.'

'Welcome, Dr Grainger,' Tara said as the Dragonsbane took his seat. 'Noah has briefed us on the circumstances of the pyrohm's presence here. Our decision lies in whether we hide it or destroy it. To do this, we need more information about the workings of the device. Could you please tell us what you know?'

Grainger nodded, wisps of wiry grey hair that had sprung free of his ponytail waving defiantly as he did so. 'Certainly.'

Noah studied him as he spoke. His hair betrayed his advancing years but his eyes certainly didn't. The intensity of his gaze was inescapable.

'For the benefit of the new king at the table,' Grainger began, with a nod in Severine's direction, 'I will briefly relate the events that have landed me here today.'

'That would be appreciated, Dr Grainger,' Severine said. 'Thank you.'

'I accompanied Noah on a venture to Tisaan,' Grainger said, 'the ancient Pyranhi city of the Elanu. We undertook this journey to recover the thirteen pieces of firestone that now form the basis of this Alliance. The mission was by no means simple. The city was accessible only via a portal under Dragonhall.

'Though I wasn't convinced of the merits of retrieving the firestone, I *was* interested in the portal. You see, it's not just one portal. The portal to Tisaan is one in a cluster of twenty-three portals, and the cluster is unstable. When it implodes – and one day it will – the results will be catastrophic. It is my goal that during my tenure as Talisker's Dragonsbane, I will stabilise the portal cluster.'

'A worthy objective for our Dragonsbane,' Tara said. 'We certainly don't want imploding portals waking Xan. We applaud your efforts in maintaining the dragonsong that keeps our great dragon at rest.'

'Thank you, Your Highness,' Grainger said. 'Our journey to Tisaan gave me a taste of Pyranhi magic. Since our return, I have done much research – both in Dragonhall and in the royal archives.'

'So you are now an expert on Pyranhi magic?' Severine asked.

Grainger shook his head. 'Far from it, Your Highness. Pyranhi magic is very different from the raiki that we use now. And although goblin records on the Pyranhi culture are far superior to human records, there is still limited information available.'

Catriona leaned forward to rest her elbows on the table. 'Noah has told us that the pieces of the illestial are linked and protected by magic. Do you think you could undo the Pyranhi spell?'

Grainger held Catriona's gaze. 'I would like the opportunity to try.'

With a glance at the artefact on the table, Catriona said, 'Could you make your assessment with just that piece?'

'I could make a start,' Grainger replied, 'but ultimately, if they're bound together, I'd need to assess all the pieces.'

'You want to go to Somyni?' Tara asked.

'I don't *want* to go to Somyni,' Grainger said, 'but I would *need* to go there to analyse the spell thoroughly.'

'Could Dragonhall survive your absence?' Tara said.

'My apprentice is very capable,' Grainger said. 'I would trust Yeti to monitor things until I returned.'

'Assuming you did return,' Henrik said.

'Sachin,' Mallory said, 'do you think the spell *can* be reversed?'

Sachin pursed his lips. 'I don't know,' he said at last, 'but I agree with Grainger that the only way to find out is to go to Somyni.'

'Taking that to Somyni,' Henrik said, pointing at the artefact, 'sounds like we're playing into Jong's hands.'

'Does it have to go to Somyni for an assessment to be made?' Anok asked.

All eyes went to the Mellifont's most senior adept. The octogenarian inventor of the 'carry everything' trousers that all adepts wore, spoke little but when he did, people listened.

'Could *this* piece be analysed and left here,' Anok continued, 'and then the other pieces analysed onsite in Somyni? Perhaps after that, we could make an informed decision on the fate of this device?'

Henrik tapped his chin. 'Your idea has merit, Major,' he said, 'but it is my understanding that expeditions to Somyni are ... difficult.'

'Meaning no one returns,' Sachin said. 'If we're going to Somyni, we've got one shot and we need to make it count.'

'Jacin can give you the stats on missions to Somyni,' Noah said.

Henrik waved to the door guard. 'Bring him.'

Jacin leapt through the doorway and bowed with the flamboyance of a stage actor on his third encore.

'Major Jacin at your service, Your Highnesses and other assorted dignitaries,' he said.

'We could do without the theatrics today, Major,' Mallory said. 'Please sit and tell us about access to Somyni.'

'Right. Yes. Okay,' Jacin said as he settled himself into his chair.

Noah sighed. If Jacin managed to contain himself for the duration of his testimony, the Alliance would have used up its quota of miracles. In his time as king's adviser in Carai, he'd spent almost as much time in the dungeon as he had in his suite in the palace. As with most high-functioning individuals, Jacin's talents came at a cost. Noah couldn't decide if it was his goblin genes or human genes – or a combination of them – that made him so wilful. He had a good heart though. Jacin's unwavering loyalty to her had seen him appoint himself as her protector on her mission to Tisaan. And, as her raiki apprentice, he'd been a model student – attaining the rank of Major in just eighteen months.

'Major Alan,' Henrik said, 'have you updated the attendance list to reflect—'

'Yes,' Alan said curtly.

Noah winced. The animosity between Alan and Jacin as they vied for Noah's affection was excruciatingly embarrassing. A kingly reprimand might put Alan in his place but Noah knew it wouldn't happen. All the kings knew of the spat but it was beneath them to acknowledge it.

Jacin looked at Grainger. 'Did you tell them about our trip to Tisaan?'

Grainger nodded.

'Excellent,' Jacin said. 'Well, as you can probably imagine, venturing into a Pyranhi city is pretty exciting. It gave me a … taste for it, you could say. So when we returned from Tisaan, I was keen to see Somyni too. Of course, Noah and Sachin and I were doing a lot of research into how to reverse the effects of the ilanxis worm but—'

'And me,' Alan interjected. 'I was integral to that project too.'

'But I still found time to assist Dr Grainger,' Jacin continued smoothly, 'with his work on the Pyranhi culture.'

He opened a pocket on his trousers to retrieve several books. When he dropped the musty tomes on the table, a dust cloud mushroomed into the air around them.

As the gritty residue settled, Jacin said, 'After scouring the library, these are the only books I could find that were relevant. I believe many records were destroyed or stolen' – he pointed to the journal Noah had brought back from Earth – 'after a disastrous expedition about two and a half thousand years ago.'

'What happened?' Tara asked.

'Two hundred goblins, accompanied by human slaves, set out. One goblin returned … mostly.'

'Mostly?' Severine said. 'What does that mean?'

'His body returned, Your Highness,' Jacin said, 'but his wits didn't. His mind was addled – he just babbled and screamed a lot. The city of Somyni was intact when they found it. But the adventurers found a clutch of eggs … that were still warm.' He smiled and shivered. 'One of the goblins took an egg from the nest and all hell broke loose! Ghosts of dragon-riding Pyranhi assaulted the group, leaving only one expeditioner alive to return with a message. Don't come back!

'The lone survivor escaped – with the stolen egg – and returned to Carai. All access to Somyni was subsequently destroyed. All the tunnels were collapsed and spells now deflect any would-be trespassers who might be of a mind to find a way in.'

'Who collapsed the tunnels?' Sachin said.

Jacin's eyes widened. 'The ghosts of the Pyranhi.'

'But you think the city survived?'

'I do. I think they wanted to protect their city from invaders.'

'And the egg?' Severine asked.

'A dragon egg,' Jacin said.

Severine flinched. 'Did it hatch?'

Jacin shook his head. 'No. When they eventually cracked the egg open, the baby dragon was dead.'

Noah watched reactions around the table. She'd heard the story from Jacin before. Apart from Severine, expressions remained neutral. *They must be surprised,* Noah thought. *They're just too experienced to show it.*

'Accessing Somyni will be challenging,' Tara said. 'Perhaps it's time we heard from your prisoner, Catriona?'

Montana stood up. 'Before you do that,' the high priestess said, 'may I speak?'

Tara bowed her head. 'Your counsel is always welcome, Montana.'

'All talk this morning has been about destroying the illestial – which I believe is the correct *long-term* strategy. Perhaps though, we could give some thought to … securing it … while we figure out how we can destroy it.'

'Hiding it, you mean?' Sachin said.

Montana smiled. 'Hiding it somewhere secure, Major.'

Sachin reached across the table and picked up the pyrohm. 'For how long? What does "long term" mean to you?'

Though it was probably a fair question to ask of someone who was over eight hundred years old, Noah still thought it was rude.

Unruffled, Montana said, 'Long term means … until you know what you're doing. So that's really up to you.'

'You have a secure location in mind, Montana?' Henrik said.

'I could take it to Aoratia,' Montana said. 'The elves could hold it until such time as an appropriate strategy is in place. Given the nature of the device, they might even offer counsel on how to deal with it.'

Montana sat down to stunned silence. Noah studied everybody at the table in turn. In every case, their shock mirrored her own. But Noah's consternation was twofold. Not only had Montana suggested a visit to the land where her life was forfeit, but if she got her way, she'd have blindsided Brinn too. No small feat.

'Not an option,' Noah said.

'While counsel of the old ones holds some appeal, Montana,' Tara said, 'I think I'd prefer to send them a message and have them come here. I, for one, am not prepared to sacrifice you for this thing.'

'I serve Talisker,' Montana said. 'If it needs to be done, I'm prepared to do it.'

Tara looked at Alan. 'Record Montana's offer. Also note that it has no support at the table.'

'You didn't ask for a vote,' Montana said.

Tara snorted. 'We don't have time to waste.' The king twisted in her seat and addressed the door guard. 'Bring King Catriona's prisoner, please.'

Avril entered the chamber with her chin up, shoulders back and eyes on Noah. When she reached the only vacant seat at the table, she stood in front of it.

'The attendance of Avril Jane of Earth is noted,' Alan said.

Mallory tapped the table. 'Sit.'

Avril stared at Melwick's dark-skinned king as she sat down.

'I believe you've come to discuss some disputed items?' Tara said, inclining her head towards the table.

'Yes,' Avril said, 'and once they're returned to me, I'll be on my way.'

'This isn't so much a negotiation as an information-sharing session,' Henrik said. 'From our perspective, Ms Jane, your options are these … option one, you can return to Earth now, without these two items or option two, you can stay and make yourself useful.'

Avril's eyes narrowed. 'Useful how?'

Henrik shrugged. 'I don't know. I did say it was an information-sharing session though. I have shared our information, it's now your turn to share.'

'I will remain here,' Avril declared, 'in my role as sein-Temperance.'

'As what?' Catriona said.

Jacin clapped. 'Bold play, Avril!' He turned to the kings. 'Sein is the Pyranhi word for champion. Sein-Temperance is Temperance's champion, one who will carry on her work.'

'My grandfather has charged me with protecting Talisker by securing this device,' Avril said. 'I intend to honour his wish.'

'Protecting Talisker?' Noah muttered. 'I don't think so.'

Avril's cheeks flushed. 'What reason have you to doubt me?'

'Fun fact, Avril,' Sachin said, 'is that the last time a grandchild of Bernard Kurz came here, our world was almost destroyed. So you'll forgive us for doubting you, but we're still working through some trust issues there.'

Avril frowned as the colour drained from her face. 'What are you talking about?'

'Orville Kurz was my father's adviser,' Catriona said, 'and he plotted to destroy Talisker. There are several people at this table who still bear the scars – physical and mental – of the night that he nearly succeeded.'

Avril's shock – real or staged – evaporated quickly. 'I'm not my cousin,' she said. 'This is my grandmother's homeland and I won't stand by and watch you people destroy it.'

'Indeed,' Tara said.

'Well, I think we'll test your resolve, Avril,' Catriona said, turning away from her prisoner. 'Noah, she's all yours. Do with her what you will.'

Noah grimaced. 'Is there a returns policy on this "gift"?'

'Hey!' Avril protested. 'I'm not an object. You can't give me away to—'

'I can give you to whom I please,' Catriona said.

Well, if she can, I can, Noah thought. Aloud she said, 'Jacin, I'm leaving Avril in your capable hands.'

Jacin looked like he'd won the lottery. A big one. 'Really?'

'Re-gifting, Noah?' Sachin said. 'That's very poor form, especially in front of the person who gave you the gift.'

'Enough,' Henrik said. 'This meeting is adjourned. We kings will consider our position and get back to you.'

♪♫

Noah exhaled sharply as Emir found another knotted muscle in her back.

'Sorry,' he said.

'Keep going,' Noah wheezed. 'Just fix it.'

She buried her face in the pillow and clenched her teeth in preparation for the next round.

'You're really tight through your shoulders,' Emir said.

Noah turned her head to one side. 'I can't imagine why.'

'I thought you'd be relieved that you didn't have to confess to being the 13th key to get the Alliance to approve the mission to Somyni.'

'That *is* a relief,' Noah said, 'but the expedition itself … it's not going to be a picnic.'

'No.'

'Even if we *can* get there,' Noah said, 'there's no guarantee we'll be able to destroy the illestial.'

Crash!

Noah twisted and sat up. 'What the …?'

Emir planted himself protectively in front of Noah. She craned her neck to see around him. Catriona stood in the doorway of their suite, cheeks flushed and eyes wide. Noah held her breath. Catriona's un-regal demeanour spelled trouble.

'Have you seen Montana?' Catriona said.

'I thought she was with Sachin,' Noah replied.

'She's *supposed* to be,' Sachin said, appearing beside Catriona.

'You can't find the pyrohm either, can you,' Noah guessed.

Catriona shook her head. 'No.'

'Ardis?' Emir asked.

'Also missing,' Catriona said.

Noah swore. 'We have to find her. We can't let her go to Aoratia. They'll kill her.'

'None of us wants that, Noah,' Emir said, 'but it's Montana. Defying her is second only to defying Brinn.'

'Who won't be happy about this either,' Sachin added.

'Well, that's hardly breaking news,' Noah snapped. 'Maybe Brinn could find it in her heart to *actually* help us … rather than just telling us what to do all the time.'

Emir put his hand on her shoulder. 'Noah.'

'I'm calm.'

He raised an eyebrow.

Noah turned her attention to Catriona. 'We can't just do nothing. We have to try to stop her.'

Catriona let out a long breath. 'Tell me what you need.'

Chapter 10

'We're too late,' Jacin said.

Noah shielded her eyes. Montana's galleon made a striking silhouette against the vibrant blue ocean but Noah was in no mood to admire the view. The high priestess hadn't been far ahead of them after all. Her ship was only a few kilometres out to sea and the onshore breeze was hampering its efforts to make headway. Noah dismounted and handed her horse's reins to Jacin.

'Return the horses to the village and get back here as fast as you can,' she said.

'But the ship is gone,' Avril said. 'What are you going to do? Swim after her?'

'Yep,' Noah replied. 'You go with Jacin.'

Avril's jaw dropped as Emir and Dragonsbane Grainger dismounted.

'Juno's not going to like your plan, Noah,' Grainger said.

The hawk ruffled her feathers as she tightened her grip on Noah's shoulder, her claws digging harmlessly into the padding Noah had sewn into her jacket.

'I don't think she'd be a good swimmer anyway,' Noah said, coaxing the bird onto her gloved hand. 'She can take a message to Montana instead.'

Emir took a pencil and notebook from his pocket. 'What do you want the message to say?'

'Tell her that I'm going to keep swimming until she comes back for me.'

'You'll probably get eaten by a sabrefish,' Grainger said.

'I doubt it,' Jacin said. 'Sabrefish would have more taste, I reckon.'

Noah spun round to face him. 'Are you still here? You should be back at the village by now. *Go!*'

Emir wound the message into the cuff on the hawk's leg. 'She's ready,' he said.

Noah clicked her fingers and the bird looked at her. She signed two words – 'ship' and 'go' – before launching the hawk into the air.

'I can't believe you taught her sign language,' Grainger said, shaking his head.

Noah watched Juno as she took flight. 'I've only had her for a year and a half so I haven't taught her as much as I'd like,' she said. 'But hopefully it'll be enough.'

Anok had given her the hawk when she had moved to Carai and the bird had proven herself indispensable.

Noah kicked off her shoes before stripping down to her sports top and leggings.

'You're not going to try to stop her?' Grainger said to Emir.

Emir shook his head. 'If you want to try … be my guest.'

'Point taken,' Grainger said with a shrug.

Noah waded into the water up to her knees. 'It's a bit chilly.'

'Well, you'd better hope Montana comes back for you,' Emir said. 'It's only going to get colder the further north you swim. King Henrik did offer you a ship … remember?'

'We need to be *with* Montana, not *behind* her,' Noah said, shivering as she took another few steps.

'Just dive in then, Noah,' Grainger said. 'Get on with it.'

'Right,' Noah said.

She took a deep breath and launched herself into the salty water off Orian's west coast. *That's ridiculously cold,* she thought. *I hope Montana comes back.*

Noah focused on keeping her breathing steady and her strokes regular. *One, two, three … breathe. One, two, three … breathe. One, two, three … breathe.* She paced herself. While reasonably fit, she hadn't done a lot of swimming and her arm and chest muscles burned in protest. She glanced up occasionally to make sure she was heading in the right direction but when something brushed against her thigh, Noah squealed into the water.

Kicking faster, she prayed that it was seaweed but an image of the fearsome sabrefish with its mouth full of razor-sharp teeth filled her mind. She hoped that Jacin was right in thinking the sabrefish would find her unpalatable and kept swimming.

Noah glanced up again. Was the ship turning?

Something bumped her shoulder. *That's not seaweed,* she thought. The water was too salty for her to open her eyes underwater so she quickened her pace. Whatever it was, it hadn't bitten her yet.

A large body glided over her back and then underneath her. Noah stopped. Treading water, she scanned the water to identify her tormentor. A whiskery snout appeared in front of her.

Awk! Awk!

'You nearly gave me a heart attack,' Noah said to the seal.

Awk!

The seal swam a circle around her and popped up again – right in front of her face this time. Noah recoiled to avoid its probing muzzle.

'Stop that,' she said, pushing its face away. 'I don't want to smell what you had for lunch.'

Awk! Awk!

Noah glanced at the ship, which was now heading her way. Thankful that Montana was coming for her, Noah focused on her new companion.

'Want to play?' she said, as the seal swam around her.

Awk!

The young seal dived under the water and Noah reached out her hand. Its sleek fur was smooth to touch. *Pity it doesn't have a fin I could hold onto,* Noah thought. *It'd be fun to go for a ride.* No ride was on offer, but the pup was playful. It jumped over her head, swam under and around her, and smothered her with whiskery kisses. The game continued for several minutes as Montana's ship closed in. But suddenly, the seal vanished.

Noah thought the ship had spooked it, until she saw the fin in the water ahead. She swore. She'd have to contend with the sabrefish until the ship arrived. As the sabrefish approached, Noah waved to the ship's watch to signal her location. If they didn't hurry though, they'd be following a blood trail to find her.

The fin cut the water cleanly as it sped towards her. Noah held her position. She'd move at the last possible moment. When the fish was upon her, she threw herself left and drew her legs up to her chest. She kicked hard.

Got him, she thought. *Maybe that'll scare him away …*

Noah twisted round, panting hard. The fin arced before turning her way again. Noah pumped her legs to keep herself as high out of the water as she could. She dived left again and kicked but cried out as her foot connected with the fish's teeth, which sliced through her flesh.

'*Noah!*' Montana yelled. 'Get out of the way!'

What do you think I'm doing? Noah thought.

She spun again, looking for the sabrefish, but a whirring sound caught her attention.

Smack!

Only a metre or so from her, the fish thrashed violently to free itself of the harpoon. Noah struggled to put more distance between them but her muscles were spent. She could barely keep her head above water. As she rolled over, she saw someone dive from the ship.

Splash!

Noah rolled onto her back and waited for the warrior to reach her.

'Grab this,' Ardis said, thrusting a paddleboard towards her.

'Thanks,' Noah said as she pulled herself onto the wooden board. 'You know you could've warned me that Montana was going to do a runner.'

'No I couldn't,' Ardis said. 'She's my boss.'

Noah sighed as he dragged her towards the ship. When the hulking wooden galleon loomed over them, Ardis secured a harness around her and then signalled for the crew to hoist her up. Noah dangled in the air, shivering as the breeze embraced her. Two warriors met her at the top and pulled her on deck. On her hands and knees, Noah felt a blanket draped over her.

'What am I going to do with you, Noah?' Montana said. 'You are utterly impossible.'

'Yeah … well … you missed me with the harpoon,' Noah said breathlessly, 'so I guess you'll have to try something else.'

'We *were* actually aiming for the fish.'

Noah rocked back on her haunches. 'Sure you were.'

Montana folded her arms. 'I suppose we're to go back for the others?'

Noah nodded as she wrapped the blanket around herself. 'We're here to help.'

'Inform the captain,' Montana said to the warrior closest to her, 'that we're returning to shore.'

The woman saluted before heading for the helm.

Ardis, with a towel over his shoulder, arrived at Montana's side bearing a medical bag. 'Want me to sew her foot back together, Boss?'

'You any good at sewing?' Montana asked.

'I've watched my wife do it often,' Ardis replied. 'It doesn't look too difficult.'

'No,' Noah said. 'Absolutely not. I'd rather do it myself.'

Montana took the medical bag from her warrior. 'It's okay. I'll do it. Go find some dry clothes.'

'Yes, Ma'am,' Ardis said, bowing before leaving.

Juno landed on the rail next to Noah as Montana got to work.

'Hey Juno,' Noah said. 'Nice job. If you want some fish though' — she inclined her head towards the sabrefish that had been hauled onto the deck – 'you might have to ask Montana yourself. I think I've used up my quota of favours.'

'You got that right,' Montana said, squirting a gooey brown gel on Noah's foot.

Noah winced. 'That stings.'

'That means it's working,'

'I can't believe you'd just run off on me like that. I thought we were a team.'

Montana sighed. 'I'm trying to buy us time, Noah. Humans tend to act quite … impulsively. Elves take more time, because they have more time. They also have a lot of knowledge that humans don't. We need their knowledge.'

'There's more,' Noah guessed. 'You want to go home?'

'No. Aoratia is my father's home. Not mine.'

'Do you think you'll see him?'

'He's probably still in jail. I can't imagine they'd let me see him.'

Noah shook her head. 'I couldn't imagine being in jail for over eight hundred years.'

'Mmm,' Montana said. 'Perhaps my mother was the lucky one after all.'

'They must have really loved each other,' Noah said, 'to take such a risk.'

Montana threaded her needle. 'Yes. They did love each other. Knowing that intimate relationships between elves and humans was the worst rule on Aoratia they could break, they broke it anyway. My mother, at least, had no regrets. She loved my father until her dying day and swore she didn't regret anything.'

'She died of a broken heart?'

'Hardly. My mother – Erin – was a formidable human. She lived to one hundred and three and died picking apples in her orchard. She fell off a ladder.'

Noah smiled. 'You must take after her.'

'What do you mean?' Montana said. 'I've never fallen off a ladder.'

Chapter 11

Noah didn't dare admit it but she was almost glad to be going ashore. Aoratia – the island of the elves – lay far to the north of the seven states, and after nearly three weeks on a ship, Noah was keen to be on solid ground again. The treacherous seas and vicious storms had tested not only the ship but the fortitude of the crew as well. Butterflies stirred in Noah's stomach as Montana's warriors prepared the skiff for the trip to shore.

'I'd be happy to row,' Jacin said.

Noah ignored him. She refused to be drawn into the argument again.

'We'll stick to the plan,' Montana said. 'Noah, Emir, Grainger and I will go ashore. We should have an indication of the elves' response to the illestial by tonight. Send Juno so we can send a message to you with instructions on which phase to enact next.'

'If Juno can *find* you to get the message,' Avril said. 'It's going to be difficult if they separate you all.'

Montana tightened the sash around her waist. 'Juno will find Noah.'

When the skiff was in the water, Emir climbed over the rail and down the rope ladder.

'Noah,' Grainger said, gesturing for her to go next.

Despite the cold, Noah's hands were clammy which made her descent precarious. Emir helped her to her seat when she reached the craft.

'You ready for this?' he asked.

'Ready as I'll ever be,' Noah said, huddling inside her coat.

Once Grainger and Montana were settled, Emir took the oars. Noah squinted through the mist as the boat coasted towards the elves' stronghold. As more foggy vapour cascaded down the mountainsides from ice-capped peaks, the mist near the foot of the coastal range swirled mischievously. The shifting curtain of fog revealed tantalising glimpses of a lone figure on the rocks at the water's edge.

No one spoke as the boat ride wore on. Only the occasional splash of the oars disturbed the silence. When the wooden hull grazed the rocks in the shallows, Noah inhaled deeply. *Here goes nothing,* she thought as Grainger jumped out first and dragged the bow clear of the water. Noah followed Montana as Emir stowed the oars.

The elf approached them, the fur-trimmed hood of the hide cloak framing his angular face. His complexion was flawless, his emerald eyes searing. Noah was mesmerised. He was so perfect it seemed impossible that he was real.

'I am Torbin, of the woodland elves,' he said. 'What is your business here?'

Montana bowed her head. 'I am Montana, High Priestess of the Order of Elani. With me are Noah Chord and Grainger Brimblecombe – both Dragonsbanes of Talisker, and Emir Delorian – my adviser. We come seeking counsel regarding this.'

Montana produced the pyrohm from the pocket of her robe and handed it to the elf.

Torbin turned the relic over in his gloved hands and said, 'Do you know what this is?'

'It is part of the illestial,' Montana said.

'Where did you find it?'

'Noah found it on Earth,' Montana replied.

The elf's expression remained neutral. *Perhaps that's why he has no wrinkles,* Noah thought. *I bet he never frowns.*

'This is a matter for the Council,' Torbin said at last.

He reached inside his coat and took out a slender metal rod about the length of a pencil. A small piece of firestone adorned one end.

Noah felt Grainger's gaze on her and understood his warning. Though she sometimes still referred to his baton as a 'wand', she knew better than to make any 'wand' jokes here.

Torbin traced a large circle in the air as he uttered words Noah didn't understand. Within heartbeats, the air within the circle shimmered. Colours swirled to form a picture. A female elf sat at a desk, reading from a parchment. Her ebony locks were braided and coiled on top of her head. White and yellow flowers punctuated the elaborate hairstyle, reminding Noah of something out of one of Aunt Polly's cake icing magazines.

The elf looked up and Noah gasped. This wasn't just a picture. The elves obviously possessed powerful magic.

'I'm sorry to interrupt you, Councillor Talyn,' Torbin said, 'but I bear an important message.'

Councillor Talyn put the parchment down on her desk. 'What is it?'

Torbin held up the pyrohm. 'Four humans have brought this to us. They seek counsel.'

'Indeed,' the lady said, her brown eyes smouldering. 'Take them to the Council Chambers. I will summon the other Councillors.'

Without waiting for an answer, the councillor stood up and the circle vanished.

'Was that an elf charm or Pyranhi magic?' Grainger asked.

'The doorways are Pyranhi spells,' Torbin said. 'They allow us to communicate – and travel – over great distances.'

'How much firestone do you have here?' Noah said.

Torbin wove another circle with his wand. 'More than humans have,' he said.

Not that it's a competition or anything, Noah thought.

Another doorway shimmered into view. The picture crystallised and in the room beyond the doorway, a lively fireplace beckoned.

'The Council meet in the woodland lodge,' Torbin said. 'After you.'

Montana stepped through the doorway and Noah followed, the transition from arctic shoreline to cosy lodge a welcome relief. Noah loosened her scarf as Emir and Grainger arrived.

An elaborately carved table dominated the room, the frieze across the front of the immense wooden slab depicted a myriad of woodland animals. A cursory glance revealed bison, wolves, bears and snow leopards. But Noah wasn't interested in the intricate carving.

'How many councillors are there?' she asked.

'Three,' Torbin said. 'And you shouldn't speak to them unless they tell you to.'

Noah glanced at Montana who raised an eyebrow but said nothing.

Talyn arrived first, through a doorway that appeared behind the middle seat at the table. She sat down without acknowledging her guests. Instead, she spoke to Torbin.

'You have the device?' Talyn said.

Torbin crossed the floor and bowed his head before placing the pyrohm on the table.

Talyn nodded. 'Thank you, Torbin. Dismissed.'

'Thank you, Councillor. Good day.'

Torbin took his leave as two more doorways appeared within seconds of each other. A female elf entered and sat down on Talyn's right, and an older male elf settled himself in the chair on Talyn's left. Noah searched their faces for any imperfections – scars, wrinkles, broken capillaries – but found none. She wondered what the elves thought of their human visitors. If they were bothered by the sight of inferior folk, they didn't show it.

Talyn nodded curtly. 'Humans,' she said. 'Attend!'

Noah flinched at the elf's tone.

'I am Talyn of the woodland elves,' she said, 'and I represent my clan on the Council. With me are Councillors Vance and Linden of the mountain elves and lake elves respectively. This Council serves as government here. We speak for, and make decisions on behalf of, all Aoratia's elves.'

She paused as her fellow councillors nodded.

'This object you have is no trinket and it is right that you brought it to us. The Council will take this into account as we decide your sentence.'

'Sentence?' Noah said. 'For what?'

'Trespass,' Councillor Vance said, tapping his fingers on the table. 'You do not have permission to be here.'

'We didn't know who to ask for permission,' Grainger said.

'Ignorance is no excuse,' Vance replied.

Councillor Linden pointed at Montana. 'But *your* crime is more serious,' she said. 'Are you hoping that perhaps we'll reduce your penalty to life imprisonment?'

'I'm happy to accept the original penalty,' Montana said, 'if my friends go free.'

'Yes, very noble,' Talyn said with a wave, 'but irrelevant. You are in no position to negotiate.'

Vance leaned forward. 'You are an abomination, Montana. But since it wasn't *your* fault that you were born, we didn't exterminate you. Though it pained us deeply to know that you defiled this world with your presence, we let you live.'

'For which I am truly grateful,' Montana said.

'Well, it doesn't look like it,' Linden said. 'Your return speaks to your disregard – no, your contempt – for our generosity.'

Generosity? Noah thought. *That's a bit rich.*

Talyn's eyes flicked to Noah. 'Your face betrays your thoughts, human,' she said. 'You doubt our generosity?'

'I don't know about your generosity,' Noah said, 'but your manners could do with some work. I have a name.'

'And I would have asked for it if I'd cared to hear it,' Talyn said.

Noah held the elf's gaze. 'My name is Noah Chord and I am a Dragonsbane of Talisker. While our presence here may offend you, there are bigger things to worry about. Our world faces a great threat.' She pointed to the pyrohm. 'Now you can sit here deliberating on how best to punish us … or we can just get down to the business of working out what's to be done about the illestial.'

Talyn's nostrils flared. 'That's just one of your many human flaws, *Noah*. You're too hasty. Now that the pyrohm is with us … it is safe. We will decide – in our own good time – how to deal with it.'

'We didn't come here to *give* it to you,' Emir said. 'We came for counsel – to work together.'

Linden snorted. 'Humans are inferior to elves in every way. We would not consider working with you.'

'We allow humans to work *for* us, but not *with* us,' Talyn said.

Noah frowned.

Vance raised his hand. 'Humans who are foolish enough to come here,' he said, 'are given an opportunity to be useful. We understand the fundamentally flawed nature of humans and so we *generously* extend them one chance to be of service to this world. Most of them work on reservations – hunting, farming and producing goods we require. Some, if they can be unobtrusive, are permitted to work in our communities doing menial tasks.'

'So as long as you don't have to look at their ugly faces,' Noah said, 'they can do all the crappy jobs that you don't want to do?'

'In return for following the *natural order* of things here,' Vance said, 'humans enjoy sanctuary on our beautiful island. Given that they shouldn't be here at all – I'd say that is extremely generous.'

'Well, I'd respectfully suggest to you that *these* humans,' Emir said, gesturing to his companions, 'have more to offer than most. They are extremely talented and capable individuals who should not be dismissed lightly.'

'Is that a threat?' Talyn said.

'I am simply giving you information,' Emir said calmly. 'Noah and Grainger outwitted the Guardian in Tisaan to retrieve thirteen pieces of firestone that the Pyranhi had hidden there.'

Vance stood up and walked around the table. He stopped in front of the group.

'If you are all so clever,' he said, 'why bring the pyrohm to us?'

'We are … resourceful,' Noah replied. 'Humans are very capable but we recognise our limitations. Once we know *how* to deal with the illestial – we'll get the job done.'

'The arrangement should suit you,' Montana said. 'That's basically what happens now anyway. You provide the tools and humans do your dirty work for you.'

The corners of Vance's mouth twitched as he studied them. Noah wondered if he was trying to smile.

After a long moment, Vance said, 'For now, Noah will go to a female reservation on Talyn's lands. The men will be put to work on one of Linden's reservations. Montana, you are for the dungeon.'

'Will I see my father?' Montana asked.

'Yes,' Talyn said. 'We'll make sure your cell is right next to his.'

♪♫

'Hold still,' the woman said. 'You want a nice brand, don't you?'

Noah wanted to tell the woman that she'd happily forego the brand, but the gag made that impossible. Under the watchful eye of a lone elf overseer, four of the reservation's women fought to subdue Noah while another stirred the branding iron among the coals.

'If you want to be one of us, this ceremony is necessary,' the lead woman said.

I don't want to be one of you! Noah thought as she wriggled desperately to get free.

Talyn's woodland reservation was possibly the most picturesque countryside Noah had ever seen and the women seemed content. The accommodation was basic but clean. Stone dormitories sported fireplaces that protected the residents from the harsh winter elements. Bedding was comfortable, food was fresh and abundant. Seemingly, it was an idyllic existence for those who'd left human civilisation in search of a better life.

But Noah sensed an undercurrent of … wrongness. She didn't even brand the cows on her farm. How could these women think it was okay to brand their fellow human beings?

Strong hands pushed Noah's head onto a flat rock.

Determined not to cower, Noah glared at the brand as it got closer. She thought of Jacin. He'd been branded to mark him as a goman – half goblin, half human. Noah would now bear a scar in the shape of a leaf to mark her as one of Talyn's 'employees'.

'Now this *will* sting a little …' the branding woman said.

White light exploded inside Noah's head when the brand struck her neck. She screamed, almost choking on the gag.

'There, there,' someone said. 'All done now.'

Breathing hard through her nose, Noah glowered at the woman as her gag was removed and tossed into the fire. The woman smiled at her as she put the brand in the snow. It hissed and sizzled briefly before falling silent again.

The elf overseer stepped forward, wand pinched between her delicate fingers.

Noah's eyes narrowed. 'Can you magic up some ointment?' she said. 'That really hurts.'

The elf didn't answer. She traced an elaborate pattern with her wand and chanted softly.

Noah's pain eased. 'Ah, that's bet—'

Tingling around her burn alerted Noah to a new problem. *That elf magic is not just for healing,* Noah thought. Memories of Orville Kurz's compliance spell flooded her mind. His blood magic had been crude but effective. When near him, she'd been compelled to do whatever he'd demanded of her. The elf's magic had the same undertones but was much more sophisticated. Noah touched her neck gingerly.

'Better?' the branding woman asked.

Noah nodded, trying to look amazed rather than concerned. If the elves suspected she understood anything about magic, she'd be in a good deal more trouble.

'Well, Noah, now that the formalities are out of the way,' the woman said, 'we can get to work. My name is Ren and I'll be your mentor. If you have any questions – I'm here to answer them for you.'

'Let's get started then,' Noah said. 'What's the first job?'

'An excellent question,' Ren said, glancing at the elf overseer. 'I think you're going to do just fine here, Noah. Just fine.'

Ren's words were encouraging, her tone was syrupy but her look at the overseer told Noah everything she needed to know. Noah suddenly understood the wrongness here. There was a system. If she conformed and did a good job, Ren would be rewarded. Noah didn't know what the reward was, but that didn't matter. The only thing that mattered was that Ren wanted it. Ren didn't care about Noah. She only cared about the reward that would come if she could successfully mould her charge.

'We have to catch a bison for Talyn's table,' Ren said.

'Catch a bison?' Noah said. 'And kill it?'

'Yes, but don't worry – it's a team effort. I'll tell you what to do.'

♪♫

Noah peered between the trees. Even a hundred metres away, the bison looked imposing. It appeared content as it nibbled the leaves of a hardy winter bush, but Ren had warned her about their contrary nature.

'That's a lot of animal,' Noah said. 'Are you sure you want to kill that one?'

'There are many mouths to feed in Talyn's household,' Ren said. 'Bigger is better.'

'Smaller ones would be more tender,' Noah said. 'I thought elves would go for quality over quantity.'

Ren frowned. 'Elves have more respect for life than humans do, Noah. They like the bison to live long, happy lives before they end up on a table. And anyway, elves are extraordinary cooks. Give them any cut of meat and they'll turn it into something magical.'

'Right,' Noah said as she studied the beast.

Although the bison was herbivorous, Noah counted three ways it could kill her. Goring her with its horns would be the most spectacular, while a solid kick from its hind legs would probably deliver the quickest end. Failing that, if it fell on her … well, she wouldn't have long to worry about it.

'Repeat the plan,' Ren said, 'so I know you remember what to do.'

Noah turned to her. 'I wander down there and get its attention. Then I lure it up here. You and your crew lasso it and bring it down.'

Noah glanced back at the bison.

'And?' Ren said.

'Then I jump on it and cut its throat.'

Ren nodded. 'Yes. It needs to be quick. We don't want the animal to suffer.'

We don't want the animal to suffer. This from the person who only an hour before had pressed a red-hot iron against Noah's throat.

'Of course not,' Noah said, shaking her head. 'Are you ready then?'

'Ready,' Ren said.

Noah tramped through the snow towards the bison. She didn't need to sneak up on it. The more noise she made the better, she reasoned. She was bait, annoying it was a priority.

The bison swung its head in her direction, snorting plumes of vapour from its nostrils. Noah quickened her pace. Bison had poor eyesight so she flailed her arms.

'Over here,' she called. 'Mr Bison … this way.'

The beast snorted again and shook its shaggy head.

'I'm the bearer of bad news, I'm afraid,' Noah continued. 'The elves are hungry and they've sent me to—'

Without warning, the bison charged.

Noah spun round but slipped as she tried to run.

'Crap!' Noah said as she scrambled to her feet and pushed off more carefully.

'Run, Noah!' Ren cried. *'Faster!'*

Noah didn't look back. Thundering hooves compelled her. She pumped her arms harder. With her slight build, she was supposed to have an advantage over the lumbering bison on the inclined trail. But bison were deceptively fast.

I have to outrun it, she thought. *I have to.*

'Come on!' Ren yelled.

Cold air seared Noah's lungs but she ignored the pain. She focused on her feet. If she were to make it to the trap ahead of the bison, she needed to stay upright. The hoofbeats were getting louder. Noah chanced a peek behind her.

The bloody thing is taller than me.

Adrenaline surged through her, but as she pushed for more speed she slipped again. She rolled to the side of the trail and the beast thundered past her. Noah clambered to her hands and knees. She watched the bison pull up and turn around. Springing to her feet, she dashed across the trail and leapt at a tree branch. She found a foothold on the trunk and levered herself onto the branch. She crouched, breathing hard.

'What are you doing?' Ren called.

Noah didn't answer. Her attention was on the bison. He'd picked up her scent again.

'That's right,' Noah said, bracing herself on the branch. 'Come to me.'

The animal walked to the tree and rammed the trunk with its head.

'I really hope you've had a long and happy life, Mr Bison,' Noah said.

The bison rammed the trunk again.

'Neither of us wants this,' she said, 'but I have to live long enough to help my friends. I am sorry.'

When the animal rammed the trunk a third time, Noah whipped her dagger from its sheath and dropped onto the bison's humped shoulders. It bellowed as it bucked. Noah jumped … landed … stabbed. With both hands clutching the hilt, she dragged the dagger through the thick muscle around the beast's throat.

The bison bawled and Noah screamed as blood spurted over her. She pulled her dagger free and leapt aside as the beast staggered. Blade poised, she set her stance. The injured bison was now much more dangerous. Enraged, it lunged at her. Noah dodged. Just. It swung its head, trying to gore her with one of its horns. She ducked and rolled. As the animal turned, Noah raised her dagger.

We don't want the animal to suffer.

She squeezed her eyes shut and thrust the blade into its flesh. It bellowed again as its knees buckled. When it collapsed on its side, Noah pulled out the knife. She wiped her bloody hands on her trousers before kneeling beside the dying bull. Running her fingers through its shaggy fur, she let her tears flow. She rested her head on its side and sobbed as the bison drew it final breaths.

A hand squeezed her shoulder.

'Noah,' Ren said.

Noah tried to shrug off the hand. 'Go away.'

'We are here to pay our respects to this beast.'

Steadying her voice, Noah said, 'Do it then. Just leave me alone.'

As Ren and her crew commenced their tribute, Noah buried her face in the bison's thick fur and cried. The magnificent beast whose blood stained the snow deserved not just to be respected, but to be mourned. And Noah planned to do just that. Ren could wait. The elves could wait.

Chapter 12

Noah closed the door gently before stealing out into the darkness. There would be no sleep for her tonight. Each time she closed her eyes, she saw the dead bison. She'd searched for solace in the embers of the dormitory fireplace for hours but found none. If anyone challenged her for being out of the dorm, she'd claim she needed some fresh air. She doubted she'd encounter anyone though. Ren had told her there was no *rule* about staying indoors at night. It was just a good idea. Wolves roamed the woodlands at night.

Noah stuck to the trail, scanning the moonlit trees on the hillside. She hoped she wouldn't find Juno this close to camp but she needed to keep watch. After a few hundred metres, Noah turned from the path and headed uphill. The snow was deceptively deep in places and she stumbled several times. *I need to be careful,* she thought. *I can't afford to roll an ankle here.*

She focused on her feet, testing each step. It was slow going but she trudged on – putting more and more distance between herself and the dormitory. At the sound of fluttering wings above her, Noah looked up. Her heart beat faster as Juno came to rest on her arm.

'Hey girl,' Noah said.

The hawk sidled up Noah's arm to her shoulder.

'It's good to see you too,' Noah said, as the bird rubbed its head against her face. 'I've got a job for you though.'

Noah sat down on a log and removed one of her gloves. As Juno preened herself, Noah took paper and pencil from her jacket pocket and composed a note.

Jacin. We've been separated. Montana is in the dungeons. Emir and Grainger are on the lake elves' reservation. I'm on the woodland elves' reservation. Hold your positions. Send Juno again tomorrow night for update. Noah.

Noah clicked her fingers and the hawk hopped down onto the log.

'I need you to take this to Jacin,' she said, rolling the note into Juno's leg cuff. 'Make sure he gives you a treat.'

Once Noah had secured the note, Juno put her head in Noah's lap. *She's like a puppy,* Noah thought as she stroked the bird's wings.

A wolf howled. Juno flinched.

'Time to go,' Noah murmured.

She clicked her fingers and made the hand signs for 'ship' and 'go'. Noah watched the hawk launch herself skyward. Juno would be safe from wolves at least. Noah shuddered. She hoped there were no archers around.

'What are you doing?' a voice said.

Noah spun round, almost slipping off the log. An elf emerged from behind a tree as Noah got to her feet. He walked – almost glided – towards her and stopped right in front of her.

'Who are you?' Noah said.

'I am Seamus. What are you doing out here? Don't you know there are wolves about?'

Noah looked him in the eye. 'Someone did mention it, but I get claustrophobic. I needed some fresh air.'

'You're new here?'

Noah nodded.

'You're not going to last long at this rate, I'd say.'

'I don't mean to. Once we've got what we came for, we'll be on our way.'

Seamus raised an eyebrow as he studied her. 'And what have you come for?'

Noah held his gaze. There was nothing to be gained by keeping their mission a secret. That would play into the Councillors' hands. She needed to shake things up.

'We've come for advice on the illestial,' she said.

'What do you know of the illestial?'

'I found part of it – the pyrohm.'

The elf frowned and said nothing for nearly a minute. 'Did you bring it here?'

'Yes.'

'Where is it?' Seamus said.

'The Councillors have it.'

Even in the moonlight, Noah saw the colour drain from his face.

'What is your name?' he said.

'Noah Chord of Leninstar. I am a Dragonsbane of Talisker.'

Seamus reached inside his cloak. 'Indeed.'

Noah whipped her dagger from the sheath strapped to her boot. Seamus flinched.

'You don't need that,' he said.

'I'll keep it all the same,' Noah replied. 'What are you doing?'

The elf withdrew his hand slowly to reveal a sliver of metal. It looked like an oversized dressmaking pin with a firestone bulb on the end. He traced the outline of a doorway as he muttered under his breath. Pulsating white light framed the portal he created. Beyond the gleaming border, a wizened elf lay on a simple cot.

Seamus held out his hand to Noah. 'You need to come with me.'

As Noah considered her options, wolves howled a chorus from the hillside. *They're close,* she thought. *Too close.*

Noah stepped through the doorway and into the small bedroom. Seamus dissolved the doorway once he too was through.

'Grandfather,' Seamus said. 'The pyrohm has come to Aoratia.'

The old elf's eyes snapped open. He sat up and swung his legs over the edge of his bed. A thick, white plait draped over his shoulder and curled in his lap. When he looked at Noah, he seemed to look *into* her rather than *at* her. She shivered.

'*You've* brought the pyrohm?' the old elf said.

Noah nodded.

Without taking his eyes off Noah, he said, 'What's your name?'

'Noah Chord of Leninstar.'

'She's a Dragonbane,' Seamus added.

The old elf's eyebrows twitched. 'I am Theo, an Elder of the wood-land elves. I hope you are stronger than you look, Noah. We have a difficult job ahead of us.'

'And what job is that?' Noah asked.

Theo got to his feet and stretched. 'Destroying the illestial. May I see the piece you've brought?'

'The Councillors took it,' Noah said.

Theo froze, eyes bulging. 'The Councillors have it?' he whispered.

'Yes,' Noah said. 'When my friends and I arrived here looking for counsel, they confiscated the pyrohm. They've imprisoned the high priestess in the dungeons and two of my friends are captive on another reservation.'

'Montana is here?' Theo said.

Noah nodded. 'You know her?'

'I know *of* her,' Theo said. 'Why would she come here? They'll kill her.'

'She thought it was important that the pyrohm got here,' Noah said, 'and she wanted to make sure that it did.'

'Montana escorted you here?'

'Not exactly,' Noah said. 'She took it, intending to bring it here by herself. We had to chase after her.'

Theo coiled his plait into a knot. 'Who is "we"?'

Noah listed her companions and their roles. She described how she'd found the pyrohm but omitted her conversation with Jong.

Theo looked at Seamus. 'We have no time to lose. Get what you need.'

Seamus bowed his head. 'Yes, Grandfather.'

Theo returned his attention to Noah. 'So sein-Temperance, what magic do you—'

'Wait, hang on a second,' Noah interrupted. 'Why did you call me that?'

'Sein-Temperance?'

'Yes.'

'Because that's what you are.'

Noah frowned. 'What makes you think that?'

Theo buttoned his cloak. 'It has long been Temperance's will that the illestial be destroyed. It was one of her Pyranhi champions – the sein-Temperance – who stole the pyrohm in the first place. When they discovered that they couldn't destroy it, they hid it. The elves have always believed that when the time was right, Temperance would send another champion to destroy it … and here you are. *You* found it, *you* brought it – *you* are sein-Temperance.'

'But what about Montana? Surely she is sein-Temperance?'

'The high priestess heads the Order of Elani,' Theo said, shaking his head, 'so *she* is sein-Elani. You and Montana are friends?'

'Yes.'

'Good. We're going to need all the help we can get.'

'We're going to rescue her?'

'Of course,' Theo said, snatching up a satchel from the floor next to his bed. 'We'll collect your male companions too. Another Dragonsbane certainly won't go astray. We must hurry though.'

'Why? What's the rush?'

Theo sighed. 'We elves are not so different from the Pyranhi. Some of us await the return of the pyrohm to destroy it, but there are those who would pick up where the Jongu left off.'

'But the Councillors will keep it safe, won't they?'

Theo scowled. 'I wouldn't count on it. The Jongu in Aoratia are secretive – no one openly admits to being one, but many suspect that Councillor Talyn is their leader.'

'Talyn? Really?'

'Yes.'

Noah's stomach churned. 'I'm surprised elves would want to destroy Talisker.'

'Some elves think this world is not the glorious place it once was – because it's been overrun by humans and goblins,' Theo said as Seamus returned. 'They think it would be a good thing for elves to start afresh somewhere else.'

'Do you know how to get to Somyni?' Noah said.

Theo nodded gravely.

Panic rising inside her, Noah said, 'Do you think Talyn might be there already?'

'No,' Theo said. 'It'll take her a little while to assemble her supporters. It's a clandestine network – if she moves too fast she risks drawing attention that might expose their operation. We shouldn't dawdle though.'

Noah inhaled deeply and then exhaled slowly. 'Montana first?'

'No,' Theo said. 'We'll get your friends first. Once we spring Montana, we'll have to move very quickly to retrieve the pyrohm as well.'

'We have to find it first,' Seamus said.

Theo slung a pack over his shoulder. 'Talyn will have it.' Turning to his grandson, he said, 'A doorway please, Seamus.'

♪♫

Noah studied the terrain as the night's grip on the mountain eased. Rescuing Emir and Grainger had been relatively easy, but saving Montana promised to be much more difficult.

'Déjà vu,' Emir said.

Noah turned to him. 'Hmm?'

'Breaking Montana out of prison. I feel like we've done this before.'

'That's because we have done this before,' Noah said. 'But Leninstar's jail was dirt and stone – this one is protected by elf magic.'

'At least there are no goblins,' Emir said.

Noah nodded. That was something to be thankful for. Though she now had many goblin friends in Carai, goblins in general were still to be feared.

'Grainger,' Theo said, 'may I see your device?'

Noah watched as Grainger removed his baton from a pocket inside his coat and offered it to the old elf. Theo took the piece of olluka wood, staring at it as he turned it over in his hands. Noah was keen to see what he thought of it. He hadn't approved of her viola. Appropriate for an adept, Theo had said, but not fitting for a Dragonsbane.

'A workable device,' Theo said at last. 'The firestone bulb doesn't need to be quite so big but it is well crafted.'

'I could perform elf magic with it?' Grainger asked.

Theo nodded. 'Yes. And you'll need to if we're to destroy the illestial. There is much you must learn. You will come with us to rescue Montana and watch what I do.'

'Lesson one?' Grainger said.

'Yes,' Theo said as he handed the baton back to Grainger and turned to face the group. 'The Dragonsbanes will come with me. Seamus and Emir will wait here.'

'Are there guards?' Noah asked.

'Only one,' Theo replied. 'A troll.'

Noah glanced at Emir. 'Goblins might have been better,' she said.

'We'll be able to walk into the chamber without challenge,' Theo said. 'All elves are permitted entry to the dungeon to view the prisoners. It's only if visitors try to break prisoners out that the troll appears.'

Grainger tapped his baton against his cheek. 'So we'll have some time to prepare once we're inside?'

Theo nodded. 'Some. It is not a place to loiter though.'

'Well, let's get on with it then,' Noah said.

'Yes,' Theo said. 'Follow me.'

Emir grabbed Noah's hand as she turned to go. She looked at him.

'Be careful,' he said.

Noah smiled. 'Always.'

He kissed her cheek before releasing her.

Noah walked between Theo and Grainger as they approached the opening at the base of the mountain, the butterflies in her stomach getting more agitated with each step she took. Thoughts of retrieving the pyrohm and outwitting Jong distracted her as she fought to focus on the job at hand. *Montana first,* she thought.

They crossed the threshold and the temperature dropped.

'I thought it would be warmer inside,' Noah said as she turned up the collar of her coat.

'It's not meant to be inviting,' Theo said as he illuminated the passageway with his device.

'What do you call that?' Noah said.

'What?' Theo said.

Noah pointed at his glowing metal pin. 'Your device. What do you call that here?'

Theo looked at the rod and then at Noah. 'It's a wand. What would you call it?'

'A baton,' Grainger said before Noah could answer.

Theo shook his head. 'Why would—'

'How many prisoners are here?' Grainger interrupted.

'Five,' Theo said.

'Five?' Grainger said. 'Only five?'

'Only the worst crimes are punishable by imprisonment here,' Theo explained, 'and very few elves commit those crimes – and if they do, they usually take their own lives to avoid coming here.'

'What kind of crimes?' Noah asked.

'One prisoner here has murdered an elf,' Theo said, 'and three have fraternised with humans. And then there's Montana.'

'Is Montana's father one of the three who has "fraternised with humans"?' Noah said.

Theo nodded. 'Yes.'

Noah's pulse quickened. Montana had hoped to see her father again someday, but not under these circumstances.

When the passageway ended, Noah gasped. Dozens of translucent crystal pillars sprouted from the floor of the cathedral-like cavern and speared the ceiling high above. Five of the massive columns were occupied. Elfin faces stared out at them from their crystal cells.

'This is your dungeon?' Grainger said.

'It's not mine,' Theo said, 'but this is Aoratia's dungeon.'

Noah raced to Montana and put her palms on the cool, clear quartz. From inside her cell, Montana placed her hands to Noah's.

Creases marred the high priestess's forehead. 'Noah,' she said, 'you shouldn't have come here. Your priority is the illestial.'

'No,' Noah said, shaking her head. 'My priority is you.'

A voice from another column intruded. 'So this is the friend you've been telling me about?'

Noah turned to face the elf in the adjacent column. She had only to look at his eyes to know he was Montana's father.

'Yes, Father,' Montana said. 'This is my friend, Noah.'

'Nice to meet you, Noah,' he said. 'I am Kafir.'

Introductions were made as the remaining three prisoners watched on with interest.

'Now,' Kafir said to Noah, 'you have no time to dally.' Looking at Theo, he said, 'You have come to help?'

Theo nodded.

'Then, my good elf,' Kafir said, 'make haste. Get my daughter out of here and secure the pyrohm.'

Noah leant in close to Theo. 'Could we take Kafir too?' she whispered.

'No,' Theo said. 'The crystals all have different … frequencies. Breaking down one will be difficult enough.'

Noah winced but didn't argue. 'What do you want me to do?'

'Watch and learn,' Theo said as he readied his wand, 'and you'll want your sword when the troll arrives.'

'Has anyone done this before?' Grainger asked as he drew his sword. 'Busted someone out of here?'

'Once,' Kafir said.

'You saw how it was done?' Noah asked.

'No,' Kafir replied. 'It was before my time. Theo, get on with it.'

With a nod, Theo raised his wand.

'Noah,' Grainger said, 'you listen to the words, I'll note the actions.'

'Right,' Noah said, closing her eyes to focus her attention on her hearing. 'Just tell me when the troll arrives.'

Noah cleared her mind and readied herself to catalogue what she heard. She wouldn't recognise any of the elvish words, so she'd have to memorise the sounds. *I'll never remember them all,* she thought. But as panic spread through her, an idea squirmed free of her doubt.

'I've been inside a piece of firestone …,' she murmured to herself, 'so to get an elf inside a piece of crystal … it can't be that different, can it?'

Noah's raiki training kicked in. Though she'd risen to the rank of Major relatively quickly, she'd earned it. She'd studied hard – that had to be worth something. Noah inhaled deeply. Everything on Talisker was made of music. She just had to analyse the music of the elvish magic – visualise it as a piece of fabric – and then weave in the sounds she heard. Noah focused her perceptions on Montana's crystal column and chose her fabric. She started with a plain white landscape of a cotton and angora blend.

Theo got to work. Noah's ears accepted each new sound and her mind embellished the fabric with a symbol or pattern. A small pink daisy here, a spiral of ochre there … By the time Theo was done, her print was a chaotic mix of plants, animals and geometric designs – certainly not the elegant elvish spell she'd expected.

'*Noah!*' Grainger cried. 'Eyes front!'

The floor trembled as thunder ripped through the underground. Sword raised, Noah's eyes flicked to Montana. The high priestess leapt free of the crumbling crystal and dashed to her father's column. Noah scanned the cavern. All the other crystals remained intact.

Grrrrrrrrrooooooooooaaaaarrrrrr!

Noah spun round. A lumpy, puffy troll barrelled through the entranceway, its squat legs and disproportionately long arms giving it a gorilla-like gait. Red blazed from sunken eye sockets in its flat head and brown mucus coated its long fangs.

'That's repulsive,' Noah said, gripping her sword more tightly.

The creature roared again.

Grainger glanced at her. 'Maybe you shouldn't insult it, Noah.'

The troll glared at them, eyes blazing. 'The penalty is *death*,' it roared, raising its fists in the air.

'Noah,' Montana said. 'Do you have a spare sword?'

Noah shoved hers into Montana's hands and drew her dagger. Montana winked at her. 'Three against one. Should be easy.'

'Four against one,' Theo said. 'I'm old but I can still fight.'

'Four against *two*,' one of the prisoners said. 'This should be good.'

A second, much fatter troll struggled to squeeze through the entranceway. Doomed to fail, it held a beefy, mould-covered arm towards its mate. 'Little help?' it growled.

The first troll clutched the other's wrist and yanked its companion into the cavern. The dumpy troll rolled to its feet and snarled.

'You never said anything about *two* trolls,' Noah said to Theo.

'I didn't know there were two,' Theo said. 'Let's just hope there aren't any more.'

Noah shuddered. 'Well, two at a time is enough. Let's deal with these two now just in case there are more.'

Without waiting for an answer, Noah ran towards the first troll. It swung its arm as she approached. She dodged and slid between its legs, dragging her dagger across its ankle as she went. It bellowed as it stamped its injured foot. Noah rolled clear and sprang to her feet.

'Hey, troll!' she cried. 'I'm behind you.'

The troll roared as it turned.

Noah balanced her weight. This wasn't a bison. The troll was easily three times bigger. And its skin was tough. She'd scratched its ankle but inflicted no lasting damage. When the beast glowered at her, Noah could almost feel the malevolence radiating from it.

'Got it!' Montana yelled.

The creature bawled. Montana screamed.

'Montana!' Noah cried. She backed towards an exit, the troll blocking her view of the cavern. 'What's wrong?'

'I lost the sword,' Montana called. 'It's stuck in the troll's back.'

Noah swore softly.

No matter how good Montana's shot was, one blow wouldn't be enough to finish the troll. Noah turned and raced into the tunnel.

'Come get me,' she yelled over her shoulder.

Once inside the tunnel, Noah channelled the firestone in her veins and sang a tonic to illuminate her dagger. She ran until the troll bellowed again. Spinning back to face the creature, Noah held the dagger in front of her. The troll was wedged in the entranceway. It wriggled and writhed, trying to get back into the tunnel. Thumping its boulder-like fists on the floor, it howled in frustration.

Noah's eyes darted back and forth, watching its fists. Her timing had to be perfect. If she misjudged her run, she'd be squished. The troll bellowed again, blasting another gale of putrid wind down the tunnel. Noah gagged. *Too much more of this,* she thought, *and I'll pass out from the smell.*

She took a deep breath and launched herself at the beast. She dodged … ducked … and scrambled until she was within reach of its face. Squatting before it, Noah exhaled sharply before springing onto the creature's snout. It flinched in surprise and Noah slipped on its slimy skin. She kicked out as she fell, flinging herself to the right.

'Take that!' she yelled as she stabbed her illuminated dagger into its eye.

The troll screeched as Noah hit the floor. She rolled, tossing her dagger aside to avoid injury. Noah crouched and watched the beast thrash its head from side to side. She reached for her blade as the creature bellowed.

'Need a hand?'

Noah jumped. 'Emir! How did you get in here?'

'Found a back door,' he said. 'Need some help?'

'Help is good.'

Emir peered up at the troll. 'You're trying to blind it?'

'Yes.'

He held up his sword. 'There's two of us now. Let's finish it quickly.'

Between them, they opened the creature's throat – its sticky, black blood seeping into the tunnel like lava oozing from a volcano.

'Is there another way back into the dungeon?' Emir said, as the troll lay still.

Noah shrugged. 'I don't know.'

Noah strained to hear beyond the gruesome plug in the entrance-way. 'I can't hear anything,' she said.

'Cover your ears,' Emir said.

Noah did as he said.

'MONTANA!' he yelled. 'GRAINGER! Can you hear me?'

Noah lowered her hands and listened.

Nothing.

Emir called again.

Still nothing.

'We should go back to the rendezvous point,' Emir suggested. 'Theo might have taken the others back out the front way.'

'Let's hope so,' Noah said, stomach churning.

She scooted along the tunnel after Emir. *Please let them be okay,* she thought. The sound of their footsteps echoed off the ancient stone and Noah strained to hear anything that would indicate her companions were alive. Nothing. Once outside, she overtook Emir – desperate to reach the meeting point.

When they reached Seamus, he was alone.

'Where are the others?' he said.

'We were separated,' Noah said, panting.

Seamus frowned. 'We need to go and find them.'

Emir held up one hand. 'Wait,' he whispered. 'Do you hear something?'

'Someone – or some*thing* – is coming,' Noah said.

'Get down,' Emir said.

Swords at the ready, the trio ducked behind a stand of boulders as the footsteps grew louder.

'Seamus!' Theo cried. 'Doorway!'

At the sound of the old elf's voice, Noah scrambled to her feet. Relief washed through her as Theo, Montana and Grainger raced towards her. Seamus whipped out his wand and had a doorway ready when they arrived.

'Ladies first,' Seamus said, nodding at Noah.

Noah didn't hesitate. With Montana at her heels, she leapt over the threshold.

Chapter 13

'So, sein-Elani, do you see why we cannot linger here?' Theo said. 'We need to retrieve the pyrohm before Talyn gets her house in order.'

Montana sighed. 'I have been a fool.' She looked at Noah. 'I took the pyrohm to save it from human rashness … but in my haste, I have made things worse. I am so sorry.'

'You couldn't have known that there were Jongu here,' Noah said. 'And anyway, Theo knows the way to Somyni. At least we've got a guide now.'

Montana reached out and took Noah's hands. 'But we don't want to go there yet. We're not prepared. We don't know how to destroy the illestial.'

'There's no rush to go to Somyni,' Grainger said. 'We must retrieve the pyrohm first.'

'Agreed,' Emir said. 'Seamus, can you take Grainger and Montana back to the high priestess's ship through one of your doorways?'

The young elf nodded. 'Of course.'

'Good. Wait for us there. Theo, Noah and I will bring the pyrohm as soon as we can.'

As Seamus prepared his doorway, Emir turned to Theo. 'Where would Talyn hide the pyrohm?'

'In her lodge,' Theo said.

Emir nodded. 'Take us there.'

Theo traced an outline of a doorway with his wand, chanting softly as he did so. When he was done, he peered through the breach. Satisfied it was safe, he turned and beckoned.

'Stay close,' he said.

Noah followed Theo into a forest with Emir behind her. She touched the brand on her neck as she surveyed the massive oaks and her pulse quickened. Winter had stripped the foliage from the trees, but the leaf on her skin remained, marking her as a slave.

Smoke drifted from the chimneys of the cottages that lay nestled among the forest's ancient oaks. Huts sprouted and bungalows dangled from branches high above. Some elves had carved their homes out of the gargantuan trunks. On the forest floor, the tentacle-like roots of the oaks snaked over and around multistorey chalets, gripping the structures in a possessive embrace.

'I thought you were taking us into Talyn's lodge,' Emir said.

'Too dangerous to go straight there,' Theo said. 'Security is tight. There are spells in place to deflect anchors – a doorway would fail or be easily identified.'

'But Torbin took us straight inside,' Emir said.

'His anchor was detected and permission was given,' Theo said. 'We would not be granted access though.'

'Where is the lodge?' Noah asked.

'On the far side of the village. You can't see it from here.'

'So what's your plan?' Noah said.

Theo tucked his wand under his belt. 'We'll skirt around the village. That'll take us to the south tower. I think the pyrohm will be there.'

'And we'll get inside how?'

Theo drew his dagger. 'Fight our way in – I'll make a doorway to get us out once we have the pyrohm.'

Noah thought of her friends aboard Montana's ship. 'Can they track your destination after you've closed your doorway?'

'Anchors can be traced,' Theo said, 'but I've got a few tricks that should throw them off our scent.'

♪♫

Noah peeked around the tree trunk. Across the snow-covered forecourt, four elfin soldiers guarded the entrance to the southern tower.

'We've got a fair bit of ground to cover,' she said, 'and it's pretty exposed. They're definitely going to see us coming.'

'I'm faster than I look,' Theo said.

Emir glanced at him. 'You'd better be.'

'They're still going to spot us way before we get there,' Noah said. 'We should lure them away from the door.'

'A distraction?' Emir said.

Noah drummed her fingers on her thigh before turning to Theo. 'They can track *your* magic here,' she said, 'but what about mine?'

Theo frowned. 'Yours?'

'Raiki,' she said, reaching into a pocket on her trousers. 'A tonic could create a diversion.'

'They'll hear it,' Theo said as Noah snapped open the clips on her viola case.

She plucked the instrument from its case. 'Yes, but they won't be able to decipher it … much less counteract it.'

'Could you just conceal us until we get to the doorway?' Emir said. 'That way we could at least surprise the guards.'

Noah scanned the surroundings as she extracted her slider from her locket and lodged it in the bridge of her viola. 'There's plenty of snow around,' she said. 'That should make it easy.'

Concealment was all about bringing the background to the foreground. Snow made it simple. A blanket of white would be enough to camouflage them. Noah tucked her instrument under her chin and drew her bow lightly across the strings.

'I hope this is a quick one, Noah,' Theo said. 'You've got the guards' attention.'

'Let's see how many of them we can draw out,' Emir said. 'That'll work in our favour.'

Theo squinted. 'Two coming this way. Two still at the door.'

'Let them get to the tree line here,' Emir said as Noah wove the next phase of her tonic, 'so we can neutralise them. Then we can dash across and take the other two.'

'Assuming Noah doesn't take too long,' Theo said.

Noah lowered her bow. 'I'm done.'

As she packed her viola away, Emir signalled to Theo which guard he'd take. Theo nodded.

'I'll take the other guard,' Noah said.

'You sure?' Theo whispered.

Noah nodded as she pressed her back against the tree trunk. 'Save your strength. You're going to need it once we get inside.'

Heart hammering in her chest, Noah waited. She held her position as the elf guard entered her peripheral vision before launching herself at him and knocking him to the ground. She cut short his cry of surprise with a sharp punch to his temple. The guard slumped to the ground.

On her hands and knees, Noah peered around the tree again. The two remaining guards sprinted towards them as the tower door flew open and more armed elves emerged.

'Run,' Emir said.

Noah leapt to her feet and bolted, taking a different line across the clearing from her companions. Her tonic would obscure their bodies but not the footprints they left in the snow. Tracks too close together might snag the guards' attention. *Please let them focus on their fallen comrades,* she prayed.

The soldiers fanned out and Noah veered sharply to avoid running head-on into one. Being invisible had its disadvantages. More guards streamed across the forecourt, so close to Noah that she was buffeted by gusts of wind as they rushed by. She pumped her arms and focused on breathing as quietly as she could. If they heard her now …

Emir reached the door first and wrenched it open.

'In!' he ordered.

Noah followed Theo through the doorway before Emir slammed the door and shoved the bolt across.

'Now, we just need to deal with whoever's inside,' Emir said.

Noah peered through the relative gloom of the tower's interior and picked out the stairway hugging the stone wall. 'There!' she said, drawing her sword.

Emir charged towards the stairway and made it halfway up before the next wave of guards appeared from the level above.

'Be gone!' an elf cried as he stabbed his spear at Emir.

Emir grabbed the spear, grunting as he twisted and pushed the elf off the staircase. Noah ducked around him to take on a guard brandishing a mace. She stabbed him in the thigh and barely dodged a blow he levelled at her head. The spiky metal ball lodged in the stone only centimetres from her. As the elf wrestled to retrieve his weapon, Noah jumped two steps. She pressed her back against the stone wall and kicked the elf.

'Off you go!' she said as he plummeted towards the floor.

Another three elves went the same way before the trio continued up the stairs. They met more guards on each level. Only on the fourth level, did their injury-free run end.

'*AAAAARGH!*' Theo cried.

Noah spun round to see a knife handle protruding from his chest.

'*NO!*' she screamed as he clutched the handle. '*Leave* it!'

Noah sprang at him, knocking him on his back. She grabbed his wrists. 'Don't pull it out,' she panted. 'You'll bleed out right here.'

He groaned. 'I'm going to die. Please let it be quick.'

'You're not going to die,' Noah said as Emir impaled an elf on its own spear. 'I can fix that – just not right now.'

'You can't—'

Noah leant over to shield him from a falling elf. 'Shush!' she said. 'Not far to go now.'

She glanced at Emir who wiped his brow with the back of his hand before helping her get Theo on his feet.

'Come on, Theo,' Emir said. 'Next floor is ours.'

Between them, Noah and Emir dragged Theo to the top level of the tower.

'Well, you were right, Theo,' Noah said as she stepped off the stairs onto the dusty tiled floor. 'The pyrohm is here.'

'I don't think they were expecting guests,' Emir said.

Grimy windows blocked much of the sunlight that would otherwise have illuminated the chamber. The four carved pillars that supported the domed ceiling were netted in cobwebs that could have dated back to

Desceran times, and a disused fountain slumbered on the room's central dais. Above the fountain, under lightless chandeliers, the pyrohm swivelled lazily in mid-air. Its dragonscale core glittered cheerily in contrast to its dreary surroundings.

Noah looked at Emir. 'Can you hold him?' she asked, nodding her head towards Theo.

'No problem,' he said, taking the elf's weight.

As Emir eased Theo onto the floor, Noah padded across the tiles to the fountain. The bronze sculpture of the diminutive Pyranhi in the fountain's centre seemed to study her as she approached. Ageless eyes stared out from its angelic face. The disproportionately large pointed ears on top of its head reminded Noah of Kane's ears when he was a puppy. A silky mane cascaded down the creature's back, ending in a luxuriant, long tail. The statue's arms extended out from its sides, palms up – as if exalting in the glittering light raining down from the firestone hovering over its head.

Noah stepped onto the foot of the fountain and reached up. As she clenched her fist, her hand passed through the metal triangle.

'What the …?' she murmured.

She tried again, catching nothing but dust.

'So it's an illusion?' Emir said. 'It's not really here?'

Noah folded her arms and frowned. 'It is here. I can feel it … it's just not *there*,' she said, pointing to the spinning triangle.

'Having fun?'

Noah spun round at the sound of the unexpected voice.

'I can see I need better guards,' Talyn said, as she stepped through a glimmering archway.

'Yes,' Emir said. 'The ones you sent were barely even bothersome.'

'Indeed,' she said.

Talyn extinguished the doorway with a flick of her delicate wand before turning her attention to Theo. She shook her head.

'You make me very sad, Theo. You've disgraced the woodland elves with your treachery – but at least it looks like you've saved me the trouble of issuing you a death penalty. In all my years as a councillor I've never given one, and I don't want to spoil my record.'

Theo sucked in a shuddering breath. 'My treachery? What about *your* treachery, sein-*Jong*?'

Talyn slipped her wand into the braided bun on her head and smiled. 'This time was always going to come,' she said, 'and it is my honour to lead the elves to a better place. Talisker is swarming with humans and goblins … it is time for a new beginning.'

'You know, I've spoken to Jong,' Noah said. 'A couple of times. He doesn't seem like the type to look out for others. If he gets free of Talisker – he's going on his own.'

Talyn reached up and plucked the pyrohm from the air. Noah frowned. The elf walked over to Noah, her silver robe clearing a trail in the dust behind her. Talyn looked like an angel. Her lustrous dark locks were coifed to perfection and her pale skin was flawless. The moonlight sheen of her robe dazzled despite the poor lighting in the tower. Only her eyes betrayed her rotten core. Contempt and arrogance smouldered in the elf's gaze.

'Jong would not save humans,' Talyn said, tracing the outline of the metal triangle with a slender finger, 'because they are a scourge. Elves are superior. He will deliver us.'

Noah shrugged. There was no point arguing.

Talyn kept her gaze on Noah as she tossed the pyrohm over her shoulder. Noah watched it sail towards the fountain. It stopped above the bronze Pyranhi sculpture and began swivelling again.

'Now,' Talyn said, drawing her wand from her hair, 'I have things to do and I don't intend wasting any more time on you.'

The elf traced a doorway and clicked her fingers. A dozen guards marched through the void.

Talyn pointed at Theo. 'Take him to the dungeon.'

When Emir stepped in front of the injured elf, four guards wrestled him to the floor. Though he landed a couple of good punches, he was quickly subdued. Two guards approached Noah. Not prepared to be taken without a fight, she kicked – catching one in the shin – and then punched the other on the jaw. Pain shot through her hand. *That probably hurt me more than it hurt him,* she thought.

As the guards tied Noah's arms behind her back, Talyn created another doorway. Noah's heart thumped as the guards dragged Theo away.

'No!' she cried.

Theo twisted his head around to look at her. His face was ashen. He wouldn't last much longer. Noah struggled against her bonds. She could save him, but she needed to do it now.

'Let me *help* him,' she pleaded.

Theo smiled at her weakly as the guards hauled him through the doorway. Talyn dissolved her spell as soon as he was through.

'And you two,' Talyn said, glancing between Noah and Emir, 'will return to your ship. You will leave Aoratia's shores, and if you dare to return – it will mean your death.' She turned to her remaining soldiers. 'Capture the elf that is aboard with the humans and bring him to me.'

'And the high priestess?' one guard asked.

Talyn traced the outline of another doorway. 'Leave her.'

'But her death penalty?'

Talyn smiled as she nodded towards the pyrohm. 'We have more important things to focus on now. Soon, we'll be in Somyni and there'll be nothing any of them can do about it.'

'Yes, Councillor.'

Talyn created another doorway. 'Take them.'

Hands still tied behind her, Noah charged at Talyn, but she didn't make more than five steps. Though she pumped her legs as hard as she could Noah made no progress. She looked down. Her feet weren't touching the ground. Noah turned her gaze on Talyn as a guard gripped her arm.

Talyn smiled. 'I can control you, Noah,' she said, lowering her to the floor again. 'Don't forget that.'

The skin on Noah's neck tingled. Her brand.

'Move,' the guard said, tugging on Noah's arm.

Noah turned towards the doorway, allowing the guard to escort her. The deck of Montana's ship shimmered beyond the breach. As she passed the fountain, her gaze lingered on the pyrohm. Noah held her breath as she crossed the threshold.

The guard pushed her aside once they were aboard the ship. Jacin caught Noah as she stumbled.

'Noah!' he said. 'Are you okay?'

Noah ignored him. 'Seamus!' she called. 'Look out!'

The guards shoved Emir face first onto the deck as their comrades ambushed Seamus. Talyn's soldiers pounced, securing their quarry before Montana's warriors could intervene. One blow to the head was all it took to subdue him.

'No!' Noah cried as they hauled Seamus away.

She watched helplessly as Talyn's elves dragged Seamus through the doorway. Montana's troops converged but they were too late. The doorway evaporated.

Noah hung her head. Montana knelt beside her and cut her bonds. 'Are you hurt?'

'My heart hurts,' Noah said without looking up. 'Seamus is gone, Theo is dying and Talyn has the pyrohm.'

Montana sighed. 'Noah, I'm so sorry. This is all my fault.'

'No. You were just doing what you thought was right.'

'Yes, but this is a mess. Without Theo, we don't have a way to Somyni – we'll be so far behind Talyn.'

'Don't worry about that yet,' Noah said. 'I assume Brinn will give us some advice on what to do next.'

Chapter 14

Noah adjusted her scarf to protect her face from the icy night air. She peered out into the darkness from the ship's crow's nest as she considered what explanation she would give the Alliance on their return to Mellifont. Over dinner, her companions had all offered advice on what she should say, but ultimately the decision was hers. This mission was on her head.

'Could you have found a worse place to wait for me?' a voice said.

Noah recoiled. '*Brinn!* You took ten years off my life!'

'If that were true every time you said it, Noah,' the cat said, 'you'd still be a couple of centuries away from even being born.'

'Right now,' Noah mumbled, 'I wish I *hadn't* been born.'

'Sit down, please.'

Noah planted herself on the wooden floor of the lookout and crossed her legs. Brinn crawled into her lap.

'That's better,' Brinn said.

For you maybe, Noah thought.

'Things aren't quite going to plan.'

'No,' Noah said, 'but it's not totally my fault this time. So if you're going to get stroppy, I don't think it's fair that you just rip into me.'

Brinn purred. 'When have I ever ripped into you, Noah?'

'When *haven't* you? You're always giving me a hard time.'

'Nonsense,' Brinn said, 'I think I've been very helpful. And I don't think I've ever been stroppy.'

Noah stared. 'Never been stroppy? You're always stroppy! You're like … fur-coated vitriol!'

Brinn's eyes narrowed. 'That's a bit harsh. Anyway, if it makes you feel any better, I've had a word with Montana about her … intervention.'

Noah sighed. It probably should have made her feel better, but it didn't.

'I can take you to Somyni,' Brinn said.

Noah frowned. 'Just me?'

'We'll need Emir and Grainger as well.'

'Montana?'

Brinn swished her tail. 'No. The Alliance will need her.'

'Jacin wants to come,' Noah said.

'No chance,' Brinn growled.

'Avril thinks she should come too, in her role as sein-Temperance.'

Brinn sat up. 'She's sein-Temperance? Says who?'

'Her grandfather. Old Bernard charged her with protecting the pyrohm.'

Brinn hissed. 'She is *not* sein-Temperance.'

'Try telling her that.'

'You didn't tell her?'

'Not my place.'

Brinn hissed again.

'Stop that!' Noah said. 'It's really—'

'What do you mean it's not your place to tell her?' Brinn said. 'As sein-Temperance – you're the best person *to* tell her!'

'Me?'

'Yes, you.'

Theo had thought she was sein-Temperance, but Noah had dismissed the idea.

'Look, I'm not sein-Temperance,' Noah said. 'That's totally ridiculous.'

'You *are* sein-Temperance,' Brinn said.

Exasperated, Noah said, 'Says who?'

Brinn licked her paw nonchalantly. 'Says *me*.'

'Right,' Noah said, 'so now you speak on behalf of the gods? You can appoint their champions?'

'Only my own,' Brinn said.

Noah stared at her for a long moment. She could barely find enough breath to say, '*You're* Temperance? Jong and Elani's sister? *You're a god?*'

Brinn scowled. 'Why do you look surprised? Is that really so difficult to believe?'

Though utterly ridiculous, Noah found it actually wasn't so difficult to believe. Brinn appeared and disappeared at will. She was bossy and arrogant and had everyone doing her dirty work for her. But above all, she defied rules. All rules. Even rules of nature.

'So I should call you Temperance now?' Noah said.

'No,' the cat said. 'Call me Brinn. No one else can know who I really am.'

Hope stirred inside Noah. 'We're going to do this.'

'Don't get ahead of yourself,' Brinn said, shaking her head. 'Though I try to keep the peace between my brothers, it is tricky. Jong has been contained here for a long time – and as charming as I am, I doubt I can talk him into seeing reason. I need to be very careful what I do. If I use my power here, I could destroy Talisker.'

Thoughts clattered through Noah's mind but shock prevented her making sense of them. One clawed its way to the top.

'Why me?' she said at last.

'Hmm?'

'Why me?' Noah said. 'Of all the people you could have picked on, why me?'

'Most people would be flattered,' Brinn said.

'I'm not "most people".'

'Exactly. And that's your answer.'

Noah chewed her lip. 'So is Elani here too? Does he hassle Montana the way you hassle me?'

'Elani doesn't come here,' Brinn said, grooming her whiskers.

'Then why do *you* come here?'

Brinn rubbed her head against Noah's leg. 'Because humans are wonderful yet fragile creatures, Noah. Your short lives deprive you of the opportunity to *individually* build knowledge and wisdom. Over generations, humans achieve amazing things but one lifetime is too short to master the magic of this world.'

'Why do you even care if we master the magic of this world or not?'

Brinn turned her hypnotic gaze on Noah. 'Talisker is in grave danger.'

Noah rolled her eyes. 'What's new? It's *always* in danger.'

'Not *this* kind of danger. Jong is actually not Talisker's biggest problem.'

'Shock me,' Noah said.

To her horror, Brinn stretched her front paws up on Noah's shoulders. Noah flinched as Brinn's nose touched hers.

'You must tell no one of what I tell you now,' the cat said. 'I didn't tell you this before because I didn't want it to … cloud your testimony to the Alliance.'

Noah's eyes narrowed. 'You wanted me to lie without knowing I was lying?' she guessed.

'I didn't want to burden you—'

'Just tell me,' Noah said.

'There is a vortex not far from Talisker,' Brinn said. 'Soon, it will suck this world into it.'

Noah stared. 'A world-devouring vortex? Suddenly the illestial doesn't seem that big a deal …'

Eyes blazing, Brinn said, 'As luck would have it, the illestial is key to solving both problems – Jong *and* the vortex.'

'So, we're *not* going to destroy the illestial?'

'Correct. We're going to use it to extract Jong from Talisker and … re-home him in the vortex.'

'*What?*'

'Elani and I think that Jong's violence could stabilise the vortex. If we can stop it growing – Talisker will be saved. And, if Jong is in the vortex, Xan can finally rest.'

Noah shivered. 'And Gillette?'

Brinn stepped down from Noah's lap. 'It is remotely possible that you could save him, but Talisker is a bigger priority.'

Noah stood up. She leant on the rail and sucked in a lungful of the salty ocean air. Moonlight shimmered on the water but she barely noticed nature's artistic endeavour. Her mind was clogged with fear.

'What am I supposed to tell the Alliance?' Noah said.

'The same thing you told them last time,' Brinn replied. 'Tell them that you will go to Somyni to destroy the illestial.'

'But that's lying.'

'Yes.'

Noah tapped the rail with her gloved fingers. 'Do we have time to return to Mellifont?' she whispered. 'How fast will Talyn move?'

'We have time,' Brinn said. 'Elves don't rush things.'

The cat leapt up onto the railing, balancing easily on the cold metal. She followed Noah's gaze out over the ocean.

'When we're in Mellifont,' Brinn said, 'you need to say your good-byes without saying your goodbyes.'

Noah's chest tightened. 'We're not coming back.'

'It is possible that you could return, but it is unlikely.'

'Raven …' Noah murmured.

'If it's any consolation,' Brinn said, 'I *am* sorry, Noah, but this task was destined to fall to someone in your family …'

Too heartsore to be angry, Noah looked at the cat. 'Just bad timing for me then?'

'Depends how you look at it,' Brinn replied. 'You'll have done your family proud. You've racked up quite the resume since you've been here.'

The tears in Noah's eyes made it difficult for her to glare at the feline.

'The 13th key, King's Tailor, Dragonsbane, King of Carai, Major of Raiki, sein-Temperance …' Brinn said.

'But I'm only nineteen,' Noah said. 'Chase was going to make me her child's godmother. I don't want to die.'

'You're going to die one day, Noah – you're mortal,' Brinn said. 'But you've proven to be pretty hard to kill. It's by no means certain that this mission will be the end of you … it's just very unlikely you'll come back here.'

Noah's head pounded. 'You're doing my head in, Brinn,' she said, massaging her temples. 'So … am I supposed to be grateful that you're letting me take Emir?'

'He's not a pet, Noah. We need him.'

'For?'

'Let's just say that you two are a good team.'

♪♫

'I thought that was never going to end,' Noah said as she closed the door to Elani's Chamber.

Emir nodded. 'It was a long meeting.'

After five hours of negotiation, the Firestone Alliance had recommitted to sending a mission to Somyni to intercept the pyrohm and destroy the illestial. Again, Noah had avoided revealing that she was the 13th key, but it was little consolation. The expedition weighed heavily on her as they wound their way through Mellifont's corridors.

Emir opened the door to their bedchamber and gestured for Noah to enter. When she crossed the threshold, Chase and Ardis rose from the sofa. Kane barked excitedly.

'Chase!' Noah said. 'When did you get here?'

'A couple of hours ago,' Chase said, struggling to dodge Kane to hug her friend.

'What are you doing here?' Noah said.

'I needed to see that you were all okay.'

Woof! Woof!

Chase smiled. '*We* needed to see that you're all okay.'

Noah kissed her friend's cheek. 'We're fine. See?'

Chase cupped her hands around Noah's face. 'But for how long?'

Noah frowned. 'Do you know something I don't?'

'Brinn came to visit us at the farm,' Chase said, 'and she was actually very pleasant. That tells me that something is wrong … very wrong. What is it?'

'She didn't tell you?' Noah said.

'I said she was pleasant,' Chase said, 'not cooperative.'

'Right.' Noah waved towards the lounge. 'Maybe you should get comfortable.'

'I'll pour some drinks,' Emir said.

Chase rubbed her belly. 'Just water for me, please.'

Emir nodded as he turned and made his way to the kitchenette. While Noah silently rehearsed her lines, she watched Ardis arrange cushions for his pregnant wife. Once Emir had returned with the drinks, she took a seat beside Chase.

'So, what's going on?' Chase said.

'The Alliance has authorised a mission to Somyni to destroy the illestial,' Noah said, 'but we have the added excitement of having to retrieve the pyrohm from the elves first.'

Chase frowned. 'Retrieve it? Won't they help you destroy it?'

'Unfortunately not,' Emir said. 'The elves are Jongu. Their plan is to use the illestial to release Jong.'

Colour deserted Chase's face. 'I can't believe that elves would destroy Talisker. I thought they were gentle, peaceful creatures.'

'They are in some ways,' Noah said, thinking of the elves' attitude to livestock and allowing them a long life before putting them on the table, 'but they are totally up themselves and think they deserve to go to a lovely new world that isn't overrun by humans and goblins.'

'Oh,' Chase said. 'That's rude.'

'Yes,' Noah agreed.

'So how many are going on this mission?' Chase said.

'A hundred,' Noah said, glancing at Emir. 'Officially.'

Chase pursed her lips. 'And unofficially?'

'Brinn has authorised four,' Noah said. 'Five – if you count her.'

'Let me guess,' Chase said, 'you, Emir, Raven and …'

'Grainger,' Emir added.

'Not Jaxon?' Chase said.

'My brother might … complicate our mission in Somyni,' Emir said.

'You're not going to rescue Gillette?' Ardis said.

'Of course we're going to try,' Noah said, 'but we don't think Jaxon will add to the rescue effort. He'd more likely be collateral damage.'

Ardis frowned. 'I think he'd rather die trying to save his son than be left behind when you are risking your lives.'

'No doubt,' Emir said, 'but in this situation, the fewer people going, the better.'

Noah's heart pounded as she watched Chase. Tears pooled on Chase's lower eyelids as her frown deepened. Noah knew how her friend felt. She'd cried herself when Brinn had given in to Raven's demand that he join the unofficial expedition. Noah didn't want to be separated from her twin but the thought of any harm coming to him on this mission terrified her.

'But you're going to come back,' Chase whispered.

Noah reached out and squeezed Chase's hand. 'That's my plan,' she said. 'I wouldn't be much of a godmother if I didn't, would I?'

'I think this is a good plan,' Ardis said.

All eyes went to the Elani warrior.

'A small group is what's needed here,' Ardis continued. 'All those other people the Alliance wants to send will just get in Noah's way.' He looked at Chase. 'You are right to worry for your friend. The failure rate for expeditions to Somyni is high, but none of those expeditions had Noah in them. Have faith, Jem.'

Chase nodded as tears slipped down her cheeks. 'No one believes in her more than I do.'

Noah's stomach clenched painfully. *Faith.* Brinn had no faith that they'd return, and she was a god. Who was Noah to be giving assurances that they'd come back? *I just have to,* Noah thought. *I just have to get back somehow.*

'So, when do you leave … unofficially?' Ardis asked.

'The day after tomorrow,' a voice said.

Noah didn't flinch at Brinn's appearance this time.

'Noah and Chase can spend another day together,' Brinn said, 'and then we're off.'

Chapter 15

The setting sun cast murky shadows across the crater's swampy floor. Noah peered into the gloom, searching for signs of danger. Brinn had warned them about the malevolent creatures that lurked under the slime and spiny shrubs here. The desolate landscape in the heart of Orian bore the scars of the Pryanhi magic that severed access to Somyni thousands of years ago. Three sides of the illestial lay in a temple nearly one hundred kilometres below her feet. At least, Noah hoped there were still only three sides there. If Talyn had already arrived … Noah shuddered.

Raven appeared at her side. 'Dinner's ready.'

Smoke from the campfire tingled inside Noah's nose. 'I'm not hungry.'

'Let me rephrase that,' Raven said. *'Brinn's* ready.'

Noah groaned.

Raven nudged her with his elbow. 'Don't worry, Sis. I'll protect you from the cat-god.'

'Shush!' Noah said. 'I wasn't supposed to tell anyone.'

'How many people did you tell?'

'Three – you, Emir and Chase.'

'It's alright,' he said, shining his fingernails on his tunic, 'I'll smooth it over with her if she finds out.'

Noah rolled her eyes. 'After three years of shameless sucking up, you got one favour out of her. I wouldn't count on getting another one anytime soon.'

It hadn't really been a favour, Noah knew. Even Brinn realised the futility of trying to separate the twins. Raven had always protected Noah and he wouldn't abandon her now.

Raven took her hand and pulled her gently towards camp. 'I always knew there was something special about Brinn.'

Noah groaned again. 'Don't start,' she said. 'You didn't know she was a god.'

'I knew she was more than just a cat.'

Noah took a seat on a log beside Emir as Grainger dished up dinner.

'So, Brinn, now we're away from … everyone,' Noah said, taking the bowl Grainger offered, 'how about you tell us about Somyni.'

From her perch atop a stump, Brinn swished her tail from side to side. 'Did you know,' she said, 'that the first expeditions to Somyni didn't return because they didn't want to? They were happy to stay and enjoy the beauty of the Pyranhi city, but they were even more happy to be with the dragons.'

'Dragons?' Grainger said. 'They really still exist?'

'Yes,' Brinn said, 'and everything was fine until someone tried to steal a dragon egg.'

'And the ghosts of the Pyranhi acted to protect Somyni?' Noah said.

'The enduring *magic* of the Pyranhi acted to protect the dragons,' Brinn said. 'The result is what you see here. This crater is a result of the collapse of all the physical tunnels that led down to the city.'

Grainger scratched his chin with the end of his fork. 'And then there are the shields. As far as I can tell, the spells in place here will make any magical entry impossible too. I don't know how we'll create a doorway to bypass them.'

Grainger had practised what he'd learned from Theo, creating a series of doorways to skip the group across the continent from Mellifont to Orian. His growing confidence using elf magic had taken a hit on arrival though. He'd spent several hours probing the protective magic around the site and was pessimistic about entering Somyni.

'Getting in is the least of our difficulties,' Brinn said. 'Somyni is a dangerous place these days. At the beginning, when explorers first arrived, there was unity. They shared in the wonder of the place and resolved to care for the dragons and also to guard against the return of the last piece of the illestial.'

'It's hard to imagine humans and goblins being united,' Emir said.

Brinn nodded. 'That should tell you how special a place it was.'

Noah stirred her stew. 'Was?'

'The settlers' initial fervour in protecting against the return of the pyrohm eventually turned to complacency. When no enemy appeared after centuries of vigilance, the Somynians lost interest in the quest.'

'Understandable,' Emir said.

'And it would have been better if that complacency had continued,' Brinn said, 'but eventually it turned to paranoia.'

'What happened?' Noah asked.

Brinn squirmed on her log to get more comfortable. 'When Somyni was sealed off after the attempted theft of the dragon egg, attitudes changed. Some Somynians – now trapped – wanted to leave.'

'*Choosing* to be in a place is one thing,' Raven said, 'but being *forced* to be there is very different.'

'Correct,' Brinn said. 'Once the city was sealed off, the Jongu rose again and the slaughter began.'

'And what's the situation now?' Emir asked.

'Tensions run high,' Brinn said. 'Most Somynians promote themselves as Elanu but there is a significant number of Jongu in the city. Like in Aoratia, they are secretive so it is hard to tell how many of them there are, but they're there.'

'It's going to be a disaster when the Jongu elves turn up,' Noah added.

Brinn's whiskers twitched. 'Yes. And to make things even more complicated, there are the dragon riders.'

Grainger tossed another log on the fire. 'Whose side are they on?'

'Xan's,' Brinn said.

'That figures,' Noah said, 'but what do they do?'

'They try to eliminate any Jongu they find while avoiding the Elanu,' Brinn said.

'What have the Elanu got against the dragon riders?' Emir asked.

Brinn stretched. 'Jealousy. One doesn't choose to be a dragon rider, *dragons* choose their riders.'

'So being a dragon rider is a big deal,' Grainger said.

'There is no greater privilege on Talisker,' Brinn replied, 'and now the *un*chosen see the dragon riders as elitist rogues who need to be wiped out.'

'Sounds like a fun place,' Raven said. 'Are we going to have any friends there?'

Brinn nodded. 'The dragon riders will help us.'

♪♫

Noah gasped and sat up. She scanned her swag, unsure what had woken her. The moonlight revealed nothing crawling on her. She looked to her left and her heart froze. A gossamer film of green light cocooned Emir's sleeping form. Noah clambered out of her swag and reached out one hand towards him.

'No,' she whispered. 'No, no.'

Sparks spewed from the cocoon when her fingers touched it.

'Ouch!'

She wrenched her hand back, balling her burnt fingers into a protective fist.

'Noah?' Raven said.

Without looking at her brother, she said, 'We've got a problem here.'

'You got that right,' he said. 'And Grainger's got the same problem.'

Noah turned her head towards the remains of the night's campfire. Grainger, who'd drawn the first watch, stood motionless within a translucent green shell. Eyes open and arm pointing in their direction, his mouth framed a silent warning.

'Brinn?' Noah said.

Raven crouched beside her. 'Can't see her anywhere.'

Noah surveyed the campsite. Specks of green light glimmered among the spindly tufts of grass that sprouted haphazardly across the rocky landscape.

'I think I'd have preferred to fight a troll,' she said.

'I didn't see a menu,' Raven replied. 'I don't think you get to order the monster you want.'

Zzzzzap!

'What was that?' Raven said.

Noah peered at the green shield. 'A bug.'

'Nasty.'

Fingers throbbing, Noah said, 'I know how it feels.'

'Have you got a tonic that will get rid of that thing?'

'Maybe,' Noah said, reaching for a stick, 'but let's try something else first – something that won't attract as much attention.'

She squatted near Emir's feet and poked the glowing shell. The twig caught alight instantly.

'Let's try water,' Noah said, stabbing the burning end of the stick into the dirt.

Raven retrieved his water skin from a pocket on his trousers. 'Here.'

Noah took it and twisted off the lid. Without time to marvel at how Anok had adapted his miniaturising technology to allow them to carry hundreds of litres of liquid in such a small pouch, Noah splashed water onto the cocoon. Steam sizzled off it but a tiny hole appeared. She squirted more water and was rewarded with a bigger opening.

'Looks to be working,' Raven said.

'Yep. Have you got another water skin?'

'I have a few.'

'Good,' Noah said. 'Go and help Grainger.'

Noah shuffled up to start working near Emir's head. When his face was free of the glowing green hue, she breathed a little easier but maintained her focus. She spurted the water in measured strokes but a few stray droplets landed on his cheek. His eyes fluttered open.

'Noah?' he said.

'Stay still.'

Emir grimaced. 'Yes, well … I *can't* actually move.'

'What?'

'I can't move my arms or legs, Noah. I can't even wiggle my fingers.'

Noah exhaled slowly. 'Okay. Let's worry about that after I get rid of this thing.'

Within a few minutes she was done, and Raven returned soon after with Grainger draped over his shoulder.

He lay the Dragonsbane on the ground beside Emir. 'He can't move.'

'Can you cure this, Noah?' Grainger asked.

'I'll give it a shot,' she replied.

'It'll have to wait,' Brinn said, appearing between the stricken men. 'A hundred goblins are headed this way. We have to move.'

'They're not my goblins then?' Noah said.

'They're not from Carai, no,' Brinn said. 'Noah, make a doorway, please.'

'A doorway?'

'Like the elves make,' Brinn said. 'That's our fastest way out of here with two people who can't walk.'

'I wasn't paying that much attention,' Noah said. 'Grainger was—'

Brinn glared at her. 'No time to argue. Just get us out of here.'

'Get my baton, Noah,' Grainger said. 'Do it.'

'Anywhere in particular you'd like to go?' Noah asked as she fumbled through Grainger's coat pocket.

'As long as it's not Aoratia,' Grainger said.

'Or Mellifont,' Brinn added.

Raven hoisted Emir to his feet. 'Leninstar's probably not a great idea either.'

Noah shook her head. 'Sorry I asked.'

She traced the outline of a doorway as she fought to remember Theo's incantation. Shrill screams erupted nearby.

'Faster, Noah,' Grainger said. 'The goblins are close.'

'Yeah, yeah.' She closed her eyes, trying to block out the inhuman screeching of the goblin horde. 'Baby steps.'

'What?' Grainger said.

'I'm not going to go too far.'

Noah visualised a spot on the other side of the crater and whispered the words she'd learned from Theo. Her doorway glistened to life.

Brinn inspected the portal. 'Nothing moving, nothing glowing green – go.'

Brinn disappeared. Noah couldn't tell if the cat had used the doorway or her own usual vanishing trick. She tucked the baton in her ponytail and braced herself to lever Grainger off the ground. She sat him up before wedging her shoulder under his armpit.

'Ready?'

'Ready,' Grainger said.

Noah grunted as she dragged him to his feet. The ground trembled under them as the goblin swarm pounded over the last few metres to their quarry. Beyond the doorway, Raven lay Emir on the ground and turned back as Noah sprang at the portal. Raven clutched at Grainger.

'I've got him,' Raven said. 'Close it!'

Noah whipped the baton from her hair and stabbed at the doorway, but three goblins cleared the threshold before it vanished. Raven dumped Grainger on the ground with a hasty apology as drew his sword. Noah did likewise.

'First to two, wins,' Raven said, lunging at the tallest of the hideous creatures.

Noah slashed at the goblin nearest her, opening a gash on its forearm. It shrieked as she raised her blade again. The goblin swung its sword at her head. Noah ducked and the weapon whistled past her ear. She drew a knife from her boot with her free hand and took aim.

'Throw it, Noah!' Emir called. 'Throw it now!'

Noah hurled the knife but missed her target. The small dagger whirled through the air, lodging in a tree trunk. As the creature bore down on her, Raven charged – spearing the goblin in the side. It crashed on its back, clutching at the sword as Raven rolled clear.

Noah raced to her brother and pushed the hilt of her sword into his hands. 'Take mine.'

Raven grimaced. 'Giving up so soon, Noah?'

'Yep,' Noah said.

'Fine,' Raven said as the next goblin charged. He pushed Noah aside. 'Get Emir and Grainger on their feet. I'll protect you.'

'Deal.'

Noah raced to her patients and found Brinn sitting on Grainger's chest.

'I've got Grainger,' Brinn said. 'You work on Emir.'

'What are we dealing with?' Noah asked.

'Swamp flies,' Brinn said. 'They attack the nervous system – focus your attention there.'

Noah nodded and pulled out her viola.

'No,' Brinn said. 'That's going to be too noisy. Do it the other way.'

Noah cursed as she stashed her instrument back in her pocket. She placed her hands on Emir's chest and closed her eyes, focusing on the firestone in her veins. Humming softly, she assessed his condition. Relief washed through her that he'd suffered no permanent damage. It would take her a little while to coax his nerves back into action though, so she got to work.

As Noah hummed her tonic to repair Emir's frayed nerves, she was aware of Grainger's scrutiny.

'What's she doing?' Grainger asked.

'Healing,' Brinn replied.

'How?'

'I'll explain once we get to Somyni,' Brinn said as she stepped off his chest, 'but right now – your job is to find us a way there.'

Grainger sat up, testing his limbs. Apparently satisfied, he retrieved his baton from its temporary home in Noah's ponytail and set to work on a doorway to the ancient Pyranhi city. While Grainger laboured, Noah continued Emir's therapy. Conscious of the danger around them, she worked quickly.

When she was satisfied she'd fixed what she could, Noah said, 'Stand up and tell me how you feel.'

Emir got to his feet and shook his arms and legs. He leaned his head to one side and then the other, stretching his neck muscles.

'Feels pretty good. You're—'

'More goblins!' Raven called.

Emir drew his sword. 'You and Grainger get that doorway sorted. The sooner we're out of here the better.'

Noah frowned as Emir sprinted towards Raven. *I'll be glad to be away from here,* she thought, *but I think where we're going will be worse.*

Chapter 16

'Got it!' Grainger cried.

'Raven! Emir!' Noah called. 'Time to go!'

The forest clearing beyond the shimmering doorway looked inviting but Noah's stomach churned at the thought of what might be lurking there. Somyni was only a dozen steps away, but even with another goblin horde descending on them, Noah hesitated.

Raven raced to the doorway, grabbing Noah's wrist as he neared the threshold. Noah stumbled as he dragged her along, but she remained upright. Raven released her once they were through, then raised his sword defensively. Noah, with her sword at the ready too, surveyed Somyni's landscape with apprehension and wonder. Although the canopy hid the sky from view, there was ample light in the understorey.

Brightly coloured birds swooped and wheeled in an hypnotic display. Noah's eyes followed a troupe of monkeys as they scampered among the branches. *They're clearly not worried about falling,* she thought as the primates leapt from one bough to another. The drone of insects and sonorous bird cries gave the forest a vital, cheerful atmosphere.

Noah lowered her sword. 'It's beautiful.'

Emir stepped beside her. 'Stay alert. The vegetation here could conceal any number of nasty surprises.'

Something rubbed up against Noah's leg and she jumped. Brinn purred loudly.

'Nasty surprises alright,' Noah mumbled.

'Grainger,' Brinn said. 'Great job. Mount Jubilee isn't far from here.'

'Mount Jubilee?' Raven said. 'That sounds festive.'

'It was in the past,' Brinn said, 'but these days, it's a command post. The dragon riders have much to fear nowadays.'

'Well,' Noah said, 'let's see if we can offer them some assistance. They've got plenty more trouble coming their way.'

Brinn rubbed her whiskers. 'Yes, but we won't head straight to their headquarters. We'll pay a visit to a couple I know first. Twigg and Olive are both dragon riders. The best way for you to understand what they're up against, is to talk to them.'

Raven nodded. 'Lead the way.'

Brinn sauntered off along one of the paths from the clearing. Noah followed Grainger with Emir and Raven behind her. For almost an hour, they trekked through the forest without conversation, mostly because they'd have had to yell at each other to be heard over the frogs that had become increasingly vocal.

As their path steepened, the trees thinned and Noah had her first glimpse of Somyni's sky.

She gasped. 'Oh … my …'

'You're impressed?' Brinn said.

Noah nodded as Emir said, 'How could you not be impressed?'

Somyni had been built under a dome of firestone. The dragonscale sky bathed the countryside in shifting colours. While there was no day and night underground, the light from the scales ebbed and flowed in line with the dragon's fluctuating consciousness. Noah gazed at the twinkling landscape over her head, transfixed by its ancient power and splendour.

'Do you see the cottage up there?' Brinn asked.

Noah scanned the mountainside. 'Yes. I see it.'

'That's where we're going,' the cat said. 'But from here we must be very careful – there are booby traps.'

'Of course there are,' Raven said, eyes gleaming. 'What sort of booby traps do they have here?'

Noah shook her head. No doubt her brother was looking for anything that would boost his army's arsenal back in Leninstar. *At least he's thinking we will go back home,* she thought.

'First trap is sinking sand,' Brinn said with a swish of her tail. 'I'll show you where to get off the path to avoid it.'

They'd walked for only a few minutes when Brinn indicated a detour.

'I don't see any sinking sand,' Grainger said. 'The dragon riders are good.'

'To stop enemies invading their headquarters, they've had to perfect their defences,' Brinn said. 'Follow me.'

Noah fought her way through dense scrub as they skirted the concealed sand trap.

'Try not to break any branches,' Brinn said, slinking easily between the crisscrossing vines and foliage, 'we don't want to leave a trail for anyone to follow.'

'Easy for you to say,' Noah said as a thorny branch snagged her sleeve.

Noah's relief when they finally emerged from the scrub was short-lived. Only a few hundred metres down the trail, Brinn stopped again.

Raven raised an eyebrow. 'What is it now?'

'Mangeray,' Brinn said. 'Three of them.'

Emir frowned. 'What's a mangeray?'

Brinn sauntered down the path a short way and scraped in the leaf litter. 'Come,' she said. 'See for yourself.'

Raven led the way with Noah close behind him. Emir and Grainger brought up the rear. With the leaves and twigs cleared, the group peered into the exposed crevice. Hundreds of long, brown, barbed spikes protruded from the earth like thick porcupine quills. They pointed downwards, ensuring that anything that fell into the crack went only one way.

'What's at the bottom?' Noah asked.

'A stomach … of sorts,' Brinn said. 'It's like a giant Venus flytrap.'

'Can you grow those?' Raven asked.

Emir's eyes narrowed. 'Tell me you're not thinking of trying to take a cutting back to Leninstar …'

Raven patted his trousers. 'I've got plenty of pockets.'

'No, you can't grow them,' Brinn said. 'And anyway, we need to keep moving.'

The group set off again and Noah focused on the clearing ahead. Beyond the scrubby outskirts of the forest, a rocky hillside beckoned. *Surely there can't be as many booby traps up there,* Noah thought.

'Duck!' Brinn called.

Noah crouched instantly, as did her companions.

Whoosh!

'What the hell?' Grainger said.

Noah twisted and sprawled on her back as a massive log swung less than a metre off the ground.

'A bit more warning might have been helpful there, Brinn,' Emir said.

'Yes,' the cat agreed, 'but I thought it was further along the track.'

'What else have we got to look forward to?' Noah asked as they waited for the log pendulum to slow down.

'Archers and a bed of daggers,' Brinn said, cleaning her whiskers with her paw.

'Archers?' Raven said. 'I don't think that technically qualifies as a booby trap.'

'You can point that out to the dragon riders if you wish,' Brinn said.

'Hmm,' Raven said. 'Maybe not.'

'How do you know about all these traps?' Grainger asked. 'I imagine you've spent some time here in Somyni, Brinn, but I don't imagine you walk around the forest much.'

'I just find it useful to *know* things,' Brinn replied.

'For times like this?' Emir guessed.

Brinn purred. 'Yes. Now, about the archers,' she said, 'when we exit that clearing ahead, you need to have a fern frond in your hand to wave above your head. If you don't have one, you'll get an arrow in the neck.'

Noah rolled clear of the swinging log and found her requisite piece of fern. When everyone had their frond, they marched along the track behind Brinn. Noah clutched her fern, praying that the archers wouldn't make any mistakes. At the foot of the mountain, she inhaled deeply. The thought of being watched unsettled her.

Brinn meandered off to her left.

'Where are you going?' Noah asked. She pointed to the cabin on the hillside to her right and said, 'I thought you said we were going up there.'

'We are going up there,' Brinn said, 'but not up that way. There are four traps on the hillside, but only one if we go through the tunnel.'

'The bed of daggers?' Emir said.

Brinn nodded. 'If we walk in the wrong spots, thirty blades attached to a rectangular metal frame will drop from the ceiling.'

Noah winced. 'Let's not trigger that one.'

At the entrance to the underground, Noah took a torch from one of her pockets and lit it. Raven, Emir and Grainger did the same. In the cool darkness, Noah concentrated on walking exactly where Brinn walked. It was slow going, but with the cat's guidance they cleared the bed of daggers without incident.

'We're through,' Brinn said. 'Now we just have to follow the tunnel and we'll come out right near Twigg and Olive's house.'

'Great,' Grainger said, 'let's move it then.'

Brinn trotted off into the darkness and Noah jogged after her. The tunnel was narrow and there was barely any room above Noah's head. She glanced behind her. The boys were keeping up the pace, despite having to stoop.

'We're making good time,' Brinn said, 'only another few minutes and—'

Crash!

A metal door dropped from the ceiling, slamming into the floor in front of them. Noah shrieked and Grainger yelled as water from above pummelled them to the ground. The room dimmed as the water extinguished some of the torches.

Brinn yowled. 'Retreat!'

'Can't!' Raven yelled over the gushing water. 'Door behind as well!'

Emir, fighting to stay on his feet, wrenched Noah's arm and pulled her upright. 'Can you stop the water?' he yelled.

'I don't know!' Noah yelled back. 'I can try.'

Emir nodded before turning to Raven. 'See if you can get that door open!'

Raven saluted while trying to keep his torch close to the wall and out of the water. 'Where's Brinn?'

'Gone!' Grainger cried. 'Hopefully she's outside trying to open the doors.'

Doubt it, Noah thought. *She's got no thumbs. Hopefully she's gone to get help!*

Noah struggled to stay on her feet. The water was already halfway up her thighs. *The doors must've damned an underground river running above the tunnel,* Noah thought, *and once they dropped …* Her viola wasn't an option to stop the torrent gushing in through the gaping hole overhead.

'Can't open it!' Raven called.

Emir spun round. 'Me neither! Noah? The water?'

Darkness descended as the last torch died. Noah drew her sword. *I can't stop the water with this,* she thought channelling the firestone in her veins, *but I can at least get some light in here.* Eyes closed, her sword glowed.

'I think we'll have to swim for it!' Noah shouted.

'What!' Grainger cried.

'Once this chamber is full,' Noah said, 'we can swim out. Follow the river.'

'What!' Grainger cried again. 'Are you crazy?'

'Got any other suggestions?' Noah yelled back, the water lapping at her waist now.

Grainger waded over to stand beside her, baton in hand. 'How about a doorway?'

'Great idea!' Emir said. 'But can you make one underwater?'

Grainger pursed his lips. 'I'll try.'

'Hurry,' Noah said. 'I reckon we've got less than a minute before we have to go with my plan.'

'Baby steps,' Grainger said as he flicked his baton.

Noah fought to steady her breathing as Emir and Raven converged. *I wonder if he can chant underwater,* she thought as the water level continued to rise. Noah clutched her sword. It was the only thing she could control at the moment. She focused on the light, blocking out everything else. Until Emir put his mouth next to her ear.

'Take a deep breath,' he said.

Heart pounding, Noah nodded. The water kept rising. Careful to keep her nose clear of the water, she inhaled. Soon, they'd be sucked into the underground river. Shimmering light under the water caught her attention.

A doorway.

Raven dragged Noah close to the doorway and the water did the rest. Noah clutched her sword as they surfed the torrent cascading through the magical opening. Tangled in near darkness, Noah tried to roll onto her hands and knees. Water continued to pour through the doorway but here – wherever here was – there was room to breathe. Grainger slipped through, almost crashing into her.

'Watch out!' she cried as the shimmering doorway dissolved and darkness returned.

Grainger groaned. 'Ouch.'

'Where are we?' Raven asked.

'Hopefully,' Grainger said, 'in the tunnel just beyond the door that trapped us.'

'Hopefully?' Noah said.

'Baby steps,' Grainger said. 'I didn't think it was safe to go too far.'

Noah sang softly, channelling more dragonsong into her sword. Warm light glowed in front of her. She stared at the metal door, then at the puddles on the ground.

'I hope we're not on the side heading back to the forest,' Noah murmured.

'No,' Raven said. 'Look at the incline. We're headed up – that's where Brinn wanted us to go.'

'Yes it is,' Brinn said, reappearing behind Noah.

Noah rounded on her. 'You're dry. Lucky you.'

'I went for help. Twigg is on his way.'

Noah nodded.

'Was that a test?' Grainger asked.

'A test?' Brinn echoed, tail twitching.

Grainger frowned as he tucked his baton inside his vest. 'You never mentioned that booby trap. Why not?'

'It's new,' Brinn said, 'and no one thought to mention it to me. We'll wait here for Twigg. He'll escort us the rest of the way so we don't have any more "surprises".'

Noah hadn't met Twigg but she already felt sorry for him. Brinn was clearly unhappy.

When the dragon rider arrived, he was out of breath. The young man with curly blonde hair and warm brown eyes bowed to Brinn.

'I'm glad to see your friends are safe, Temperance,' he said.

'Of course they're safe,' Brinn snapped. 'Make sure they stay that way.'

The cat disappeared.

Twigg held out his hand to Noah. 'I'm Twigg,' he said. 'It's nice to meet you at last, Noah Chord.'

Noah shook his hand before introducing her companions.

'Well,' Twigg said, 'we'd better get back or Temperance will be *really* cranky.'

The group organised torches, changed into dry clothes and set off. Noah was thankful to make it to Twigg's cottage without any more excitement.

'Here we are,' Twigg said, opening the door and ushering them inside.

A young woman stood up from a large table cluttered with tools and straps of dyed leather. Her hide trousers and linen top cloaked her slight build and a braid of dark hair hung like rope to her waist. But it was her eyes that captured Noah's attention. Irises of pale lavender twinkled under perfectly shaped eyebrows.

'Welcome,' she said, extending her hand. 'I'm Olive.'

Noah shook her hand. 'I'm Noah. Pleased to meet you.'

'Excuse the seating arrangements,' Twigg said once all introductions had been made, 'my sister and I don't entertain much here.'

Wooden stumps, called into service as stools, surrounded the table. Noah wasn't surprised to see Brinn grooming herself in front of the fireplace.

Noah perched herself on a stump. 'This is perfectly fine.'

Twigg brought a tray of cups from the kitchen bench while Olive filled a pitcher with water.

'Temperance has told us much of what's happened in the uplands,' Olive said as she poured water into Noah's cup, 'but we're really interested to hear Noah's account of how she found the pyrohm.'

Noah looked at Brinn, who'd now settled herself in Raven's lap.

'Tell them, Noah,' Brinn said. 'Tell them everything.'

Noah nodded and commenced her story. She detailed how they'd seen the pyrohm at the museum and her connection to the Kurz family. And she told them how she'd liberated the relic and brought it back to Talisker. She recounted Jong's appearance and ultimatum and neither Twigg nor Olive interrupted until Noah mentioned Gillette.

'Who's Gillette?' Twigg asked.

'He's my nephew,' Emir replied. 'My brother's son.'

Twigg's brow furrowed. 'Right.'

Noah continued her narrative, describing their adventures in Aoratia in exhaustive detail.

Olive shook her head. 'The elves aren't what I'd imagined them to be. I thought they were kind, and wise and … good.'

Noah loosened her scarf to reveal her brand. 'This is how the woodland elves mark their slaves,' she said. 'And it's the leader of the woodland elves who now has the pyrohm. Talyn is sein-Jong and she means to come here to free him.'

Noah turned to Brinn. 'Is that everything?'

Brinn raised her head and crossed her front paws on Raven's leg. 'Almost.'

'What did I miss?' Noah said.

Brinn's ear twitched. 'You didn't tell them that you're the 13th key.'

Twigg and Olive stared at Noah as Grainger gasped.

'The 13th key?' Grainger breathed.

Noah winced as she looked at him. 'If I'd realised it wasn't a secret anymore,' she said with a glance at Brinn, 'I would have told you before.'

Grainger shook his head to free himself of the fog of bewilderment that had descended on him.

'That's how you cured Emir without your viola?' he said.

Noah nodded.

As the vacant stare faded from Grainger's eyes, Noah braced herself for an angry outburst, but he said, 'Suddenly, a lot of things make a lot more sense.'

'You're not angry?'

Grainger shook his head slowly. 'No, Noah. I'm just even more glad that I'm not you.'

'Hang on,' Olive said, 'are you telling us that the 13th key is a *person*?'

'Yes,' Brinn said.

'How did that happen?' Twigg asked.

Raven raised his hand. 'I can tell you that,' he said. 'I helped to make her the 13th key.'

Grateful for a reprieve from story-telling, Noah gestured for him to continue. She listened to her brother's recount – to make sure he didn't embellish it too much – as she studied the assortment of items on the table. Fittings of iron and brass lay scattered across the surface, in amongst rolls of leather strapping. An array of hammers, chisels and blades was neatly arranged in pockets of a rolled-out tool pouch. She hadn't needed any such tools to become the 13th key.

Noah shuddered as she remembered stepping into one of the pockets on Raven's Academy trousers. The nausea she'd experienced at the time washed through her again now. Raven had rolled up his trousers and tucked them into Cecil's pouch. Cecil, phoenix and guardian of Dragonhall, had then dived into a river of lava. Surrounded by dragon's blood, Noah had infused her own blood with the dragonsong in her piece of firestone.

As Raven wound up his narrative, Noah's gaze landed on a brass ring and realisation struck. *Bridles,* she thought, *they're making bridles here.* Noah shivered in delight. *They're making dragon bridles.*

When Raven was finished, all eyes turned to Noah. Olive reached over and poked her gently in the arm.

'That's amazing,' she whispered.

Keen to turn the attention away from herself, Noah said, 'So what do we do now?'

'Later,' Twigg said, 'we will take you to the elders to discuss how we will prepare for Talyn's arrival.'

'Later?' Emir said. 'Today? Tomorrow?'

Olive smiled. 'Such words mean nothing here. We talk of time differently. We don't have days or weeks or years. Things are past … or now … or later – sometimes, *much* later.'

Raven leaned forward and rested his elbows on the table. 'So if I were to ask how old you were, what would you say?'

Emir frowned. 'But you *wouldn't* ask a lady her age, Raven.'

'It's fine,' Olive said. 'I am an adolescent. Twigg is now an adult because he has started growing a beard.'

'And when my body is frail and I cannot work,' Twigg said, 'I will be an old man.'

'Right,' Raven said, frowning.

'I see this troubles you,' Olive said, 'but maybe I can help. The light in our dragonscale sky fluctuates with Xan's consciousness. We say gleaming and waning to describe the brighter time compared to the darker time. We work during the gleaming and rest during the waning.'

'Gleaming and waning sound like our day and night,' Raven said, 'so that makes sense at least.'

'Waning approaches,' Brinn said. 'I will go and inform the elders of your arrival. You will all eat, sleep and then visit the elders after breakfast.'

'The elders are dragon riders?' Grainger asked.

'No,' Twigg said. 'The elders are *dragons*. There are twelve of them.'

Raven whistled softly. 'That ought to be something.'

Chapter 17

Noah checked her watch. Though the Somynians didn't measure time, she wouldn't be shaking the habit anytime soon. Two hours. She'd been staring at the ceiling of Twigg and Olive's cabin for two hours. In only a few more hours, she'd be standing before the dragon elders. Her heart fluttered again at the thought of it. *I think I might* actually *explode,* she thought. Deciding it wouldn't be polite to explode inside the cabin, Noah eased herself out of her swag and tiptoed to the door.

She pulled the latch across and opened the door. A look behind her revealed no movement. Her companions appeared to be sleeping peacefully. Noah slipped outside, carefully pushing the door closed behind her before venturing out into the twilight. She stood for a couple of minutes marvelling at the sky. It was almost impossible to believe there was so much firestone in one place.

Though she could easily have stood and sky-gazed for hours, Noah knew there was more to see. The main city of Somyni lay on the other side of the mountain somewhere and she was keen for her first glimpse of it. She followed a well-worn path for a couple of kilometres, with the sounds of the forest for company.

Something above her caught her attention. Noah looked up.

'Oh my god ...'

'Are you talking to me?' Brinn asked.

Noah flinched but didn't take her attention away from the sky. 'Get over yourself.'

'Ingrate,' Brinn mumbled. 'I bring you to Somyni to see *this*, and that's the thanks I get.'

'You didn't bring me here to see *this*,' Noah retorted. 'You brought me here to die.'

Brinn hissed. 'That's not true.'

Noah ignored her. Captivated, for the moment, by the spectacle overhead, she didn't care what Brinn's true motives were. Gods were powerful and Noah knew she should have been in awe of them. But both Brinn and Jong were complicated and contrary individuals and Noah resented them manipulating her. She needed a distraction and this was it. With her heart thumping in her chest, Noah's eyes tracked the airborne creature. *I never thought I'd see this,* she thought.

'You need to come back inside,' Brinn said. 'It's not safe out here.'

'Yeah … soon,' Noah said.

'Now!' Brinn said.

Noah shook her head in wonder. 'That is amazing! Xan's little cousin …'

She watched as the pale blue dragon twisted and turned, surfing the air currents on powerful wings. When it was directly above her, it banked – tracing an elegant loop against the firestone backdrop. Each successive circle constricted as the dragon's altitude dropped and Noah held her breath. It spiralled down … down … until she could see her reflection in its scales. The downdraft of its beating wings buffeted her as it landed but Noah stayed rooted to the spot.

The dragon landed a few metres away, coming to rest on its four clawed feet. It shook its head – almost like a dog, Noah thought – before shrieking at the sky. Noah took a step towards the creature as it tucked its wings against its sides. She took another step. When it swung its head in her direction, she stopped.

Ice-blue eyes studied her as the dragon's snout touched her nose.

'You are a strange dragon,' it said. 'What is your name?'

Noah coaxed her voice into action. 'I'm Noah. What's your name?'

'My name is Piper. How is it that there is dragon blood in a human body?'

Brinn said, 'Noah has absorbed the power of firestone with Xan's blessing.'

Piper snorted a gentle stream of smoke around Noah. 'Well,' she said, 'that would make us … sisters then.'

'Sisters?' Noah said.

The dragon nodded. 'Sisters.'

'Are you an Elder?' Noah asked.

'No,' the dragon said, shaking her head. 'I am a fledgling.'

'And fledglings,' Brinn said, 'are not supposed to be out alone. It's not safe.'

Piper pointed to Noah and then to Brinn. 'But I'm not alone, Temperance. What better company could I be in, than a god and another dragon?'

Noah glared at the cat.

'What?' Brinn said. 'What's your problem?'

'What's *my* problem?' Noah said. 'My problem is you lecturing someone on following rules. *You* don't follow *any* rules!'

Brinn's eyes narrowed. 'I follow some rules.'

'Only by accident,' Noah said.

Piper bared her teeth and Noah recoiled.

'Relax, Noah,' Brinn said. 'She's smiling.'

Noah unclenched her fists, but without taking her eyes off the dragon's terrifying dental hardware, said, 'Right.'

'So, little sister,' Piper said, 'since you can't fly, would you like me to take you for a ride? I could show you the city?'

'Absolutely,' Noah said as she strode to the dragon's side.

When Brinn's objection didn't come, Noah glanced behind her. The cat had disappeared. *Probably gone for backup,* she thought.

Piper crouched as Noah fought to steady her shaking hands. She studied the dragon's back. The height wasn't a problem. It would be like mounting a tall horse. And in the absence of stirrups, she'd use its scales to climb up. Large, saddle-shaped scales ran the length of Piper's spine, each one sprouting knobs on both sides. *Perfect handholds for human riders,* she thought.

Noah wiped her sweaty hands on her trousers and took another deep breath.

'Here goes,' she murmured.

The blue scales were cool to touch. Noah climbed up and eased herself into place close to Piper's shoulders and gripped the scaly knobs. *Chase would love this,* she thought as she tucked her legs up and squeezed them against the dragon's sides.

'Ready,' Noah said.

'Right,' Piper said. 'Hang on.'

Noah clung to the handholds as the dragon sprang into the air. She felt the power of Piper's muscles as the dragon beat her wings to gain altitude. It was a rocky ascent, each wing stroke threatening to fling Noah from her seat.

When are we going to be high enough? she wondered.

By the time Piper reached cruising altitude, Noah's hands ached but she maintained her grip. She tensed her leg muscles and leaned forward. Wind stung her eyes and whipped her hair across her face as the dragon glided around the mountain. Making a mental note to find goggles for any future flights, Noah squinted through slitted eyelids to survey the countryside below.

She was surprised to find that Mount Jubilee wasn't Somyni's only high point. Several peaks protruded from the lush floor of the undulating underground landscape. Veins of ice-melt streaked the mountains, pooling in shimmering lakes across the sprawling valley farmlands.

'Is this where the dragon riders live?' Noah called, raising her voice to make herself heard over the rush of the wind.

'No,' Piper said. 'The dragon riders all live at Mount Jubilee. It's not safe for them out here.'

'But it looks so peaceful.'

'The landscape is peaceful,' Piper said, 'but the people are not.'

'I heard no one likes the dragon riders. Jealousy, right?'

'It's worse than that,' Piper said. 'Envy and paranoia among the common folk has almost exterminated the dragon riders.'

'How many dragon riders are there left?'

'Five hundred and twelve.'

Noah tried in vain to spit hair from her mouth. 'And how many … people live in Somyni?'

'About fifty thousand.'

As they soared towards the heart of Somyni, Noah wondered how many elves Talyn would bring with her. The dragon riders didn't need any more enemies.

'The city is on the other side of the next mountain,' Piper said. 'Not far now.'

Noah's heart fluttered as the dragon skirted the craggy, ice-capped megalith.

'That's … incredible,' she whispered.

Jong's temple dominated the city centre. Perched on an elongated plateau, the transparent structure appeared to have been wrought from glass. The central building was shaped like a wasp's abdomen with its stinger pointed towards the sky. Noah's stomach churned as Piper descended and the apparatus inside it became clear.

A circular slab of firestone – maybe five metres in diameter – pulsed in the middle of the floor of the massive temple. Through watery eyes, Noah studied the monumental tripod that straddled it. The Pyranhi love of art shone through. Braided metal struts came to a peak about thirty metres above the firestone slab. Though there were no regular stairs on the struts, the textured design would allow easy walking access to the circular platform at the top. In the centre of the platform was the cradle containing three pieces of the illestial, and an empty space for the pyrohm.

Images of Talyn ascending the structure, pyrohm in hand, flashed in Noah's mind. The elf reaching the top and inserting the final piece into the cradle … a flash of light … Jong blasting free of the firestone slab … Gillette's lifeless body in his grasp …

No, she thought. *I am* not *going to let that happen.*

The crystalline cylinders around the main building reminded Noah of the prison cells in Aoratia, though much bigger. The colours varied and their spires looped and coiled. They were breathtakingly beautiful.

Something struck the sole of Noah's boot. Carefully, she shifted her head to her right to inspect her footwear. An arrow protruded from the sole of her boot.

'Archer!' she yelled.

'Time to go then,' Piper replied, veering left and flapping hard.

Noah tensed every muscle she possessed and flattened herself against the dragon's scales. Getting shot was one thing, but plummeting to one's death was quite something else. She closed her eyes and willed Piper to fly faster. Perhaps embarking on a bareback dragon ride with no training had been a little rash. If she survived this flight she'd talk to Olive about a bridle, reins and saddle.

'We're out of arrow range,' Piper announced.

Noah sighed in relief.

'Now all we have to worry about is the cannons!' the dragon said.

Noah stiffened again. *Cannons? Really?*

Noah doubted anyone could hit a flying dragon with a cannonball, but this wasn't the time to argue. She huddled against Piper's pearlescent blue armour and prayed they'd make it back to the cabin. At least now, if she lived to meet the elders, she had a clearer understanding of what the dragon riders were up against.

Chapter 18

'It's pretty impressive,' Raven said. 'Apart from the smell.'

Noah took one large step away from him.

'What?' Raven said.

'If one of these dragons takes offence and decides to roast you … someone needs to try to put out the flames,' Noah said.

Raven folded his arms. 'Hmm. I think you're just trying to save your own skin.'

Noah didn't answer him. Instead, she turned her attention to the dragons filing into the chamber. From inside Mount Jubilee, its volcanic past was clearly evident. The round opening far above gave a glimpse of the firestone sky beyond. But it was the inner walls of the sanctum that were most impressive. Archways carved into the rock – many now occupied by dragons and their riders – reminded Noah of balcony seating at the theatre. Piper had said there were currently five hundred dragon riders, but the chamber could have accommodated four times that number.

As Noah scanned the alcoves, Piper appeared in a second-level entryway. Relieved to see a familiar face, even if it was reptilian, Noah waved to her. The blue dragon flapped her wings before settling herself on the rocky outcrop.

Olive arrived at Noah's side. 'The elders will be here soon.'

Noah nodded. 'Great.'

'Are you nervous?'

'A little.'

Olive smiled. 'You'll be fine.'

Noah decided not to tell the dragon rider that her primary concern was for her brother's safety. He was in grave danger of being incinerated for one of his trademark wisecracks. She looked at Emir and Grainger, who stood either side of Twigg, and wondered if they felt as calm as they looked.

When something pressed against Noah's leg, she looked down.

'Pick me up, please, Noah,' Brinn said.

'Wouldn't you prefer one of the balcony seats?' Noah asked.

'Actually I *would* prefer a balcony seat,' Brinn said, 'but it's more important that I keep a close eye on you.'

Noah scooped the cat up in her arms. 'Thanks for the vote of confidence.'

'You're welcome.'

'Here they come,' Olive said.

A procession of dragons entered the chamber through an archway to Noah's right. Her heart swelled in her chest as the elders took their places around the central platform. *Chase should be here,* she thought. A pang of sadness gripped her as she thought of her friend. Brinn had said she'd probably never see Chase again. As tears stung the corners of her eyes, Noah fought for composure. This wasn't the time to be emotional.

An emerald dragon stepped onto the stage and the dragons roosting in the alcoves above fell silent.

'I, Horatio,' the dragon said, 'speak on behalf of the elders in welcoming you to today's assembly. We have some special guests to meet. So without further ado, I request dragon riders Olive and Twigg to join me on the dais.'

The dragon riders strode to the stage and bowed to the Elder before taking their position beside him.

'Today,' Olive said, 'it is our honour to welcome Temperance to the chamber, and our great privilege to introduce you to her allies from the uplands.'

An excited murmur swirled around the cavern, punctuated by several shrieks.

When silence returned, Twigg began the presentations.

'Elders, dragons, dragon riders … our first guest is Dr Grainger Brimblecombe, Dragonsbane,' he said.

Grainger walked to the stage amid a cacophony of growling and screeching. If Noah's hands hadn't been full of cat, she'd have covered her ears.

'Our second guest,' Olive said, 'is Emir Delorian, former adviser to the Kings of Leninstar and Carai.'

Emir bowed to the elders when he reached the stage and then stood next to Grainger.

Twigg said, 'I would request Raven Chord, Leninstar's Army Commander, to join us.'

More whooping and cheering erupted as Raven made his way onto the dais. Noah trembled as her brother lined up next to Emir.

'Relax, Noah,' Brinn said.

'I'm fine,' Noah murmured.

'Your arms are shaking.'

'My arms are *tired*,' Noah said. 'Did you have a big breakfast?'

Olive held up her hands for quiet. 'And lastly, with Temperance, is her champion – Noah Chord, sein-Temperance and the 13th key!'

Noah's legs seemed to move of their own accord as she drifted across the stage. Light sparkled around the chamber as hundreds of dragons flamed their appreciation. The elders joined in, creating a ring of fire around the dais. The smoke stung Noah's eyes but she managed to find Olive in the haze.

Twigg raised his hands and the kerfuffle died down.

'Friends,' he said, 'as you know, Somyni doesn't receive casual visitors. Those who venture here are either friend or foe. There is no in-between. Olive and I have heard their story' – he gestured towards Noah and her companions – 'and we think it is one that you all must hear.'

'You can put me down now,' Brinn said.

Noah placed the cat on the floor and stepped forward. As Brinn climbed up onto the green dragon's back, Noah acknowledged the dragon elders, bowing to each of them in turn.

'My friends and I bring news of the pyrohm,' she said.

'We would hear everything you know of the relic, Noah,' Horatio said. 'Please tell us.'

Noah told her story again, hoping it was the last time she'd have to do it.

When she was finished, Horatio padded across the stage to her. Noah looked him in the eye as he studied her.

'You bring grave news,' the emerald dragon said, 'but also hope. We have much to think about.'

A soot-coloured Elder climbed onto the dais. 'I am Fontina,' she said. 'We have long believed that the illestial must be destroyed. It seems we will be given a chance to do so at last.'

Noah nodded politely. Brinn's plan to use the illestial to transfer Jong from Talisker to the vortex was still a secret it seemed.

'You are the strangest-looking dragon I've ever seen,' Fontina continued, 'but perhaps your disguise serves you well?'

Unsure what to say, Noah just nodded again.

Horatio sprang into the air, fire blazing from his throat. As he flew around the chamber, he quelled his flame and said, 'Dragons and dragon riders! There is much to do. We elders will now discuss our strategy. Go to your stations and await directions from your lieutenants!'

Dragons screeched and flamed their acknowledgement while their riders cheered.

'Go!' Horatio commanded.

Piper and four other dragons fluttered down onto the chamber floor as the audience retreated into the archways.

'Piper,' Fontina said, 'you're dismissed.'

'But Noah is my rider,' Piper said. 'I must stay with her.'

Fontina shook her head. 'Just because Noah rode with you once, doesn't make it a permanent arrangement.'

'But she *is* my rider,' Piper insisted. 'Noah is the one I hatched for.'

'Hatched for?' Noah said, frowning. 'What does that mean?'

Olive patted the snout of her bronze-coloured dragon. 'There is a bond between dragons and their riders,' she said. 'Dragons sense the birth of the rider they are destined to take, and when they do, they hatch.'

'So … dragons who aren't destined to have a rider don't ever hatch?' Emir asked.

'No, no,' Twigg said. 'Those dragons just hatch when they're ready. But dragons destined to have riders, just delay hatching until the time is right for them to meet their mate.'

An apple-green dragon broke away from the others on the dais and nuzzled Twigg's hand as Piper and the other dragons looked on.

'And they always find their rider?' Raven said.

'Unfortunately not,' Olive said, shaking her head. 'Unless riders are born in Somyni, there is little chance of them meeting.'

Emir rubbed his chin. 'So you're saying that potential riders are born in other places?'

'Yes,' Olive said. 'Many riders, like you, are born in the uplands.'

Emir frowned as Noah's heart rate kicked up a gear.

'I'm not a dragon rider,' Emir said.

The black dragon beside Piper walked over to Emir and squatted in front of him. 'I'm Chain,' he said. 'We are destined to ride together.'

Emir stared at the dragon for a long moment before dropping to one knee.

Brinn rubbed against Noah's leg. 'That's what *you* should have done when you met Piper,' she said.

'How was I supposed to know?' Noah whispered.

'How was Emir supposed to know?' Brinn countered.

Noah looked at the cat. 'This is why you wanted Emir to come?'

Brinn nodded.

Another dragon approached Raven. As Emir had done, Raven bowed his head and knelt before the red dragon, who introduced herself as Vespa.

'So, Brinn,' Noah said, 'if both Emir and Raven are destined to be dragon riders, why did you want Emir to come, but not Raven?'

'Raven will no doubt be useful,' Brinn replied, 'but he isn't necessary. He might just as well have stayed with Catriona and protected Leninstar.'

One of the elders in the cordon around the stage flapped its wings. 'Horatio,' it said, 'we have much to discuss. While the new dragon riders go to practise their manoeuvres, Dr Grainger will remain here with us. As Dragonsbane, we would welcome his counsel.'

Grainger smiled. 'I would be honoured,' he said.

Noah relaxed her shoulders. She felt bad for him that he'd missed out on a dragon, but he appeared genuinely pleased to be included in the elders' discussions.

'There is still the issue of the fledgling,' Fontina said, looking at Piper. 'She can't carry a rider unless she's supervised.'

'Twigg and I will supervise,' Olive said.

Piper trembled with excitement. 'I'll be a trainee-pilot at last!'

'Supervision for practice is fine,' Fontina said, 'but what about later?'

Noah ran her hand along Piper's neck. 'Later?'

'We will have to do battle to defeat the Jongu and destroy the illestial,' Fontina said.

'When it comes to that,' Horatio said, 'I think we'll have more to worry about than supervision procedures.'

'I think that's probably Fontina's point,' another of the elders said. 'Can we entrust the safety of sein-Temperance to a fledgling when such a great battle is imminent?'

'Trainee-pilot,' Piper said.

Noah climbed up onto Piper's back. 'I trust her. She's fast, agile and—'

'Reckless,' Fontina said.

'—brave,' Noah finished.

'Perhaps there is no harm in letting them practise,' an Elder said. 'We can defer our decision until later?'

'We have limited time,' another argued, 'Noah needs to practise on the dragon she will go into battle on.'

'But *I'm* bonded to Noah,' Piper said.

'But that doesn't mean another dragon couldn't take her, Piper,' an amber-coloured Elder said. 'It's obviously not ideal, but it's possible.'

Fontina sighed, sending a delicate puff of smoke from her nostrils. 'I understand your devotion to your destined rider, Piper,' she said, 'but time is our enemy.'

'I won't ride any other dragon,' Noah said.

Silence.

'If I can't ride Piper,' she added, 'I'll be going into battle on foot.'

'Well,' Horatio said, 'sein-Temperance has spoken. By the sounds of things, Noah has prevailed in many difficult situations. Perhaps, fellow elders, we should show some faith in her judgement? Any objections?'

No one spoke. As all eyes went to Fontina. Noah wondered if she'd just made an enemy.

'I have aired my concerns,' Fontina said, 'but I will accept the decision of my peers.'

Noah slid down from Piper's back to find Brinn waiting.

'Well, *that* was direct,' the cat said. 'I think being king went to your head, Noah.'

'Or maybe,' Noah said, squatting down and rubbing her hand the wrong way up Brinn's back, 'I've just been hanging out with you too long.'

'Leave us, dragon riders,' Horatio said. 'You will receive your orders in due course.'

Noah jumped to her feet as Brinn attended to grooming her ruffled fur.

Horatio shook his head. 'Not you, Noah,' he said. 'You need to stay with us.'

Though keen to start practising with Piper, Noah sat on the floor and crossed her legs. *Might as well get comfortable,* she thought. *This could take a while.* Brinn parked herself to Noah's right, out of arm's reach.

'So, Temperance,' Fontina said, 'how long do you think we have until the elves arrive?'

'It's difficult to say,' Brinn said. 'The elves are not rash creatures, but they have been awaiting the return of the pyrohm for a long time and already have a plan. Talyn will send scouts to gather intelligence on what is happening here in Somyni, and then they'll strike.'

Horatio snorted. 'Well, the elves aren't the only ones with a plan,' he said. 'Once we get the pyrohm, we have the spell to destroy it.'

'Which is a credit to you,' Brinn said, 'but might I suggest an alternative?'

'We will always listen to your counsel, Temperance,' Fontina said.

Noah tensed, fearing Brinn would tell her to share the crazy plan, but to her relief the cat held the floor.

'As you know, Jong's presence here means that Talisker's existence has always been precarious,' Brinn said.

The elders all nodded.

'But Talisker faces another more imminent threat,' Brinn continued. 'You have a rapidly expanding vortex on your doorstep.'

For a few moments, the dragons were silent.

Fontina was first to respond. 'Can we assume you have a crafty solution to alleviate both these problems?' she said.

'Yes,' Brinn said. 'Noah will use the illestial to extract Jong from his prison here and then transport him to the vortex and re-home him there.'

'And the vortex could contain him?' Horatio said.

'Elani and I think so,' Brinn said. '*And* we hope his wrath will stabilise the vortex.'

All eyes turned to Noah.

'You can do this?' Horatio said.

Noah glanced at Grainger as she tried to swallow the lump in her throat. 'Not alone,' she said.

Horatio nodded slowly. 'What do you need from us?'

'Noah and Grainger need to master some Pyranhi spells to contain Jong within the illestial long enough to transport him to the vortex,' Brinn said. 'They're also going to have to redirect one of the olluka pathways to get within range of the vortex.'

'Redirect an olluka pathway?' Grainger said. 'Which one?'

'One of the Genja pathways,' Brinn said.

Grainger shuddered. 'We wouldn't want to get that wrong,' he said. 'If we end up on Genja, we're dead.'

Brinn purred. 'Correct.'

'And where is the portal for this pathway?' Noah asked.

'It's one of the portals in the cluster under Dragonhall,' Grainger replied.

The colour had drained from the senior Dragonsbane's face, and Noah knew why. The portal cluster was unstable. They'd risked using it to get to Tisaan and had been very lucky to survive it. Grainger had tinkered with it since their return but it was still incredibly volatile. The power needed to divert a pathway attached to one of the portals could easily blow the whole thing.

'I have never heard of Pyranhi magic that could achieve this,' a rust-coloured Elder asked. 'Is it even possible?'

'The Pyranhi are the ones that activated the pathways,' Brinn said.

'How did they do it?' Noah said.

'Olluka trees grow in many places,' Brinn said, 'and their branches reach across space, connecting worlds. Even though the branches aren't visible in space, the Pyranhi knew they were there and used magic to create the portals – they called them portal gates – to access the branches and use them to move between worlds. As you know, there are many portals on Earth, Noah, and that's because there are many branches, or pathways connecting Talisker and Earth – and many other worlds too.'

Noah frowned. 'And we're supposed to move one of these branches so we can get to the vortex?'

'You need to move one of the pathways so you can get *within range* of the vortex,' Brinn said. 'You don't want to get sucked *into* the vortex, do you?'

Noah shook her head. 'No.'

'I'm afraid we don't know this kind of magic,' Horatio said. 'How are we to help?'

Brinn turned her gazed on Piper. 'Noah needs to go to the city to get a book.'

Piper shivered. 'It will be an honour to assist the sein-Temperance in this venture,' she said.

'And where is this book exactly?' Noah asked.

'Ion Tower,' Brinn replied. 'Sorcerer-master Percival's stronghold.'

Fontina snorted a plume of sooty smoke. 'The sein-Jong.'

'Oh, this ought to be good,' Grainger said. 'Talyn thinks she's sein-Jong … we should definitely get those two together.'

'Yep,' Noah said. 'If we let them duke it out, maybe we just fight the winner?'

'Don't underestimate either of these adversaries,' Horatio said. 'Percival is wily and sadistic. His campaign against the dragon riders has seen our ranks reduced by two-thirds. If he finds out the elves are on their way bearing the pyrohm, he will seek to eliminate us before they get here. He won't want to be fighting them and us.'

Brinn's tail swished from side to side. 'Talyn will send scouts,' she said. 'She'll want to know what resistance the elves will face here.'

'So any Jongu we take out here,' Fontina said, 'we're doing the elves a favour?'

'Unfortunately, yes,' Brinn said. She looked to Horatio. 'You asked before what you can do to help Noah?'

The emerald dragon nodded.

'Withdraw all your spies from the city and have them return here,' Brinn said. 'Keep them safe. We're going to need everyone we can get once the elves arrive.'

Chapter 19

'So you're really going to break into Sorcerer-master Percival's chambers to steal a book?' Olive said.

Noah glanced sideways at her companion and nodded. 'Yep.'

Olive frowned. 'I don't envy you.'

Noah shrugged, returning her attention to the path. She prodded the leaf litter on the forest floor with a stick she'd found. Not only was the detritus slippery, but it could conceal any number of perils – spiders, scorpions, centipedes, snakes … and that was just the things that moved. Sinking sand, tree roots and mangerays also lurked beneath the layer of organic matter.

Their return to the woodland at the foot of Mt Jubilee to reset the log pendulum booby trap they'd triggered the day before, generated excited chatter amongst the resident birds, apes and amphibians. In the canopy, baboons gibbered while the frogs croaked their chorus from the creeks and pools below. Parrots screeched as they swooped to get a closer look at the five intruders.

Only a few steps in front of Noah, Twigg led the way, with a tomahawk tucked in his belt and coils of rope looped over his shoulders. Emir and Raven brought up the rear, also bearing hatchets.

'What do you know about the Sorcerer-master?' Noah said.

Olive skirted a lichen-covered rock. 'Percival is a tyrant,' she said. 'He's brought the Four Houses to heel and rules Somyni by the might of his magic.'

'Four Houses?'

'There are four powerful families with a long history in Somyni,' Olive said. 'I've been a "servant" in the Ascit house for the last three harvests – they own all the distilleries hereabouts. The Grooters preside over a pastoral empire, the goblin clan Huble own the mining conglomerate and the Overills operate a construction consortium.'

Noah frowned. 'Brinn asked Horatio to withdraw all spies from the city. If you're a spy, how come you're not there?'

'Holidays,' Olive said, smiling. 'Much-needed holidays.'

'The Ascit's are hard to work for?'

'That's putting it mildly. I only know of Lord Ascit by reputation. He's not at the estate much – spends most of his time micro-managing the stills. Probably to get away from his wife, I reckon.'

'She's not very nice I take it?' Noah said.

Olive snorted. 'She's awful. "Lady" Ascit is anything but a lady. She's a cruel, vindictive woman … enjoys beating servants for work she considers sub-standard.'

'And I don't suppose the pay is very good either?' Noah said.

'Correct. Though I did find a way to supplement my salary.'

Noah raised an eyebrow. 'How's that?'

'I *might* have procured a stash of top-shelf whisky.'

'You stole it?'

'Not exactly,' Olive said. 'It was a gift from Reuben – the Ascit's son and sole heir. He's taken a special interest in me.'

'Sounds creepy.'

Olive shrugged. 'It's not that simple.'

'What do you mean?'

'I'm there because Reuben's secretly working for Percival,' Olive said, 'which sounds really bad. But part of me feels sorry for him.'

When Olive went quiet, Noah prompted her. 'Because?'

'He's young, Noah. Like us. I don't think he's joined Percival's clandestine network because he's evil. Reuben's a rebel looking for a cause. And with the parents he's got – I'm not surprised he wants to cut loose.'

'Is he like his parents?'

'Reuben is handsome, intelligent and charming,' Olive said, 'but he does have a mean streak which comes out when he's drunk.'

'And what's his special interest in you?'

Olive's cheeks flushed red. 'Romantic.'

'I can't imagine his parents would approve of that,' Noah said.

'They wouldn't,' Olive agreed, 'and I'm sure that's part of the attraction.'

Emir's voice came from behind. 'And joining Percival's network of Jongu?' he said. 'Would his parents approve of that?'

'No,' Olive said. 'Lord and Lady Ascit – like the older generations of the other Four Houses – want rid of Percival. They would love nothing more than to strip him of his power and re-take control of Somyni.'

Noah's opportunity to ask her next question was lost as Twigg raised his hand to signal a stop. The log booby trap was further down the track, so the unscheduled stop put them all on notice. Noah scanned the forest as she stood close behind Twigg, with Olive at her side. Emir and Raven took their defensive stance at the rear.

Noah caught Olive's eye and cocked her head. A silent question. The dragon rider tapped her sword in reply and adrenaline coursed through Noah's veins at the prospect of a fight. Emir nudged her. She glanced at him but his attention was elsewhere. Following his gaze, Noah glimpsed movement behind a stand of ferns in the distance.

'Show yourselves, cowards!' Twigg called. 'Stop skulking around in the undergrowth.'

Thwack!

An arrow lodged in a tree trunk to Twigg's left.

Noah's eyes darted to the high branches where a lone archer squatted, nocking another arrow to her bow. Rustling in the understorey distracted Noah. Black-clad warriors waded through the ferns towards them, swords drawn. Without speaking, Noah and her companions armed themselves as they formed a defensive circle.

'Who are these guys?' Raven said.

'Elanu,' Twigg muttered.

'Dragon rider scum!' a young woman cried.

Noah studied the warriors as the cordon closed. The girl who'd called out was probably no older than Noah, and her sword gleamed menacingly despite the relative gloom in the understorey. As Noah scanned the group she shuddered. Of the eight she could see, most were young but they moved with the fluid grace of seasoned fighters.

'They seek to capture us,' Twigg whispered, 'so they can lure and kill our dragons. We will not suffer this. We fight to the death. On my mark …'

Noah tightened her grip on her sword.

'Charge!' Twigg bellowed.

Noah pushed forward, sword raised in front of her as two young men bore down on her. Legs pumping, she drew her weapon back behind her right shoulder. The fighter to her left mirrored her action while the other levelled the point of his blade at her head. As Noah swung her sword, she skidded to her knees, ducking her head to avoid being decapitated. Something whizzed past her ear, landing beside her with a thud. Blue feathers fluttered on the end of the arrow that protruded from the ground. *That's not fair,* she thought. *I can't fight three at once.*

'Noah! Stay down!' Raven cried.

Noah scrambled out of the path of the closest warrior.

Thwack!

A young man sprawled in front of her with a knife handle protruding from his neck. Desperate hands grappled for the handle as the victim attempted to dislodge the blade. From experience Noah knew that winning the battle would mean losing the war. If he succeeded in removing the blade, he'd bleed to death in minutes. Raven was a crack shot.

Noah gagged as swords clashed above her.

'Run!' Raven hissed.

Noah panted as she leapt to her feet. 'I don't run away!'

Raven didn't reply, his attention now fixed on his opponent.

Olive appeared at her side. 'Come on, Noah,' she said, tugging on her wrist. 'Follow me. We'll get behind them – attack from the rear.'

Noah stumbled the first few steps before Olive released her. At a crouch, the girls scurried through the undergrowth.

Noah vaulted a rotten stump as an arrow slammed into it. 'I'd like to get that archer,' she muttered as she swatted a fern aside.

Olive turned. 'Could you?'

Noah almost crashed into her. 'Sorry … what?'

'Could you get the archer?'

Noah cocked her head. 'I could try.'

Olive nodded. 'Do it. I'll get behind the line.'

The dragon rider dashed off as Noah considered her task. She couldn't climb the tree. The archer would pick her off before she got even halfway up. She had no rope and there was no time to retrieve any that Twigg had brought. Noah glanced behind her. Twigg was still fighting, as were Emir and Raven, but they were outnumbered. The archer fired another arrow. This one speared Twigg's thigh. The dragon rider grunted but kept fighting. Noah swallowed the large lump in her throat.

She dropped to her knees and rummaged through the leaf litter until she found some decent-sized rocks. Noah stepped back and took aim. She pitched the first stone, striking the archer's shoulder.

'What?' the girl said as she spun on her branch.

Noah pursed her lips. The girl couldn't have been more than ten. It felt wrong to throw rocks at a child. But this child had just shot Twigg. Noah's fingers clenched tighter around the second rock. She hurled it but missed, and the girl whipped another arrow from her quiver. Noah dived aside as the arrow came. *I probably can't knock her down,* she thought, *but if I can keep her busy, Emir and Raven will be okay.*

She brushed leaves aside in her quest for more rocks.

'Die! Dragon rider scum!' the girl snarled as she fired more arrows in quick succession.

Noah pegged rocks and dodged the lethal darts until a scream split the air behind her.

'Olive!' Noah called.

When there was no answer, Noah spun round. Raven, Emir and Twigg battled on, a knot of seven warriors around them. Olive was nowhere in sight. Noah surveyed the understorey, watching for any sign of movement. Nothing. Noah frowned. Olive had been behind the line. If she hadn't been cut down … perhaps she'd tripped and fallen.

Noah glanced up the tree. If she went searching for Olive, the archer would return her attention to Raven and Emir. *Or if I run, maybe she'll try to skewer me rather than them,* she thought.

Noah pitched one more rock at the archer then bolted in the direction of Olive's cry. She scrambled amongst the ferns, eyes scanning the forest floor for any sign of the dragon rider. When she spied two hands protruding from the ground up ahead, Noah ran faster. She dived and slid, coming to rest on the lip of a mangeray, and grabbed Olive's wrists.

'Interesting hiding spot,' Noah said.

Olive snorted. 'Very funny,' she said. 'Just get me out so we can help the others.'

Noah eyed the downward pointing spines. They weren't doing Olive any damage at present, but if she tried to pull the dragon rider out, her flesh would be torn to pieces.

'Okay,' Noah said. 'And how do you suggest I do that?'

'Banana leaves.'

'Did you say—'

'Yes, Noah – banana leaves. Hurry!'

Noah glanced behind her and clutched at a fern frond. 'It'll have to do,' she muttered, pulling the frond towards the crevice. 'Hold onto this so you don't fall in any further.'

'Okay,' Olive said. 'I got it. Go!'

With the clanging of swords behind her, Noah raced to the nearest banana tree and hacked off half a dozen of the biggest leaves she could reach.

'Slide them down,' Olive said when Noah returned. 'Front and back.'

'You've done this before?'

'More than once, I'm embarrassed to say.'

Noah wiggled the leaves into place, but it was slow going. 'Bark would be better,' Noah said. 'Not so bendy.'

'Beggars can't be choosers,' Olive said. 'Try that – pull me out.'

Noah straddled the carnivorous monstrosity and crouched by Olive's side.

'Straight up,' Olive said. 'Too much angle far forward or backward and the pressure will push the spines through the leaves.'

'Got it,' Noah said, wedging her shoulder under Olive's armpit.

Noah straightened her back and tensed her leg muscles. She grunted. 'I feel like I'm lining up for the clean and jerk at the Olympic weightlifting,' Noah said.

'What?'

'Never mind,' Noah said, straining to pull Olive free.

Once the dragon rider was clear of the crevice, both girls collapsed on the ground.

'We can't lie here,' Olive said. 'We need to get back to help the boys.'

'Uh-huh,' Noah said as rolled onto her hands and knees and staggered to her feet. 'Oh … wait.'

Olive appeared at Noah's side. 'Mmm.'

'It seems our services are no longer required.'

Emir, Raven and Twigg – still with an arrow protruding from his thigh – ringed the tree where the now arrowless archer still perched.

Olive sighed. 'Not for the fight, but the clean-up is the worst part. Come on.'

'Clean-up?' Noah asked as they tramped through the undergrowth towards their companions. 'You bury the bodies?'

Olive shook her head. 'The mangeray missed *me*, but they won't go hungry today.'

'And the girl?' Noah said, inclining her head towards the archer.

'Twigg will offer his condolences for the lives lost, and then let her go.'

Noah frowned. 'Condolences? For those who tried to kill him?'

Olive shrugged. 'We don't like taking lives.'

Chapter 20

'It really is magnificent,' Noah said, eyeing the ancient tower from her park bench as she nibbled a tart from a nearby street stall.

'Indeed,' Brinn said. 'Just remember – don't get caught.'

Noah didn't reply. She knew Brinn had already vanished again. Piper had dropped Noah as close to Somyni city as she dared. The dragon would await her return at the rendezvous point, but until then Noah was alone. She took a deep breath as she surveyed the streetscape below Ion Tower.

The city was swarming with foot traffic and carts. Street vendors cajoled potential patrons, waving signs and calling out specials. From artwork to apothecary, tools to homewares and food to fashion – Somyni seemed to have everything. And humans and goblins were buying.

Noah was aghast at what passed for fashion among the high society types in Somyni though. Men and women alike looked to have been decorated rather than dressed. The women looked like bejewelled meringues, the bell-like skirts of their dresses so wide that they couldn't hold hands with their suitors. Not that they had a free hand to hold. They clutched elaborately embroidered purses in one hand and lacy parasols in the other. And while the kaftans favoured by the men were slimmer fitting, they were still ostentatiously jewelled, beaded and embroidered.

Noah had borrowed her outfit from Olive. The tailored linen trousers and smock the dragon rider had worn in her undercover role in the Ascit's household were – in Noah's opinion – tasteful and practical.

With a final glance at the ten-storey brick tower, Noah collected the wooden box from the seat beside her. Lord Ascit's whisky was a highly prized commodity in Somyni and Olive had donated one from her stash to the cause. Noah threaded her way through the crowd, hoping to look like any other servant delivering a parcel, and when she arrived at the tower door, she rang the bell.

The door opened almost immediately. A young woman in a black robe stood in the entranceway. Below her dark fringe, eyes of cobalt blue regarded her guest. Two crossed sticks through the coiled bun on top of her head caught Noah's attention. One appeared to be obsidian, the other definitely firestone. The wands marked her as a high-ranking sorcerer in Percival's order.

'Yes?' the sorcerer said.

Noah bowed her head. 'I have a delivery for Sorcerer-master Percival.'

'From whom?'

'Lord Nelson Ascit,' Noah replied.

The young woman turned her head and studied something on the wall. 'This delivery is not scheduled this gleaming.'

Noah's pulse quickened. 'Lord Ascit's household is very busy making final preparations for his Harvest End Ball. He hoped that an early delivery would not be too much of an inconvenience for the Sorcerer-master.'

The sorcerer frowned. 'Lord Ascit should have formally advised the Sorcerer-master if he wished to alter the regular delivery schedule.'

'Are you attending the Harvest End Ball?' Noah asked.

The young woman nodded. 'I am.'

'Then I'll let you tell Lord Ascit that yourself.'

'Fine,' the sorcerer said, holding out her hand. 'Leave it with me then.'

'I am to deliver this to Sorcerer-master Percival personally,' Noah said. 'Lord Ascit has instructed me to wait for his convenience.'

The woman's frown deepened. 'He could be some time.'

'That's fine.'

Blue eyes considered Noah for a long moment before the woman relented. She stepped out of the entranceway and gestured for Noah to enter.

'Thank you,' Noah said as she crossed the threshold.

The sorcerer drew her obsidian wand and chanted a few lilting phrases in a language Noah didn't understand. 'Follow me and don't touch anything.'

Noah didn't need to ask what spell had been put on her. She'd had more than enough experience with compliance spells. *Orville did it with blood magic, Talyn can control me with a brand and now this!* Noah thought.

The young woman strode towards the spiral staircase with Noah in her wake.

On each level apart from the ground floor, robed figures went about their work, different coloured robes identifying the different ranks. Noah struggled to recall what Olive had told her about Percival's minions. Acolytes wore red, mages wore blue, wizards wore grey, sorcerers wore black and the Sorcerer-master cloaked himself in white. Few of Ion Tower's residents noticed Noah though, and not one acknowledged her.

By the time Noah reached the top storey, her leg muscles burned. She scanned the walls. Books filled every shelf. An ornate wooden desk dominated the middle of the room. More books lay scattered across the wooden expanse along with an array of chalks, inks, feathers, beads and twine, but Noah was most interested in the lamp.

The sorcerer pointed to a chair. 'Sit,' she said. 'Stay.'

Noah sat. The sorcerer, confident in her spell, left Noah alone in the Sorcerer-master's chambers. Still cradling the box containing the whisky, Noah adjusted the scarf covering the brand on her neck. Satisfied that the leaf wouldn't be visible, she turned her attention to the lamp on the desk. It was quite plain, and according to Brinn, that was why none of Somyni's human sorcerers had discovered its true purpose. A small flame burned inside the throat of the glass chimney and a wooden carving adorned the white porcelain base.

How can that be a book? she wondered, shaking her head. She sighed. It didn't matter *if* it was a book, or *how* it was a book … Brinn had told her to take it, so she had to take it. With all the candles in Percival's chambers, the lamp contributed relatively little light, so Noah hoped Percival wouldn't notice its disappearance straight away. If only she could reach it.

She'd concealed a pocket from her Academy trousers in the pocket on her smock. Once the lamp was inside, Noah had only to hand over the whisky to Sorcerer-master Percival and be on her way. As long as he didn't miss the lamp before she'd cleared the tower, all would be good.

For several minutes Noah stewed on how to circumvent the wizard's compliance spell as well as snatch the lamp. The chamber door opened. A dark-haired man in a white robe drifted towards Noah, stopping a couple of metres from her. While the skin on his face protected an intricate network of capillaries, it did nothing to hide them. It wasn't so much pale, as translucent. Grey eyes languished deep in their sockets under a severe brow ridge. His dark eyebrows were bushy and unruly, in contrast to his long hair which cascaded down his back like a sheet of polished onyx.

'And what do we have here?' Sorcerer-master Percival asked.

'A delivery from Lord Ascit, Sorcerer-master,' Noah said.

Percival slipped his firestone wand from his belt and chanted softly. Noah rose from her seat and floated into the air. The sorcerer stepped forward and held out his hand.

Stomach churning, Noah handed him the wooden box and Percival accepted it without thanks. He removed the lid.

'Lovely,' Percival said, turning his frosty gaze on Noah. 'I shall put it with the bottle Lord Ascit sent earlier.'

Noah frowned. 'He sent another bottle?' she said. 'Who delivered it?'

'His son, Reuben.'

Noah shook her head slowly. 'That's vexing.'

'Indeed it is,' Percival said. 'Which begs the question … what are you really doing here?'

Noah thought about the lamp. 'I really want to learn magic,' she whispered.

Percival snorted. 'And you think I'd accept someone who gains access to my tower with so simple a ruse? Have you any talent?'

'My mother was a practitioner,' Noah said.

'Well,' Percival said, 'perhaps a little test is in order. Let's see if you can escape from this.'

Percival flicked his wand, tracing figures of eight in the air and chanting as he did so. Still suspended in mid-air, Noah felt something slithering around her wrists and ankles. She stared at the spaghetti-like green luminous strands that looped themselves around her wrists and then pulled her arms behind her back. Noah tugged and wriggled to slip free of her bonds but they held tight.

'Can you get free, would-be sorcerer?' Percival taunted.

Noah stopped struggling. She *could* get free, but should she? Using raiki now would blow her cover, but if it meant freedom …

Percival twirled his wand and Noah's body turned to the right, slowly at first but the revolutions soon picked up speed. Noah squeezed her eyes shut as her axis shifted. The sorcerer rotated her to a horizontal position, but didn't stop there. Noah felt her feet rising skyward until she was spinning upside down. The whirling and gyrating continued until Noah vomited.

'Urgh!' Percival exclaimed as Noah crashed to the floor. 'That's disgusting!'

Face down on the floor, Noah threw up again.

'Look at you!' Percival said. 'Lying in a pool of your own filth. As if I'd waste my time training the likes of you.' He turned to the door. 'Kalvin!'

The smell of vomit made Noah's stomach heave again. She tried to roll clear of the mess but her arms tied behind her back made that impossible. Brinn's voice echoed inside her head. *Don't get caught … don't get caught … don't get—*

A new voice interrupted Noah's internal torment.

'What is your bidding, Sorcerer-master?' a man asked.

'Kalvin, remove *that!*' Percival said.

Strong hands gripped Noah's ankles and dragged her across the floor.

'Pick her up!' Percival said. 'You're smearing that putrid mess everywhere!'

'Yes, Sorcerer-master.'

Kalvin slid one arm under Noah's back and the other behind her knees. He grunted as he lifted her. Too woozy to resist, Noah lay limp in his arms.

'Wait,' Percival said. 'What's that?'

'What's what?' the man replied.

'That mark on her neck …'

A fingernail brushed Noah's neck then tugged at her scarf.

'Well, well, well,' Percival said, '*that* is interesting.'

'Her tattoo?'

'That's not a tattoo. That is a brand. We have an elf slave here.'

'Shall I … dispose of her, Sorcerer-master?'

'Not yet,' Percival said. 'I think I'll have a little word to her first. Put her in the chair and then clean up the mess. Let me know when you're done.'

'Is it safe?'

'The bonds I've put on her will hold.'

'What if she does some magic while you're gone?'

'She won't,' Percival said. 'Elf slaves can't do magic.'

When Noah heard the door close, she opened her eyes. The man pumped water from a faucet to fill a wooden bucket.

'Look who's awake,' he said.

Despite her throbbing head, Noah glared at him. His clothing marked him as a servant so she didn't need to concern herself with any more magical intervention for now. She scanned the room. Percival was gone. Her eyes went to the desk. The lamp was still there. *I need to get that before Percival returns,* Noah thought.

She rested her head against the back of the chair and closed her eyes again. Percival's magic had dissolved the compliance spell at least, so once the servant was finished cleaning she'd burn off her bonds and steal the lamp. While she waited, she fought to focus her hazy mind on the glowing filaments that held her. The more she understood them, the better chance she had of dispelling them quickly. And she'd need to be fast. Percival would be keen to interrogate an elf slave.

'All done,' the servant said, throwing his cloth into the bucket of murky water. 'I'll let the Sorcerer-master know you're ready.'

'You do that,' Noah said.

Before he'd closed the door behind him, Noah started humming her tonic. The firestone within her answered instantly, focusing heat at her ankles and wrists. It took several minutes but the bindings on her wrists finally gave way. She bent over, reaching for the ties around her ankles, which vanished at her touch.

Noah leapt from her chair. Still disoriented from being spun, she stumbled and crashed into the desk. She winced as pain flared in her hip. Ignoring it, she stretched over the piles of books towards the lamp. She picked it up gently and cradled it in both hands. Though Percival could arrive at any moment, Noah was captivated by the carving on the porcelain base.

A Pyranhi sorcerer.

The carving had been sculpted from young olluka wood, but had long since petrified. Fine etchings in the wood gave the creature's torso and head a shaggy fur covering. Ears peeked through the luxuriant mane atop its head. Green eyes, fashioned from what looked like jade, seemed to regard her with curiosity. Powerful arms were crossed in front of its chest and, in one hand, it held a wand. The tiny firestone rod glinted in the candlelight.

Noah opened the pocket on her smock and slid the lamp inside.

Click.

Noah buttoned her pocket before she turned around.

Percival strode into the room, wand raised menacingly. 'What are you doing?'

'Looking for something to read,' Noah said. 'I got bored waiting for you to come back.'

'How did you break your bonds?'

Noah inspected her wrists. 'Magic.'

Percival's lips pressed into a thin line. 'Whatever information the elves have sent you to collect,' he said, 'they won't get it.'

'Maybe not from me,' Noah said, 'but the elves will get what they're after. I'm not the only scout.'

Percival regarded her, eyes burning with malice. 'Not the only scout,' he murmured. Realisation, when it came, made him smile. 'The elves are coming here?'

Noah nodded.

Percival's smile broadened. 'That can mean only one thing,' he said. 'They have the pyrohm.'

Noah's stomach churned as Horatio's words came back to her. *Percival is wily and sadistic. His campaign against the dragon riders has seen our ranks reduced by two-thirds. If he finds out the elves are on their way bearing the pyrohm, he will seek to eliminate us before they get here.*

The sorcerer pointed his wand at her. '*That* changes things. I think I'd like to send the elves a message – and *you* will be my messenger.'

Noah rubbed her chin thoughtfully. 'For the right price, I'd consider it.'

Percival sneered. 'I will not pay you, slave. You will simply be doing the job the elves sent you to do.'

Noah sighed. 'And what would you have me tell them?'

'Well, as I see it, the elves have the pyrohm, but I control the other three pieces of the illestial. They can join me as equal partners or be vanquished by the might of Sorcerer-master Percival.'

'May I offer some advice on your wording there?' Noah said.

Percival waved dismissively. 'No.'

'Fine,' Noah said. 'I should warn you though – elves don't respond well to threats.'

'Just as I don't respond well to having spies sent into my realm,' Percival retorted, as he advanced on her. 'You can tell your—'

Noah grabbed a book from the desk and swung it at Percival's head. His eyes widened in surprise but he had no time to muster a defensive spell. Noah grunted as the book connected with the sorcerer's temple. He slumped to the floor.

'Sometimes you just have to keep it simple,' Noah said as she plucked the firestone wand from the unconscious man's hand.

Elvish words tumbled from her mouth. Noah visualised the rendez-vous point where Piper waited as she drew a doorway. Her heart pounded as a glittering ring appeared. Once it was whole, she jumped through.

'Noah!' Piper said. 'What are you doing?'

'Improvising,' Noah replied as she considered what to do with Percival's wand.

'Creating doorways here is dangerous. If Percival follows the trail …'

'Good point,' Noah said.

She stabbed the wand at the doorway to close it. As the circle shrivelled away, Noah pitched the wand through it. The firestone rod landed near the sorcerer's hand.

'Climb aboard,' Piper said once the doorway was gone. 'We must get back to Mt Jubilee quickly.'

Noah scampered up to her seat. 'Hopefully Percival won't figure out how I escaped.'

'You'd better hope Temperance doesn't find out either,' Piper said.

Chapter 21

Noah set the lamp on a flat rock and settled herself on a stool in front of it while Grainger lit the torches in the cavern. They were deep under Mt Jubilee, in an ancient hall that the dragon riders hadn't used in centuries. Noah's knees ached from the punishing six hour descent and she shivered in the chamber's cold embrace.

Brinn monitored proceedings from a ledge above Noah's head. 'It's fine there.'

'I still don't see how you think this is a book,' Noah said.

'It's a book,' Brinn said, 'because it contains information. It's a book of Pyranhi spells. You just need to learn how to read it.'

Even though Brinn had said the elves wouldn't be hasty in coming to Somyni with the illestial, Noah didn't think she had time to decipher a book in which there weren't actually any words. She studied the image of the Pyranhi sorcerer on the lamp's base.

'Show me something,' she said to the lamp.

The wooden figure wriggled off the lamp and jumped onto the floor. Noah scrambled backwards and tumbled off her stool. The miniature Pyranhi pointed his wand at her as she fought to regain her composure. Heart hammering inside her chest, Noah stared.

He stood erect but looked like a cross between a lion and a horse. The short, rust-coloured hair that covered his arms, hands, legs and feet was horse-like, as was his tail. His mane, claws and teeth would have been the envy of any lion and the shaggy fur that covered his body protected his modesty, saving him the bother of wearing clothes. He looked at Brinn and said something Noah didn't understand.

'Hello, Hildebrand,' Brinn said. 'It's good to see you again, too. This is Noah.'

Hildebrand rattled off another series of sounds, a combination of clicking and chittering.

'She's part dragon, part human,' Brinn said.

Noah imagined the Pyranhi's next question was probably "what's a human?".

Brinn leapt down onto the floor and sat beside Hildebrand. 'See for yourself,' she said.

Grainger righted Noah's stool before sitting on his. Noah sat beside him without taking her eyes off the animated wooden carving. Hildebrand levelled his wand at her head. Noah squeezed her eyes shut and clamped her hands to her head as her brain vibrated violently inside her skull. She felt as though she'd been engulfed by a swarm of enraged cicadas. Ribbons of pain raced down her arms and legs. Heat consumed her torso. Noah clenched her jaws, determined not to scream.

Then, as quickly as it had started, it stopped.

Noah opened her eyes. She checked her arms to make sure her skin hadn't peeled off and then peered at Hildebrand.

'You're a strange creature,' the Pyranhi said.

Noah frowned. 'You should talk.' She leaned forward. 'I couldn't understand you before, but I can now. What did you do to me?'

'He made a connection between you and him,' Brinn said.

Hildebrand turned to the cat and said, 'I could have explained it to her.'

Brinn licked her paw. 'Yes,' she said, 'but humans age quite quickly. She'd be dead long before you finished.'

Hildebrand smiled. 'You haven't changed at all, Temperance.'

'Of course not,' Brinn said. 'Why would I?'

Hildebrand shook his head as he turned to Grainger. 'And who's this?'

'Grainger Brimblecombe, Dragonsbane of Talisker,' Brinn said.

'Let's see what you're made of,' Hildebrand said, pointing his wand at Grainger.

Grainger's eyes widened but otherwise he remained perfectly still as Hildebrand tested him.

'No dragon in that one,' the Pyranhi said at last. Then he returned his attention to Noah. 'So this is your new champion, Temperance?'

Brinn swished her tail. 'Yes. And she's also your new apprentice.'

'Apprentice?' Hildebrand said. 'Do you think that's wise? Her dragon blood is strong but from what I can see, the human body is weak and the mind – very primitive.'

Noah glanced at Grainger. 'You'd think they'd have had this conversation *before* we could understand what they were saying, wouldn't you?'

Grainger shrugged. 'Well, look at it this way … they're probably not going to say anything behind our backs that they wouldn't say to our faces.'

'I guess not,' Noah said.

'Humans lack the strength of body and mind that the Pyranhi had,' Brinn said, 'but Noah … has proven resourceful and quite difficult to kill.'

'Sounds like a challenge,' Hildebrand said.

Noah folded her arms across her chest. 'I have enough enemies,' she said. 'I don't need you trying to knock me off, too.'

Brinn growled. 'We don't have time to mess about,' she said. 'Hildebrand, the last piece of the illestial has returned to Talisker and the elves are on their way here with it.'

Hildebrand tapped his wand against his cheek. He shivered. '*Noah's the 13th key?*'

Brinn nodded. 'Yes, she is.'

'Not what I expected,' he said, shaking his head.

Noah scooped him up in her hand and lifted him up to her eye level. 'Got a problem with that?'

'Nothing I can't resolve,' Hildebrand said, tapping her on the nose with his wand. He turned and pointed to Grainger. 'And what about him, Temperance?'

'Another apprentice,' Brinn said. 'You won't find anyone more dedicated to Talisker or more devoted to learning Pyranhi magic.'

'And what would you have me teach them?'

Grainger raised his hand. 'We need to contain Jong within the illestial long enough to transport him to the vortex.'

'What vortex?' Hildebrand asked.

Brinn took over the commentary again, giving the most concise version of her plan for Jong, the illestial and the vortex that Noah had heard yet. Hildebrand shook his head, his lustrous mane catching the torchlight as it swished from side to side.

'Let me see if I've got this,' Hildebrand said. 'You want to contain Jong inside the illestial and then take it through an elfin doorway to the portal cluster under Dragonhall. You're going to divert one of the pathways attached to the portal cluster so it is within range of the vortex … the idea being that you get close enough to throw the illestial in there … but no too close because you don't want to get sucked in with it?'

'Yes,' Brinn said.

Hildebrand scratched his ear with his wand. 'Okay. Let's get started then. Grainger, do you have a wand?'

'I have a baton,' Grainger said, pulling his device from one of his pockets.

After a moment's consideration, Hildebrand said, 'That will suffice.'

When Noah retrieved her viola, Hildebrand screwed up his face. 'What is that?'

'It's my key,' Noah said.

'What do you mean it's your key?' Hildebrand said. 'You *are* a key. Do you not use the firestone inside you for your magic?'

'Occasionally,' Noah admitted, 'but I'm better channelling it through my viola.'

Hildebrand's lips curled in disgust. 'Not anymore. You don't need a key *or* a wand, Noah. Learn what I teach you – Pyranhi magic will serve you well.'

♪♫

Noah wiped the perspiration from her forehead with her shirt sleeve.

'What's next?' Grainger asked.

Noah stared at him. Grainger was three times her age and had worked as hard as she had to master the spells Hildebrand had taught them so far, yet he'd barely raised a sweat. *He's not drawing on his own power like I am,* she thought.

'I've taught you what you'll need, you just need to practise … a lot,' Hildebrand said.

'You don't think we can do this, do you,' Grainger said.

'I don't think two of you will be enough,' Hildebrand said. 'Even *if* you master what I've taught you, the scale of what's required …'

'Brinn,' Noah said, 'what about the dragon riders? Can we train any of them?'

'They are brave and true warriors,' Brinn said, 'but unfortunately there is no talent for magic in them.'

Grainger reached out and squeezed Noah's shoulder. 'We'll just have to practise. You did really well with the whirlwind.'

Noah smiled. Hildebrand had taught them to conjure wind, control it and then contain it. Noah's slender wind spout had wound its way around the cavern like a belly-dancer, its gyrations dizzying and hypnotic. It was currently contained in an adjoining cave, awaiting her next command.

Brinn leapt up onto a ledge on the wall. 'One more lesson, Hildebrand,' she said. 'Teach them summoning.'

Summoning? Noah thought. Goosebumps broke out all over her body as adrenaline coursed through her. 'Gillette,' she whispered.

Grainger tapped his baton against his temple. '*This* is going to be great.'

'If by "great", you mean terrifying,' Brinn said, crossing her front paws, 'then I agree.'

Noah grimaced. 'If you're so worried about what we might summon, why are you still here?'

'It's *because* I'm so worried about what you might conjure up that I'm still here,' Brinn said.

Noah pointed her finger at the cat. 'As long as we don't summon Elani, I reckon we'll be fine,' she said. 'You and Jong are enough trouble. I can't imagine anything worse than the three of you together.'

'Then you clearly lack imagination,' Brinn retorted.

'Are we ready to begin?' Hildebrand said.

'I'm ready,' Grainger said. 'Noah?'

Noah nodded. 'I'm ready.'

Hildebrand clapped his hands twice. 'Very good,' he said. 'Firstly, we'll move back towards the wall, so we've got a clear space in the middle.'

Noah and Grainger followed Hildebrand to a spot directly across from Brinn. *If we stuff up and she has to save us, we're never going to hear the end of it,* Noah thought.

'Now,' Hildebrand said, 'let's start with something simple – a potato.'

'A potato?' Noah said, eyeing the expanse of open space in the cavern.

'A potato,' Hildebrand confirmed.

Noah looked up at Brinn. 'Brace yourself,' she called. 'This could be really terrifying.'

Brinn's tail twitched but she said nothing.

'The thing about summoning,' Hildebrand said, 'is that you can summon a *general* thing or a *specific* thing. For instance, I could summon just any old potato, or I could summon a specific potato if I knew its true name.'

'True name?' Grainger said.

Hildebrand nodded. 'There is great power in names,' he said, 'and the Pyranhi relied on this for summoning. If a Pyranhi sorcerer knew someone's – or some*thing's* – true name, he or she could summon them.'

'Like a particular dragon?' Noah said.

'Correct,' Hildebrand said. 'But it must be their true name.'

'You couldn't summon your dragon using the name Piper, Noah,' Brinn said. 'You'd have to use her true name.'

'But if I knew that,' Noah said, 'I could summon her to wherever I needed her?'

'Yes,' Hildebrand said, 'but the spell is very intricate – and if even the slightest thing were to go wrong and you didn't reconstruct your subject quite right – they would have to live with the "defect" for the rest of their lives. I don't recommend you do it. Try a horse instead.'

Noah frowned. 'Horses don't fly.'

'Horses with wings do,' Grainger said.

'And horses run faster than dragons do,' Hildebrand added.

'Can you teach us to summon a flying horse?' Grainger asked.

Hildebrand nodded as he readied his pin-like wand. 'We'll get to that. Let's start with a potato though – and work our way up.'

'Just start with the horse,' Brinn said. 'We're on the clock here.'

'Okay,' the Pyranhi sorcerer said, 'but you'll have to listen *very* carefully. There is a lot of detail in this spell.'

Noah closed her eyes to help her concentrate on the sounds first. She pictured a plain piece of fabric and, as Hildebrand wove the spell, she catalogued the barks, clicks and chirrups as best she could with different colours, shapes and patterns. This spell was much more involved than any of the others Hildebrand had taught them and when he was done, Noah opened her eyes to see his creation.

A dappled grey and white horse extended its wings, testing them tentatively, and whinnied. Noah reached out and stroked its velvety muzzle.

'She's beautiful,' Noah murmured, feeling the creature's warm breath on her hand.

'Could a person really ride her?' Grainger asked.

'A child would be fine on this one,' Hildebrand said, 'but she wouldn't get far carrying an adult.'

The Pyranhi chittered as he waved his wand. Particles like luminous bubbles drifted from the horse's mane and floated towards the ceiling, slowly at first but they soon became a gushing stream. Noah looked away, not wanting to witness the creature's demise. She kept her eyes on Grainger.

Once the horse was gone, Grainger rubbed his chin. 'I'd need to hear the spell again.'

'Maybe we could break it into sections?' Noah said, frowning. 'I can't keep track of this one. It's kind of … slippery.'

'We're "constructing" the horse from the bottom up,' Hildebrand explained. 'Start with the hooves and legs – remembering to build strong limbs with powerful muscles. Then move onto the body and wings. Head last.'

'Right. Do it again,' Noah said.

Hildebrand repeated the spell, in sections, several more times.

Grainger twitched his baton. 'Ready to give it a go, Noah?'

'Sure,' Noah said. 'What could possibly go wrong?'

Brinn stood up on her ledge and stretched. 'Do you want me to start with the most likely or least likely thing that could go wrong?'

Noah ignored the cat, instead concentrating on a spot in the middle of the floor. Visualising the fabric she'd constructed in her mind for the spell, she launched into it. The sounds were difficult for her mouth to make and tracing the wand movements with her index finger was awkward, but she persevered. When hooves shimmered into view on the floor, Noah's heart beat faster. *It's working,* she thought. The legs appeared next, but her growing excitement made it difficult to concentrate on the spell. A draught ruffled Noah's hair as invisible particles rushed past her to take their place in her creation.

Noah scowled. The animal was smaller than she'd anticipated. She wouldn't be able to ride this horse. Its body was about the size of a pillow and its scrawny legs would only have come up to her knees. *Keep going,* she told herself. *You have to start somewhere.*

The distraction cost her as she strove to create the wings and head. When she was finished, she lowered her hands, frowning in consternation. Brinn slunk towards the creature, stopping a metre away from it.

'It looks like a goat with dragonfly wings,' Hildebrand said.

Grainger patted her shoulder. 'I think it's an admirable first attempt.'

Noah gestured to Brinn. 'Move back,' she said. 'I'm going to try to fix it.'

'I rather think you should put this one out of its misery,' Brinn said, 'and start again.'

Noah saw the sense in the cat's suggestion but looking into the creature's lopsided eyes, she knew she couldn't destroy it. She'd created a living thing. It was now her responsibility. Noah chewed her lip as she considered where to start.

'Fix the wings first,' Hildebrand suggested, 'and then the size.'

'Repeat the wing part for me again,' Noah said.

She listened carefully, checking it against her mental pattern. After making the necessary amendments, she got to work. The insect-like wings transformed into something more bird-like and the animal flapped its new appendages in delight. Heartened, Noah turned her attention to size. With long, vertical finger strokes, she lengthened its legs and then bulked out its muscles. She did the same for its body, neck and head.

'That actually looks like a horse,' Grainger said.

Noah smiled as she put the finishing touches on her spell, but as she was about to utter the final cadence, something in her mental pattern changed. The geometric shapes swirled into jagged, irregular figures. Noah hesitated. Her creation wavered, like she was looking at it through a heat haze. *I have to finish the spell.* She followed her mental pattern through a series of odd clicks and growls.

'Noah,' Hildebrand said, 'what are you doing?'

The horse continued growing as its coat turned from brown to black. Smoke curled from its body and its eyes glowed red. Three sets of gruesome horns sprouted from the sides of its head.

Brinn hissed. 'Noah! Stop!'

Noah shook her head. The spell had hold of her. She couldn't stop. Her arm moved of its own accord and ancient, foreign words tumbled from her mouth. The creature's body elongated as its wings sprouted lethal spines.

Grainger seized Noah's wrist but it was too late. Though the stench of sulphur made her gag, Noah didn't take her eyes off the demon that had hijacked her spell. It towered over her, bristling with menace.

'Thank you,' the creature said. 'It's good to be whole again.'

Brinn crouched just out of strike range of the creature's barbed tail. 'Be gone, demon,' she said. 'You're not welcome here.'

'Ah, Temperance,' it said. 'Meddling again, I see. Did the death of your precious Pyranhi disciples teach you nothing?'

Brinn glared at the demon but said nothing.

The creature stretched its wings. 'I see you have some new friends now,' it said. 'You haven't got these poor souls chasing around after the pyrohm too, have you?'

'That's no concern of yours,' Brinn growled.

'I think it is,' the demon said. 'You almost destroyed the world last time and I'd hate to think you might succeed this time. I like coming here.'

Brinn hissed. 'You've already outstayed your welcome, dem—'

Without warning, the demon sprang at Noah, skittling Grainger and Hildebrand out of the way with its tail as it reached for her. Grainger hit his head on the cavern wall before slumping to the floor on top of Hildebrand. The demon's claws closed around Noah's upper arms and it lifted her into the air.

Noah grunted. 'Put me down.'

She glanced below her. Grainger lay still on the floor while Brinn dodged the demon's sweeping, barbed tail.

'You look tasty,' the monster said.

'I'm hard to swallow,' Noah said, as she tried to wriggle free of the creature's grip.

It bared its fangs. 'I promise I'll chew you up properly first.'

'That's generally when the trouble starts,' Noah said, wincing as claws pierced her flesh. 'I've got firestone in my veins.'

The demon cocked its head to one side and regarded her with blazing red eyes. 'Is that so,' it said. 'Well, that *does* change things. I'll just kill you so you can't destroy me … and then I'll eat your friend instead.'

'He'll taste worse than me,' Noah said.

Hildebrand began chanting in ancient Pyranhi and the demon shook its head.

'Stop that!' it roared.

Noah, straining to look over her shoulder, saw Hildebrand race across the floor away from Grainger, chanting and waving his wand as he went. The demon lifted his foot and stomped on the Pyranhi spell-master.

'*No!*' Noah cried.

The demon twisted its foot from side to side, grinding Hildebrand's body to dust on the rocky floor.

Brinn appeared on top of the demon's head. 'Noah!' she said.

Noah looked at her, surprised the cat had made it there without the monster noticing.

'Time to *wind* this up,' Brinn said.

'You don't say!' Noah retorted. 'But I'm a little stuck, in case you hadn't noticed.'

'Temperance,' the demon said, releasing one of Noah's arms so it could swat at Brinn, 'you are annoying me.'

As the demon tried to dislodge its feline parasite, Brinn said, 'I sense the *wind* of change coming.'

'Oh, *wind*,' Noah said. 'Gotcha.'

'Finally!' Brinn said as she leapt onto a nearby ledge and scampered away.

Noah chanted softly as she waved her index finger. The demon jolted her in its new quest to snare Grainger for its supper so controlling her strokes was difficult, but her whirlwind answered her call. It entered the cavern tail first, the upper spout following like a limbo dancer under the low entranceway.

The demon growled. Noah chanted a few phrases, hoping to shield Grainger's unconscious body with the whirlwind. But the monster shook her, compromising her hand motion. The twister tightened and pitched left.

'Crap!' Noah said as the whirlwind dragged Grainger into the demon's path.

She made a quick adjustment and the whirlwind skated right again, taking Grainger with it. The demon snarled in frustration and flapped its wings, wrenching Noah's arm painfully as it took to the air. It turned and flew a few metres away from the gyrating wind spout before banking sharply to its left.

The demon skirted the whirlwind and dived towards Grainger. Noah felt faint from the pain in her arm, but she focused on her spell. She tightened the twister's grip on Grainger and then sent the whirlwind back to the adjoining cave.

The demon howled as its dinner disappeared and it threw Noah at the wall.

'Aaaaaargh!' she screamed as she sailed through the air.

Noah heard the crunch as her shoulder slammed against the wall and the explosion of pain blinded her momentarily. Her head hit something soft. She slid to the floor as Brinn landed beside her.

Noah groaned.

'You're welcome,' Brinn said. 'Now get up. You need to destroy the demon.'

'Is Grainger okay?' Noah said, clutching her shoulder.

'Safe for now,' Brinn said, 'but *you're* not.'

Noah looked up and shuddered. The demon, deprived of its dinner and infuriated to find Noah still alive, slunk towards her on all fours. Barely able to lift her right arm, she twitched her finger to recall her whirlwind. Once it cleared the entranceway, she chanted one phrase over and over to constrict the spout.

'More speed, Noah,' Brinn said. 'Much more.'

The demon was almost upon her. Noah recited the sounds Hildebrand had taught her and jerked her finger back and forth. She tensed her leg muscles, pressing her back against the wall as the whirlwind's intensity increased. The twister caught the monster's tail.

'You can't do this to me!' the demon roared.

Its talons scored the cavern floor as it scrabbled to resist the twister's pull. Noah kept chanting and the whirlwind grew.

'More,' Brinn said.

'I can't,' Noah snapped. '*I'll* get sucked into it too.'

Brinn flopped across Noah's lap. 'Now … do it.'

'You're much heavier than you look,' Noah said.

Brinn hissed. 'Just get on with it.'

Noah barked the spell, ignoring the hair that stuck in her mouth as the driving wind whipped it across her face. The whirlwind wobbled, then billowed, swallowing the demon. Mesmerised, Noah watched the monster being churned around inside the twister.

'You've caught it,' Brinn said. 'Now, destroy it.'

Without hesitation, Noah used the shearing wind to shred the demon. Once that job was done, she dismantled the whirlwind. As the last wisps of wind carried away the particles she'd borrowed for her spells, Noah relaxed her hand and slumped against the wall. Silence returned to the cavern.

'I think that's enough for today,' Brinn said.

Noah reached into a pocket on her trousers, wincing as pain shot through her shoulder. She pulled out the Pyranhi lamp. The flame was out. Gently, she placed the lamp on the floor. Hildebrand's outline was visible on the porcelain but his carving would never return.

'I killed him,' she whispered.

'He wasn't alive,' Brinn said. 'It's a book. An animated book.'

Noah sighed. 'Not anymore.'

'No,' Brinn said. 'Not anymore.'

Chapter 22

Noah lowered her hammer and chisel. With sweat trickling down her back, she massaged her injured shoulder as she surveyed her work. Deep under the mountain, in the wall of a dark cave, she'd located a substantial vein of firestone. She shuddered, wishing Grainger had been well enough to join her. After a waning and a gleaming he was still very unsteady on his feet following his encounter with the demon and certainly in no shape for summoning.

While Emir, Raven and the dragon riders laboured to reinforce Mt Jubilee's defences in readiness for Percival's assault, Noah focused on her personal quest. The muted lavender, blue and gold in this part of the dragonscale vein twinkled in the dancing light of Noah's torch. She reached out, caressing the stone with her fingers. The colours swirled at her touch.

'The coast is still clear,' Piper called from the entranceway.

Brinn growled. 'Of course it is,' she said. 'No one has been down here for thousands of years.'

'One can't be too careful,' Piper said.

Ignoring the banter, Noah inhaled deeply and released her breath slowly. Her preference was to enter the firestone, find Gillette and then extract him, but Jong would catch her. The only way to draw Gillette out was to use the summoning spell Hildebrand had taught her.

'Whenever you're ready, Noah,' Brinn said.

Noah closed her eyes and pushed her worries aside. She visualised the mental pattern she'd created for the spell, reviewing the sounds the shapes represented. Summoning a specific person was difficult and dangerous. Silently, she practised her hand movements – over and over. She needed to summon every fibre of Gillette's being and reconstruct it perfectly. If she didn't, Gillette wouldn't be himself. As if recreating a person wasn't challenging enough, she also needed to guard against interference. She didn't want him to turn into a demon like the horse had.

You need a person's true name, Hildebrand had said.

Noah's heart hammered against her ribcage. She didn't know anything about 'true names'. *Surely a musical signature is the same thing?* she thought. Everyone on Talisker had a unique musical signature and though Noah's raiki training had given her some expertise in manipulating them, she had years more study ahead of her before she could claim to be a true expert.

'Don't *doubt,*' Brinn said, 'just *do.*'

Noah opened her eyes. 'Easy for you to say,' she said. 'Gillette's life isn't in your hands, is it?'

'Luckily, because I don't have hands,' Brinn said. 'By the way, I think you should have your viola ready … just in case.'

'Just in case what?'

'Just in case you need to fix something,' Brinn said. 'You're much better at raiki than at Pyranhi magic.'

'I guess it couldn't hurt.'

Brinn purred. 'You're welcome.'

Noah took her viola case from her trouser pocket and set it on the floor beside her. She opened the lid and inserted her firestone slider into the bridge. Noah knew now that she didn't need the slider, but it would conserve her own energy stores.

'Now get started,' Brinn said.

Please let this work, Noah thought.

She pushed all other thoughts aside and uttered the opening phrase of the Pyranhi spell. Brinn would monitor the firestone window for signs of Jong and let her know of anything untoward in the cave behind her.

Like she'd done with the horse, Noah started with Gillette's feet. She adjusted the pitch and tempo of her incantations to incorporate the boy's musical signature. Long, sweeping finger strokes were needed for his legs. As Noah moulded his lower limbs, panic gripped her. Had Gillette grown while he'd been in captivity? She decided that he probably had and added a little extra length to what she remembered.

Noah took her time with his torso. All his organs needed to be in the correct position and be properly connected. The construction of such an intricate system while weaving in his musical signature as she went, took immense concentration. Noah's head pounded with the effort.

Once she'd finished his arms, Noah moved onto his head. Though she was pleased with what she'd done so far, this would be the most difficult part. Only when his head was complete would she know if she'd succeeded.

Muscle cramps in Noah's arms and shoulders tormented her, but there was no stopping to stretch them out. She'd gotten Gillette into this mess; she had to get him out. His return – whole and hale – was the only way to extinguish her debt. She chanted until her throat was raw and then chanted some more. The overlay of his musical signature on her mental template made the spell excruciatingly complex.

Keep going, she told herself. *Not far to go now.*

Noah scoured out every bit of stubborn within herself to finish her work, and when she was done, she slumped onto the cool, dirt floor with barely enough energy for another breath.

'Where are my clothes?' a voice cried.

Noah didn't look up. She didn't have the strength to lift her head. Something tugged at one of the pockets on her trousers but she ignored it.

'Oh. Thanks, cat.'

Noah felt a hand on her arm.

'Noah? Is it really you?'

Noah opened her eyes, smiling as she stared at the boy's face.

'You got me out!' Gillette said.

'Mmm.'

Gillette hooked his arms under her armpits.

'No!' Noah said. 'Sore shoulder. I'll move.' She dragged herself into a sitting position against the wall. 'That's a lovely dress, by the way, Gillette, but not really your colour.'

Gillette's cheeks reddened. 'Yeah, well … the cat gave it to me.'

Noah's head rolled sideways until she could look at Brinn. 'You're terrible.'

Brinn said nothing, but pawed at one of the pockets on Noah's trousers.

Why won't she just talk? Noah wondered. *I'm too tired for this.*

'Gillette,' Noah said, 'she wants you to get something out of my pocket.'

The boy rummaged in her pocket and retrieved a water skin. He opened it and dribbled a few drops of water onto Noah's parched lips. She licked it unenthusiastically. She needed it, but it was too much effort.

'You have some,' Noah said, leaning her head back against the wall and closing her eyes.

Gillette trickled water on her scalp. 'I think you need it more than I do.'

Noah sighed contentedly. Gillette was back, there was no sign of demons and the cool water on her head told her she'd survived the experience.

'So, where are we?' Gillette asked.

'Somyni,' Noah said.

'Where's that?'

'Underground.'

'Is Dad here?'

'No.'

'Emir?'

'Yes.'

'Can I see him?'

'Soon.'

Piper's voice cut in. 'Did you do it, Noah?'

'Who's that?' Gillette said.

'Piper,' Noah said. 'My dragon.'

More water streamed over Noah's head and down her face. 'Right,' Gillette said. 'You've lost it, haven't you?'

Noah opened her eyes and pushed his arm away. 'Go and look if you don't believe me.'

Gillette dropped the water skin into her lap. 'I reckon I will.'

Noah watched him until he disappeared around a rocky outcrop, and then waited. She'd only just had time to realise Brinn was gone again when Gillette cried out.

'Holy crackers!'

Noah smiled as Gillette raced back into the cave, wide-eyed.

'There's a dragon out there,' he said. 'A real one!'

Piper's head appeared around the rock. 'Thanks for noticing,' she said, snorting a plume of smoke into the cave.

'Stop that,' Noah said. 'We'll suffocate if you keep doing that.'

Gillette reached out a tentative hand and stroked Piper's neck. 'Whoa!' he said. 'That's so cool.'

'I'm Piper,' the dragon said. 'Hopefully you're Gillette?'

Noah rolled her eyes. 'Yes, Piper. This is Gillette. I didn't just summon up a random twelve-year-old.'

'I'm twelve now?' Gillette said, not taking his eyes off the dragon. 'How long have I been away?'

'Eighteen months,' Noah said.

'Man, I had two birthdays,' Gillette said, shaking his head, 'and Jong didn't even get me a present.'

'I'm pretty sure—' Noah began before an unwelcome voice intruded.

'—that you didn't deserve a present,' Jong finished.

Noah scanned the cavern as Gillette flinched, but the god was nowhere to be seen.

'Hello, Noah,' Jong said. 'You've made it to Somyni, I see.'

'Yes,' she said.

'And you've rescued Gillette. Clever girl.'

Small pieces of rock cascaded down the walls as Jong's voice rattled around the cave. *He can't break free yet,* Noah thought, *but he's obviously going to push the boundaries.* Talking like this threatened the cavern's structure. It would collapse if he disturbed the foundations too much.

Noah waved at Piper. 'Go! Take Gillette!' she hissed. 'Go *now!*'

Gillette didn't hesitate. He dashed out of the cave.

'Did you forget something, Noah?' Jong asked. 'I asked you to bring me the pyrohm.'

'I didn't forget it,' she said. 'The elves stole it. They'll bring it here though. The pyrohm *will* be here.'

The god's guttural rumble shook the cavern. 'Hmm.'

Noah clenched her fists. 'You're not going to win,' she said. 'I'm going to get the pyrohm back and when I do, you're going to be sorry.'

Jong chuckled. 'I doubt that, Noah. In all the aeons of my existence, I haven't yet found anything to be sorry for. In fact, I will enjoy destroying you.'

'I'm pretty hard to kill,' Noah said.

'*Mortals* find you hard to kill,' Jong said. 'I'm a god – I won't have any trouble.'

Noah's blood ran hot, and it had nothing to do with the firestone in her veins. She took a deep breath and let it out slowly. *Calm,* she thought. *I need to be calm.*

'Well,' she said. 'I suppose I should be flattered.'

There was a pause before Jong said, 'Flattered?'

'You seem to think so little of mortals – of humans,' Noah said, 'and yet you'll *enjoy* killing me. Makes me feel pretty special really.'

Jong snorted. The cavern rattled again.

'It's not about you,' he said. 'It's about my sister. Temperance has grown fond of you, so by destroying you, I can put her in her place.'

Noah laughed.

'You think that's funny?' Jong said.

'Yes, I do,' Noah said, nodding. 'This is just sibling rivalry. You think humans are petty – *you're* no better.'

'Your death is certain,' Jong said coldly, 'but I've yet to decide on the *manner* of your death. You might consider that before you say anything else.'

Noah did consider it and decided she didn't want to be buried alive in a cave. Finally, she said, 'We're done here.'

Chapter 23

'Hold on!' Piper called. 'Mt Jubilee ahead. We're coming in to land.'

Noah held on as best she could with only one good arm. Her injured shoulder ached mercilessly but her main concern was for Gillette. It would be a grave injustice to be rescued from Jong's clutches only to then plummet from a dragon's back. Noah didn't fancy having to explain that to Emir.

On one of the mountain's lower landing platforms, Emir waited with Raven. They'd both be excited to see Gillette. Noah's heart swelled with joy. So much that had happened recently made her heart sore, but today they had something to celebrate. Regardless of the trials ahead, Noah intended to savour this victory.

Piper had barely touched down when Gillette slid from the dragon's back. Emir and Raven were ready to help him but their assistance wasn't required. Noah watched Gillette give his uncle and army commander Leninstar's salute. Emir and Gillette then shook hands and clapped each other on the shoulder. No hugging, Noah noticed. Though only twelve, Gillette seemed older. He was tall for his age and had spent a good deal of time with Raven's soldiers before his kidnapping by King Franco. And his time as a hostage had also affected him. Tears welled in Noah's eyes and she made no attempt to wipe them away.

Emir reached up to help Noah down from Piper's back. Once she was on solid ground, he kissed her tenderly.

'You're amazing,' he whispered. 'I'm so glad you're both safe.'

'We're *all* safe,' Piper said.

'She has exceptional hearing,' Emir said.

'Yes,' Noah agreed. 'Just remember that.'

Raven squeezed her uninjured shoulder. 'Good job, Sis,' he said. 'I knew you'd do it.'

'I'm glad it's finally done,' Noah said. 'I really need to rest now though.'

Chain and Vespa flew overhead and beckoned for Piper to follow them.

'See you soon, Noah,' Piper said as she launched herself into the air. 'Rest up.'

Noah saluted with her good arm before turning to Emir. She frowned. 'Okay, what is it now?'

Emir raised an eyebrow. 'What do you mean?'

Noah's eyes narrowed as she glanced between her boyfriend and her brother. 'You both have a look – there's something going on. What is it?'

'We're just so happy you're both back,' Raven said.

'No,' Noah said. 'There's more.'

Raven sighed. 'You're no fun sometimes, Noah. You know that?'

'So, what is going on?'

'A miracle,' Emir said. 'Another miracle, I mean. You rescuing Gillette was obviously a miracle, but we had another one here while you were gone.'

'Brinn's in a good mood?' Noah guessed.

Emir smiled. 'Sorry to disappoint you, Noah, but you're going to have to wait a bit longer for that one.'

Noah chewed her bottom lip. 'Grainger's recovered?'

Both Emir and Raven shook their heads.

'Is my dad here?' Gillette said.

Emir and Raven looked at each other before turning to him.

'He is,' Emir said, 'and he's brought a few friends.'

Noah's knees felt like they might give way. 'Who?' she whispered. 'Who else is here?'

Emir shook his head. 'We're not telling, are we Raven?'

'Nope,' Raven said. 'She'll have to come inside and see for herself.'

'Well, what the hell are we waiting for?' Noah said. 'Let's go!'

'You don't want to bathe first?' Raven said.

Noah swatted him on the arm. 'No! If they are true friends, they won't care that I'm a bit grimy.'

'Fine,' Emir said, taking her hand. 'Come along then.'

Noah shuffled along at Emir's side. Though she wanted to run, her exhaustion meant she could barely walk.

When they reached a large wooden door, Emir stopped. 'Close your eyes,' he said. 'You too, Gillette.'

Noah squeezed her eyes closed. 'Hurry up!' she pleaded.

She heard the hinges grind before Emir led her forward. 'Open your eyes.'

Noah scanned the crowd, eyes wide and mouth agape. 'How did you all get here?'

Chase and Montana rushed to her first.

'You didn't really think we'd abandon you, did you?' Montana said.

Chase hugged her. 'I had to check up on you,' she whispered in Noah's ear.

'Chase, why are you here?' Noah said. 'This is seriously dangerous. What about your baby?'

Chase pulled back and looked Noah in the eye. 'I need to make sure there is going to be a world for my baby to be born into. I have as much right to fight for it as you do!'

Ardis appeared at his wife's side, dressed in his warrior's uniform. 'I tried to keep her away, but you know how she is.'

Noah smiled. 'Yes, I do. So by the look of you, you're here in your official capacity as an Elani warrior, not as Chase's escort?'

Ardis nodded. 'The high priestess has brought her army.'

Noah gasped and stared at Montana. 'You did?'

'You need fighters don't you?' Montana said.

Noah laughed. 'Yes, we do!'

Jaxon appeared beside Noah, wrapped one arm around her and kissed her forehead. 'You're the best, Noah. I can't thank you enough for rescuing my son.'

'Believe me,' Noah said, 'no one is more relieved than me to have Gillette back.'

From behind her, someone ruffled her hair. Noah spun round to find Sachin grinning at her.

'Surprise!' he said.

Noah shook her head. 'I didn't think you'd be able to tear yourself away from the Academy, Chief Examiner! But I am so glad you're here.'

'Yeah, well let's wrap this thing up as quickly as we can. I've left Alan in charge …'

Noah's eyes widened. 'You left *Alan* in charge?'

Sachin raised his hands in surrender. 'Elani knows I didn't want to, but it was the only way I could keep him from coming here. He really wanted to be here for you, and since "you-know-who" is here too …'

Jacin popped up beside Sachin, and Emir and Raven each clapped a restraining hand on his shoulders.

'No hugging,' Emir said. 'She's injured.'

'Totally understand,' Jacin said, 'but I'm here to fix that shoulder – among other things – and then I'll get my hug.'

'And what will your girlfriend think of that?' Sachin asked.

Noah's eyebrows both shot up. 'Girlfriend? You have a girlfriend? How long have I been gone?'

When Avril appeared at Jacin's side and took his hand in hers, Noah's heart lurched.

'Seriously?' Noah said.

Jacin winked at her. 'You're not jealous are you, Noah?'

Noah snorted. 'Don't be ridiculous.'

'You've only got yourself to blame, Noah,' Sachin said. 'You're the one who gave her to him.'

Avril frowned. 'I'm not an object.'

'No,' Noah said, 'you were a *prisoner* – a prisoner that's supposed to be *secured*.'

Silence cloaked the room as all conversation and celebration ceased.

'You can trust her, Noah,' Jacin said.

Noah inhaled deeply, aware that everyone was watching her. 'Trust is earned.'

'I'm not my cousin,' Avril said.

'She's nothing like Orville,' Jacin added.

'Jacin, how can you know that?' Noah said. 'You never even met Orville.'

Jacin's smile faded. Noah had rarely seen him look so serious. 'Maybe not,' he said, 'but I know *her*. Do you not trust my judgement?'

Noah's breath caught in her throat. Jacin had been one of her advisers in Carai – she wouldn't have survived the goblin city without him. He'd risked his life for her countless times. He'd been her raiki apprentice, helping her find a cure for ilanxis worm poisoning. His loyalty was beyond question.

'Of course I trust you,' Noah said at last.

'Yes, yes,' another voice said. 'Very touching, but we have work to do.'

A path cleared for King Catriona as she made her way towards Noah.

'Your Highness,' Noah said, bowing her head. 'I am surprised to see *you* here.'

'Well, someone had to escort my army here,' Catriona said, 'since my Army Commander was conspicuously absent.'

Noah noted Catriona's military dress. This king was no figurehead. She'd fight alongside Raven and her army. In a flagrant breach of protocol, Raven put his arm around Catriona's waist.

'The king is right,' Raven said. 'We have work to do. The fight is coming to us.'

Montana nodded. 'We have eight thousand warriors awaiting instructions – and we need to discuss our strategy with the dragon riders.'

Catriona scanned the room. 'And where is this Brinn character I've been hearing about?'

'You'll meet her soon,' Raven said.

That's one meeting I don't want to be at, Noah thought.

Jaxon waved a journal in the air as he came to stand beside Montana. 'Can I just say something?'

Emir nodded to his brother. 'Of course. Go ahead.'

Jaxon scanned the faces of everyone in the room before he spoke again. 'Before we all go off to fight,' he said, 'I just wanted to share a

story with you all.' He tapped the journal. 'A story that my son wrote –
his take on how this world was created.'

Gillette groaned. 'Come on, Dad. It was just a stupid homework
task. Do you really have to read that?'

'It's a great story, Gillette,' Noah said. 'You were really proud of it
when you wrote it.'

'I want to hear it,' Chase said. 'I love stories.'

Jaxon nodded. 'Gillette wrote this story the day before I was captured
by goblins at the t'Amos mine,' he said. 'I was poisoned by ilanxis worm
and am lucky to be alive. It's only because of Noah, Sachin, Jacin and
Alan that I am standing here talking to you today. It took them a year to
find a cure – and to be honest it's incredible that a cure was even possible.'

Those who had seen the condition of the poisoned miners nodded.

'By the time I was healed, Gillette was long gone,' Jaxon continued.
'He'd been abducted by King Franco and then taken hostage by Jong.
Every day since my recovery I have read this story' – he flicked through
the pages in the journal – 'and today, it seems fitting that I share it with
you all – a reminder of what we're fighting for.'

Chase clapped as Jaxon cleared his throat and read from Gillette's
journal.

*Jong drew his sword as he stomped across the frozen ground towards
his brother.*

'What's going on here?' he demanded.

'I won't be part of your destruction anymore, Jong,' Xan said.

'But I am your master,' Jong said. 'If I say you must, then you must.'

'I am no longer your servant,' the dragon said.

*'Why not? We've been destroying failed worlds – like this one – for
ages. Why the change of heart?'*

Elani spoke. 'They weren't all failed, Jong.'

*'Life could come back here,' Xan said. 'There is hope. That's what
Elani has showed me.'*

Jong spat. 'Life? Hope? Absolute rubbish!'

*'You should change your ways, Jong,' Elani said. 'This is your
chance to be a creator rather than a destroyer. Work with us.'*

'Us? Us!' Jong screamed in rage. 'There is no US!'

'Calm down,' Elani said.

'Fight me,' he said, challenging Elani with his lethal sword.

Elani shook his head. 'No. I won't fight.'

Anger exploded inside Jong and he lunged at his brother. 'If you won't fight, then you will DIE!'

Xan stepped in between the two gods. 'Stop!' she commanded.

Jong slashed at the dragon and his sword scraped across her scales. Sparks flew. The god overbalanced and fell over, skidding on the icy ground. He stood up. He was really angry now.

'Jong, you don't need to do this,' Xan said.

Jong set his stance and raised his sword ready to strike. 'Stand aside, Xan. This is between me and my brother.'

The dragon crouched. 'If you want him, you'll have to get through me first.'

'Okay,' Jong said and thrust his sword at her shining scales.

Xan swiped at him with her claw, easily blocking him. Jong kept his balance. He slid one foot across the other as he looked for a better position. He needed to find a soft spot to strike. Unfortunately it was cloudy so he couldn't use the sun to blind his opponent. Xan lashed out with her talons and Jong parried. Be patient, Jong told himself.

Jong and Xan circled each other while Elani watched on. Jong kept his sword raised as Xan swished her long tail. Suddenly, Xan crouched and then sprang at Jong. At last, Jong thought. He ran forward and caught the dragon by surprise. As Xan landed, Jong raised his sword over his head and it pierced the dragon through her shoulder joint. Jong twisted and wrenched his sword, trying to cut off Xan's front leg. The dragon roared in pain as she collapsed on the ground. Jong jumped out of the way just in time and then stabbed Xan in the eye.

But Jong underestimated the dragon. Xan flicked her head up and he was thrown into the air. Up and up he went, still clutching his *sword … and then down and down again. He looked down and screamed. The dragon's open mouth was below him.*

When Jong landed in Xan's mouth she swallowed him instantly and then collapsed on the ground again.

'Help me,' she said to Elani. 'Jong is still fighting. Help me to stop him escaping.'

Elani patted the dragon's head. 'I will put you to sleep and then remake this world around you, Xan,' he said. 'You will be safe and Jong will not escape. And even better – your blood and scales will warm up this world and life will return.'

Xan wheezed a puff of smoke. 'Do it,' she said. 'Do it.'

And that is how Talisker was created.

Jaxon turned the journal around so his audience could see the script.

'Actually, you can see where "the end" has been crossed out,' he said, 'and then replaced with "the beginning".'

Chase put her arm around Gillette. 'That is a wonderful story,' she said. 'Truly wonderful.'

Gillette's cheeks flushed red as he mumbled his thanks.

'That *was* the beginning of Talisker,' Montana said, 'and now it's time for a *new* beginning. What we fight for now is a world free of Jong and the constant threat that he poses.'

'Exactly,' Raven said. 'Catriona, Emir, Montana, Ardis, Jaxon and Gillette will accompany me to meet with the dragon elders to coordinate our troops.'

Emir nodded. 'Chase, Sachin, Jacin and Avril – go with Noah. See if you can get her and Grainger back on deck. We're going to need them.'

Chase put her arm around Noah, steering her towards the door.

'I just need a good sleep,' Noah said.

'Piffle,' Chase said. 'You need a lot of work on that shoulder by the look of it.'

'I'll take care of that,' Jacin boasted, waving a baton similar to Grainger's. 'If I can get eight thousand warriors to Somyni, fixing a dodgy shoulder should be a cinch.'

Chapter 24

Noah studied herself in the wall mirror. Olive's face stared back at her, thanks to Jacin's concealment spell. Undercover as a servant in Lord Ascit's house in Olive's place, Noah frowned as she despaired of her outfit for Somyni's most prestigious social event – the Harvest End Ball. The puffy, frilly lilac dress was a perfect fit, but that was all it had going for it. *I feel like I'm dressed for a fancy dress party rather than a high society event,* Noah thought.

She turned her head slightly to let the light shine on her neck where her brand had been. Jacin had removed Talyn's leaf motif when he'd healed her shoulder. She jiggled her shoulder. A slight twinge, but otherwise fine.

'I'll need to be in good shape,' she murmured to herself. 'Tonight could go really wrong.'

Noah picked up the white velvet choker from the bedside table and undid the clasp, but a knock at the door interrupted her preparations.

'Who is it?' she called.

'It's me,' the voice said.

Noah shook her head. 'Come in.'

The door creaked opened and Reuben's face appeared. The sole heir to Somyni's whisky empire tucked an errant lock of his golden hair behind his ear as he slipped inside the small room and closed the door behind him. His hazel eyes drank her in as he crossed the floor.

'Ready for my parents' boring party?' he said, taking her hands and kissing her cheek.

'Almost,' Noah said.

'Olive, you look stunning,' he whispered.

Noah smiled. 'Thanks. You look pretty dashing yourself.'

Taking the necklace from her, he said, 'May I?'

Noah raised an eyebrow. 'To be honest, I don't think it goes with your outfit.'

'Very funny,' he said. 'Turn around.'

Noah spun on the balls of her feet to face the mirror again. Reuben stood behind her, so close that she could feel the heat from his chest against her back. He looped the choker over her head and secured the clasp at her nape. Once his task was done, he rested his hands on her shoulders and kissed her neck, just below her ear.

Noah froze. Though thankful she had a Pyranhi spell rather than a flimsy glamour to protect her identity, she didn't want to spend the entire evening fending off Reuben. She knew Olive had subtle ways of deflecting Lord Ascit's son's advances, but Noah was out of her depth. Jacin was the only one who'd ever made any unwanted advances towards her and she hadn't needed to be subtle to deflect him. Being king had had some advantages.

Reuben slid his hands down her arms and stepped back.

Noah turned. 'Shall we go?'

'Let's,' he said. 'The sooner we get there, the sooner we can leave – and find a real party to go to.'

Reuben took her hand and escorted her to the banquet hall. About the size of a small football field, the hall was lavishly decorated. Lanterns and ribbons adorned the ceiling while the tables sported gleaming silver cutlery, sparkling crystal goblets and gold-trimmed white crockery.

'We're over the far side,' Reuben said, 'with a view of the valley. Come see.'

Noah surveyed the room as they walked towards the terrace. Sachin, Grainger and Jacin were attending the ball too – also in disguise. She found Sachin without any trouble. He was currently serving drinks at the bar as he masqueraded as Twigg, who was still recovering from his arrow wound.

'Reuben, my boy!' someone called.

A tall man with a cherry-red nose clapped Reuben on the shoulder.

'Hello, Father,' Reuben said.

The man cradled his whisky tumbler with slender, manicured fingers as he raked his eyes over Noah. 'And who do we have here?'

'Father,' Reuben said, 'this is Olive. Olive, this is my father, Lord Nelson Ascit.'

Noah curtsied. 'A pleasure to meet you, Lord Ascit.'

'Hmm,' the man said, swirling the whisky in his glass. 'And what do you do, Olive? Besides pretending to be important by keeping company with people above your station, I mean ...'

Above my station? Noah thought. *That's rude!*

'Well, as you can probably imagine, sir,' Noah said, 'pretending to be important keeps me pretty busy. But in my spare time, I work for you.'

Lord Ascit glared at his son. 'We'll talk later. I'd keep her away from your mother if I were you.'

He skolled the last of his drink before tottering away.

Reuben smirked. 'That was brilliant.'

The dinner gong sounded before Noah could respond.

'Let's get some grub,' Reuben said.

Noah followed him to the table and took her seat. Jacin was sitting two tables across from her and Grainger was seated closest to the dignitaries' table. Sorcerer-master Percival sat in the central position at the main table on an ornate throne, flanked by the lords and ladies of Somyni's four ruling houses. Power practically radiated from the table, and Noah hoped that Montana and Catriona knew what they were doing.

Noah half listened to Lord Ascit's welcome as she made a flower out of her napkin. Then she picked at her dinner and made polite conversation with the other guests at her table as the minutes dragged by.

'Olive,' Reuben said, pouring mead into her goblet, 'are you okay? You're not eating much.'

'I'm fine. I just—'

Crash!

'Some oaf has dropped a tray,' Reuben muttered as he turned in his seat. 'Mother will have them thrashed for that.'

Noah's heart raced as she watched Montana and Catriona wind their way between the tables with Ardis and Emir behind them. Conversation in the hall stalled in the wake of the odd procession, several hundred diners silenced by four strangers.

'Who are *they*?' Reuben said.

Lady Ascit lumbered to her feet as Catriona's entourage approached the dignitaries' table. Noah winced. The designer who'd won the bid to outfit Lady Ascit for the Harvest End Ball had faced an impossible challenge. Noah still hadn't figured out why anyone had bid for the job at all. She certainly had no desire to outfit someone with the physique of a wine barrel.

'What is the meaning of this?' Lady Ascit demanded. 'Who *are* you people?'

Montana stopped and curtsied. 'I am Montana, sein-Elani and High Priestess of Talisker and I come with grave news.'

Murmuring rippled around the banquet hall.

Percival dabbed his mouth with a napkin. 'I am Sorcerer-master Percival, ruler of this realm,' he said, 'and before we hear your "grave news", perhaps you should introduce your companions, sein-Elani.'

Montana bowed her head and motioned to her left. 'This is King Catriona, of Leninstar. We are accompanied by our advisers, Ardis and Emir.'

Lord Ascit swigged from his whisky glass, obviously enjoying the unscheduled entertainment while Lady Ascit, whose bluster had deserted her, plonked herself back in her seat.

Percival's expression remained neutral. 'We don't often receive visitors here,' he said. 'Your news must be grave indeed. What is it?'

'The pyrohm has been found and is on its way here,' Montana said.

The banquet hall was instantly abuzz with animated chatter. Noah did her best to look shocked as Reuben's gaze locked on her.

'Did you hear that, Olive?' Reuben hissed. 'The pyrohm!'

Noah nodded but kept her focus on the main event.

When the noise died down, Percival said, 'And how do you know this?'

Montana shared a heavily sanitised version of the pyrohm's journey since Noah had discovered it in Sayle's Museum. There was enough detail to be convincing without giving away too much information about Noah or her friends.

'Well,' Percival said when Montana had finished, 'if the elves dare to come here thinking they can throw their weight around, they are in for a treat.'

'A treat?' Montana said. 'What do you mean?'

Percival waved his hand dismissively. 'We are more than capable of dealing with a few elves.'

'It will be more than "a few",' Montana said, 'and their goal is to use the illestial to release Jong from his prison. Do you understand what that means?'

'I do understand what that means,' Percival said. '*If* the elves were to succeed in releasing Jong, he would destroy this world. But I can assure you, sein-Elani that I would not suffer the elves releasing Jong.'

No, that's because you want to steal the pyrohm from them and release him yourself, Noah thought.

'I admire your confidence, Sorcerer-master Percival,' Montana said, 'but the fate of this world is a shared responsibility. We're here to offer assistance.'

Percival stabbed a piece of roast potato with his fork. 'What kind of assistance?'

'King Catriona and I have brought our armies. Eight thousand armed soldiers are on your doorstep, ready to fight the Jongu.'

Noah scanned the room, gauging reactions and knowing that Sachin, Grainger and Jacin would be doing the same. The hall almost crackled with tension. The Jongu in Somyni were secretive and not used to being challenged.

Percival's lips curled into a smile. 'A generous offer,' he said, 'but unnecessary. Please feel free to join us for dinner, and then you can take your armies home.'

Percival took a sip from his goblet before resuming his meal and Noah noted the slight straightening of Catriona's back – never a good sign.

'To my shame, I do not know much of Somyni's customs,' Catriona said, 'but I feel your hospitality is lacking.'

Lord Ascit staggered to his feet. 'You dare!' he said.

'I dare!' Catriona said, chin raised. 'We have suffered much to be here, to offer help – and you think it's okay to simply dismiss us?'

Lord Ascit sneered. 'We didn't ask you to come here,' he said. 'You have brought a formidable army, if what you say is true. That could be interpreted as a threat.'

'Only Jongu need fear our army,' Montana said.

The goblin to Percival's left who appeared to have a peacock nesting on her head said, 'Why should we trust you? Who's to say you're not here to use the illestial yourselves?'

'We want to ensure the illestial is destroyed,' Montana said, 'so that no one can ever use it.'

The goblin harrumphed. 'So you say. But why should we trust you?'

'The High Priestess is beyond reproach,' Ardis said. 'Her life has been one of service to Talisker, to upholding the Score by promoting peace and harmony.'

'Yet she has an army,' Lord Ascit said. 'That doesn't sound very peaceful or harmonious to me.'

'And by her own admission,' Lady Ascit said, 'she's the one that took the pyrohm to the elves in the first place. She's responsible for this mess!'

'Montana's life is forfeit in Aoratia,' Emir said evenly, 'but she went there anyway, seeking counsel on how to destroy the illestial. No one could have foreseen the elves' treachery.'

'Do you know how to destroy the illestial?' Percival asked.

'No,' Montana admitted, 'we do not.'

Percival raised an eyebrow. 'Do you have any *talent* in your ranks?'

Noah held her breath.

'Talisker's current Dragonsbane is with us,' Montana said. 'He is of the opinion that your people would have the knowledge and skills to undertake this task, but he is keen to assist.'

'He's here to spy on us!' someone in the audience called. 'The uplanders want to steal our magic!'

Percival leant forward, resting his elbows on the table and interlacing his fingers. 'Okay,' he said, 'I've heard enough. We need action, not words.'

'Agreed,' Catriona said.

'Hospitality and trust appear to be the two most immediate issues before us,' Percival said, 'so this is what I propose.'

Noah's stomach churned. Percival exuded calm, and his audience hung on every word.

'Firstly, your Dragonsbane will report to me in Ion Tower at the beginning of next gleaming,' the sorcerer said. 'With respect to accommodation, the sein-Elani and her closest confidantes can take Uon Tower as their temporary residence. It might need a bit of a dust and sweep out but, other than that, it's quite functional. *And* it's close to my quarters, so we can be in regular contact.'

Catriona nodded. 'Excellent! We will need to work together to come up with the best strategy to secure your city against the elf invasion.'

'And to continually revise the strategy,' Emir added.

'Indeed,' Percival said. 'And as for your army, the catacombs are available. Again, maybe a bit grimy as they haven't been used in a few millennia, but since your soldiers won't have much to do before the elves arrive ...'

'Sounds workable,' Ardis said.

Sounds workable? Noah's eyes nearly popped out of her head. *There are about ten thousand Jongu that need to be detained before the elves arrive. How is that workable?*

Montana nodded. 'The accommodation arrangements are acceptable. We thank you.'

Percival sat back in his throne and crossed his legs. 'And now to the trust issue. If your mission truly is to bring the Jongu to account, then you will detain and deliver Somyni's remaining dragon riders – and their dragons – to me.'

Noah gasped, along with several hundred other guests.

Unflappable, Catriona said, 'How many are there?'

'A few hundred,' Percival replied.

'And they're all Jongu?' Montana said.

'No,' Percival said, 'but if you do this, you will be doing our city a great service and will, thereby, win our trust.'

'While earning trust is important,' Montana said, 'so is being true to our values. On what grounds would you have us detain them?'

Percival smiled. 'The dragon riders promote themselves as moral crusaders or holy vigilantes,' he said, 'but they are, in fact, just vicious murderers.'

Vicious murderers? Noah fought for calm as anger coursed through her.

'All of them are murderers?' Catriona said, her voice betraying her scepticism.

'I would say *most*,' Percival said.

'With all due respect,' Ardis said, 'detaining an entire population sounds like persecution.'

For the first time since the group's arrival, Percival frowned. 'You know nothing of what my people have endured at their hands.'

'Trust goes both ways,' Emir said. 'You've been very focused on us proving ourselves to you. Well' – he met the gaze of each dignitary at the table – 'you need to show you're worthy of our trust as well. So we will offer you this … we will detain the dragon riders, and their dragons, and we will secure them in the catacombs. You can send a panel of three judges at a time to try each case, under our supervision.'

'That's preposterous!' Lord Ascit said.

'The dragons will bewitch you!' peacock-woman said.

'Waste of time!' another dignitary moaned.

Reuben leapt to his feet. 'Man, who do you think you are?'

Noah's heart raced as Emir turned around.

'I'm a king's adviser,' Emir said. 'And you are?'

Reuben sneered. 'Someone you don't wanna mess with, pal!'

'Noted,' Emir said as he turned back to the main table.

Montana stepped forward. 'Sorcerer-master Percival, do you accept the terms that Emir has outlined?'

Nearly a minute past before Percival spoke. 'Yes,' he said at last. 'I accept.'

Chapter 25

Reuben raised his empty tankard for yet another garbled toast. The alehouse was quiet now but for the snoring of the dozen or so revellers who'd passed out under the tables.

'To all my friends who share my vision for …' Reuben began.

The tankard slipped from his grasp as he too passed out. His head made an audible thud as it hit the wooden table.

Finally, Noah thought as she eased herself off the wooden pew and crept to the back door of the alehouse. With a furtive glance around her, she retrieved her Academy trousers from her purse and slipped them on under her frilly lilac gown. She unbuttoned the bodice of her dress with trembling fingers. The drunken soiree had gone on much longer than she'd anticipated and now she had to hurry. Grainger, Sachin and Jacin were waiting for her.

Noah donned a jacket, then stuffed her gown into a pocket on her Academy trousers before stealing out through the back door. She'd like to have dumped the offensive garment but she didn't want to leave a trail for anyone to follow. Gleaming wasn't far away now.

The alley behind the alehouse was quiet but Noah was taking no chances. Walking the streets alone at this hour was dangerous so she climbed a stack of wooden crates to get to the roof. From the alehouse roof, Noah leapt across the laneway to the building opposite and then scaled a pylon to access the second storey. Somyni city was crammed with two-storey and three-storey buildings. The narrow laneways and gentle slope of the shingled roofs invited pedestrian access for those who were nimble and not afraid of heights.

Noah surveyed the rooftops, catching glimpses of movement here and there. She wasn't the only one using the elevated pathways. Wondering if she might actually be better off on the street, Noah set off. When she reached the end of the current block of buildings, she stopped and peaked around the corner. *Clear,* she thought. *Keep going.*

The bakery where her companions were waiting was several blocks away. She'd meant to be there well before this but Reuben's afterparty had dragged on and on. Grainger had an appointment with Sorcerer-master Percival and Noah intended to join him. She scooted along the rooftops, careful to stay low, tread lightly and stick to the reinforced lines. By the time she reached the bakery, her leg muscles burned from the continual crouching.

Noah eased herself down from the roof into the laneway and entered the bakery. Despite the early hour, the bakery was abuzz. Six staff scampered back and forth to keep the customers moving through. Sachin – still masquerading as Twigg – gave her a wave as he served a young boy.

'Be right with you, Miss Olive,' Sachin said, handing a bag of bread sticks to the boy. 'Lord Ascit's order is all ready for you.'

Noah winked at him as she walked around the counter and into the kitchen behind. Once Sachin had finished serving the boy, he joined her in the kitchen.

'Where have you been?' Sachin said.

Noah snorted. 'Having less fun than you,' she said. 'I'd much rather have been posing as a baker than enduring Reuben and his mates.'

'Not a great party then?'

'No.'

Sachin nodded. 'Let's talk about it upstairs. We don't have much time.'

Noah followed Sachin up a narrow staircase to the workers' quarters. Jacin opened the door as Noah raised her hand to knock.

'Spooky,' Noah said.

'Hardly,' Jacin said. 'You two are about as sneaky as a pair of elephants. Hurry up and come inside.'

'Noah,' Grainger said, 'about time. I thought I was going to have to go to Ion Tower without you.'

'I'm glad you didn't,' Noah said to the only one of her companions not in disguise.

Resplendent in his Dragonsbane's cloak, Grainger appeared calm. His clean-shaven face and slicked-back hair made him look youthful, and at odds with the resolve in his steely gaze.

'After your last visit there, Noah,' Jacin said, 'I'm surprised you want to go back.'

'That should tell you how terrible Reuben's party was,' Noah said. 'But anyway, Percival's not going to catch me this time.'

'Well, if he does,' Jacin said, 'at least he won't recognise you.'

Sachin rubbed his chin. 'So what did Reuben and his crew think about the show?'

Anger simmered in Noah's belly as she recalled the drunken conversations about Montana and Catriona's appearance at the Harvest End Ball.

'We'll get no support from them,' Noah said.

'From Reuben's outburst at dinner,' Jacin said, 'I got the impression he didn't like Emir very much.'

Noah nodded. 'That's putting it mildly.'

Reuben had spent a good deal of the night plotting ways to kill Emir, and the more ale he drank, the more macabre his schemes had become.

'Are they a real threat though?' Sachin asked. 'Or are they all talk and bluster but ultimately pretty useless?'

Noah took a steadying breath. 'They're no match for our soldiers but I wouldn't dismiss them. They could be a nuisance.'

Sachin patted Noah's shoulder. 'Jacin and I will keep an eye on things here and get word to our crew in Uon Tower if we need to.'

'Good,' Noah said.

'Now, Noah,' Grainger said, 'it's time for us to go. We need to be in Percival's chambers before him.'

'Agreed,' Noah said.

Grainger drew his baton from under his robe and created a doorway. 'Ready?'

'After you,' Noah said.

Grainger stepped through the doorway and into Percival's private quarters in Ion Tower. After a cursory scan of the room, Grainger beckoned for Noah to join him. She shuddered.

'Go, Noah,' Sachin said, 'and don't mess up my plan.'

Noah scowled at him before she stepped through the doorway. *It is a good plan*, she thought, *but does he have to be so smug about it?*

Though Percival had decreed that the Dragonsbane report to him, he would no doubt expect Grainger to knock on the tower door and then wait to be escorted to the Sorcerer-master's chambers. Sachin, however, had other ideas.

Grainger, Sachin had said, *you need to truly annoy Percival. Show him that you're a man of talent and not to be trifled with. And be pro-active. Show him that you'll do things when you're ready, not when it's convenient for him.*

There had been a subsequent discussion about the difference between 'pro-active' and 'precocious', but Sachin would not be swayed. He had another motive.

And Grainger, you also need to distract the Sorcerer-master, Sachin continued. *If he's fuming at* your *audacity, perhaps he won't notice a spy inside his tower.*

Grainger turned to Noah once he'd closed his doorway. 'You'd better hide. Percival will be along very soon, I imagine.'

Noah smiled. 'No doubt.'

'Go.'

Noah opened a closet between two bookshelves and squeezed in amongst the multitude of white robes before sliding the door closed again. *How long until Percival arrives?* she wondered. After Noah's previous visit to Ion Tower and Montana's and Catriona's performance at the Harvest End Ball, Percival would have enhanced surveillance. He couldn't have missed Grainger's magical entrance.

Within a dozen heartbeats, the chamber door opened.

Percival's voice was unmistakable. 'You're the Dragonsbane?'

'Yes,' Grainger said. 'I heard you wanted to see me.'

'Indeed,' Percival said.

'And who is this?' Grainger asked.

'I am Sorcerer Sagan,' a woman replied, 'second in command here in Ion Tower.'

'A pleasure,' Grainger said.

'Do you have a wand?' Sagan asked.

Grainger's response was immediate. 'I have a baton.'

'Which you will surrender to me,' Percival said, 'so it can be examined and then – depending on what we find – registered.'

Noah clenched her fists, willing herself not to crack the door open for a peek.

'And how long will that take?' Grainger asked.

'Not long,' Percival replied. 'But until the examination is complete, you can settle in to your new quarters.'

'Settle in?' Grainger said. 'I'd rather just get straight to work.'

'Once we've assessed your usefulness,' Percival said, 'we'll get down to business. There is a servant outside who will escort you to your room now.'

Noah winced. Percival's tone was as condescending as it was dismissive.

The chamber door closed with a click.

'Will there be anything else, Sorcerer-master?' Sagan said.

'Yes, Sagan,' Percival said. 'We need to do some more packing. I think it will not be long until the pyrohm arrives.'

Noah's skin tingled. *Packing?*

'What would you like to pack next, Sorcerer-master?'

'This room,' Percival said. 'We must take the ancient knowledge of the Jongu with us to our new world.'

Noah heard two clicks. She held her breath and slid the closet door open a crack. Peering through the gap, she watched Percival scoop something out of a velvet-lined case. When he held it aloft, it twinkled in the torchlight. A blue crystal, about the size of Noah's index finger.

'Do you remember what I taught you, Sagan?' Percival asked.

'Yes, Sorcerer-master. I can do this.'

'Then what are you waiting for?'

The woman moved into the light and Noah almost gasped. Sagan was the sorcerer who'd answered the door when Noah had delivered the whisky. She extracted both her wands from her hair and began her spell. Noah watched, mesmerised, as the young sorcerer plied her craft.

Dazzling colour burst from her firestone wand and Noah shielded her eyes. Even through the small gap, the light was blinding. Sagan's chanting continued and Noah risked another peek through the crack. With her obsidian wand, Sagan pointed at a book on one of the many shelves. The book floated free of the stack and sailed towards the blue crystal in Percival's hand. When it struck the crystal, it disappeared.

Noah gasped, then clamped her hands over her mouth, but neither Percival nor Sagan seemed to notice. Their attention was wholly on their task. Another book flew from the shelf and then another. Each vanished when it struck the crystal. What started as a trickle quickly escalated, until the room became a blur of books. Books whizzed and swirled around the room like a blizzard. And it continued until every text from the walls and Percival's desk was contained within the blue crystal.

Noah gaped. She'd thought that the miniaturising technology Anok had pioneered to create the Academy trousers and water skins was unique. But it seemed the Somynians had crystals that did a similar thing. The crystal now pulsed eerily in the stillness and it was no longer blue. Its new, variegated appearance was a consequence of the kaleidoscope of books it contained.

'Excellent work, Sagan,' Percival said, inspecting the crystal, 'but the room looks a bit bare, don't you think?'

Sagan smiled and nodded. 'Yes it does. Luckily, I have a remedy for that.'

The sorcerer commenced her next task and Noah watched as the bookshelves sparkled to life once again. Noah shook her head. The illusion was flawless.

Sagan returned her wands to her hair and folded her hands in front of her. 'Will that be all, Sorcerer-master?'

'Yes, Sagan,' Percival replied, placing the crystal back into the case on the table, 'that will be all.'

'Very good,' she said, bowing her head.

Percival selected another crystal and tossed it to his protégé. 'Perhaps you should organise your own belongings.'

Sagan caught the crystal and clutched it to her chest. 'I will do that.'

'Dismissed,' Percival said.

Sagan closed the door gently behind her as Percival inspected some of the other crystals in the case. How long would he stay? Noah wondered. Would he sense her scrutiny? Sweat trickled down her back.

The Sorcerer-master closed the case and secured the clasps. He withdrew his wand from inside his robe and muttered a spell as he strode to the door.

'Just let someone else try to open a doorway in here,' he said.

A low rumble echoed around the room as he closed the door. Noah sucked in a shuddering breath and let it out slowly. She took two more deep breaths before she slid the closet door open. A quick scan of the room revealed that she was alone. *Well, I can't stay in here forever,* she thought.

With a prayer that Percival's spell only prevented doorways – and not people – accessing his chambers, Noah tiptoed to the table. Her hands shook but she unfastened the clips and opened the case. Dozens of crystals gleamed in the room's warm light. Some were empty but many had been used. Noah picked up one at random and held it close to her eye.

Hundreds of glass jars of different shapes and sizes were filled with seeds, powders and dried leaves. *Medicines,* Noah thought. She selected another crystal for study and was surprised to discover farming equipment and tools inside it. The next one held food stores – grains and legumes, preserved fruits and meats, as well as massive cheese wheels. Each successive crystal revealed another element of Somynian society. Percival had been busy.

Noah's stomach churned. When she found the crystal Sagan had just filled with Percival's library, an idea struck her. Noah shoved the crystal in her pocket before resealing the case. *Let's see what Sachin thinks of this,* she thought.

Chapter 26

Lady Ascit waddled into the stateroom, nose in the air. 'Have you finished polishing those trays yet, girl?'

Noah inspected the silver tray in her hand, ignoring Olive's reflection. If the job wasn't perfect, there'd be no supper.

'All done, Ma'am,' Noah said, placing the tray on the sideboard and removing her gloves. 'How may I serve you next?'

'Report to the stables,' Lady Ascit said. 'The Horse-master is short-staffed today and there is mucking out to be done.'

'Yes, Ma'am,' Noah said evenly.

The lady of the house studied Noah, who bowed her head to hide her smile. Reuben's vindictive mother revelled in antagonising her staff. And after Noah had accompanied Reuben to the Harvest End Ball, the lady of the house was keen to remind Noah of her place. If she discovered that Noah was pleased with the new assignment, she'd send her elsewhere.

'Go now,' Lady Ascit said, 'and be quick about it.'

Noah collected the polish and rags she'd been using as Lady Ascit waddled out of the room. *I really hope there is lots of mucking out to be done,* Noah thought. *The longer I'm out of this house, the better.*

The last week had dragged torturously. Apart from one visit to the bakery when she'd given Percival's crystal to Sachin, Noah had been confined to the Ascit's mansion. Menial tasks around the house meant

Noah had had plenty of time to fret about Emir and his crew in Uon Tower, as well as Raven and his army in the catacombs. And she'd had no news of the dragon riders either. If the army *had* rounded them up, it wasn't common knowledge yet. The isolation was wearing her down. She'd even have been happy to see Brinn.

Noah strode along the corridor with the prospect of some physical activity putting a spring in her step, but when she rounded the corner her heart sank.

'There you are,' Reuben said. 'I've been looking for you.'

Noah forced a smile. 'Here I am. Fancy walking me to the stables?'

Reuben's eyes widened. 'The stables?'

'There's mucking out to be done,' Noah said, 'and your mother thinks I'm the best qualified to do it.'

'Well, not for much longer,' he said.

'You're better qualified?'

Reuben snorted. 'That's not what I meant.'

'Then what did you mean?'

Reuben winked at her as he drew a folded sheet of parchment from his pocket. 'This,' he whispered, 'is our ticket out of here.'

Goosebumps broke out all over Noah's body. 'When?'

'Next waning!' Reuben hissed. 'Can you believe it? The time has finally come!'

'Show me,' Noah said.

Reuben unfolded the parchment and handed it to Noah.

Dear Reuben,

You are invited to the New Beginnings Bash!

Please bring your friends and join in the festivities!

Who: Henry, Olive, Saffron and Julius

Where: The Huliana Caverna

When: next waning

Now that Harvest End had passed, New Season parties were all the rage. This one looked like a typical party invitation, but Noah knew better. The New Beginnings Bash didn't herald the start of the new season, but the start of a new civilisation.

'Go to the stables now,' Reuben said, 'and act like everything is normal. Meet me at the graveyard at the start of waning. Our ride will meet us there.'

Noah nodded. 'Got it.'

Reuben squeezed her hand. 'And remember,' he said, 'pack light.'

♪♫

Noah watched Reuben skol another drink. So far, this party was much like the one they'd attended after the Harvest End Ball. It was awash with alcohol, the crowd chorus drowned out the band and the improvised acrobatics display looked likely to result in death. At least the excessive noise minimised conversation, something Noah was relieved about.

Reuben slammed his goblet down on the stone table. His fellow drinkers cheered.

'Another!' one cried.

'All around!' Reuben said.

They all cheered again as the young man next to Reuben picked up a tray. 'Load your empties,' he said.

Keen for refills, the drinkers shoved their goblets on the tray.

'Olive?' Henry said. 'Your goblet?'

Noah gripped the goblet protectively. 'Get me next round.'

Those around her booed as Reuben put his arm around her shoulder and leant in close. 'Nervous?' he said.

'A little,' she admitted.

'No regrets though?'

Noah knew he meant joining Percival's breeding program, but she thought of her quest to remove Jong and the illestial from Talisker. 'No,' she said at last. 'No regrets.'

'Good. I'd hate to think that—'

A sheet of lightning lit the ceiling of the cavern, distracting the revellers. The venue for Percival's New Beginnings Bash was an abandoned Jongu temple under the city. Ageless Pyranhi buildings surrounded the square where hundreds of young men and women celebrated their imminent journey. The Huliana Caverna wasn't a legitimate business, just a name created for the invitation. Any outsiders who tried to find it would have no luck.

Another flash of lightning – pink this time – drew an *Ooh!* from the crowd, before a female voice distracted them.

'Welcome!' the woman said.

The crowd cheered as Noah tried to locate the voice's owner. When she spotted Sagan on a dais at the far end of the square, she wasn't surprised. The black-robed sorcerer still wore her two wands in her dark hair and Noah was even less surprised to see Sorcerer-master Percival standing beside her.

'I'm pleased to see you are all having a good time,' she said, her voice clearly audible despite the distance it travelled across the square, 'as you have much to celebrate.'

The crowd cheered again, raising their tankards and goblets. Henry, who had just returned with the drinks, was ambushed by his friends who hurriedly joined the salute.

'But I will not take any more of your time,' Sagan said, gesturing to her left. 'Instead, I will hand over to Sorcerer-master Percival – our master and saviour!'

Noah hollered her approval along with everyone else, though it pained her to do so. *Don't let your cover slip now,* she reminded herself.

The Sorcerer-master clasped his hands in front of him. 'This, my good people, is where our new society begins. Savour this waning's festivities,' he said, 'because the memories you create here are ones that you will cherish forever. In Talisker's long history, no one has had this opportunity. No one! We are the privileged generation. It is in *our* time that the pyrohm has returned.'

Noah thought she might be sick as a fresh round of spirited applause and whooping echoed around the cavern.

'For centuries,' Percival continued, 'the Jongu in Somyni have awaited the return of the pyrohm. Plans were made, only to gather dust as generation after generation passed away without being able to fulfil their dreams of starting anew in a better place. But now we, with the gifts we've inherited from our forebears' – he held aloft the case containing the crystals – 'we can realise this dream!'

Noah wondered if Percival had missed the crystal that she'd taken. But before she could ponder it further, Henry stood up and swayed, spilling some of his ale on Reuben's head.

'And what of the elves?' Henry called. 'And the up*starts* from the up*lands*?'

He chuckled at his own joke and a few of his mates joined in.

Percival glanced at Sagan and nodded before addressing Henry. 'You can rest assured that those … issues are being dealt with by the appropriate people,' he said calmly.

'Which people?' Henry said.

Percival's demeanour didn't change. 'Different people have different skillsets,' he said. 'Some are skilled in magic, others excel in strategy and it is *those* people who are dealing with the issues you've highlighted. So relax, friend – you people *will* get to make your contribution to the new world.'

Your contribution to the new world. The words swirled around inside Noah's head. This group was the breeding stock and it took all her self-control not to grimace.

'Cheers to that!' Henry said, raising his tankard. 'I'd hate to get this close and then miss out.'

Percival nodded as Henry sat down.

'So again, enjoy your celebrations this waning – make worthy memories,' Percival said. 'When gleaming comes though, be ready to start preparations in earnest!'

Noah didn't like the sound of that and she hoped Montana's warriors arrived before preparations progressed too far. The tracking device Avril had used to follow her to Talisker was sewn into the hem of her tunic, so Montana could pinpoint her location. When Ardis and his crew arrived to capture Olive, Percival would be left in no doubt as to the high priestess's resourcefulness. If she could track a dragon rider to this clandestine location, the Sorcerer-master would certainly get the message that he should not underestimate her.

The revelry resumed and Noah pretended to take a sip from her goblet. *This is beyond tedious,* she thought.

'Olive, have you finished that drink yet?' Henry asked. 'I'm just about ready to go for another round.'

Reluctantly, Noah drained her goblet and put it on the tray.

'Great party, hey?' Reuben said.

'Yeah,' Noah said, 'but by the time gleaming comes, I don't think Henry will remember any of the memories he makes.'

Reuben laughed, but when Noah didn't join in he said, 'What's bothering you?'

'This is a test,' she said, watching Henry wind his way towards the bar.

'A test?' Reuben said.

She nodded before turning to face him. 'Anyone who doesn't "behave" appropriately here will be eliminated from the program.'

Reuben's smile faded. 'But we're the *chosen,*' he said. 'The Sorcerer-master has brought us here to celebrate and he certainly wouldn't mind us having a few drinks. He's very keen on my family's whisky.'

'A few drinks is one thing,' Noah said, 'but I guarantee you – Percival won't tolerate anyone who goes too far. He's not going to want our "new society" to be full of drunks.'

'Maybe you're right,' Reuben said as he put his tankard down on the table. 'The Sorcerer-master has high standards. He must be satisfied that we are worthy.'

Noah nodded. 'Exactly.'

Reuben took Noah's hand and squeezed it. 'Well, *we* are going to be fine,' he said. 'He'll know what a diligent worker you've been at my parents' house – following every ridiculous command that my mother could come up with, and as for me ... I've done something pretty special.'

'What's that?' Noah said.

'I poisoned the water supply in the catacombs.'

Noah's heart thudded in her chest as she withdrew her hand from his grasp. 'You did *what?*'

'I poisoned the water supply in the catacombs,' he said again, smiling broadly. 'Impressive, hey?'

Raven, Noah thought. *Please be okay.* The army had a number of Anok's water skins but the skins were tricky to make and though they'd procured as many as they could from Mellifont's adepts, they wouldn't have enough to sustain eight thousand soldiers for an extended period. Noah wondered how many soldiers would die before the act of treachery was discovered.

'Why didn't you tell me before?' she said.

Reuben winked at her. 'I knew you'd want to help,' he said, 'but that would have compromised your job at the house. I needed to protect you.'

Shouting behind them saved Noah the trouble of responding.

'What's going on?' Reuben said, swivelling in his seat.

Noah leapt to her feet. 'Fight!' She squinted, surveying the scene. 'Henry's involved. Let's go.'

Reuben grabbed her wrist. 'No! Stay here. If we get involved, Percival might—'

'Henry's our friend!'

'Who's made a poor choice!' Reuben cried. 'Do you really want to risk our place in Percival's ranks?'

Noah glowered at him. 'I can't believe you'd abandon your friend.'

She twisted free of his grip and pushed her way through the crowd, but she'd closed less than half the distance when Sagan intervened.

'Enough!' the sorcerer cried.

Sagan flashed her wands and within seconds, four drunken combatants floated into the air. Still kicking and throwing punches, Henry and the other fighters seemed not to notice that they'd been separated.

'Brawling will not be tolerated,' Sagan said. 'The party is over for you four.'

The crowd watched in silence as the three men and one woman floated higher into the air and then soared towards one of the ancient Pyranhi towers before disappearing through different windows on the top floors.

'Anyone else need to cool off?' Sagan asked.

The revellers dispersed, returning to their tables.

Reuben appeared at Noah's side. 'Still planning a rescue?' he said.

Noah sighed. She knew she shouldn't do anything that would compromise the force that Montana was sending, and that definitely included breaking out prisoners from a tower. But if the army's water supply had been poisoned, who knew how long it would be until troops arrived. Or if they arrived at all.

If Noah did nothing, she knew Henry and his friends would die. Percival could not afford to release them back into Somyni's generation population. Noah's conscience taunted her. Could she leave them to die? Though all of these people had chosen to follow a path that condemned everyone else on Talisker to death, not all of them were evil. Most were her age – teenagers – looking for adventure. Impressionable young people who were easily seduced by the charismatic Sorcerer-master. He'd fed them lies about Talisker's fate and instilled in them a false sense of destiny.

Noah gritted her teeth. Jong and the illestial were her priorities. Henry's choice to follow Percival – regardless of his motivation – had consequences. Noah's time as king had taught her that she personally, could not save everyone. Not that that sat well with her. She'd rather serve justice than deliver it.

'We could "investigate" after the party's over?' Reuben suggested.

Noah turned to look at him. 'You're brave all of a sudden,' she said. 'Why the change of heart?'

Reuben shrugged. 'You were right. Percival is looking for the highest quality people to seed our new world. If we don't look after our friends, how could we be worthy of such an honour?'

Highest quality people. Noah smothered her surprise. Was this the same person who'd openly threatened Emir's life and then committed a criminal act in poisoning the water supply in the catacombs?

Chapter 27

Reuben stepped off the final landing of the spiral staircase and scratched his head.

'They're not here,' he said.

Noah joined him in the room that, apart from an undisturbed layer of dust on the stone floor, was empty.

'They were never here,' Noah said. 'Look at the floor.'

Reuben nodded slowly. 'If anyone had been here, there'd be footprints or something.'

'Yes.'

'But we saw them fly in through the windows.'

Noah strode to the window and stuck her head through the gap. Craning her neck, she looked up.

'This isn't the top floor,' she said as she pulled her head back inside. 'I think they're still here – just upstairs.'

'Well, the staircase ends here,' Reuben said. 'Do we have to climb up the outside of the tower to get to them?'

Noah returned to the landing and glanced down at the staircase from the floor below. She turned around, faced where the stairs should have continued and took a step forward.

Reuben stared. 'How did you do that?'

Noah stepped up again. 'There *are* stairs,' she said. 'We just can't see them. Come on.'

Walking up an invisible staircase was tricky. Noah took her time, measuring each step, to avoid injury. When she reached the next floor, she found Henry dozing on the floor.

'Henry?'

The young man stirred as Noah knelt beside him. 'Henry,' she said again.

'Olive?'

'Yep. It's me.'

'And me too,' Reuben said.

Henry rubbed his eyes. 'I must have had way more to drink than I thought,' he mumbled.

'On your feet, man,' Reuben said. 'Once I get the others, we'll be on our way.' He nodded to Noah. 'Wait here.'

'What's happening?' Henry said as Reuben continued on up the invisible staircase, gradually vanishing from the head down as he passed between levels.

'You got into a fight,' Noah said, 'and Sagan put four of you in separate rooms in this tower to "cool off".'

Henry muttered something Noah didn't hear.

'What's that?' she said.

'That's embarrassing,' he said. 'Has the Sorcerer-master summoned us?'

'Not exactly,' Noah said. 'We're more what you'd call "free agents".'

Henry winced and cradled his head in his hands. 'I really appreciate the thought,' he said, 'but I reckon we'll all be in trouble if we leave without permission. Perhaps it's better if we just wait here … and accept the consequences?'

Noah shrugged. 'If you're ready for a funeral, then feel free to stay.'

Henry scowled. 'That's a bit dramatic, Olive.'

'Have it your way,' Noah said, folding her arms across her chest.

While she awaited Reuben's return, Noah cursed her predicament. No one had said that those involved in the melee *couldn't* receive visitors, but the invisible staircase was a big clue. The illusion was probably intended to keep the residents in, but they had the added benefit of deterring potential rescuers. Noah assumed that Sagan would be watching the tower, so she and Reuben had dispensed with stealth on their way in. Sneaking into the tower would have made them look guilty – like they knew they were doing the wrong thing.

Getting out again would be the bigger problem though. Once the sorcerer realised they'd circumvented her magic, there would be trouble.

When Reuben returned with the other brawlers, Noah said, 'Ready to go?'

The woman and two men nodded.

'I'm still not sure it's a good idea,' Henry said. 'The Sorcerer-master is already disappointed in us. If we leave without permission, he'll be really annoyed.'

'He's already really annoyed,' Reuben said. 'I did a little eavesdropping after the party. You've all been … cut from the program.'

Henry and the others stared at him.

'Cut?' Henry said. 'Really?'

Reuben nodded. 'Really. So you can stay here and wait for Sagan to deliver you to your deaths or you can come with us now – and make a run for it.'

'They won't kill us,' the woman said. 'Not for something as trivial as a fistfight.'

'Do you really think Percival is going to let you return to the city?' Noah said.

The woman hung her head. 'He might think that we would try to join with the elves – to find another way to the new world.'

'Or that we might side with the dragon riders,' one man said, 'to take revenge against him for abandoning us.'

Henry sighed. 'The Sorcerer-master does not tolerate dissent. He will not risk that we might stir up resistance against him.'

'Correct,' Reuben said, 'so what's it to be?'

Bleary-eyed, Henry said, 'I'm coming.' He held out his hand. 'Help me up?'

Reuben pulled him to his feet. 'Follow me.'

Reuben led the way down the staircase with the prisoners behind him. Noah brought up the rear, each level they descended heightening her anxiety.

When they reached the ground floor, Reuben jogged across the floor to the outer door. He reached for the doorhandle but didn't open the door straight away. He turned to Henry and his fellow outcasts.

'Once the door is open,' Reuben said, 'run!'

Without waiting for a response he wrenched the door open, but no one moved.

'What is that?' Henry whispered.

Noah pushed past the others to see what the problem was. Beyond the doorway, the underground landscape had been replaced with a white ice sheet that stretched away in all directions, contained only by the dazzling blue sky that hemmed it in at the horizon.

'Magic,' Noah said.

'Illusion? Reuben said. 'Like the staircase?'

Noah shrugged. 'Only one way to find out.'

She stepped over the threshold, placing a tentative foot on the ice.

'It's slippery,' Noah said. 'Be careful.'

Once her companions had all made it onto the ice, the tower disappeared. Noah scanned the featureless landscape as the others studied the blue dome overhead.

Henry shivered. 'I thought the sun was supposed to be warm?'

'It probably would be if it were closer,' Noah said, rubbing her arms.

'So what do we do now?' Reuben said.

Noah pursed her lips as she considered options. 'We move,' she said at last.

'Which way?' Henry asked.

'Doesn't matter,' Noah said, sweeping her gaze across the ice again.

She felt very small. The six humans were the only blemish on the pristine white landscape. There were no shrubs or trees, no buildings or shelters. *Nowhere to hide,* Noah thought. *Not that there's anything to hide from. Yet.*

'Olive's right,' Reuben said. 'There's no point just standing here. Let's go.'

Carefully, they started walking but they'd made it less than a couple of dozen steps before the ground began to tilt. In her mind, Noah visualised a giant ice seesaw, where the group had just moved off the balance point in the middle. Her feet slid out from under her and she crashed on her backside.

'Ouch!' Noah cried as she scrabbled in vain for a handhold or foothold.

It was an instinctive but ultimately futile endeavour. The ice was perfectly smooth.

Reuben crashed into her as the ice tilted further. They rocketed down the icesheet like they were on a giant slippery slide.

'Ahhhhhhh!' Noah yelled, as she fended off Reuben's grasping hands.

Her companions screamed too as they accelerated. *How far?* Noah wondered. *And what's at the bottom?*

Noah fought to keep her feet pointing downward as she careened down the ice. *Maybe we'll fall forever …* As Noah contemplated this adrenaline-pumping eternal punishment, her descent stopped abruptly. The icesheet was now vertical behind her as she dangled in the air, and the horizon traced an arc under her feet. 'What's happening?' Reuben asked. 'How are we just floating here?'

'Magic,' Noah said as she studied the sun that blazed directly in front of her.

Oddly, even though she peered into the roiling pools of magma, it didn't burn her eyes.

A wavering spot near the sun's centre caught Noah's attention.

'What is that?' she murmured, squinting at the dark stain.

Another blemish appeared and then another. Within moments, dozens of spots marked the sun's surface. To Noah's horror, the spots elongated into long tendrils which wriggled free of the churning molten pools and waved menacingly.

'That can't be good,' Reuben said.

Noah clenched her fists as the snakelike ribbons broke free of the sun and sailed towards the group.

The woman beside Noah whimpered. 'What's happening?'

'Close your eyes, Carrie,' one of her male companions said.

'How will you fight with your eyes closed?' Noah said.

'We're to fight?' she said.

Noah frowned. 'Up to you – but I doubt they're friendly.'

The finger-thick filaments swarmed towards them, then stopped a few metres from the group and hung in the air, twisting and coiling.

'Why aren't they attacking?' Henry said.

A voice echoed from beyond the sun. 'I can answer that.'

A woman cloaked in black glided towards them and the writhing sun snakes parted to let her through.

'Sagan,' Noah muttered.

The sorcerer hovered before her prisoners, smiling benignly. She met the eye of each of her six captives before she said, 'Now that I have your attention, I would suggest you listen very carefully.'

'We're listening,' Reuben said.

'Sorcerer-master Percival is very disappointed in all of you,' Sagan said, extracting her firestone wand from her hair, 'and planned to cut you all from the program. But as he is a compassionate leader, he offers you a chance to redeem yourselves.'

This ought to be good, Noah thought.

'How?' Henry asked.

'A test,' Sagan said. 'An obstacle course, to be more precise. If you complete the course successfully, you may re-join the others, journey to the new world and fulfil your destinies.'

Noah's eyes narrowed. 'And if we don't complete it successfully?'

Sagan spread her arms. 'Then this will be your new home.'

Reuben turned to Noah. 'The Sorcerer-master cut them from the program,' he whispered. 'Why would he change his mind?'

'Maybe he's saving face,' Noah said. 'He's personally chosen everyone for the program, and it looks bad for him if some of us don't meet the grade.'

'If we pass the test and return, his reputation remains intact,' Reuben mused. 'If we don't, he still looks good. He's given us a second chance but he won't be seen as letting us off easy.'

Noah nodded. 'Exactly.'

'Are you ready to get started?' Sagan said.

'Yes!' Henry said.

The sorcerer muttered under her breath while waving her wand. Suddenly, the icesheet lurched before crashing back to its horizontal position. The violent impact launched chunks of ice high in the air and sprayed frosty splinters like the detonation of a hundred grenades. Thunder rolled all around as the landscape underwent its cataclysmic transformation. Noah shielded her head with her arms as the turbulence continued.

When the landscape finally settled, groans and whimpering were the only sounds.

'Is everyone okay?' one of the men said.

'I've been better,' Henry replied.

'Stand up!' Sagan said.

Noah clambered to her feet. While the ice was still slippery, the uneven surface made negotiating it a bit easier. Noah surveyed the terrain. *A good start for an obstacle course,* she thought. Mountains of ice rubble sprouted from amongst the jumble of blocks strewn across the landscape. Deep crevasses cut jagged swathes through the frosty detritus while sunlight sparkled off splinters of ice that pierced the ground like the spears of arctic warriors.

Sagan drew her second wand from her hair and began chanting. The wands flashed side to side, up and down and then round in dizzying circles. Noah held her breath as Sagan charmed the wriggling sun snakes. Some joined together to form a fiery circle, reminding Noah of the doorways the elves made. More of the glowing filaments connected within the circle to create a blazing, shifting web.

'This,' Sagan said, 'is the gateway back. If you can get through it, you can return to claim your destiny.'

'When you said it was an obstacle course,' Reuben said, 'I didn't think there'd only be one obstacle.'

Sagan smiled. 'It is a significant test,' she said. 'The gateway itself will change size and shape, and the strands that form the web in the middle will continually shift.'

'They look hot,' Noah said.

'Indeed they are,' Sagan said. 'Drawn from the sun itself, these filaments will incinerate anything that touches them.'

Henry held out his hand and eyed the glowing gateway. 'I wouldn't even get my hand through one of those gaps,' he said. 'There's no way I'll get my body through.'

The youngest man in the group took two steps forward and the gateway zipped away to his right.

Noah gasped, along with her companions.

'That's going to be impossible,' the young man mumbled.

Impossible doesn't even begin to cover it, Noah thought.

'Well, I'll leave you to it,' Sagan said. 'Perhaps we'll meet again?'

With precise wand movements and a string of undecipherable sounds, Sagan vanished … only to reappear on the other side of the gateway. Noah squinted to get a better view of their destination. Inside the cavern, hundreds of young people milled about, drawn to the spectacle of the glowing portal.

'They can see us,' Reuben said.

'That figures,' Noah said. 'Percival is making an example of us.'

To Noah's right, the youngest man in the group dropped to his hands and knees. 'I have an idea,' he said. 'If I pack ice inside my clothes, I might be able to jump through the gateway without being burned.'

'If you can get close to the gateway,' Henry said.

'It's a test of worthiness,' the man said. 'If it's a good idea, I might be allowed close enough.'

Noah scooped up handfuls of pulverised ice to contribute to the frozen body armour. The group worked in silence for several minutes, packing as much ice as they could around his back, arms and legs. When they'd filled his clothing to near bursting, the young man took a deep breath.

'Wish me luck,' he said.

Reuben ruffled his hair. 'Good luck.'

The rest of the group echoed his sentiments before the young man turned his back on them. He lurched forward, almost stumbling on his first step. As he ran the gateway moved towards him. Noah held her breath. The gateway glowed brighter and showered sparks that sizzled on the ice.

The man cried out as he launched and twisted, turning his ice-packed back towards the portal. His back hit the snaking web and light exploded from the gateway. Noah turned away, shielding her eyes with her hands. *Please let him have made it,* she thought. She counted to five before risking a peek at the gateway.

Steam from the man's charred corpse wafted into the air. Noah's stomach heaved. She hadn't even found out his name.

Henry dropped to his knees and the others followed his example. On the other side of the gateway, many chosen did the same.

'Anyone else got any brilliant ideas?' Henry said.

The words were no sooner out of his mouth when the gateway moved again. It hovered right before the group, spitting and crackling. Heat washed over Noah and she backed away. Without warning, the portal expanded – doubling in size in an instant.

'What is happening?' Henry said.

The gateway ballooned again, the fiery webbing stretching to near breaking point. The strands became hairlike with wide gaps between them.

Movement beside Noah snagged her attention. It was the other man in the group whose name she didn't know. He was on his feet. Before anyone could react, he sprang at the glowing ring. Noah reached for him but Reuben rammed her with his shoulder, knocking her to the ground. She watched the man sail towards the gateway, arms outstretched like he was diving into a pool. His arms made it through, and then his head and shoulders. Then his chest was clear. But as his hips passed the boundary, the portal shimmered and shrank.

'No!' Noah cried.

The man's legs fell onto the ice while his torso dropped onto the cavern's dirt floor. There was no blood though. The burning tendrils cauterised the flesh as they sliced through.

The man wailed and Noah hung her head. He'd probably live for a couple of minutes more. His heart would labour to pump blood around his truncated circulatory system but with so many veins and arteries severed, the system couldn't work. Blood would pool in his extremities and it wouldn't be until his brain was starved of oxygen, that the man's misery would end.

'No more,' Reuben whispered. 'Promise me, no one else will attempt the crossing until we've had time to think.'

'Retreat is a good idea,' Henry said, turning his back on the gateway. 'If for no other reason than to deprive *them*' – he jerked his thumb over his shoulder towards the chosen in the cavern – 'of a spectacle. And … I think we should split up.'

'What?' Reuben said. 'Why?'

'Divide and conquer,' Henry said. 'If we split up, it can't follow all of us.'

'He's got a point,' Noah said.

Henry turned to the other woman in the group. 'What do you say, Carrie? We'll go one way, Reuben and Olive can go another.'

Carrie nodded. 'It's worth trying.'

Henry took Carrie's hand, then faced Reuben. 'Good luck.'

Reuben saluted the departing couple while Noah eyed the portal. The glowing filaments quivered and sparked before the structure collapsed into a smouldering sphere. Smoke wafted from it as the snakelike tentacles curled and twisted around each other. The mass glowed brighter, radiating more heat.

Noah stepped back.

'What's it doing now?' Reuben said.

'I think it's going to—'

The sphere split in two.

'—replicate,' Noah finished.

Reuben groaned as one of the balls expanded into the now familiar weblike portal. 'Henry won't be happy,' he said, as the second ball zipped off after its prey.

'No, he won't be,' Noah murmured, turning her attention to the sky.

'What are you looking at?'

Noah squinted. 'Does the sun seem closer now?'

Reuben nodded. 'I think it could be. It feels warmer.'

'Sagan's trying to unnerve us. Let's move.'

Reuben glanced at the portal as they set off. 'It's following us.'

'Ignore it,' Noah advised. 'We're going to have a bigger problem soon.'

'Which is?'

Noah sploshed in a puddle. 'Depending on how much of this ice melts … do you know how to swim?'

Reuben scowled.

The ice melted more quickly as the sun's heat intensified. Water trickled down frozen spires until the spires disappeared, and Noah and Reuben waded through ankle-deep water as the gateway stalked them. They slogged on, ignoring the audience at their backs. As the ice mountains surrendered their peaks and the rivulets running down their sides joined forces to create dangerous torrents, Noah struggled to stay out of the main flow of water. A misstep now spelled certain death.

'Olive,' Reuben said, 'we can't outrun this thing.'

Noah sighed. 'I know, but we can't breach it either.'

'We're going to have to face it at some st—'

Reuben slipped and crashed on his back, hitting his head on a block of ice. Unconscious, he slid towards a fast-moving stream.

'Reuben!' Noah called as she dropped to her knees and reached for him.

She caught his collar and his momentum pulled her forward onto her stomach.

'Nooooo!' she screamed as they both skated downward.

An instant before they hit the water, Noah sucked in a deep breath. She tumbled in the current as her lungs burned in protest. Swept along in the swift flow, Noah lost her grip on Reuben. She fought to find the surface and, when her head was free, she gulped in another lungful of air. Reuben was nowhere in sight. The water pulled her under again. She released her breath in short bursts, desperate to conserve oxygen.

Suddenly, the current released her, but Noah's relief at being able to breathe fresh air evaporated quickly.

Oh crap! she thought as she plummeted downward, fighting to stabilise her freefall. There were plenty of chasms in Sagan's landscape and Noah hoped this was a shallow one. But a glimpse below her shattered that hope instantly. The bottom – wherever it was – was shrouded in darkness.

Noah closed her eyes. *It's now or never,* she thought, summoning the power in her veins. She visualised the wind spell Hildebrand had taught her. *This better—*

Pain in her lower leg wrenched her attention away from the spell. Her descent stopped and she hung in mid-air. Almost too afraid to see what the next horror might be, Noah looked up. A blue claw encircled her ankle.

'Piper?' she breathed. 'Is that really you?'

The blue dragon flamed. 'Of course it's me,' she said, beating her leathery wings hard. 'And I'll have you back on solid ground in a flash.'

Chapter 28

Piper landed close to the gateway and eased Noah onto the ice.

'You're hurt,' Noah said, stroking the dragon's blackened scales.

'I'll be fine,' Piper said. With a nod towards the portal she added, 'It was hotter than I expected.'

Noah crouched in front of the dragon. 'Why are you here?'

'I had to save you,' Piper said.

Noah hung her head. Montana had intended to send her warriors to intercept her, but Piper hadn't been part of the plan.

'What about the soldiers?' Noah whispered. 'Raven … Ardis? The water supply was poisoned—'

Piper winked. 'Ardis is on the other side of the portal, and Raven is fine. Reuben is a pretty ineffective operator as it turns out.'

Noah nodded, relief flooding through her. 'Well, we need to get out of here,' she said, eyeing the portal, 'but I don't fancy going back that way.'

Piper nodded. 'I must say I'm not keen on another pass.'

As Noah weighed her options, Piper began to glow.

'Noah, what's happening to me?' Piper said, her voice wavering.

Noah's stomach tightened as the air shimmered and acrid smoke swirled around them.

The dragon whimpered. 'That's not my smoke.'

Noah scrambled to mount her dragon. *Magic,* she thought as she collapsed against the Piper's back. Between heartbeats her body seemed to have turned to rubber, refusing to respond to her brain's commands. Only her stomach was active. It churned mercilessly.

'I can't move!' Piper cried.

'Me either,' Noah said.

Zrip!

'Ahhhhhhh!' Noah screamed as her body rocketed headlong towards the portal.

Before her stomach had the chance to revolt, Noah found herself sprawled on the ground beside Piper.

'Noah?' Piper said.

Noah held up one hand. 'Give me a second,' she mumbled.

A woman's voice responded. 'I don't think so.'

Noah looked up.

Sagan's eyes loomed over her, two dark voids ringed by dazzling blue irises. 'Cosy in there, is it?'

Noah rolled onto her hands and knees and clutched her stomach. She squeezed her eyes shut as waves of nausea washed through her.

'What have you done to us?' Noah said.

'I have apprehended a dragon and its rider,' Sagan said. 'It's never been done this way before, but it appears to be very effective.'

Piper snorted. 'Never been done what way?'

'What way?' Sagan echoed. 'I would have thought it was *crystal* clear.'

We're in a crystal, Noah thought, *like the books in Percival's library.*

'Anyway,' Sagan said, 'we've foiled your plot to compromise the Sorcerer-master's next generation of apprentices, and now it's time for you to face justice.'

Noah cocked her head to one side. 'Next generation of apprentices?' she said. 'What are you talking about? They're not apprentices, they're breeders!'

Sagan smiled. 'No one will believe your lies, dragon rider.'

Noah turned towards the portal and peered into the cavern where Ardis was talking with Percival. Sagan's performance was for Montana's warriors, and Percival was most likely backing her claim that the group's presence in the secret cavern was legitimate.

'I haven't had the chance to test myself against the portal yet,' Noah said.

Sagan sniffed. 'And nor will you get the chance, *dragon rider*. You shouldn't have been here in the first place. Only the *acolytes* were entitled to an opportunity to redeem themselves.'

Acolytes, Noah thought, anger flaring inside her. Percival's scheming had killed at least two of their companions. And Sagan's lies as she covered for him were the ultimate insult. Reuben and his companion weren't innocent, but their crimes should have been tried before a jury. They deserved more than to be sacrificed to preserve the Sorcerer-master's image.

Piper crouched next Noah. 'You have a plan, don't you?'

Noah frowned. 'I have an idea …'

'That'll have to do,' Piper said. 'Get on with it.'

Noah dredged through her memories for the spell Theo had used to bust Montana out of her cell on Aoratia. Eyes closed, she chanted softly. She hadn't seen the wand movements – that had been Grainger's department – so she improvised. If she got it wrong and made the crystal implode rather than explode … Noah pushed on, despite the doubts that plagued her.

'Sagan's moving,' Piper said.

Noah nodded but didn't open her eyes.

'Looks like she's opening another doorway,' Piper said. 'She's taking us back to Percival.'

Sweat rolled down Noah's back as she ground out all the Pyranhi words she remembered. She made her hand movements more sweeping, hoping to speed up the process. Noah's heartbeat echoed in her ears as the pressure inside the crystal intensified. She struggled to breathe, but kept chanting.

'What are you doing?' Sagan asked.

'She's trying to get out,' Piper said. 'What does it look like she's doing?'

Noah opened her eyes and glared at the dragon. 'Well, there goes the element of surprise.'

Sagan laughed. 'As if a dragon rider could do magic. There's more to it than chanting random words and twiddling your fingers around. Ridiculous!'

The pressure inside the crystal was so high that Noah's ears felt like they were clogged with cotton wool, making Sagan's words difficult to decipher. But the scornful tone was unmistakable.

Sagan waved a wand over the crystal for her prisoners to see. 'And now,' she said, 'you will face justice.'

Piper screeched, long and loud. Noah clamped her hands over her ears.

What the hell? she thought as smoked enveloped her. Admonishing the dragon wasn't an option. If she tried to speak, she'd choke on the smoke. But as the shrieking continued, Noah's brain registered the escalation in pressure. Piper could finish what she'd started. Noah curled herself into a ball and prayed that she'd stay conscious long enough to witness a miracle.

She counted her heartbeats. *One, two, three, four—*

Bang!

Sagan screamed.

Free of the crystal, Noah drifted towards the ground like a falling leaf – being so small had some advantages.

'All aboard!' Piper cried, swooping beneath her.

Noah clutched the dragon's pommel-like scales and hauled herself into place. She gazed at her surroundings. Everything looked so big.

Sagan screamed again, drawing Noah's attention. Crystal shards protruded from the sorcerer's face and neck; blood streaked her cheeks and throat. Noah cupped her hand over her mouth at the sight of a wedge lodged in Sagan's eye.

The black-robed sorcerer stumbled back. One step … two steps …

'*No!*' Noah cried. 'Look out!'

Sagan appeared not to hear the warning. She stumbled back into her fiery portal. Noah averted her eyes as light flashed.

Noah stroked Piper's neck. 'We're in big trouble now.'

'What do we do?'

Noah stared at the web's glowing filaments. 'We're small enough to fly through without getting burned,' she said. 'Let's go back to the cavern so Ardis can take us to the catacombs.'

Piper darted towards the web, unable to suppress a shudder on the way through. Her scorch marks and the charred remains of those who'd perished were evidence of what happened if one touched the burning filaments.

Once inside the cavern, silence met them. Noah took several deep breaths as they flew towards the Sorcerer-master.

'Should we land?' Piper asked as they neared Percival.

'Not on the floor,' Noah said. 'I don't want him to step on us.'

Percival raised his wand and chanted. Noah's body convulsed and then swelled to its proper size before she tumbled from Piper's back. As she lay in the dirt battling nausea, soldiers ringed her and her dragon. The only sound in the cavern was the clinking of chains as Ardis's soldiers shackled them.

'Well, we've got what we came for,' Ardis said. 'We'll take our leave, and secure these with the others, Sorcerer-master.'

'Actually, *I'll* take care of this,' Percival said. 'Dragon rider, look at me.'

Noah lifted her head and glared at him. He flinched before his eyes narrowed.

'The elf slave,' Percival said. 'How did *you* get in here?'

Elf slave? Realisation struck like a blacksmith's hammer against an anvil. Sagan's magic had disrupted the spell that Jacin had woven to give her Olive's appearance. Her cover was blown.

'Pretty easily,' Noah said. 'I was disguised as a servant.'

'Elf slaves can't do magic,' Percival said. 'What we just witnessed is proof of that. You clearly have no talent – the dragon had to save you.'

'Maybe you should pay your acolytes more,' Noah said. 'Then they mightn't sell their services on the side to people like me.'

Noah marvelled at how easily that lie had come to her. She just hoped that she'd delivered it convincingly.

Percival rubbed his chin. 'How an elf slave came to be in the company of a dragon is curious, but ultimately of little consequence. What *is* of consequence, is that this dragon' – he pointed to Piper – 'murdered Sorcerer Sagan and that *you* are its accomplice. All present here witnessed it. The penalty is death.'

Noah stared at him. 'We escaped from unlawful imprisonment,' she countered. 'Sorcerer Sagan was collateral damage. We didn't intend for her to fall against her portal.'

'The agreement was for us to secure all the dragons and their riders,' Ardis said, 'until their trials could be arranged.'

'Yes,' Percival agreed, 'but you can tell Montana that in *this* case, no trial is necessary.'

Noah felt Piper's gaze on her but she kept her attention on Ardis. The success of Montana's strategy to win Percival's trust depended on what he said next.

'I'm not here to negotiate,' Ardis said. 'I have my orders.'

The muscles in Percival's jaw bulged as he clenched his jaws. 'I'm not here to negotiate either,' he growled, 'but I'll tell you what I'll do. We'll take these two back to the city now and explain the situation to your mistress. In fact, we'll do it in the city's main square. If you're so keen on a trial, let's do it publicly.'

Chapter 29

Noah kept her head down and eyes closed as her cage rattled its way along one of Somyni's main boulevards. She sat cross-legged on the wooden floor of the horse-drawn cell as the crowds that lined the street jeered and taunted her. Their words didn't bother her as much as the rotten fruit and excrement they threw at her. Piper followed in a cage behind her and Noah wondered how the dragon was holding up. She didn't dare turn around though. She didn't want to get any more putrid filth in her eyes.

Percival had kept his word of holding a public hearing for Sagan's murder. And it was very public. The city was swarming with humans and goblins of all ages, and it disturbed Noah to see young children heckling and pelting food.

She steadied her breathing. Once they reached the main square, the trial would begin. Emir would be there with Montana and Catriona, and with the majority of their armies also present, Raven and Ardis were bound to be there also. She inhaled deeply and wondered what had become of Sachin, Jacin and Grainger. Would they be there? If everything had gone to plan, Chase and Avril would be incarcerated with the dragon riders and under the protection of Leninstar's army in the catacombs. Hopefully Gillette and Jaxon were there watching over them.

'Death to the dragon riders!' someone cried.

'Burn her and butcher the dragon!' another yelled.

The vitriolic hatred the Somynians harboured towards the dragon riders shocked Noah. She shuddered. The procession continued inexorably until it finally reached Somyni's main square.

When her wagon stopped, Noah kept her head down. The crowd berated her as she was dragged from her cage. Rough hands clamped around her arms and hauled her along a cobblestone path. The soldiers escorted her up a flight of stairs as, behind her, Piper roared. The noise from the crowd subsided. Noah mounted the stage and her footsteps echoed in her ears as she stumbled to the centre of the wooden platform where her escorts forced her to her knees. Noah surveyed her surroundings. Emir, Raven, Montana, Catriona and Grainger stood grim-faced on the far side of the stage. At the back of the platform – behind Percival – three sorcerers sat on ornate chairs behind a bench. Nearest to the stairs was a guillotine.

Noah didn't let her eyes linger on the gleaming blade, turning instead to the crowd. Thousands of soldiers waited in formation. Noah's heart swelled to see the familiar uniforms of Leninstar and the Order of Elani. Even though most of their troops were in attendance, they were outnumbered by at least three to one by Somynians. Noah wondered if Jacin was in the crowd. He'd be surprised to see that his concealment spell had been dismantled.

Percival raised his hands and addressed the crowd. 'Today we are holding a public trial. It is alleged that this dragon' – he pointed to Piper – 'murdered Sorcerer Sagan. You will hear testimony from dozens of people that will settle this matter beyond doubt. And this woman' – he indicated Noah – 'is the dragon's accomplice.'

'Are you missing a lamp?' Noah said.

Percival lowered his arms. 'What?'

'Are you missing a lamp?' Noah said again. 'A white one with a carving of a Pyranhi sorcerer on it?'

Percival didn't answer, but drew his wand.

'And what about the crystal containing your library?' Noah asked. 'Did you think you'd misplaced it?'

The square fell silent. No one spoke – no one moved. Noah doubted the Somynians had ever witnessed someone openly challenging the

Sorcerer-master. Undermining him would not be easy, but she had to start somewhere.

'I might know something about their whereabouts,' Noah continued, 'and I'd consider sharing that information … for the right price.'

The wizard attending Percival frowned. 'Attempting to bribe an official?' he said. 'Shall I add that to the list of charges, Sorcerer-master?'

Noah ignored the wizard. 'What do you say, Sorcerer-master?' she said. 'After all, you're going to need those texts once you get to Jong's new world.'

Percival flicked his wand and chanted. Light shimmered before Noah's eyes and a faint buzzing sound tickled her ears.

'It's time to progress with the trial,' Percival said, 'so we'll have no more nonsense from you.'

'We'll see about that,' Noah said.

Percival smiled and cupped his hand around his ear. 'What was that?'

Noah frowned as her words echoed around her, like she was talking with a bucket over her head. She tested the Sorcerer-master's spell with her perceptions. The invisible bubble around her head would contain her words, preventing her testimony being heard.

Noah glanced at Emir and Raven. They stared straight ahead, their faces grim. Noah turned to Piper. She crouched on the floor, iron shackles around her neck, ankles and tail. In spite of her predicament though, the dragon was not cowed. The fire in her eyes might well have been the source of the delicate plumes of smoke that snaked from her nostrils.

'First witness,' Percival said with a wave of his hand.

A young man Noah didn't recognise mounted the stairs to the stage. The crowd hung on every word as he described how Piper had caused the explosion that had slammed Sagan against her own gateway, incinerating her. *Never mind the other people who also died,* Noah thought. As the trial continued, and witness after witness gave the same testimony, it became clear that there'd be no justice for the two chosen who'd also perished.

'That concludes the witness statements,' Percival said, turning to the judges at the bench. 'It is time for a verdict.'

Montana stepped forward. 'If the court would indulge me,' she said, 'I am curious as to how this dragon and its rider came to be in Sagan's company in the first place. We have heard much about the *end* of the story, but I'd like to know more of what happened before.'

Noah studied the Sorcerer-master's face, but his expression betrayed nothing.

'What are you implying, High Priestess?' Percival said.

Montana held her head high. 'I'm not *implying* anything. I just want to understand all of what happened in the secret cavern where this event occurred. How did one of your most talented sorcerers end up in the company of a dragon and a dragon rider with a lethal gateway between them and a few hundred young people?'

Several people in the crowd booed.

'We've heard enough,' one cried. 'The dragon is guilty!'

Percival held up one hand. 'Stop!' he said.

The crowd quietened again, awaiting the Sorcerer-master's response.

'High Priestess,' Percival said, 'as your commanders no doubt reported to you, with the imminent arrival of the elves, I thought it best to protect my next intake of apprentices. That underground cavern seemed the perfect place. I thought they would be safe there. What we didn't realise was that this spy' – he point to Noah – 'had infiltrated the group.'

'Filthy dragon-rider scum!' someone in the audience yelled.

'Liar!' Noah screamed inside her bubble. 'They weren't *apprentices* – they were *breeders!*'

Percival's wand twitched and Noah winced as the pressure inside the invisible helmet increased.

'When Sorcerer Sagan discovered this spy,' Percival continued, 'she acted promptly to secure her beyond a gateway. Sagan was questioning her when the dragon and your army showed up. In fact, one might question the timing of your army's arrival, given that it coincided with the appearance of the dragon. If we thought you were colluding with the dragon riders …'

Well, if people weren't thinking it before, Noah thought, *they certainly will be now.*

Montana maintained her composure. 'And as *you* were no doubt informed,' she said, 'we have been monitoring, tracking and securing the dragons and their riders, as per our agreement. My warriors were simply chasing down this dragon.'

'I was informed,' Percival agreed, 'and now that everyone's role in this horrendous event has been aired publicly, I see no further reason to defer judgement.'

All eyes went to the judges' bench and the judge closest to Percival stood up. He had one eyebrow – the only hair on his face or head – that looked like two hairy caterpillars joined together. Noah held her breath as he rested his fingertips on the table.

'We find the dragon guilty of the murder of Sorcerer Sagan,' he said, 'and that its accomplice shares the guilt in equal measure. The penalty is death.'

The judge sat down as the crowd cheered. Noah's stomach churned as wizards chanted incantations designed to immobilise Piper's limbs. Muscled thugs then yanked Piper's chains, dragging her towards the guillotine.

'*NO!*' Noah screamed. '*NO!*'

Time seemed to slow down as Noah watched the final preparations. To restrain the dragon behind the guillotine, the hooded executioner drove iron spikes through the links in Piper's leg irons and into the wooden floor. Three men tugged the chains attached to her neck shackle and then fastened the headlock in place. Another man wound the tail chain around a wooden pylon several times before securing it with a linchpin.

Behind Noah, the crowd took up a chant.

'*Guilty! Guilty! Guilty! Guilty!*'

Percival crouched beside Noah and shouted into her ear. 'Enjoy the show,' he said. 'You're next!'

'Screw you!' Noah yelled.

She turned her head towards Emir and Raven. Both had their hands on their sword hilts, as did Catriona. Montana's hands were behind her back. Grainger though, had disappeared. Noah twisted round. The square was a seething crush of humanity. It looked like a rock concert.

A flicker of light in the distance caught her eye. Noah looked beyond the throng to the crystal temple on the far side of the square.

'Oh my god,' she breathed. 'What are they doing?'

Inside the transparent temple, Sachin was perched on top of the tripod, while Jacin was a third of the way up one of the legs. Sachin tossed a triangle to Jacin, who caught it and shoved it inside his tunic. Noah squinted through the shimmering haze in front of her. Only one piece of the illestial remained in place.

A glance back at the guillotine showed final preparations were complete. Piper had only moments left. Noah swore.

Raven rushed across the stage towards Percival, waving both arms above his head and Emir was right behind him.

'The illestial!' Raven yelled. 'They're stealing the illestial!'

Noah's heart hammered as Percival spun round. *This is the plan?* she thought. As distractions went, this was as audacious as it got.

Percival pointed towards the temple. 'Stop them!' he roared as he strode to the front of the stage.

The crowd frenzy made it impossible to hear him. Percival screamed his order several times, but it was his animated gesticulations towards the temple that finally got the mob's attention. They turned around and the cheering faltered.

Noah barely had time to notice the ring of light on the floor around her before she fell and crashed heavily in the dirt. Footsteps on the wooden planks overhead told her she was now under the stage.

'What the hell?' she wheezed.

Grainger's face appeared out of the gloom. He waved his baton, rattled off a string of Pyranhi words and the globe around Noah's head vanished.

Grainger's gaze bored into her. 'Are you okay?'

'I've been better,' Noah said.

He gave her a curt nod before he opened another doorway. A small room containing only a cot and a chair appeared beyond the gleaming circle. Grainger hooked his arm under Noah's armpit and dragged her through. Once he'd closed the doorway, he set to work on her shackles.

Noah scanned her surroundings. 'Where are we?'

'Ion Tower,' Grainger said.

'What are we doing here?' Noah said. 'We need to get back to the square! We have to save Piper and the others.'

Grainger shook his head. 'Summon her, Noah.'

Her shackles gave way and clattered onto the floor.

'What?' Noah said.

'If you want to save Piper,' Grainger said, 'you'll have to summon her here.'

Noah stared at him. 'There's no time for that.'

'We've bought you as much time as we can. Capitalise on the confusion, Noah.'

'What are you going to do?'

Grainger winked. 'Steal the rest of Percival's crystals.'

♪♫

'Hold on!' Emir said as he pushed his way through the crowd still milling about in Somyni's main square.

Noah clutched his hand as she followed in his wake. At least that stopped one of her hands shaking. Summoning Piper from the guillotine had sapped most of her energy and she could barely stand, let alone push her way through the throng. Though she'd seen her beloved dragon flying back towards Mt Jubilee, Noah was heartsore at her condition. Thanks to Percival's thugs, Piper was now missing a front foot and both her horns. A couple of her wing membranes were puckered in places where Noah had erred in her spell too. But at least Piper was alive – and able to fly.

'Hey! Watch out!' a man said.

'Sorry,' Emir said, 'my girlfriend's sick. Need to get through.'

Noah had changed her clothes and tidied her hair before returning to the square but she kept her head down. She didn't want anyone to recognise her. Hands gripped her shoulders and pushed her forward.

'Come on, Sis,' Raven said. 'Keep moving.'

'How far?' Noah asked.

'The temple's close now,' Raven replied.

'What's happening?'

'The Sorcerer-master and all his wizards are inside, and the doors are closed.'

Percival's focus was on returning the illestial to its rightful place. Sachin and Jacin had pretended to be opportunistic thrill-seekers, claiming that stealing the illestial had been a lark, and had given all the pieces back. The pair had subsequently been taken away though, and Noah hoped Jacin found an opportunity to open a doorway for their escape before the local constables thrashed them.

Emir turned around. 'We can't get any closer,' he said. 'These folks are wedged in tight.'

Hemmed in by people a head taller than her, Noah said, 'Tell me what you see.'

'Percival is standing on the circular walkway at the top of the tripod and reattaching the three pieces of the illestial to the cradle,' Emir said.

Talyn will be thrilled, Noah thought.

'And what are the sorcerers and wizards doing?' she asked.

'They're standing around the edge of the firestone under the tripod – five or six deep – waving their wands and … chanting by the looks of it.'

An old crone beside Noah elbowed her in the ribs. 'They'll be warding off the Pyranhi Jongu spirits,' she wheezed. 'A good thing the Sorcerer-master is here to protect us all.'

'Yeah,' Noah said. 'Lucky.'

'What are they *really* doing?' Raven whispered in Noah's ear.

Noah shook her head. 'I don't know. I can't tell from here.'

Time dragged on, but the crowd in the square remained. After the failed execution and the theft of the illestial, it seemed no one was willing to risk missing what might happen next.

When a tremor rippled under their feet, Noah said, 'What are they doing now?'

'They're on their knees, waving their arms in the air,' Emir said.

Noah closed her eyes and concentrated. The crowd chatter was hard to block out but she focused on the temple and detected a low hum.

'Pressure's building inside,' she murmured. Her eyes snapped open. 'He's going to blow the temple!'

Emir frowned. 'That doesn't make sense. He's locked the doors to keep everyone out. If he destroys it, he leaves the illestial exposed.'

The humming in Noah's head grew stronger.

'I don't know *why* he's doing it,' she said, 'but he is going to do it.'

'If that thing explodes,' Raven said, 'casualties will be high.'

'Percival's ready to clear the decks,' Emir mused. 'Anyone he wants to take with him, is either in there with him, or in a safe place. But *these* people out here, he wants rid of.'

Raven ran a hand through his hair. 'We need to warn the others.'

'No time!' Noah said. 'Get—'

BOOM!

The blast triggered a human tsunami. The shockwave knocked over those closest to the crystal temple and the rest fell like dominoes. Noah fell and, crushed between Emir and Raven, fought for breath. She wriggled free as crystal shards rained down and the screaming started. Emir hauled Raven to his feet.

'Multiple fatalities at the front,' Emir reported, 'but many more will die in the stampede.'

Raven nodded. 'No matter what you do, stay on your feet.'

'We need to get to Percival,' Noah said.

'We'll go with the flow of the crowd to the side of the square,' Emir said. 'Then we can double back.'

Noah wrapped her arms around Emir's middle and huddled against his back as he led the way through the melee. Only once they reached the edge of the square did she let go.

'Where did all this water come from?' Raven said.

Emir knelt and dragged his fingers through the liquid. 'I don't think it's water.'

He's right, Noah thought as she tested it. It was colourless and odourless, but too viscous to be water. Movement beside her caught her attention. She jumped to her feet, staring at two rippling puddles about half a metre apart. The larger puddle shimmered, then oozed towards the smaller one, consuming it.

'Noah?' Emir said. 'What's happening?'

Noah's eyes darted from puddle to puddle. Everywhere she looked, puddles joined together.

'It's liquid crystal,' Noah said. 'Percival melted the crystal.'

'And now what?' Raven said.

Noah stared at him. 'Now it's coming to life.'

Crystal globs, like giant jellyfish bells, skated haphazardly across the forecourt. They continued joining until they were big enough to engulf a person. Raven leapt out of the path of one oversized blob. The young woman behind him wasn't as quick though and the gooey crystal enveloped her, solidifying almost instantly.

'Look out!' Noah cried as another glob skidded towards Emir.

Raven grabbed Emir's arm and wrenched him aside. Noah watched as the crystal ensnared another helpless victim.

'We need to move,' Emir said. 'This stuff is everywhere.'

The trio angled their way towards the tripod, but it was slow going. Hysterical Somynians darted in all directions as they battled to clear the square, but most were heading away from the temple ruins.

'Ever feel like you're swimming against the tide?' Raven said as he shoved Noah out of the path of another panic-stricken local.

Noah didn't answer, focusing instead on avoiding trampling the dead and the dying. Some had been crushed in the stampede, others speared or shredded by crystal shards. Hundreds of others were encased in crystal – wholly or in part – and many more would soon join them as the crystal slime did its work.

As they neared the tripod, Percival's voice rang out.

'Bravo! Bravo!' he said, clapping his hands. 'You've put on a great show so far … don't stop now! Let's see who can get the closest, shall we?'

Noah's eyes flitted across the square. Aside from her, Emir and Raven, scores of soldiers from Montana's and Catriona's armies approached the ruins too. Ardis saluted them. Noah nodded before returning her attention to the Sorcerer-master.

Percival stood in the centre of the firestone floor under the tripod. The dragonscale circle was about five metres across, dazzling colours swirled and glowed in its depths. Noah's blood ran hot, the dragonscale in her veins reacting to this stone's ancient, elemental power. The

Sorcerer-master's wizards knelt on the ground around the stone, chanting and waving their wands to channel the molten crystal where it was needed.

As Percival cast his gaze across the group, Noah ducked behind her brother.

'What are you doing?' Raven said.

'I don't want Percival to see me yet.'

Noah peeked around her brother's shoulder as the Sorcerer-master pointed to a young man to her right.

'You,' Percival said with a wink. 'I've got my money on you.'

The man leapt forward and made half a dozen strides before one of the transparent blobs whizzed across and caught his foot. Instantly, the blob solidified, encasing the man's foot. Momentum carried his body forward and his knee bent at an awkward angle. He screamed as he went down.

Noah turned away. As Percival deliberated over his next victim, she took off. She wouldn't reach the sorcerer. That would have to wait. She focused on her feet, negotiating the obstacles carefully. When she was only metres away from the wizards, she heard Percival gasp.

Noah looked up. The sorcerer smothered his surprise. Noah smiled at him as he whipped his wand in small circles. Several globs sped towards her.

As they crystallised around her ankles, Percival said, 'You again.'

'I'm closest,' Noah said. 'Is there a prize?'

Unfazed, Percival said, 'There is and I can't wait to show it to you.'

The sorcerer closed his eyes, raised his wand and began chanting. The gelatinous globs on the ground around Noah oozed up her legs, and then coated her torso and arms. This time it didn't solidify completely, but it was viscous enough that she couldn't break out of it. Noah winced as her jellylike suit took control of her limbs.

It spun her around in a half circle, then marched her across the forecourt. Emir, Raven and all the others who'd challenged Percival strutted ahead of her. Like ghoulish marionettes, they shuffled towards their 'prize'.

Chapter 30

'About time,' Emir said to Noah as Percival strode along the lakeshore towards them. 'I feel like we've been standing here for hours.'

Raven's voice came from behind them. 'That's because we *have* been standing here for hours.'

'Percival's trying to unsettle us,' Noah murmured.

Beside her, Ardis grunted. 'I'd like to unsettle him.'

Noah turned her gaze to the subterranean lake, hoping for inspiration. Lush grasses punctuated the sandy shoreline that ringed the underground pool, the clumps of green a striking contrast to the pristine white beach. In the lake itself, the deep blue at the bottom faded to a pearlescent, luminous sheen at the surface where brightly coloured fish darted about among the iridescent corals. *It's almost* too *beautiful,* she thought. *I wonder what secrets it's hiding.*

Noah whistled softly. 'That's it.'

'What's it?' Emir said.

Noah closed her eyes and sang softly to herself, drawing on the firestone in her veins.

'Noah,' Emir whispered. 'What are you doing?'

She ignored him. Percival was closing in on them so every second counted. She sang as quietly as she could, not wanting to draw the attention of the other captives or the wizards guarding them. When she was done, Noah opened her eyes and looked at Emir.

'How'd I do?' she said.

Emir raised one eyebrow. 'Why do you look like Gillette?'

'Ardis wanted to unsettle Percival. This is the best I could come up with at short notice.'

Percival surveyed his prisoners as his wizards formed up around him. Noah watched his eyes narrow. She held her breath as he studied each of them in turn. Then, he snatched his wand from his belt and levelled it at a wizard's chest.

'Where is the elf slave?' he demanded.

'I-I don't kn-know,' the portly wizard stammered. 'N-no one has g-gone anywh-where.'

'Find her!' Percival said, nostrils flaring. 'She's encased in crystal. It can't be that difficult.'

The wizard scurried to do his bidding as Percival climbed onto a rocky platform.

'Now,' Percival said, 'your prize. I'm sure you'll all enjoy a swim.'

A few words and swipes of his wand were all it took to march the group into the water up to their shoulders.

'So what's your plan now?' Emir said.

'My plan,' Percival said, 'is to leave you all there in that lake of *acid*. Eventually, it will eat holes in your crystal suits and then your flesh.'

Noah's heart thumped harder as she noticed the small bubbles congregating on the crystal.

'In the meantime,' Percival continued, 'I have important business to attend to.'

'Like?' Ardis prompted.

'Preparing for the return of the pyrohm,' he said.

'You're no match for the elves,' Emir said. 'Their knowledge is ancient.'

'As is mine,' Percival boasted. 'I have access to all the Pyranhi lore and have dedicated my life to mastering it.'

Noah whistled a few notes, dissolving her glamour. 'You might have had *access* to it,' she said, 'but you certainly haven't *mastered* it.'

The corner of Percival's mouth twitched as his eyes landed on her. 'You. I hope you don't consider disguising yourself as a boy as "mastery". Magic is—'

'I know all about magic,' Noah said. 'I'm the 13th key.'

Percival's acolytes whispered among themselves at the lake's edge. The sorcerer's face flushed with colour.

'I can honestly say,' Percival said, 'that I have never heard anyone claim to be the 13th key. And while your story is compellingly original, it is also utterly ridiculous.'

'But still true,' Noah said.

Percival shrugged. 'So you say. But either way, you're going to die in there along with all your friends. You can tell all the stories you want until the acid eats through the crystal and then starts on your skin. Now,' he said as he turned his back, 'I'm going to prepare for my guests.'

Come on, Noah, she thought to herself as she watched him go, *if he gets away from you here, you've lost.*

'The elves won't come until one of us is dead,' she blurted.

Percival stopped. Noah saw his shoulders tense under his cloak.

Without turning to look at her he said, 'Well, hurry up and die, then we can all get on with things.'

'Really? That's hardly good preparation,' Noah said. 'How are you going to defeat the elf queen if you can't even deal with me?'

Percival spun round. 'I *am* dealing with you. You're getting as good as you deserve! As if I need to waste my time on the likes of you.'

Noah wished Sachin was with her. He was the master of goading people. She looked at Raven for inspiration. His expression was grim, in contrast to the rainbow fish that circled him. As Noah contemplated how fish and coral could survive in acid, support came from an unlikely source.

One of Percival's acolytes stepped forward, a young woman with a severe, auburn bob that framed her pale face. She regarded Noah with amusement.

'She is undoubtedly unworthy of your effort, Sorcerer-master Percival,' the woman said, 'but indulge us. We, your most loyal disciples, would relish the opportunity to see you ply your craft to smite this boaster.'

Her proposition was seconded by the wizard beside her. 'Indeed,' the man said. 'How are the low-lives expected to repent with her constant yabbering?'

'Repent?' Ardis said. 'Repent what?'

'Repent your dismal, sordid lives,' another acolyte said. 'As the crystal deteriorates and the acid leaks in and eats your flesh, pain sharpens your attention – focuses your reflection. Before you die, you should beg forgiveness for your sins.'

'From whom?' Raven said.

'From Jong,' the acolyte answered.

Noah thought her eyes might pop out of her head. Ask Jong for forgiveness? The most destructive, arrogant, manipulative god in the universe … even Raven was speechless.

'Anyway,' Noah said, 'what do you say, Percival? Are we to "magic it out", or not?'

The auburn-haired acolyte smiled at Percival. 'May I?' she said.

Percival nodded and the woman stepped forward, wand raised. Within moments, Noah's crystal suit marched her out of the lake before melting away on the sand.

'And now,' the acolyte said to her, 'prepare to meet your doom.'

Noah snatched the wand from the woman's hand. 'I don't think so,' she muttered.

'Hey!' the acolyte cried as Noah raced up an embankment.

Percival began chanting and Noah whirled back round, barking the shield spell Hildebrand had taught her. A shield appeared just in time and Noah braced herself. Percival's fireball smashed into the wood, knocking Noah back several metres. She landed hard on her behind.

Noah groaned. 'Ouch.'

'Get up!' Percival said. 'And summon whatever you can to battle my … pet.'

Noah jammed the wand into the sand. *Pyranhi magic's not my thing,* she thought as she ripped her viola from her pocket. With trembling hands, she fumbled with the clasps. Hildebrand said she didn't need a key, but she needed to conserve her strength.

Percival's chanting became louder. Noah ignored him as she raced up the embankment to shelter behind a rock. She tucked her instrument under her chin and commenced a searching tonic. *There's got to be something down there I can coax out,* she thought. It took her only a few bars to find something. She smiled grimly. A giant electric eel was perfect. She peeked around the rock and down to the lake.

'Come on,' Noah said aloud as she switched tonics. 'You know you want to come out.'

Roooaarrrrrrr!

Noah glanced at Percival and shuddered. A hulking winged jackal, twice as tall as the sorcerer, squatted beside him. Thick black goo dripped from its jaws. The jackal flapped its leathery wings and leapt into the air.

'I hope you're ready to die!' Percival called.

'Not quite!' Noah called back, upping her tonic's tempo.

Someone shrieked as Noah raced to the next rock up the embankment. She chanced a peek over her shoulder. Something snakelike slithered out of the water. Long and black with orange spots lining its sides, the eel reached the shore. Fingers of lightning rippled along its body, the crackling sparks lifting Noah's spirits.

'You like that, Percival?' Noah yelled.

'It's a fish,' he said.

'It's a *big, electric* fish,' Noah clarified.

'Size isn't important.'

The hell it isn't, Noah thought. *That thing's gotta be over ten metres long.*

'Says the man with the big, ugly hyena!' she retorted as she stowed her viola.

Its target identified, the flying jackal turned her way. The beast's size compromised its manoeuvrability so Noah wound through rocks and grasses, picking out the most circuitous route she could back to where Percival was.

'Where's my wand?' the auburn-haired acolyte screamed as Noah sprinted past.

Noah pointed back over her shoulder but didn't stop running. 'Up there,' she said.

A shriek of agony reverberated around the cavern as the eel enjoyed its first meal of Jongu acolyte. Noah wondered how many it could eat. The acolytes were obviously wondering the same thing as they were frantically rescuing captives from the lake. Wands flashed and the prisoners' crystal suits marched them out of the acid before melting away at the shoreline. Noah's heart leapt when she saw Raven sprinting along the beach towards her.

'Eat the heathens!' the acolytes cried. 'Eat the unworthy!'

Raven caught up to Noah. 'Hurry!' she said. 'Get the wands off them before they get organised and conjure up something else.'

Raven saluted. 'Got it.'

'And avoid the eel,' she added.

'Thanks, Sis,' Raven said. 'Very helpful.'

The eel struck another acolyte with its tail. The man shuddered as electricity coursed through him. His eyes rolled back in his head and tendrils of smoke escaped from his collar. Percival fumed as the man slumped to the ground.

'What do you think of my fish now?' Noah said.

Percival's face turned from red to purple.

'Master! Save us!' an acolyte cried.

The sorcerer scowled. 'Save yourself and show that you are worthy of going to the new world.'

'But they've taken my wand!'

Not far from Noah, the jackal swooped. Bones crunched as the animal's jaw clamped onto a woman's shoulder. Noah winced as the woman screamed.

Emir arrived at her side, four wands in his hand. 'We need to get this cleaned up.'

Noah scanned the cavern. Though the numbers were decreasing, there were still plenty of bodies in motion. Acolytes and captives darted about. They no longer fought each other, avoiding the lethal wildlife had become everyone's individual priority.

'Get Ardis, lead the others out,' Noah said. 'I'll deal with Percival.'

Emir nodded and jogged away as Percival picked up the threads of his spell. Noah leapt forward and punched the sorcerer in the sternum. His eyes bulged as he doubled over, clutching his chest.

'Not … fair,' he said, fighting for breath.

'Surrender!' Noah said.

Percival shook his head. 'Never!' he cried, raising his wand.

Noah kicked his hand, sending the wand flying into a clump of grass nearby.

'*Now* will you surrender?' Noah said.

Percival rolled away before scrambling towards the grass. With a glance behind her to check where the eel was, Noah strode after Percival. As his hand closed around the base of the wand, Noah jumped on the end of it.

Snap!

'No!' Percival howled, holding the stub of his wand in his hand.

Noah pounced on the broken piece on the ground and snatched it up.

'You're finished,' she said, tucking the firestone inside her vest, 'but you've still got half a wand, so call off your beast.'

Still on his hands and knees, he brandished what remained of his wand. 'Never! The Jongu don't surrender.'

The jackal barked in distress. Noah turned. Two arrows protruded from the creature's neck. Raven, perched on a rock, had another arrow in his bow. The eel waited expectantly below. Its head waved cobra-like as it tracked the jackal's increasingly erratic flight path.

'Never mind,' Noah said. 'My brother will take care of it.'

'Jong,' Percival panted. 'Help me.'

'Hand over the wand,' Noah said.

'No!'

Noah booted the sorcerer in the ribs before snatching the broken piece of firestone from his grasp.

'Thank you, for your cooperation,' she said.

The jackal's barking ceased.

'If it's any consolation,' Noah said, 'I'm sure the eel is very grateful for such a … sumptuous snack.'

Percival beat his fist on the ground. 'No! No! No!' he whimpered.

Raven arrived at Noah's side, his bow slung over his shoulder. 'What do you want to do with him?'

'Tie him up,' Noah said. 'We'll lock him in the dungeon.'

'His followers might try to break him out,' Raven warned.

Noah shook her head. 'After the way he just abandoned them, I doubt it.'

Chapter 31

Jacin grinned. 'Ah, this brings back memories.'

Grainger grunted as he opened the wooden door and stepped over the threshold. Reluctantly, Noah followed him. The transition from Dragonhall's crypt to the portal cluster's eerie forest made Noah shudder. Memories of her last experience here bubbled to the front of her mind. She'd defeated the dundar – saving herself, Grainger and Jacin from the spirit-devouring monster – but she didn't want to run into it again. And the dundar was far from the worst nightmare that lurked in the portal cluster. She hoped Grainger knew where the Genja gate was so they didn't have to linger here any longer than necessary.

'So this is the infamous portal cluster,' Sachin said. 'It really is everything the brochure promised.'

Brinn growled. 'Sachin, if you and Jacin can't be serious, you can both go back to Somyni now.'

Sachin squatted beside Brinn and scratched her under the chin. 'You don't mean that.'

Brinn's orange eyes blazed, but it was Grainger who spoke.

'We've got a job to do,' he said. 'Let's get it done so we can all get back to Somyni.'

Jacin saluted. 'Lead the way.'

'Just don't touch anything in here,' Noah said, 'and if anything moves – run.'

'Don't worry, Noah,' Piper said. 'I'll protect you.'

Despite losing her horns and one foot, the dragon's enthusiasm was undented. Noah stroked her neck as Grainger led the way with Jacin close behind him. Sachin walked at Noah's side.

'Never thought I'd be messing about with olluka pathways,' Sachin said.

Noah sighed. 'I wish we didn't have to. Shifting a pathway is one thing. But cutting it to get it the right distance from the vortex is going to be next to impossible.'

'There's no choice,' Sachin said. 'If we don't do this, there'll be no way to get Jong and the illestial into the vortex.'

'Assuming we can get the pyrohm back and get Jong into the illestial,' Noah said.

Piper snorted. 'Let's worry about one thing at a time. The pathway is our priority now. Anyway, if the elves show up in Somyni in our absence, the others will keep them busy.'

That's what I'm afraid of, Noah thought. When the elves arrived they'd find only Montana's and Catriona's warriors, a few hundred dragon riders and a handful of Somynians standing against them. Percival's crystal assault had been ruthlessly effective and most of those Somynians who hadn't perished were in hiding.

The group walked in silence, each reviewing their own role in the task at hand.

'This is it,' Grainger said at last.

Noah squinted at the fist-sized opening in the olluka tree's ancient wood. Unlike other portals she'd seen, this one had an 'X' carved above the opening.

Noah frowned. 'Is that a warning?'

'Yes,' Brinn said. 'Grainger, dilate the pathway, please.'

Grainger nodded at Jacin. 'Ready?'

Jacin whipped his baton from his vest. 'Ready.'

Noah clenched her fists as the pair chanted in ancient Pyranhi. Sachin leant in so he could whisper in her ear.

'I feel a bit redundant,' he said.

'Enjoy it while it lasts,' Noah whispered back. 'Once that pathway is big enough, we're up.'

With Brinn and Piper on watch, Noah closed her eyes and opened her mind to the cosmos beyond the portal. She gasped. The branches of the olluka trees that grew on Talisker were solid, but that changed in space. To account for the movements of cosmic bodies, the pathways were flexible. *Elastic,* Noah thought. Space wasn't empty. Clumps of tangled pathways dotted the galactic landscape in every direction.

Movement caught Noah's attention. Beyond the sun, something stirred. Sweat broke out on her forehead.

The vortex.

A gargantuan swirling funnel of rock and dust warped the solar system's celestial fabric. Occasional flares of light belched from its throat as metallic elements collided in the maelstrom in its belly. Rather than being satiated by the worlds it had consumed, its appetite had grown exponentially. Eventually it would collapse under its own mass, but Talisker would fall victim to it long before that.

'Noah,' Sachin said. 'Eyes front.'

Noah opened her eyes and stared at the portal gate, which had expanded almost enough for them to walk in upright. She reached into her pocket for her viola as Sachin readied his flute.

'Don't get too close,' Brinn warned. 'It's not ready yet.'

Sweat trickled down both Grainger's and Jacin's faces as their wands flicked back and forth to manipulate the ancient Pyranhi magic that regulated the pathway.

'Almost there,' Brinn said as the portal gate stretched a little wider.

Noah retuned her viola as Grainger and Jacin laboured over their part in this crazy plan to convert a magical, spaghetti-thin pathway into a pedestrian tunnel. The circle of inky blackness continued to grow.

Brinn turned to Noah. 'Start your tonic.'

Noah glanced at Sachin as she dragged her bow across the strings of her instrument and he blew his first note. Sachin's frown betrayed his intense concentration. Noah focused on her own melody as they wove their tonic to accelerate their neural networks. Travel through the olluka pathways was not instantaneous. It only appeared that way to humans whose reflexes were relatively slow. To sever the pathway at the critical point to take their tunnel in range of the vortex, Noah needed to be able to track their progress through the pathway. Grainger and Jacin could dilate the pathway but they couldn't slow it down. She and Sachin had to boost their reaction times to align with the pathway.

'I can see the pathway,' Noah said. 'It's working.'

Where darkness had loomed beyond the portal gate, stars now twinkled.

'Go!' Grainger said. 'We can't hold this for long.'

Sachin, playing furiously, raced towards the portal. Noah was right behind him. She'd thought it would be difficult to play her viola while running, but once inside the pathway their passage was perfectly smooth. *I don't have to run,* she thought, *the pathway takes care of that.*

Noah relaxed her legs and the lights streaked by around them as they hurtled down the tunnel. She reached out for the vortex with her perceptions. It was a long way away, but they were approaching at blinding speed. Despite the augmented mental acuity the tonic brought her, Noah struggled to calibrate the distances. If she missed the mark, there'd be no second chance. Going too far meant certain death on Genja while pulling up short meant their tunnel wouldn't be within reach of the vortex.

Piper appeared at her side. 'Hurry, Noah! You don't have much time!'

No kidding, Noah thought. Her augmented neural activity would soon cook her brain – if her heart didn't fail first as it laboured to deliver the oxygen required to sustain her hypersensitive state. She glanced at Sachin, wondering if he was better or worse off than she was. Would the firestone in her veins protect her or accelerate her demise?

While Sachin continued with the existing tonic, Noah switched to a new one. She squeezed her eyes closed and immersed herself in music designed to constrict the pathway, like a string being tied around a sausage.

'It's narrowing up ahead,' Piper said.

Noah sensed the contraction, but timing was everything now. If she didn't seal it quickly enough, they'd all slip through and end up on Genja.

We're not going to make it, she thought. *We need more power.* Reaching inside herself, she drew on the firestone dwelling within her body.

Brinn's voice echoed down the tunnel. 'Noah! Don't! You'll blow the whole thing.'

Noah ignored the cat, instead channelling her power until the strings on her viola smoked. Her fingers blistered and her arm ached, but Sachin's unwavering melody kept her focused.

'Come on,' she murmured aloud. 'Just close already!'

'Noah!' Piper yelled. 'Hurry!'

Noah ignored the dragon, focusing all her energy on the task at hand. Brinn's face swam in her mind. *You'll blow the whole thing.* Noah clenched her jaws as she sawed her bow back and forth across the strings. She could sense rather than see that the translucent pathway was almost sealed up ahead.

Hoped sparked in Noah's chest. Though not totally sure the pathway was the right length, she was optimistic that she could close it and keep them from landing on Genja. She adjusted her tonic slightly. *That ought to do—*

Piper screeched, disrupting Noah's final cadence. But it wasn't what she *could* hear that made Noah's heart freeze – it was what she couldn't hear. Sachin's flute was silent.

Without his tonic, Noah's perception faltered. Her reflexes slowed only slightly but it was enough to compromise her endeavour. Noah twisted her head round. Sachin lay on the floor, motionless.

'*Sachin!*' she screamed as she sped towards the narrow opening ahead.

Piper spewed flame. 'Fix the seal, then you can attend to him!'

Heart thumping, Noah jerked back round to face the end of the tunnel and thrust her feet towards the narrow opening.

'Ouch!' she groaned as she hugged her viola to her chest.

'That wasn't quite the idea,' Piper said. 'You weren't supposed to plug the hole.'

'I didn't do it on purpose,' Noah snapped, wriggling to pull her legs back through the breach. 'And if you say anything about the size of my butt …'

Piper shook her head. 'Wouldn't dream of it.'

Noah glanced at Sachin's unconscious body. 'Stay with him, Piper. I'll close this last bit and then examine him.'

Noah wedged her feet either side of the gap and raced through the end of her tonic. When the hole was finally sealed, she crawled to Sachin. His eyes were closed and his face, deathly pale. Noah rested her head on his chest and listened. His heart-rate was so high, the individual beats were virtually indistinguishable and his breathing was shallow.

'No,' Noah whispered. 'Don't do this to me, Sachin.'

Piper crouched next to her. 'Stabilise him, and then finish what we came here to do.'

It would take a miracle to save him. She could suppress his metabolism to prevent further damage but she couldn't undo what the tonic had already done. She'd need Grainger and Jacin for that.

And it was a long way back to the portal gate.

'Come on,' Piper said. 'The sooner we're done, the sooner we can get him back to the others.'

Noah nodded. The seal she'd created had interrupted the magic of the pathway, like a kink in a garden hose. High-speed travel was no longer an option on this route so she was thankful that Piper would fly them back to the portal gate. The distance they'd travelled was too much for Noah's mind to grasp. If she'd had to walk back, she'd likely be an old woman by the time she arrived.

At least Grainger and Jacin could rest until she returned. Now that the pathway was a static tunnel, their job was done.

Noah inspected her bow. Few of the fibres remained intact. Most had burned away. *It'll have to do*, she thought. Inhaling deeply, she commenced the tonic to slow their reflexes. The music calmed her, physically at least. The pressure inside her head eased, along with her heart-rate. She monitored Sachin's breathing, watching the rise and fall of his chest.

When she was done, she put her instrument aside and checked his pulse. It was ragged, but it was slower. Noah hooked her elbows under Sachin's armpits. She dragged him over to Piper, laying him across the dragon's back.

Noah squeezed his shoulder. 'Won't be long,' she promised.

With an aching heart, Noah stowed her viola and bow in her trousers, then studied the seal she'd created. The tunnel tapered away to a dimple that reminded her of a human navel. Noah lowered herself onto the sloped floor and crawled towards it. When the space became too narrow, she lowered herself onto her belly and wriggled closer.

'Here goes nothing,' she murmured.

Noah reached towards the indentation with her index finger and summoned the firestone within her. Adapting Hildebrand's wind spell, she twirled her finger in slow circles as she chanted in ancient Pyranhi. The tunnel creaked, then lurched.

'Easy, Noah,' Piper said.

Noah frowned. 'I'm trying,' she said, 'but believe it or not it's a bit tricky to spin a tunnel that's millions of kilometres long.'

Noah refocused, increasing the speed of her finger spirals as she recited her incantations. The tunnel responded. It turned slowly at first, but quickly accelerated. The smooth surface slid under her, her Academy vest and trousers offering no resistance. Without interrupting her chant, Noah flipped onto her back to avoid friction burns on the exposed skin of her elbows.

She repeated the spell again, and again, but each time, her arm grew heavier. The effort of rotating something so immense pushed Noah to her limit. *I can't do this,* she thought. Twisting one end of the pathway to snap it at the pinch point was simple in theory, but the futility of the enterprise was becoming glaringly apparent.

'You can do it, Noah,' Piper urged. 'You're so close.'

Her reserves almost depleted, Noah steeled herself for one more round. If it didn't work this time, Piper would be taking back two patients. Her voice barely above a whisper, Noah battled through the spell one last time and when the last word was done, her arms flopped onto the floor. Delirium stalked her, an intangible predator she was powerless to fight, but exhaustion was the ultimate victor. Before it claimed her though, Noah heard the sound she'd been waiting for.

Crack!

It's done, Noah thought.

The tunnel pitched violently as the vortex sucked at the severed strand. Noah tried to turn her head to gauge their proximity to the insatiable cosmic spiral, but consciousness deserted her.

Chapter 32

Noah screwed up her nose. The herbal concoction smelled like rotting flesh. Grainger had assured her that it was the best remedy for the damage done to her nervous system during her quest to divert the olluka pathway to within range of the vortex. Sachin had languished in a coma for five days after their return and Noah suspected that the foul stench had contributed to his delayed return to consciousness.

'You're not pouring that out the window, are you?' Chase called.

Noah had considered doing that but didn't admit it. Perched on the window sill of Percival's former quarters in Ion Tower with her legs dangling ten storeys above the square below, Noah pinched her nostrils and downed the brew.

She held the mug aloft, signalling her victory over the vile potion. 'Done!'

Noah swivelled and handed the empty mug to Chase, who studied her friend intently.

'How are you feeling?' Chase said.

Noah smiled. 'Like I could wrestle a bear.'

'Yeah right,' Chase said. 'How about a cat? If Brinn finds you out of bed, she'll be furious.'

'A week in bed is long enough,' Noah said. 'And besides, if the elves arrive – I don't want to be caught in my pyjamas.'

Chase sighed.

'Anyway, it's not like I'm hiding from her,' Noah added. 'I actually came here looking for her – this is Brinn's new headquarters isn't it?'

Chase shook her head. 'Just don't say I didn't warn you,' she said before taking the cup to the sink.

Noah turned her gaze to the tripod in the square. The debris from the crystal temple had been cleared away and soldiers and dragons now patrolled the city. She wondered when the elves would arrive. Waiting was wearing thin; patience was at a premium.

More dragons soared over the city. They hadn't flown freely this close to the city in centuries and the new archers in the towers would protect the dragon riders rather than attack them.

Piper flew into view from behind the tower and hovered in front of Noah.

'Want to play?' the dragon said.

Noah raised an eyebrow. 'Play?'

'Practise,' Piper said. 'I meant practise. We should *practise* our manoeuvres.'

Noah nodded. 'I'll meet you downstairs.'

'Or you could jump from there,' Piper suggested.

Grimacing, Noah said, 'I'll see you downstairs.'

Noah swung her legs inside and slid down from the window ledge. Even though she'd come looking for Brinn, the prospect of riding with Piper had her hoping she wouldn't encounter the cat now. Luck was with her. She made it outside without being accosted.

Piper was waiting. 'All aboard,' the dragon said.

Noah climbed into the saddle and unlooped the reins from around the pommel-like protrusions on Piper's back scales.

'Goggles on?' Piper said.

'Almost,' Noah said, pulling them from her trouser pocket.

The dragon jumped and flapped her leathery wings, launching herself into the air. Adrenaline surged through Noah's body and she smiled. It seemed wrong to be enjoying herself at a time like this, but nothing compared to riding a dragon.

Once they were above Ion Tower, Noah shifted her body weight left and tapped Piper's side. Tensing all her muscles, Noah braced herself for the roll. As the ground passed above her head, she shrieked in delight. Ignoring her stomach's protests, Noah signalled another roll … and then another.

'Three is enough,' Piper said as she levelled out.

'In one direction,' Noah called over the wind. 'We need to go back the other way now to balance it out.'

Piper obliged, pitching right. As they turned, Noah glimpsed the empty triangular space in the cradle on top of the tripod where the pyrohm was destined to be. *Soon,* she thought. *Very soon.* Piper swivelled twice more before banking left and wheeling in a sweeping arc around the tower.

A horn blast as they rounded the tower startled Noah. She slid dangerously in the saddle as her body jolted in fright.

'What the—'

'Holy crap!' Piper said. 'There's a hole in the … air.'

'Well spotted,' Noah said. 'Take me closer!'

The dragon beat her wings harder. 'You got it.'

Above them, the air shimmered and peeled back further, revealing a glowing, pearlescent light.

'Pretty,' Piper said. 'Elves?'

Noah frowned. Somyni wasn't expecting any other magical visitors but it seemed an odd entry point.

'Don't think so,' Noah called as they approached the edge of the rift. 'It's a long way off the ground – a long way to fall.'

Ion Tower's horn continued sounding but Noah ignored it. Other dragon riders followed Noah's lead and circled the growing fracture. When a slender, white segmented leg appeared through the breach, Noah held her breath. More legs appeared around the rim of the tear, followed by bodies.

'Spiders?' Noah cried. 'Really?'

'At least they're pretty spiders,' Piper said.

'Pretty *big* spiders,' Noah said. 'I've seen camels smaller than those things.' Shifting in the saddle, she added, 'Back off a bit, would you?'

Piper banked left. 'I thought you wanted a closer look.'

Noah gripped the reins tighter. 'This is close enough.'

Massive snowy-white arachnids sailed downwards on glittering silken threads while dragons darted and dived to get out of the way.

'Stay back!' Noah yelled to those around her. 'Just watch!'

On reaching the ground, the spiders commenced an hypnotic dance. Climbing, jumping and swinging, their synchronised movements mesmerised the cordon of dragon riders. Every transition was evidenced by shimmering thread.

'They're building a web,' Noah breathed. 'They're going to cocoon the tripod.'

One dragon dived towards the rope of silk and burst into flame on impact.

Noah wrenched on the reins.

'Noah!' Piper said. 'What's happening?'

'Firestone!' Noah cried. 'Pull back! Everyone pull back!'

Whoever heard of spiders that spin firestone webs? she thought.

'Piper, take me back to the tower!'

The dragon banked and sailed towards the tower. When she landed, Brinn and Grainger were waiting.

'They're shielding the tripod,' Noah said, before the cat could chastise her for exerting herself when she was supposed to be recovering.

'Yes,' Brinn said. 'The elves are clever. They have conjured something special – and unexpected – to aid them.'

'The elves will open a doorway inside the cocoon?' Grainger said.

'I would,' Brinn said.

Dragons swirled overhead but Chain, Vespa, Horatio and Fontina broke from formation and came in to land by the tower. Battle-ready, neither Emir nor Raven dismounted their dragons.

Raven looked at Noah. 'How do we get that thing down?'

'I think we should let the spiders finish their work,' Noah said. 'If we damage any of it, they'll just repair it.'

'Agreed,' Grainger said.

'This is it,' Horatio said, his green eyes blazing. 'The dragon riders are standing by. We will make our final preparations.'

'And I will get word to Montana so she can mobilise her troops,' Fontina added.

Horatio and Fontina launched themselves into the air and goose-bumps prickled Noah's arms as she watched the dragon elders soar against the backdrop of the firestone sky.

Raven tapped his sword hilt as he studied Brinn. 'Before I go and set a perimeter, will there be anything else?'

Brinn's whiskers twitched as she turned her blistering gaze on him and then Emir.

'Don't die,' the cat said. Then, with a glance at Noah, added, 'She needs you two.'

'Uh-huh,' Raven said, smiling. 'Are you sure it's not actually because *you'd* miss us?'

Brinn growled. 'Go and set your perimeter, Army Commander.'

Both Raven and Emir gave her Leninstar's salute before taking off to attend to their respective tasks.

'The prophecy doesn't say anything about them,' Noah said when they were gone.

'Pardon?' Brinn said.

The thirteenth key the world shall need, for evil to be brought to heel – One of two, the Dragon's bane must rise; and the music wield,' she said. 'It doesn't mention brothers or boyfriends.'

'Quite,' Brinn said. 'The prophecy doesn't tell the whole story, though.'

'No, it's ridiculously vague, actually,' Noah said. 'I've lost track of the number of times I thought I'd fulfilled it – only to have it thrown in my face again. I really hope this is the last of it. Jong had better be the last "evil" that needs to be "brought to heel".'

'It's not that simple, Noah,' Brinn said. 'But if it makes you feel any better, the illestial is what the Pyranhi had in mind when they made the prophecy.'

Anger ignited in Noah's belly and surged through her. 'No, it doesn't make me feel better,' she said. 'Why did you let me believe all those other times that I was fulfilling the prophecy? Why couldn't you just tell me the truth?'

In her peripheral vision, Noah saw Grainger motion to Piper to follow him. The pair disappeared around the side of the tower before Brinn answered her.

'The *truth*,' Brinn said, 'is that you needed the practice. Do you think it would have been a good idea to start your training with this test? Would you have had any chance of defeating Jong before now?'

Noah's shoulders sagged as some of her anger deserted her. It wasn't even certain she could defeat Jong now.

'I guess not,' she said. 'As long as there isn't someone more evil coming along anytime soon.'

Brinn swished her tail. 'It depends what you mean by evil.'

Noah frowned. 'Meaning I shouldn't let my guard down because there'll always be evil in the world?'

'Jong's not evil,' Brinn said, 'but because he threatens the world the Pyranhi were attached to, they saw him as evil. It's a matter of perspective.'

'Perspective? Really?'

'As it's in Elani's nature to be creative, it's in Jong's nature to be destructive,' Brinn said. 'If nothing were ever destroyed, how would Elani continue to create?'

'But surely Jong doesn't have to destroy everything,' Noah argued. 'He can make choices.'

'Yes,' Brinn said, 'but life comes and goes on many worlds, Noah, and seems fleeting in the eyes of gods.'

Noah chewed her bottom lip. She didn't like where this conversation was going.

'If our destruction is inevitable,' Noah said, 'then why do you even care what happens here?'

Brinn rubbed against Noah's leg. 'Because to me, life on Talisker is interesting,' she said, 'and though it will end one day, it doesn't need to be now.'

Noah remembered what she'd read about Temperance in Carai's archives.

'You're the mediator,' Noah said. 'It's in your nature to balance out your brothers.'

'Yes.'

'Have you considered doing a refresher course?'

Brinn's eyes blazed. 'What?'

'To update your qualifications,' Noah said. 'You do have qualifications, don't you? Mediation is a tricky business, and considering how extreme your siblings are, you really should keep up to date with the latest techniques.'

'Would you prefer I left?' Brinn said. 'You've got this, have you?'

Noah sighed. 'No, you'd best stick around.'

'I'd say so,' Brinn said. 'You're the most unruly sein-Temperance I've had.'

'Hang on a minute!' Noah said. 'I'm unruly? What about you? You don't follow rules! Why should I?'

'Because I'm a god and you're not.'

Noah's anger flared again as the demon's words to Brinn came back to her. *Did the death of your Pyranhi disciples teach you nothing?*

'And how many of your champions have *died* because they followed you?'

Brinn hung her head, closed her eyes and said nothing for nearly a minute. Finally, she said, 'Too many.'

In all the time Noah had known Brinn, the cat had been demanding, caustic and unrelenting. Remorse was something Noah had never seen from her. Brinn suddenly looked small and fragile.

Noah shuddered. 'Tell me what happened when the Pyranhi tried to destroy the pyrohm,' she whispered.

'It should never have happened,' Brinn said. 'My champion at the time – Azrael – was only supposed to monitor the sein-Jong.' Her whiskers twitched as she glanced at the tower. 'But something happened. To this day I don't know what it was, but he stole the pyrohm and took it to Tisaan.'

'He stole it from Ion Tower?'

Brinn nodded. 'Ion Tower has always been the sein-Jong's residence in Somyni.'

Noah frowned. Twice she'd been in Percival's quarters – the sein-Jong's quarters. The room where – a thousand millennia ago – the mystical relic had been created and revered. Her head pounded with the effort of trying to imagine sein-Temperance Azrael skulking around in the tower, on the same stone tiles she had trod, as he discharged his duty to his god.

'In Tisaan,' Brinn continued, 'the three greatest Pyranhi sorcerers of the time undertook the task of destroying the pyrohm. Azrael, along with the entire Elanu Council, was there to bear witness. The twenty-six Pyranhi who died in the explosion that day … were just the beginning. Without the Council's leadership, emotions ran high in Tisaan. Those left behind were convinced that the Jongu had deliberately sabotaged the device, and then manipulated Azrael so he would steal it and take it to Tisaan. They declared war on Somyni. You know how that turned out.'

'The demon said you almost destroyed the world then,' Noah said. 'The explosion sounds bad, but not bad enough to destroy the world. So what did he mean?'

Brinn sighed. 'I arrived in Tisaan only moments after the explosion. Azrael was still alive … though barely. He begged me to destroy the pyrohm. He knew I had the power to do it.'

Tears pricked the corners of Noah's eyes. 'You refused his dying wish.'

'Not exactly,' Brinn said. 'I actually started …'

Noah's eyes widened. 'But using *that much* power would have destroyed Talisker.'

'Yes,' Brinn snapped. 'Healing the occasional Dragonsbane of swamp fly paralysis is one thing. But unleashing the force required to defuse the most ostentatious magical relic this world has ever seen – that was unwise.'

'What stopped you?'

'Not what. Who.'

'Who stopped you?'

'A dragon,' Brinn said.

'Xan?'

'No. Her name was Mia.'

Her heart too sore to ask about the dragon's fate, Noah said, 'I'm sorry.'

Brinn shook her head. 'Nothing for you to be sorry about … but let's set things right this time.'

'And how are we going to do that?'

'We need to get the elves here.'

Noah inhaled deeply and exhaled slowly. 'And you have something in mind?'

Brinn nodded. 'Yes.'

Chapter 33

Last time Noah had stood on this stage, she'd been shackled and headed for the guillotine. The guillotine was gone now and the mood in the square was sombre. Soldiers, dragons and dragon riders dominated the square, awaiting Horatio's address. The only resistance to the elves' plot stood in this square, and it seemed that the long-lived creatures might just wait until everyone died of old age before initiating their plan.

Not if I can help it, Noah thought.

'I wish Horatio would get on with it,' Chase muttered.

Noah took her friend's hand. 'Yeah,' she said, not knowing what else to say.

If Noah succeeded in her task, the elves would come. And the people here would face a peril greater than anyone on Talisker ever had. She shuddered as she scanned the group on stage. Raven stood by Catriona and Ardis by Montana. Noah was thankful to be between Chase and Emir. Grainger, Sachin, Jacin and Avril huddled in a knot behind the dragon elders while Brinn conferred with Horatio and Fontina. Jaxon and Gillette were among the thousands of soldiers in the square.

When Horatio and Fontina approached the front of the stage, Noah released Chase's hand. The soldiers stood to attention as the dragons took their places.

'Looks like your wish is about to come true, Chase,' Noah said.

'Friends,' Horatio said, 'this is it. The elves – when they come – will try to use the illestial to release Jong from his prison. We cannot allow this.'

'*Aye!*' the crowd roared.

Noah shivered.

'Our priorities,' Fontina said, 'are to acquire the pyrohm and neutralise the elves.'

Horatio nodded. 'The pyrohm needs to get to Noah. She and Dragonsbane Grainger will then dispose of the illestial, and Talisker will be free of its threat forever.'

Cheering broke out and the dragons flamed their support.

Fontina lifted her wings, a signal for quiet. 'And neutralising the elves does not mean slaughtering them. Take their wands and they can do no magic. Once they're disarmed, tie them up.'

'And what of the elf soldiers?' one of the dragon riders called.

Montana stepped forward. 'In accordance with the Score, you will use only the force that is required. As with the wizards, disarm the soldiers if you can and restrain them. But let's not be naive. Casualties will be unavoidable. Let's aim for as few deaths as possible though.'

'It is time to get the elves' attention,' Fontina said. The soot-coloured dragon turned to Noah. 'Ready?'

Noah nodded. 'Ready as I'll ever be,' she murmured.

Emir put his arm around her shoulders and kissed the top of her head. 'We're with you.'

Flanked by Emir and Chase, Noah made her way down the stairs. The soldiers turned ninety degrees to face the square's central pathway. As Noah and her retinue passed by on their way to the tripod, waves of fighters saluted.

Noah kept her eyes on the firestone web, ignoring the rising heat of the blood in her veins. Each step increased her trepidation. At the end of the guard of honour, Noah saw Piper waiting and her heart skipped a beat. The young dragon had endured more than her share of trauma already. If everything went to plan and Talisker was saved, Piper's horns would grow back, and new scales would replace the damaged ones. And if Jacin survived, he had promised her a new foot.

Noah stopped when she reached the firestone cocoon. She peered between the hairlike filaments as her friends formed up around her. The tripod that straddled the huge piece of firestone on the floor was about to serve its purpose.

Brinn appeared at Noah's side. 'Do it.'

Noah closed her eyes but struggled to concentrate. She slowed her breathing and counted her heartbeats as she dispelled conscious thought and let her subconscious drift into the world around her.

Hello, Noah.

Noah flinched.

'What's wrong?' Brinn said.

'Xan's talking to me,' Noah murmured.

Brinn growled. 'I wondered when she'd contact you,' she said. 'Make it quick.'

Noah nodded. 'Hello, Xan,' she said.

I sense an accumulation of dragonscale around you, the dragon said. *What are you up to?*

'The elves are bringing the pyrohm to Somyni to release Jong,' Noah replied. 'They've constructed a firestone web around the tripod to stop us interfering with their plan.'

You must stop them, Xan said.

'Actually, we're planning to *let* them release him … sort of.'

What!

'You're growing weak,' Noah said gently. 'It's time to relieve you of this burden. Once Jong is in the illestial, we're planning to relocate him. You'll be free to rest at last.'

Free to rest?

'Free to rest,' Noah said.

Where are you going to put him?

'In a vortex.'

Whose crazy idea is that?

'It's Brinn's crazy idea,' Noah said.

Brinn hissed as Xan said, *Who's Brinn?*

'Brinn is a cat—'

'Tell her my real name,' Brinn said.

'Oh, right,' Noah said. 'Xan, it's *Temperance's* crazy idea.'

Temperance is helping you?

'I don't know about *helping*,' Noah said, 'but she's—'

She shouldn't be interfering, Xan said.

Noah sighed. 'I'll let you tell her that.'

Noah, this is terribly dangerous.

'Yes.'

You could destroy Talisker.

'Yes, but the vortex is going to destroy Talisker. It's just a matter of time. *And,* the illestial needs to be put beyond anyone's reach. If we succeed here, we get rid of two threats at once.'

I wish I could help you, my child, Xan said. *But alas, I cannot.*

My child, the words echoed inside Noah's head. Her heart swelled with pride.

With a renewed sense of purpose, Noah said, 'You rest. We'll get this done.'

Take great care, little dragon, Xan said. *Jong is strong and wily – a mighty adversary.*

'Yeah,' Noah said. 'I noticed.'

Good luck …

When the dragon's voice faded, Noah surveyed the giant web. It was triple the size of the crystal temple that had previously housed the tripod. That meant Talyn was bringing several thousand elves. They could shelter inside the firestone cocoon while Talyn activated the illestial and extracted Jong from his prison. If Noah couldn't breach it, the four thousand soldiers that had survived Percival's crystal assault would only be able to watch as the elves deserted and then destroyed Talisker.

Noah pressed her hands onto the web and white light exploded in her head as its power coursed through her. *I'm connected,* she thought. *I'm part of the web.*

Jacin whooped. 'She didn't die!'

As the light in her head abated, Noah barked the Pyranhi word for 'break' and the firestone shattered, leaving a gaping hole. She moved to her right and repeated the process. With Piper at her side, Noah walked the perimeter of the dome opening more and more access points for the soldiers.

When she arrived at her starting point again, Catriona came to stand in front of her. 'We'll give you as much cover as we can,' she said. 'Just make sure you get the pyrohm from Talyn.'

'Yes, Your Highness,' Noah replied.

To Noah's shock, Catriona embraced her.

'We're counting on you,' Catriona whispered in her ear.

Noah swallowed the lump in her throat. 'No pressure.'

Catriona released her and without another word, spun on her heel and strode away towards her army. Montana, Ardis, Chase and Avril gathered around Noah.

'Talyn won't like that you've forced her hand,' Montana said. 'Be careful, Noah.'

'I'm always careful,' Noah said.

'Be *extra* careful,' Ardis said. 'Just remember … we're all here for you.'

The high priestess and her warrior both hugged Noah before stepping back to give Chase her turn. A tear slipped down Noah's cheek as her friend embraced her.

'You don't have to be out here,' Noah whispered in her ear. 'You could stay in the tower and guard the baby dragons we rescued from the hatchery.'

Chase snorted. 'They breathe fire, Noah,' she said. 'They can take care of themselves. *You* people on the other hand … need a nurse.'

Noah swallowed the hot lump in her throat with difficulty.

'Anyway,' Chase added, 'how can I take notes for my next bestseller if I can't see what's going on out here?'

'You don't need notes,' Noah said. 'You're not a journalist. Remember?'

'Look, I'm not hiding inside when everyone I love is out here.'

'But your baby—'

'Will be fine,' Chase finished.

Noah held her for several long moments before she released her. 'Please be careful.'

Chase smiled. 'Always.'

Avril appeared in Chase's place.

'Jacin believes in you,' Avril said, 'so I'll support you.'

Noah nodded. 'Thanks.'

Avril rested her hand on her sword hilt. 'You can't afford to fail.'

'Well, at least you're here,' Noah said. 'If anything happens to me, you can sort things out and make your grandfather proud.'

Avril's eyes narrowed as Montana drew her sword.

'Avril, time to go,' Montana said.

Eyeing Montana's gleaming sword, Avril said, 'You're not going to fight, are you?'

'Of course I am,' Montana said. 'What did you think I was going to do?'

'I thought you'd give the orders,' Avril said. 'You're the high priestess – surely hand-to-hand combat is beneath you?'

'I do whatever this world requires of me,' Montana said. 'I can't do magic, nor can I ride a dragon.' She held up her sword. 'But I *can* use this.'

'Yeah,' Avril said, 'I saw that during our training sessions.'

Montana tested her blade. 'Well, let's see what you've learned. Stay with me. We'll fight together.'

Noah watched the fighters go, stomach churning.

'Noah,' Grainger said.

Noah spun round to find the Dragonsbane with Sachin and Jacin beside him.

Jacin wrapped his arms around her, squeezing her so tightly she could barely breathe.

Noah thumped him on the back. 'Stand down.'

'This is so exciting,' Jacin said. 'As soon as you're ready, just give us the signal and we'll open the doorway to Dragonhall for you.'

Noah nodded. She'd have preferred to go directly to the end of the tunnel they'd created to access the vortex but Grainger had advised against it. The instability of the portal cluster made it too dangerous. It was safer to anchor a doorway in Dragonhall and go the rest of the way on foot.

Grainger waved his baton. 'Let's get this done and relieve Xan of her burden. She's earned a rest.'

'I'm still surprised you're so keen,' Sachin said. 'If Xan's allowed to rest peacefully, you're out of a job, Dragonsbane.'

Grainger pursed his lips. 'I reckon – after everything I've endured on account of you people and your shenanigans – that I've probably earned my retirement too.'

Sachin tried to look offended, but failed.

Grainger put his arms around Noah. 'Good luck,' he said before letting her go.

'You too,' Noah said.

'Don't think I'm hugging you,' Sachin said.

Noah smiled. 'So not even the threat of Armageddon is enough for you to suspend your "no hug" policy?'

Sachin rolled his eyes. 'We've been here before, Noah. Since your arrival on Talisker, Armageddon is only ever a few heartbeats away.'

Chapter 34

'There's a doorway opening inside the dome,' Grainger said.

Grey mist streamed through a bright circle of light above the centre of the firestone disc on the floor. Two elves appeared and took their place each side of the doorway. Their shiny silver breastplates bore a gold leaf, as did their arm guards and helmets. Thick, lustrous brown braids hung over each of the elves' shoulders, while dazzling green eyes and perfect complexions masked the malice they carried inside them. Muscular legs protruded from their short tunics and the spikes on their boots gleamed menacingly in the shifting light.

'Look at those spears,' Raven said. 'I reckon you could skewer half a dozen people on one of those.'

More soldiers marched through the doorway, forming up in rows of ten.

'A thousand soldiers,' Emir said, as elves – dressed in robes – made their way through the breach. 'That's not many.'

'In their arrogance, they could have underestimated us,' Piper said.

Noah thought of the dragon riders' leather armour. It was designed for close-range fighting and to be lightweight for riding. The elves, with their spears, would make short work of them.

Horses laden with household goods were led through by robed elves. After them came alpacas, bison calves and caged birds. The enormity of what was happening hit Noah when dozens of pregnant elves stepped through the doorway.

They really are planning to start a new colony on another world, she thought.

Echoing her thoughts, Raven said, 'They're really serious, aren't they?' Noah nodded.

Talyn was the last elf to arrive. Her eyes locked onto Noah as the doorway evaporated.

'You,' Talyn said.

Noah stepped inside the firestone dome with Emir at her side. 'Yes, it's me.'

'I granted you freedom,' Talyn said, 'and this is how you repay my generosity?'

Noah raised her eyebrows. 'Generosity? You branded me and stole my property. How is that generous?'

Talyn pointed her wand at Noah with one hand and reached inside her cloak with the other.

'*Your* property?' she said, holding up the pyrohm for all to see. 'You flatter yourself. It was never your property. *You're* not worthy.'

'Not worthy?' Noah said. 'How do you think I got in here?'

Talyn's lips curled into a smile. 'Well, how about we sort out, once and for all, just how *un*worthy you are.'

The elf twitched her wand. When nothing happened, Talyn frowned.

'Losing your touch?' Noah said.

Talyn repeated her action, but Noah stood her ground.

The elf's cheeks flushed pink. 'What devilry is this?'

Noah undid her scarf to reveal the unblemished skin on her throat. Talyn's eyes widened momentarily, but she quickly regained her composure.

'So you found someone to heal your skin,' Talyn scoffed. 'That—'

'The brand is gone,' Noah said, 'so you can't control me so easily. You're going to have to work harder now if you want me to obey you.'

'I warned you not to underestimate her,' Emir said, gesturing towards Noah. 'Now, you can hand over the pyrohm and leave, or we will *take* it from you.'

Talyn didn't answer. She spun on her heel and strode towards the tripod. The elf soldiers charged.

Raven's voice rang out. 'Charge!'

Positioned around the circumference of the dome, Catriona's and Montana's warriors responded.

'Piper! We need to stop Talyn,' Noah called.

'Yep!' Piper said. 'Climb aboard!'

Noah scrambled up onto the dragon's back and snatched up the reins. 'Go!'

Piper sprang into the air and flapped her wings hard. Dragons swooped and flamed inside the dome, dodging the burning arrows the elf archers shot at them. Dragon-rider archers fired volleys of arrows, but had limited success against the elfin soldiers.

As they climbed higher, Noah searched for her friends on the ground. Noah clutched the reins tighter as a doorway opened behind the high priestess.

'*Montana!*' Noah yelled. 'Behind you!'

Montana spun round as an elf lunged at her with his spear. She ducked, then slipped, crashing heavily onto her knees. Noah's heart thumped in her chest. Another elf bore down on Montana as she struggled to her feet.

'Hurry, Montana … get up,' Noah muttered helplessly.

Avril raced towards the high priestess. She dropped her sword and dived at the elf, tackling him around the knees. It was unorthodox, but effective. The elf crashed to the ground. His yelp of surprise made Noah smile.

Zrip!

'Crap!' Noah said, hunching to avoid the arrow.

'Are you okay, Noah?' Piper called.

'For now!' Noah called back.

'Hang on!'

Noah looped the reins around her hands and hunkered down lower in her saddle. Piper banked left before catching an updraft. As they soared higher, a doorway opened above them.

'*Turn!*' Noah screamed. '*Turn n—*'

An elf landed behind her and wrapped its hands around her neck. Noah squirmed to get free but her assailant dug its nails into her flesh. Pinpricks of light dotted Noah's vision as the elf's grip tightened and threatened to crush her windpipe.

'No!' Noah panted as she slapped the dragon's side.

Piper rolled, catching the elf by surprise.

'Aaaaaaahhhhhhh!' it cried, clutching Noah's arm as it fell.

Torn from her seat and dangling from the reins, Noah screamed. *'Piper!'*

The dragon righted herself, Noah and the elf slamming against her scaly side. Piper twisted her neck to assess her rider's predicament. She winked at Noah.

'Now!' Noah yelled, huddling behind the elf as best she could.

Piper fired a short burst of flame. Noah and the elf both shrieked. The elf released its grip, but kept screaming as it plummeted to the ground.

Noah fought to haul herself back into the saddle. With a precision wing swipe, Piper flicked her rider into place.

'Nice,' Noah panted, checking her singed clothes for signs of active flames. Finding none, she added, 'Thanks.'

'You're welcome,' Piper said. 'And we're almost there, by the way.'

Noah looked to her right. The top of the tripod was only metres away. Talyn stood on the top step, poised to put the final piece of the illestial in place.

When Piper was directly over the tripod, Noah slid from her seat. She flailed her arms to steady her fall, but missed her mark. She crashed onto the tripod leg to Talyn's left.

'You're too late,' Talyn said as she knelt down.

Noah scrambled half a dozen steps to the top. 'He'll never let you live,' she said. 'Jong is not a saviour. He only destroys things.'

'Elves are special,' Talyn said. 'Jong will be grateful to be liberated from his prison. He will reward us.'

'No, he won't,' Noah said, glancing at the tower where Brinn watched proceedings from a top floor window ledge. 'You're going to lose,' she added. 'Look around you.'

Talyn surveyed the space below and above her. Her smooth brow betrayed nothing of her feelings.

'Your losses are greater than mine,' Talyn said at last.

Hundreds of Montana's and Catriona's soldiers lay dead. Noah didn't look too closely. She didn't want to find any of her friends among them.

'Maybe,' Noah said, 'but I'm not trying to start a new colony.'

Talyn glared at Noah. 'No, you're not – because you lack the foresight, knowledge, wisdom and strength to undertake such a glorious endeavour. Only elves – superior beings – are capable of such wondrous feats.'

Noah groaned. 'Could you be any more full of yourself?'

A tinge of pink coloured Talyn's cheeks. 'At least I have reason to be.'

'Really?' Noah said. 'I haven't seen anything that's impressed me yet. A bit of levitation, a few doorways and fireballs. Hardly what I'd call the magic of "superior beings".'

'You didn't notice the firestone web?' Talyn said.

'I saw spiders spin that,' Noah said. 'Not an elf in sight.'

'And who do you think …'

Talyn paused, realisation dawning on her. 'You're stalling,' she accused.

'I'm not—'

Talyn chanted rapidly, whipping her arms skyward as Noah crouched. Before Noah could pounce, Talyn spun a full circle and dropped to a squat. The web splintered in a concussive blast that knocked Noah off the tripod.

'*Piper!*' Noah cried as she tumbled downwards.

Arms flailing, Noah fought to flatten herself out, but large pieces of firestone battered her as the structure collapsed. A blue blur flashed below her and she crashed onto Piper's tail – facing the wrong way. Noah desperately hugged the dragon's tail and wrapped her legs around as tight as she could. Piper darted side to side as she dodged falling debris. Noah squeezed her eyes shut as she tucked her head in.

The thundering clatter of falling firestone rolled on as Piper cleared the structure and skidded to a landing close to the tower. She'd barely stopped when Noah let go.

Too soon, Noah thought as she somersaulted over the cobbled ground. When she stopped, she lay perfectly still, measuring which part of her body hurt the least. Once the crashing subsided though, and the tortured cries of humans and elves rang out, Noah forced herself onto her hands and knees and looked up.

Chase stood over her with her hand outstretched. 'Come on, Noah,' she said. 'Get up.'

Noah clamped her hand around her friend's wrist and pulled herself up. 'Thanks. You okay?'

'I'm fine,' Chase said, pushing hair out of her eyes, 'but you have to deal with *that.*'

Noah's eyes followed where Chase pointed.

At the top of the tripod, Talyn held the pyrohm aloft.

'Jong!' Talyn cried. 'I, Talyn, of the woodland elves, call you forth! Come! Be free!'

As the elf reached forward with the pyrohm, the plateau fell silent and still. Fighting forgotten, everyone watched Talyn. The small piece of firestone in the triangle twinkled into life. The other three sides of the ancient Pyranhi relic – long dormant in their cradle – twitched in response. After several long moments, the large circle of firestone in the floor beneath the tripod began to glow.

'That can't be good,' Chase whispered.

Noah leapt onto Piper's back. 'Get me back up there,' she said.

'Wait!' Raven said as Vespa landed beside her. 'If you go back up there now, she'll just knock you down again. Wait until the *last moment.*'

Chain landed beside Vespa. 'He's right,' Emir said. 'Wait until the absolute last moment.'

Wait. The word bounced around inside Noah's head.

Brinn sauntered past as Noah slackened her grip on the reins.

'Brinn?' Noah said.

The cat continued towards the firestone without looking back. At the edge of the circle she sat down, tailing swishing from side to side.

'What's she doing?' Montana asked as she arrived with Ardis and Avril.

Noah scanned the expectant faces of her companions. 'I have no idea,' she said.

Light shot from the circle on the floor to the illestial above. Cries of shock rang out as Noah shielded her eyes. When the initial radiance subsided, and Noah dared a peek from behind her arm, she saw Talyn floating to the ground to join her surviving elves, who formed a defensive ring around the firestone. Brinn was the only blemish in their otherwise perfect formation.

Talyn smiled at Noah. 'You lose,' she said.

Noah ignored her, instead watching the spectacle beyond her. Colours swirled inside the cone of light as the illestial funnelled and concentrated the firestone's power to draw Jong from his prison. A collective gasp greeted the god when he finally floated into view.

Dark, wavy hair framed his hawklike face as eyes sparkled beneath perfectly symmetrical eyebrows. The high collar of his full-length scarlet robe was trimmed with black satin ribbon, as were the sleeve cuffs. His eyes landed on Brinn and he smiled.

'Hello, Temperance,' he said. 'How lovely of you to come. Is our brother here too?'

'No,' Brinn said.

'Shame,' Jong said as he glanced about him. 'Oh, Noah. You're still here, I see.'

'Yes,' she said.

'And Gillette?'

'I'm here,' Gillette called. 'With my dad.'

Relief flooded through Noah when she saw him push through a knot of soldiers to her right. Jaxon was right behind his son.

Jong stroked his chin. 'Well, I hope you're enjoying your time together, because it's about to come to an end. As it is for everyone else on this about-to-be-god-forsaken world.'

Brinn hissed. 'That's not funny.'

'So you did get it?' Jong said. '*About-to-be*-god-forsaken because I'm a god and I'm just about to leave, or forsake—'

'Yes,' Brinn said. 'I did get it, but you're not going to destroy this world.'

'I'm not?'

'No.'

'Because you're going to stop me?'

'Of course not,' Brinn said. 'I wouldn't use my power here.'

'Then who *is* going to stop me?' Jong said.

Brinn's ear twitched. 'Noah. Noah is going to stop you.'

Jong laughed and the elves joined in.

I don't care if he's evil or not, Noah thought, *he's* not *staying here.*

Jong brushed tears from his eyes as he regained his composure. 'Noah *isn't* going to stop me,' he said, 'because the elves are going to kill her.'

As one, the elves turned to face Jong and bowed.

'Go!' Jong said, pointing at Noah. 'Kill her! Kill her *now!*'

'That's not nice,' Noah murmured as elves raced towards her.

'Plan?' Piper said.

Noah looked around at her friends. 'Scatter!' she said. 'Spread out!'

'No chance, Sis,' Raven said. 'They're coming for you. We'll protect you.'

Well, if they won't go, Noah thought, *I will.*

'Piper! Fly!' Noah said.

Piper sprang but was barely off the ground when Talyn rocketed towards them. Wand pointing directly at Noah, the elf speared towards her. She collected Noah, ripping her out of her saddle, and they sailed through a first-storey window on Ion Tower.

Noah smashed into a stone wall. Startled baby dragons, roosting on the tops of wooden bookshelves, flapped and flamed in panic. Winded, Noah slid to the floor. Talyn stood over her.

'This is where you end,' Talyn said.

Noah didn't have the breath to respond.

'Jong has decreed your death,' Talyn said, 'and I will deliver it.'

The room dimmed. Clutching her chest, Noah looked towards the window. Piper hovered outside.

Talyn glanced over her shoulder. 'Don't worry,' the elf said, 'no one can get in. I've sealed the room so that it's just us.'

'Great,' Noah wheezed.

'Now it's going to be very difficult to disembowel you when you're crumpled on the floor like that,' Talyn said, 'so let's straighten you out a bit.'

Talyn waved her wand as she chanted, and Noah's body felt lighter. Her head and shoulders lifted off the floor, followed by her torso and hips.

'Thanks,' Noah said, 'that actually makes it easier to breathe.'

Talyn continued her spell. Noah swung her fist at Talyn's head, but the wall behind her limited her backswing. The elf tilted her head and easily avoided the blow.

'Now, you just *hang* in there, while I relieve you of your intestines,' Talyn said, pointing her wand at Noah's abdomen.

Noah looked up at the five dragons on top of the bookcases. They seemed interested in the shenanigans but made no move to get involved.

You're not going to help? she thought.

When they made no sign they'd registered her silent plea, Noah searched for inspiration elsewhere. Talyn was tantalisingly close – just out of arms' reach – if she could move forward just a bit …

Burning pain between her hips distracted her.

'No,' Noah whispered. 'I like my intestines where they are.'

Her head whipped from side to side. A torch burned in a sconce to her right. Without hesitation, Noah snatched the torch and jammed the flaming end against Talyn's throat.

'*Aaaaaaaaaaaargh!*' the elf shrieked, dropping her wand.

The spell broken, Noah dropped to the floor, landing lightly on her feet. She stood over the elf, who wailed as she clutched her throat.

'*NO!*' Talyn screamed. 'You can't do this to me!'

'I think we're even now,' Noah said as the smell of burning flesh assaulted her. 'A brand for a brand.'

A flash of light outside caught Noah's attention. A quick glance told her Jong was on the move.

'Gotta go!' Noah said.

She shoved the torch back in the sconce before jumping over Talyn to get to one of the bookcases. Noah heaved with all her strength, and when she'd shifted the bookcase forward, she squeezed behind it and pushed. Books rained down as the bookcase fell forward. Dust swirled. Deprived of their roost, the dragons fluttered around the ceiling.

Pinned to the floor, Talyn screamed again.

Curiosity got the better of the dragons. They settled on the fallen bookshelf, peering at the stricken elf. One flamed nervously.

'You can't do this!' Talyn cried, wriggling to get free.

The red hatchling dragon spewed flame, singeing the elf's hair.

Talyn screamed again.

Noah patted the dragon's head. 'Now you're getting it. Keep up the good work.'

Hoping Jong hadn't already made his escape, she turned towards the window and ran.

Chapter 35

Noah hurdled the window ledge and sailed through the first-storey window. Fighting continued on the plateau. Noah glimpsed Avril darting across the lawn with a sack in hand. She swiped a wand from a fallen elf and stuffed it in the bag before racing off again.

Make sure you get them all, Avril, Noah thought as she landed beside Piper. Sachin raced to her as Chase waddled behind him.

'Where's Talyn?' Sachin said.

'Level one,' Noah muttered as she turned her gaze to the tripod. 'She's feeling the heat.'

'I'll go and secure her,' Chase said.

Noah squinted at the shaft of light. It had narrowed as Jong floated upwards. He was now closer to the illestial than he was to the floor.

Grainger pointed at Jong. 'I think you'd better deal with *him* now, Noah.'

Noah nodded. 'Piper! Fly!'

Piper sprang into the air. 'Where to?'

'Get me as close to Jong as you can.'

'Got it.'

Piper swung left to catch an updraft as Vespa came alongside them.

'Noah,' Raven said, 'need a hand?'

'Get Emir and go wait with Grainger and Sachin,' she called. 'Once I've got the illestial, you'd better be ready at the doorway.'

Raven saluted and Vespa peeled away. Noah turned her gaze on Jong as Piper closed in on the illestial.

'Noah! Look out!' someone cried.

Noah whipped her head round a heartbeat before the fireball struck Piper. The dragon pitched sideways, catapulting Noah from her seat.

'Piper!' Noah screamed as she sailed towards Jong.

Noah twisted, trying to avoid him, but her body slammed into his.

Noah caught him around the shoulders, clutching tightly so she didn't fall. She scanned the sky for Piper. The dragon hovered just outside the light shaft, smoke emanating from a fresh burn on her belly. With her hands behind Jong's neck, Noah pointed to the cradle where the illestial lay. Piper flamed and flew off.

'Well,' Jong said, 'isn't *this* cosy.'

'I thought you'd like company,' Noah said.

Jong hooked his hands under her armpits and pushed her back. 'You thought wrong,' he said.

'I'm … floating,' she said.

'Of course you're floating,' Jong said. 'That's how this thing works.'

Noah's skin tingled as the light of the dragonscale caressed her. She tilted her head back. The small circle of firestone in the pyrohm seemed a long way above them. Beneath the pyrohm, the other three sides were converging. *That's why the shaft of light is narrowing,* she thought.

'It's amazing,' Noah murmured.

'So what's your plan to defeat me, Noah?' Jong said. 'You can't kill me, so are we to arm wrestle for supremacy, perhaps?'

Noah tore her attention from the dazzling light above her and smiled. 'It's a surprise,' she said.

'Meaning – you don't have a plan,' Jong said. 'But that's okay, because *I* have one.'

'Great,' Noah said as she surveyed the city.

The dragons flying around the tripod looked much bigger now. *I'm shrinking,* she thought.

Jong wrapped his hands around her wrists. 'Do you want to hear my plan?'

'Thrill me,' Noah said.

'I am going to protect you, so that when the illestial is at full power and blasts me free, I can drag you out with me.'

'So you *do* want company?'

'No,' Jong said. 'I want you to witness the destruction of your puny little world. The power this device unleashes will tear it asunder. And once you've seen that, you can watch me destroy Earth next.'

'I like your arm wrestling idea better,' Noah said.

As they floated closer to the illestial, Noah felt the pressure building. Containing the potency of a god would put the illestial under enormous strain. Just as the ancient Pyranhi Jongu had planned. Noah's heart hammered inside her chest at the thought of the race ahead. If they couldn't get the illestial to the vortex before the device reached full power, Talisker would be no more.

Noah put those thoughts aside as she drifted closer to the illestial. Although she didn't feel smaller, she knew she was. The sides of the device were almost closed, so the beam of light must have been pencil thin. But to her, the tunnel ahead appeared big enough to accommodate a train.

Noah held her breath as they entered the illestial. The sides joined soundlessly. Dazzling colours sparkled all around her.

'And now,' Jong said, still holding her wrists, 'we wait.'

'For how long?'

'As long as it takes.'

Noah peered out through the firestone. Piper's silhouette was as reassuring as it was unmistakable. *No time to lose.*

'You claustrophobic?' Noah asked.

'I was,' Jong said, 'but I got over it. Being trapped inside a dragon for so long …'

'Right.'

Jong sighed. 'Tell me you're not going to whine about—'

Noah leaned forward, pressing her lips against his. His grip on her wrists slackened, and she stroked his cheek with one hand as she kissed him.

Jong pulled back. 'What the—'

Noah head-butted him, compounding his shock. Before he could recover his wits, she reached for the pyrohm and thrust one hand through the firestone. The illestial rocked violently. Jong grabbed at Noah but she pushed him away.

Let me out, she thought as she propelled herself upwards. When her arm had disappeared to her shoulder, she felt something brush her hand outside and she grasped it instinctively. Piper's reins! Piper hauled her up while Noah kicked her feet to avoid Jong catching her. Once her head and chest cleared the firestone, she seized the reins with both hands.

'Piper!' she cried as her upper body began expanding to normal size. 'Pull harder – or this thing will cut me in half!'

The dragon whipped her head up, almost yanking Noah clear. But Jong caught her ankle.

Noah gasped. *'No!'*

Pain and panic gripped her. Jong couldn't pass through the firestone, but he could stop her getting free. As long he held her ankle, she was going nowhere. Not until she reached normal size and the illestial severed her foot.

Think, Noah. Think!

She planted her free foot on the narrow rail that circled the cradle and released her grip on Piper's reins.

'Noah?' Piper said. 'What are you doing?'

There was no time to explain. Noah wriggled her fingers and babbled through what her addled mind could recall of Hildebrand's summoning spell – hopeful that she'd summon her own foot and not just any foot. She knew it wouldn't be perfect but when it did appear, her breath caught in her throat. Her foot was about half its original size and was missing two toes.

No point worrying about that now, Noah thought as she swiped the illestial from its cradle. Miniature strands of lightning crackled around the device. Noah held her breath as she peered into the firestone. Jong glared out at her.

Noah took a deep breath and spun round to where Piper was perched on the circular walkway. She kicked off the shoe on her good foot and leapt onto her dragon's back.

'We're on the clock,' Noah said. 'We need to get to the tower.'

'Right.'

Piper launched herself from the tripod and swooped towards the tower. As they soared over the plateau, Noah's stomach twisted in revulsion at the carnage. The city was littered with dead and wounded soldiers, dragons, dragon riders and elves.

Behind the tower, Emir and Raven sat astride their dragons while Brinn paced back and forth. Grainger, Sachin and Jacin stood by the shimmering doorway that would take them to Dragonhall.

Piper landed beside Chain and Noah tossed the illestial to Emir.

'All yours,' Noah said.

Emir caught it easily. 'Thanks.'

Jacin's mouth was agape. 'Noah, how come you could get out of the illestial, but Jong couldn't?' he asked.

Noah shrugged. 'Jong doesn't have firestone in his veins.'

'Raven,' Brinn said, nodding towards the doorway, 'you go first.'

He saluted and Vespa darted through the doorway. Brinn nodded to Emir.

'Go, Chain!' Emir said.

Brinn jumped up onto Noah's lap.

'Ready?' Noah said.

Brinn's ear twitched. 'Let's go.'

Piper didn't need more prompting. She almost tripped over Chain's tail in her hurry to follow him into Dragonhall's crypts. Once inside, Grainger kicked open the door to the portal cluster and raced into the forest.

Piper flew past him. 'See you there!' she said.

'Go!' Grainger said, waving the dragons on.

Piper led the way to the pathway with Chain and Vespa only a body length behind. Noah glanced around her. Despite their speed, she was still wary of what lurked in the forest.

Noah pointed ahead. 'Avoid those dangling vines,' she called to Piper. 'They're really sticky and their spines sting like hell.'

'Aye, aye!' Piper said, swerving to avoid the treacherous flora.

When they reached the entrance to the tunnel, Piper barely slowed down and Noah gripped the reins tighter as the dragon banked to take the corner. Noah hoped Grainger, Sachin and Jacin made it to the tunnel without any delays. She was counting on them to guard the entrance and deter any pursuits.

Once inside the tunnel, Chain soared past while Vespa and Raven brought up the rear.

As they sped down the tunnel, Jong's voice rang out.

'Noah,' Jong said, 'I have an offer for you.'

Emir twisted in his seat and held the illestial above his head. Tendrils of lightning wriggled down his forearms.

'Marry me, Noah,' Jong said.

Noah's jaw dropped. She looked at Emir. His shock mirrored hers.

Brinn hissed.

'You've got to be kidding!' Noah said. 'After everything you've done to me ... why the hell would I marry you? And come to think of it, why would *you* want to marry *me?*'

'I admire your tenacity, Noah,' Jong said. 'You rescued Gillette, you brought me the illestial – albeit indirectly – and you outwitted Talyn. You are a formidable opponent.'

'You're scared of her,' Raven said. 'And so you should be!'

Jong chuckled. '*I'm* not scared of her. She's a formidable opponent to *lesser beings.*'

'It doesn't change the fact that you ordered Talyn to kill me,' Noah said as Piper flew alongside Chain. 'Hardly a romantic gesture.'

'But a worthy test,' Jong said. 'Which you passed. And besides, I've never met anyone who's dared to kiss me.'

Noah felt the heat in her cheeks as Emir's gaze bored into her.

'You kissed him?' he said.

'To distract him,' Noah said defensively. 'To escape.'

Emir frowned but said nothing.

Noah scowled. 'Look—'

'I promise I will spare Talisker and Earth from destruction if you agree to marry me, Noah,' Jong said.

Raven snorted. 'You *say* that,' he said, 'but you'll just kill her and then break your promise anyway.'

'On pain of death,' Jong said, 'I promise, that if Noah marries me, I will protect her and I will not destroy Talisker or Earth.'

'On pain of death?' Raven said. 'But you can't die.'

'He *can* die,' Brinn said. 'You couldn't kill him, but gods can die. If he makes a promise on pain of death, with a god as witness, he is bound to it.'

'Unless he wants to die?' Raven said.

'If he wanted to die,' Brinn said, 'he has other options.'

'Well, Noah has options too,' he said.

Jong wants me to suffer, Noah thought, as the dragons continued their flight along the tunnel. *He wants to drag me along with him for the rest of my life, so I can witness his destruction.*

'And what about the vortex?' Emir said.

'Vortex?' Jong said. 'What vortex?'

Brinn jumped from Piper's back onto Chain's and sat directly in front of Emir. The cat peered into the illestial through the firestone window.

'The vortex that will destroy Talisker if we don't put you in there,' she said.

'Put *me* in there?' Jong said. 'That's your grand plan? To transfer me from one prison to another?'

Brinn purred. 'I thought you'd enjoy a change of scenery.'

'You drive a hard bargain, Temperance,' Jong said. 'Okay, in addition to my original offer, I'll dismantle the vortex for you too. Your precious Talisker will be safe – and I'll be free. Deal?'

Noah took a shuddering breath. 'I could save Talisker right now,' she whispered.

'Or we could stick to my plan,' Brinn said.

'Which is risky,' Noah said. 'Certainty *now* versus dicing with the vortex?'

'Nothing is certain, Noah,' Brinn said. 'Every option has an element of risk.'

'But Talisker will be saved,' Noah argued.

'And what of the other worlds not covered by this proposal?' Brinn countered. 'You're happy to let many others be destroyed?'

Noah stared at her. 'Weren't you the one defending him earlier? "It's in his nature to be destructive … If nothing were ever destroyed, how would Elani continue to create?" Any of that sound familiar to you?'

'Some things do need to be destroyed,' Brinn said tersely, 'but there are many worlds that deserve a chance. If my brother has a bit more time to think about things, I think we could get a better deal.'

A better deal? Noah's head throbbed. Talisker – and Earth – were her priorities. Long-term universe management was beyond her human brain.

Noah eyed Emir. Strategy was his department.

'What do you think?' she said.

Emir frowned. 'The prophecy suggests you use the music of this world to save it,' he said. 'It says nothing about selling your soul to the devil.'

Noah blinked back tears. 'But if I fail …'

'If *we* fail,' he said, 'we'll still have done more than anyone else could have.'

'Eyes ahead!' Raven called. 'Someone's coming!'

A doorway crackled into view, completely blocking the tunnel.

Emir grunted. 'Elves! We don't have time for this.'

Piper landed and skidded to a stop.

'Noah?' Jong said. 'Do we have a deal?'

'Need a minute here,' Noah said as she jumped down from her dragon's back.

She stumbled, her shrivelled foot twisting awkwardly on landing.

Raven caught her arm. 'Are you okay? What happened to your foot?'

'I'll explain later,' Noah said pulling her viola and bow from her pocket.

The three dragons roared and flamed as what remained of Talyn's force streamed through the doorway. Emir and Raven drew their swords.

'Grainger won't be happy about this,' Raven said. 'He said it was too dangerous to open a doorway in here.'

'I'll try to close it,' Noah said.

One elf slipped through the dragon cordon and Raven skewered him on his sword.

Noah forced herself to concentrate, but she'd barely played a dozen bars of her tonic when a doorway appeared right beside her. A female elf – a head taller than Noah – stepped through and wrenched the viola from her grasp. Before Noah could react, the elf smashed the instrument against the tunnel wall.

Noah stared in disbelief as the elf tossed the broken viola onto the floor.

The elf pointed to the illestial in Emir's hand. 'Our lord *will* be free,' she cried.

More elves streamed through the doorway.

'I wouldn't have thought there were so many left,' Raven said.

Emir kicked an elf in the ribs. 'These ones have wands. We need to stop them!'

'You need to close that doorway, Noah,' Piper said, 'or we can't get any further down the tunnel!'

An elf cried out as Brinn sank her teeth into his wrist. He dropped his wand and Piper pounced. She scooped up the wand and swallowed it.

The elf closest to Noah grabbed her by the throat with one hand and pinned her against the wall. Noah clawed and kicked, trying to break the chokehold, but dizziness hampered her efforts. She needed to get free before she passed out.

The elf chanted.

'Brinn,' Noah whispered. 'Brinn …'

Piper's tail smacked the elf aside.

BOOOOOOM!

Noah slumped to the floor as the tunnel reverberated.

'What was that?' Raven cried.

'The tunnel is broken!' an elf exclaimed exultantly.

Noah panted as she lay on the dirt floor, tears welling in her eyes as the fighting continued. Beyond the elves' doorway, the severed section of tunnel would be whipped into the vortex. If she closed the doorway now, they'd all be sucked out into space. Brinn's cold nose probed her cheek but Noah ignored her.

'Jong,' Noah whispered, 'I accept—'

'—that things look pretty grim, but we're not done yet,' Brinn finished.

Noah peered at the cat. 'What are you doing? The tunnel is gone – we've got no way to get Jong to the vortex now. There's no other way.'

Brinn growled. 'Just give me a minute.'

Raven screamed. Noah rolled and pushed herself up onto her elbows in time to see her brother sink to his knees, a dagger protruding from his abdomen.

'*Raven!*' she cried.

Chain chomped an elf in half as Noah stumbled through the chaos towards her brother.

'Don't touch it!' Noah cried as she reached him.

Raven nodded, the colour draining from his face. 'Help me up,' he whispered.

'No,' Noah said, tugging his arm gently. 'Lean against the wall. I'll protect you.'

Raven grimaced. 'Emir!' he called. 'The illestial. Pass it here!'

'What are you doing?' Noah said.

Without turning his attention away from the elf he was fighting, Emir tossed the illestial over his shoulder. Noah dived and caught it. A loud buzzing sound reverberated around the cavern, making her tingle all over. Lightning streaked from the illestial.

'*No!*' Noah said.

'It seems I don't need a deal after all, Noah,' Jong said. 'Say your goodbyes. Very soon … I'll be free.'

Heart thumping, Noah turned to Emir. Another gateway opened.

'No more,' Noah whispered as she scanned the tunnel.

Chain, Vespa and Piper couldn't hold off the elves much longer. Jong was about to break free and Raven was dying. Noah squeezed her eyes shut and clutched the illestial to her chest. Even with the firestone in her veins she would never be able to contain the device when it blew, but she hugged it all the same. A vision of her parents flashed in her mind, beckoning her to come to them. They hadn't aged since she'd seen them last – since the accident that had stolen them from her. Her memories of them were so precious, and they'd be extinguished forever with her death. Grief coursed through her.

Mum … Dad … I'm coming, Noah thought. *It won't be long now.*

'Noah,' Raven said, jolting her from her despair. 'Look.'

She glanced at the newest doorway and saw dragons. Horatio and Fontina, with elves on their backs, led the host. Dozens of dragons, every colour of the rainbow, streamed into the tunnel. Their elf riders leapt into the fray, wands drawn.

'Since when?' Noah breathed.

'Noah!' the elf astride Horatio called.

Noah's eyes widened. '*Seamus?* Is that you?'

'Totally is,' Seamus replied, nodding.

Horatio eyed the illestial. 'We don't have much time.'

Noah held up the glowing pyramid.

'Noah, pass it here,' Seamus said.

Noah recoiled. 'What? Why?'

Horatio lifted his head and shot a magnificent burst of flame that reached the ceiling and cascaded down the walls. 'We'll take it,' the dragon said. 'We'll take it to the vortex.'

Noah shook her head. 'But you can't – the tunnel is gone.'

'We don't need a tunnel, Noah,' Seamus said. 'Only humans need a tunnel.'

Noah frowned as she looked at Brinn. 'But this is my job. I have to do it.'

'Your job is done, Noah,' Horatio said.

Noah glanced at the illestial in her hands. The vibrations were intensifying. 'How do you reckon that? This thing is about to blow …'

'Yes,' Seamus said, 'so hand it over.'

'But—'

'There is no time to explain now,' Seamus said. 'If you really want an explanation, come with us.'

'Humans aren't adapted to the conditions of space,' Horatio said, 'but I can protect you.'

'Noah, go,' Brinn said. 'Go now!'

Noah tossed the illestial to Seamus before squatting beside the cat. She stroked her from head to tail. 'Okay, Boss.'

Seamus chanted and waved his wand in circles around the illestial. The buzzing lost some of its intensity as Noah strode over to Piper.

'You know you're my favourite,' Noah said, rubbing the dragon's blue snout. 'I'll see you soon.'

Piper snorted smoke around her. 'Hurry back.'

Emir caught her in an embrace as she turned around and rested his cheek on top of her head.

'Take care,' he said. 'I'd like you back in one piece.'

Noah pulled back and looked up at him. 'Got it.' She smiled at him. 'A kiss for the road?'

He leant forward, kissing her tenderly on the lips.

Raven groaned. Noah released Emir and knelt beside her brother. 'Hold on,' she said. 'I'll be back soon.'

'Try not to kiss anyone else before you get back,' he whispered. 'I don't think Emir will forgive you a second time.'

Noah rolled her eyes. 'Thanks. Your relationship advice is always appreciated.'

'Go!' Raven said, as two of Seamus's elf comrades knelt beside him to attend to his wound.

Noah climbed up on Horatio's back and sat in front of Seamus, who tapped her on the shoulder. She swivelled in her seat and Seamus offered her the illestial.

'I've woven a spell that will hopefully buy us the time we need.'

Several of the newly arrived elves chanted in unison. The fire in Noah's veins ran hotter still, as ancient magic swirled around her. The blackness of the void that opened before them gave Noah a moment's pause, her stomach churned but she wouldn't back out now.

Horatio dived into the abyss. Noah held her breath as light flashed all around them.

Jong's voice crackled from within the illestial. 'You won't survive this, Noah.'

Noah didn't answer him. Vertigo consumed her. *If I open my mouth,* she thought, *I'll probably throw up.*

'Close your eyes,' Seamus said.

Noah took his advice.

'Shall I explain what I meant before when I said your job was done?' the elf asked.

Eyes and lips squeezed firmly shut now, Noah nodded.

'*The thirteenth key the world shall need, for evil to be brought to heel – One of two, the Dragon's bane must rise; and the music wield,*' Seamus said. 'Unfortunately, prophecies are tricky things to deal with. They're frustratingly vague, and mind-bendingly ambiguous.'

Again, Noah nodded.

'And on top of that,' Seamus continued, 'each being's perspective is different. What the Pyranhi had in mind when they made the prophecy, can only be guessed at. And what elves think, differs to what humans – or the Descera – would have thought. What "evil" did the Pyranhi have in mind? Who knows?'

'But you have a theory?' Noah said.

'Like Temperance, there are elves like me who don't think Jong is evil. Certainly, his agenda is repellent to us, but we believe that evil is a *choice*. It is in Jong's nature to destroy; it isn't a choice for him.'

Noah considered the bargain Jong had proposed, offering to spare Talisker from destruction in return for his freedom. *He can choose what he destroys,* she thought. *That makes him evil in my mind.*

'My grandfather used to say that conflict and disunity are the greatest "evils" on Talisker,' Seamus said. 'Elves, humans, goblins, dragons – they can't agree among themselves let alone with each other. The wars that have resulted …'

My grandfather used to say. Theo was gone. Noah's chest tightened. There'd be time to grieve for Seamus's grandfather later. Now, there was a job still to be done.

'There's still conflict,' Noah said. 'So, how is my job done?'

'Your job isn't to eradicate evil, or even defeat it, Noah – but to "bring it to heel" – to contain it. You've done that. You promote unity, Noah. You bring people together. You did it with goblins – now you've brought humans, elves and dragons together. Take us right here. You, me and Horatio … working together to improve our world.'

The illestial vibrated in Noah's hands.

'If we don't get to the vortex soon,' Noah said, 'we won't have a world left to work with.'

'Look, Noah,' Horatio said.

Noah followed his gaze. The vortex yawned beneath them.

'How are we not getting sucked into it?' Noah asked.

'Magic,' Horatio said.

Noah frowned. 'If we can resist the vortex, surely Jong can too?'

'He can do no magic *inside* the illestial,' Horatio said, 'but if he gets out …'

'Noah!' Jong said, 'I've been thinking about our bargain.'

'No deal,' Noah said.

'But I *will* dismantle the vortex,' Jong said, 'and when I do, Talisker will be top of my "to do" list unless you—'

Noah threw the illestial as far as she could.

'No deal,' she repeated as the shining pyramid dropped towards the mesmerising whirlpool below.

Jong's voice rang out through the heavens.

'This is not the end of me!' he thundered. 'When I'm done with this vortex, I will have my revenge.'

Noah turned to Seamus. 'Still think he's not evil?'

Seamus smiled at her. 'Let's argue about it later.'

'Yeah,' Noah said. 'I'm kind of worn out. Let's go home.'

Chapter 36

Noah rubbed saffron oil into her viola as she gazed out her window. Summer had come and gone since her return from Somyni, and the olives were almost ready for harvest. She was looking forward to a few more months of physical labour on the farm before she returned to Mellifont.

'Your instrument looks as good as new,' Avril said. 'I really didn't think you'd be able to fix it after what that elf did to it.'

'It was smashed up pretty badly,' Noah said, 'so a lot of the wood is new.'

Avril picked up the bow from Noah's workbench and ran her fingers along the horsehair. Noah watched the historian with an uneasy mix of admiration and apprehension. Avril had fought bravely against the elves in Somyni, but Noah couldn't quite shake her distrust of her.

'First big test today then?' Avril said, handing the bow to Noah. 'You nervous?'

'A little.'

Avril nodded. 'I think I'll go check on the dragons while you get ready.'

'Great,' Noah said.

Once Avril had gone, Noah packed her instrument away in its battered leather case and draped an embroidered ceremonial cover over it. *It'll be fine,* she thought.

Noah left her studio and crossed the upper walkway to Chase's quarters. She knocked gently on the bedroom door.

'Come in,' Chase called.

Noah opened the door and found Seamus and Raven standing by the baby's cot. The elves had healed her brother's knife wound and he didn't even have a scar to show for it. Chase, still in her pyjamas, studied a notebook as she sat cross-legged on her bed.

'Well,' Noah said, 'this looks like the place to be.'

Seamus winked at her. 'Hey, Noah.'

'Having fun?' Noah said.

The elf nodded. 'You have a lovely home and wonderful people around you. I am very grateful for your invitation.'

Noah bowed her head. 'I'm so pleased you could come.'

Seamus had no family now that his grandfather was gone. Theo's death had hit him hard, and Aoratia was no longer a tranquil paradise. In the wake of Talyn's treachery, the elfin heartland was in turmoil. Noah hoped Seamus would find solace at the farm and maybe, when Montana arrived, the pair could hatch a plan to capitalise on the unrest in Aoratia and rescue Montana's father from his incarceration.

Noah turned to her friend. 'Chase, are you going to get dressed anytime today?'

Chase waved her hand without looking up from her book. 'The ceremony's not for hours yet,' she said.

'What are you reading?'

'Our notes about the ceremony,' Chase said. 'I don't want to stuff anything up.'

'Relax,' Raven said. 'You just have to stick the baby in a hole and bury her up to her neck with dirt.'

Chase looked up from her notes and frowned. 'How is it that you can make an ancient, sacred ceremony sound like child abuse?'

Raven smiled. 'It's a gift.'

Noah stood next to Raven and studied her goddaughter's face. Her blue eyes twinkled with mischief as she smiled at Noah.

Noah wrinkled her nose. 'She smells bad.'

'Then change her,' Chase said.

Noah wiggled her index finger. 'Into what?'

Chase shook her head. 'Good grief.'

'You know,' Noah said, 'that my finger is really a *wand* … so does that make me her fairy godmother?'

Chase groaned. 'Oh, knock it off.'

Noah put her hand over her heart. 'I will grant you one wish, my child. Anything you want … just ask.'

Raven tickled the baby's tummy. 'Anything you want,' he echoed, 'as long as it's a demon or a whirlwind … otherwise you're out of luck.'

'I can do a shield too!' Noah said.

'Get out!' Chase said. 'Both of you – get out! Go and do something useful.'

'What about Seamus?' Raven said.

All eyes went to the elf, who scooped Alexis out of her cot and lay her on the change table.

'He's useful,' Chase said. 'He can stay.'

'Fine,' Raven said. 'I need to go and get dressed anyway. The contingent from Leninstar will be here soon.'

Noah closed the bedroom door behind them. 'Make sure you comb your hair.'

'Go boil your head,' Raven said over his shoulder.

Noah retraced her steps across the walkway and then headed to the kitchen where Chase's mother and Aunt Polly were preparing the evening's banquet.

'Can I help?' Noah said.

'Pass me the tea towel, would you?' Polly said as she opened the oven.

Noah caught a glimpse of the fresh loaf as she handed her aunt the towel. 'That smells awesome.'

'Are Raven and Seamus still "visiting" with the baby?' Genie Chase said.

'Raven is showering,' Noah said, 'and Seamus is changing the baby … changing the baby's *nappy*.'

Polly shook her head.

'What's wrong, Polly?' Genie said. 'You think it's strange that there is an elf upstairs, changing a baby's nappy?'

Polly shrugged. 'My niece just saved the world, and the four dragons in the yard have just eaten all the petunias—'

'Look!' Noah said, pointing to the window.

A royal carriage bearing Leninstar's crest rolled into view.

'Raven!' Noah yelled. 'Your girlfriend's here!'

'And my nephew is dating a king,' Polly added. 'So no, an elf changing a nappy is not news.'

'I'll go and greet our guests,' Noah said.

Polly tapped her fingers on the bread's crust. 'Good thinking.'

Glad to escape the food preparation, Noah jogged across the lawn with Kane at her side. Not to be left out, Juno swooped from a nearby tree and landed on top of the carriage. Jaxon climbed down from the driver's seat with Gillette close behind him. When Jaxon opened the carriage door, Montana stepped out first. She hugged Noah as Jaxon offered his hand to his king. Catriona accepted his assistance out of propriety rather than necessity. Leninstar's king could hold her own on a battlefield; exiting a carriage presented no challenge.

'Noah,' Catriona said.

Noah bowed her head. 'Your Highness.'

Catriona studied the dragons. 'Spoons would have been better.'

'Pardon?' Noah said.

'As souvenirs from Somyni. *Those,*' Catriona said, pointing to the dragons, 'are going to be trouble.'

Piper practised her manoeuvres for the evening's ceremony under Horatio's watchful eye. Chain provided additional assistance while Vespa nibbled at the last of the petunias.

'But they're magnificent,' Montana said.

'Is everyone here?' Catriona asked.

'We're just waiting on Sachin, Alan and Brinn to arrive now,' Noah said. 'Grainger can't make it – he still needs to rest.'

Catriona nodded. 'His injuries were serious. It's amazing he's alive.'

Although many elves had invaded the tunnel directly, Grainger, Sachin and Jacin had deflected many more. Grainger had suffered severe burns, and despite three months of intensive treatment, he had a long way to go yet.

'I can't wait to see the baby,' Montana said, clasping her hands over her heart.

Gillette rolled his eyes. 'All babies look the same,' he said. '*I'm* going to play with the dragons.'

As the boy trotted away, Noah said, 'Looks like he's recovered okay?'

Jaxon hugged her. 'All good. After everything that's happened – it seems impossible that we're back to normal.'

Catriona sniffed. 'Normal? *Nothing* is *ever* normal when Noah's around.'

'Where's Ardis?' Montana asked.

'Your fearless warrior is with Emir and Jacin, preparing the paddock for tonight,' Noah said. 'He's probably shovelling cow poo or something.'

Montana nodded. 'Good. My soldiers need to maintain top physical shape.'

Two figures on horseback turned onto the driveway.

'I'll get this carriage out of the way,' Jaxon said, 'and get these horses washed and fed.'

'Righto,' Noah said.

'Ahoy! Noah!' Alan called, dropping the reins to wave with both arms.

When Kane took off towards Alan and Sachin, Noah chased after him. The last thing she needed was for her Alsatian to spook the horses and send Mellifont's one-footed auditor tumbling from his mount.

Kane barked and Alan's horse shied away from the canine.

'Kane!' Montana said. 'Heel.'

With uncharacteristic obedience, the dog turned and bounded over to the high priestess.

Sachin made it to Noah first. He jumped down from his mount, eyeing the dragons as he looped the reins over his horse's head.

'Maybe Piper will be a good influence on Kane?' Sachin said.

Kane barked.

'I don't think that'll happen,' Noah said. 'He's not keen on the dragons.'

Sachin shrugged. 'Is Seamus here?'

Noah nodded. 'Yes. Seamus is here.'

Sachin stroked his horse's neck. 'Well, let's not have word of that get out. Dragons will be a big enough shock for people around here, but if they find out you're harbouring an elf …'

'It could have been worse,' Noah said. 'What if I'd brought some dragon riders from Somyni as well?'

'Olive and Twigg aren't coming?'

Noah shook her head. 'They've got a lot of rebuilding to do. No time for holidays.'

Noah reached out as Alan's horse neared her. She took its bridle in one hand and stroked the mare's muzzle reassuringly with the other.

Alan swung one pudgy leg over and lay across the saddle. He wriggled backwards, panting with the effort of manoeuvring his ample belly over the crest of the saddle. Once past the peak he picked up speed, landing hard.

'Noah,' he puffed, still gripping the saddle, 'would you mind getting me my walking stick?'

Sachin snorted. 'You don't need a walking stick, Alan. You've got a prosthetic foot.'

'Yes, but one can't too careful,' Alan said. 'Anyway, my walking stick was a gift from Noah, and it'd be rude not to use it.'

Alan turned to Noah. 'I hear that you're trying to be like me,' he said, grinning.

'Very funny,' Noah said, kicking off her shoe to show him her shrivelled foot. 'It shouldn't slow me down too much, but I'll probably never be a professional ballerina.'

'Probably not,' Alan said, 'but you've still got plenty to work with there.'

'I'll get to it eventually,' Noah said. 'Reconstructing a foot isn't a priority when people like Grainger still need treatment. Anyway, it seems that losing a foot hasn't slowed you down any.'

'Can't afford to slow down if I want to keep up with you people,' Alan said.

Noah winked at Sachin. 'Keep *up* with us, or keep an *eye* on us?'

Alan huffed demonstratively. 'Both. Do you have any idea how much work it is to monitor you and all the rascals you collect? Speaking of rascals … is Major Miscreant here?'

'Major Jacin is here,' Noah said, patting him on the shoulder, 'and I expect you both to behave yourselves.'

Alan made no attempt to hide his contempt.

'Avril's here too?' Sachin asked.

'Yes.'

Sachin raised an eyebrow. 'Is her grandfather coming?' he said. 'I'd love to meet old Bernard.'

Noah rolled her eyes. 'No. Bernard Kurz was *not* invited.'

♪♫

Noah stood by the small, freshly dug hole with her viola tucked under her arm. With her back to the setting sun, she marvelled briefly at the pink and yellow smudges of cloud peppering the sky. On the other side of the hole, Chase nursed Alexis while Ardis crooned softly.

Noah waved her bow. 'Are you ready?'

Chase smiled and Ardis saluted. 'Ready,' they chorused.

Noah turned to her guests. 'Raven and I welcome you all here tonight,' she said, nodding towards her brother, 'to witness this ceremony.'

Chase's mother dabbed her eyes with her handkerchief as Noah continued.

'Our parents performed this ceremony for us, right here, nearly twenty years ago,' Noah said. 'Tonight, we will perform this ancient ritual to bond Alexis to this world. Traditionally, a tonic is played to summon fire to tell a story – the story of Xan's sacrifice, and of her connection to Talisker. Given that we have real dragons here tonight' – she smiled at Piper – 'we've made some modifications to the ceremony.'

Emir took up the commentary as Noah checked the tuning on her instrument.

'You will see the wood stacks at the four compass points,' he said. 'Raven is sprinkling a spice mix on them now.'

'Smells like muffins,' Gillette said.

'That's the cinnamon,' Emir said. He gestured towards the corners of the diamond. 'I would ask that you all stay clear of the stacks,' he said. 'There *will* be fire.'

Montana stepped forward. 'Elani features in the ritual,' she said. 'I have asked Ardis, as one of Elani's most valiant warriors, to take that role this evening.'

'I think that is fitting,' Brinn said.

All eyes went to the wood pile at the northern point of the diamond.

'Better late than never?' Noah said as the cat sauntered towards her.

Raven scooped Brinn up in his arms.

Ears flattened, she said, 'You're not going to kiss me, are you?'

'No,' Raven said. 'I'm not like my sister.'

Noah groaned inwardly as her guests exchanged curious glances.

'It's not what it sounds like,' Noah said. 'I never kissed the cat.'

Catriona frowned. 'Then what does—'

'The sun has set,' Noah said. 'Time to start the ceremony.'

Ardis, dressed in full military regalia, stepped forward and drew his sword. *A girl couldn't wish for a more protective father,* Noah thought as she drew her bow across the strings of her reconstructed viola. Her tonic tonight was a simple one. She'd just warm the earth to make Alexis more comfortable.

Piper leapt into the air and soared over the audience. Noah continued her melody, upping the tempo as Piper wound her way skyward, towards the first of the night's stars. At the peak of her climb, the dragon banked left.

Alan clapped his hands against his cheeks. 'She's coming down!'

Piper flicked her tail and commenced her dive. Fixed on Ardis, she speared towards the ground.

Ardis raised his sword. 'Hail! Xan!' he cried. 'To honour your sacrifice, I'll build a new world!'

Within metres of Ardis's sword tip, Piper spread her wings and levelled out. The downdraft buffeted the group. Alan staggered but Jaxon caught his arm.

Piper dipped, gliding towards the northern wood stack. Spewing flame, she ignited the first pyre. The audience cheered as she banked right to light the eastern pyre. Once the southern pyre was alight, Noah could feel the heat from the flames.

When Piper lit the final pyre, Chase hugged her baby to her chest and cried, 'Ouroboros!'

'Circle of life,' Noah murmured.

The crowd applauded as Piper skidded to a stop just beyond the diamond. Noah lowered her viola and ducked away from the group to congratulate the dragon on her performance. Enveloped in smoke, Noah patted Piper's snout.

'How'd I do?' Piper said.

Noah smiled. 'You did great. Fantastic actually.'

Behind her, Kane growled. Noah rubbed his chest with her free hand while Piper snorted more smoke.

Noah coughed. 'That's enough, Piper,' she said as Kane growled again. 'And that goes for you too, Kane. You two need to get over yourselves – and get along … or it's the vortex for both of you!'

A lick of flame leaked from the side of Piper's mouth. 'You wouldn't!'

'Don't tempt me,' Noah said.

'Noah!' Raven called. 'You're going to miss the good bit.'

She pointed at Piper and then at Kane. 'Behave.'

Noah jogged back to stand between Raven and Emir. She arrived just in time to see Chase push warm, loose soil into the hole around Alexis.

'Another alien, like us, Noah,' Raven said as he cradled Brinn in his arms. 'One Earth parent, one Taliskeran parent.'

'Well, I hope she's not as much trouble as you two are,' Emir said.

Noah's eyes widened as she turned to him. 'What do you mean?' she demanded.

Emir took her hands and kissed the back of each one. 'Talisker was a quiet, tranquil place before you two arrived.'

Noah and Raven looked at each other before Noah turned back to Emir. 'In case you don't remember, *you're* the one who invited us here in the first place.'

Emir glanced at Brinn. 'It was her idea.'

'Well, my life was a lot less complicated before I came here,' Noah said. 'My biggest problem then was my English teacher. But here … firestone, adepts, kings, politics, goblins, elves, magic, dragons … the illestial!'

'Well, the illestial is beyond reach now,' Brinn said. 'Xan can rest easy, and so should you.'

'Rest easy?' Noah said.

Brinn licked her paw. 'Yes. Talisker is safe. For now.'

About the Author

Sarah Fisher lives west of Brisbane, Australia. When she's not corralling her collection of unruly fictional characters, she teaches real characters at local schools. She is living proof that while growing older is compulsory, growing up is not.